# The Book of Orphans

# The Book of Orphans



No AI tools used during the writing process.
Cover imagery generated using AI applications.

Version: 1.0

ISBN: 978-1-7395265-1-1

# Contents

# The Mysterious Heroism of Archibald Crane

Archibald casts his eyes down and sighs, tapping sodden soil with his trainer. It sinks easily, muddy water rising to meet cheap black plastic. The near torrential rain of the last couple of hours turning the generous flowerbed into a quagmire.

He looks up, over the top of the hydrangeas and the berberis, gazing at the long, elegant window nestled in the wall of the old building behind. The scene inside dimly lit, a solitary desk lamp casting a warm glow, keeping late afternoon Winter shadow at bay. Archibald watches for a moment, staring through the rain. No sign of movement still.

"Fucking hell, where are you man?"

He taps the soil again before resigning himself to crossing the muddy quicksand, shaking his head in small frustration. Stepping over a sprightly hebe, he fights briefly with the overgrown, thorny berberis, which easily snags a sleeve on his thick jacket. He pulls the arm away quickly, one trainer sinking further as he inspects the tiny damage in the material. With a sigh of exasperation, he steps further forward. Hitting firmer soil near the wall and moving up to the glass, peering into the office through cupped hands.

Impatient. "Come on, man, I'm running late…"

After a moment, the door to the room opens and a short, shadowy figure carrying a small bowl on a plate, steps inside. Archibald knocks hard on the glass, but the figure has already noticed him and walks quickly, raising an arm in acknowledgement.

"Fletcher!" Moving back, pushing a long dripping fringe to one side, shouting. "Pass isn't working again. I've been buzzing!"

Fletcher moves around the desk with the lamp and carefully places the plate and bowl on the surface. Then he steps over to the window.

"My pass, it's not working." Holding the new plastic ID up to the glass.

Fletcher glances at the card and gives a thumbs up with two hands, before pointing at Archibald and gesturing to walk round to the front again.

"Alright…"

Archibald moves back through the troublesome shrubs and over the sinking soil with as few steps as possible, hopping onto the puddle strewn concrete of the car park. He swirls his trainers in a couple of the more generous puddles on the way to the front, trying to remove the worst of the soil, sticking to the cheap material like brown glue. After a final flourish in one of the puddles, he looks up to see Fletcher, now sporting his black security cap, waving from around the edge of the large front doorway.

Archibald skips up the old, worn stone steps on one side and scampers across, heading to where a concrete ramp meets a slabbed area in front. He steps into the main entrance and shakes his jacket briskly. Then he scrapes his shoes, dragging both sides across a large, rough doormat fixed into the floor.

"Lovely weather, eh?"

Archibald mock grins, shaking water from his hands.

Fletcher smiles apologetically. "Sorry I didn't hear the buzzer or the knocking. Soup time…"

"No worries, Fletcher." Archibald bites his lip, running a hand through wet hair. "It's okay, just I'm eh, late, y'know?"

Fletcher glances at the digital display of his large watch and sniffs. Then he taps his security pass on a sensor embedded in the wall next to a glass door. The words Pendleton Gallery etched across the surface at eye level in flowing, ornate script. He holds it open for Archibald to move straight into the modest reception space.

"Yeah, didn't get away from the other office until well after five. Got to wait until the workshop clears. They've got a lot on right now."

"Where are you…"

"Busby's. Their new site? Small business park down Slaterhall Lane, at the bottom. The new bit…"

"Out past Eddingham? That's the other side of the city, you don't drive?"

"No, I drive, just that, well, Jess takes the car most days." Archibald shakes his head. "It's not so bad. One of my mates works there, he drops me off outside. It's on the way home."

"That's handy."

"Yeah."

Fletcher pulls sharply on the glass door, which slowly swings back into place with a sonorous clunk. He moves over to the tall reception counter nearby and glances briefly at a bank of CCTV monitors, each image showing a monochrome slice of the surrounding car park and garden.

"As you're running late, you can use one of the temporary passes we have in the office. I'll get your other one checked and sorted out."

"That's fine, Fletcher." Archibald lifts the smartphone from his jacket pocket and checks his notifications, swiping the screen. "Yeah, I need to get started. Jess is picking me up at eight and I don't want to have her waiting around, y'know? She'll have Jacey with her."

Fletcher brushes past and moves down a short corridor, just beyond the reception counter. "Soup must be getting cold by now…"

"Sorry Fletcher." Following behind, Archibald nods meekly. "Just that new pass hasn't worked properly since I got it."

Fletcher opens the door to the office revealing a dimly lit, but warm and pleasant room. Four large desks occupy most of the space, arranged in two groups of two, with another older and larger L-shaped desk situated off to one corner, close to the window Archibald had been staring through. Each desk has two large monitors side by side, clamped in place by a thick and adjustable monitor arm, the top of several adorned with small furry toys. The desks are mainly bare, with only one of the chairs having additional decoration in the form of a thick royal blue zip fleece, draped over the backrest. In the far corner, several filing cabinets nestle together alongside a couple of big shelving units, the latter containing rows of neatly grouped hanging folders. Along the top of the cabinets, a random collection of slightly anaemic houseplants, sitting on a variety of grubby saucers.

Fletcher moves across to the L-shaped desk, taking a crafty sip from the soup bowl sitting on top. "Mmm, not too bad now, perfect in fact."

Archibald glances over, sniffing the air. "Homemade?"

"No." Tapping his stomach instinctively. "I was rushing here myself today. It's from a tin. The shop across the road."

While Fletcher checks the temporary passes, Archibald taps and runs his fingers along the surfaces of each desk. He whispers words, boldly printed in Comic Sans and pasted to the top of one of the monitors: "Life is a journey, not a destination."

Sliding a plain plastic card into a clear wallet with a bright yellow lanyard attached, Fletcher walks over. "Right, here you go. This should be full access. Any problems, you know where I am."

"Great." Archibald arranges the lanyard around his neck.

"Don't lose it. Right, give me the other one."

Archibald digs into a damp jacket pocket and removes the plastic card, handing it over. "Not sure what's wrong with it, Fletcher."

"I'll check it for you." Returning to the L-shaped desk and taking another sip. "If there's a problem, I'll sort a new one out, easier doing that. Eight you finish? It'll be done by then."

Archibald feels the smartphone vibrate in his other pocket and removes it quickly, checking the latest notification. Nothing important. "That's fine, Fletcher. I'll crack on then…"

Leaving the office, Archibald skips along the short corridor to reception. He stops at another wide glass door, set in a pristine white wall, returning his phone to a jacket pocket then holding his pass out to the nearby scanner. With a click, the door bounces open and, as he passes through, he glances up to the CCTV camera and gives a thumbs up.

He steps into a large, cool, minimally decorated space, all clean lines and delicate LED spotlighting. Shadowy white walls interrupted only by paintings and photographs, staring from seas of blank white and scattered print. Every image a snapshot of something real or imagined from a different age. Pictures ranging from the plain and dull, to the vivid and dramatic. The natural, to the abstract.

Archibald scans the large room, taking in the selection of portraits, landscapes and other art projects that comprise Gallery A. He takes a moment, a precious second, to inhale the peaceful late afternoon ambience of the main gallery. A far cry from earlier in the day, the bustle and industry of Busby's workshop.

Moving along, damp trainers squeaking on polished wooden floor, he locates a large metal plate containing four rows of switches and flicks them on with both hands, one row at a time. The gallery immediately transforming, losing its shadow, bathing itself fully in gentle white light.

He follows a slightly curved wall to the bottom and turns along a corridor, heading towards one of two doors indicated with a yellow and black 'Staff Only' sign. Removing a line of keys from a trouser pocket, he unlocks it and twists the buffed metal handle, opening just enough of a gap to slip quickly inside.

Darkness greets him immediately. Home for the next couple of hours.

Instinctively, Archibald reaches out to his left, feeling rough unpainted stone at first before locating a light switch and flicking it downwards. Weary illumination reveals a strictly functional, grubby storeroom. Heavy-duty shelving along one wall, with a double sink and row of cupboards opposite. A couple of plastic folding chairs, all collapsed, languishing in the corner. Dotted between the units, a motley collection of buckets, mops and brushes leaning against stone and each other.

Parked in the near corner behind the door, a modest wheeled cart, all yellow and black plastic with a large flat mop and a medium-sized brush clipped to one side. Small plastic shelves and holders contain an assortment of disinfectant sprays, sponges, toilet rolls, a pair of red cleaning gauntlets and several hand brushes. Pinned and open in front of the hard yellow handles, a thick blue plastic refuse bag sits waiting, ready for the shift ahead.

Archibald removes his phone, sets the volume to modestly loud then looks over at the trolley. “And how are you tonight, Waspy?”

No answer.

After another check of the phone screen, Archibald pushes the device into a rear trouser pocket and unfolds one of the chairs, arranging his still damp jacket over the back. Then he lifts a blue polyester work coat from a wire hanger at the end of the large shelving unit and slides it on. Popping the four fasteners together along the front edge and smoothing out the material.

Like clockwork, Archibald lifts a plastic bucket from the floor and places it in the sink. Pouring disinfectant from a large square container, the air in the room thickens with a heavy scent of pine as water pours into the bucket. As the water rises, Archibald glances at his watch and prays to recoup some time – perhaps the toilets won’t require much cleaning tonight? Although only a small gallery, he knows that it only takes the actions of one visitor, one very messy or ill visitor, to taint the evening shift. If the toilets aren’t bad, Archibald might indeed reclaim some time and get back on schedule.

Turning off the tap, Archibald lifts the bucket with a playful groan, lowering it gently to the bottom platform at the front of the cart. He grabs a couple of the standard mops propped up near the sink and slips them down through a thick plastic loop on the side. Checking that everything is secure first, he gently pushes the cart forward, nudging the door open before pushing it wider with his arm. With the cart in the corridor, he flicks the light switch off and closes the door behind him, locking it securely.

"Right, Waspy. Let's see what's in store tonight..."

As Archibald pushes the cart across the wooden floor, the wheels make a curious rhythmic sound as they move. Clickety clack. Clickety clack. He ignores the many paintings and photographs, hurrying across the large space instead, holding his pass to the scanner and moving into reception.

A typical routine lies ahead. The galleries are always the highest priority, so picking any litter there and emptying the bins is a key task. Then a floor clean of one, whichever gallery happens to be next in the three-day rotation. Today, it's the turn of Gallery C, the main gallery once upon a time, situated in the oldest section of the building. When the galleries are done, the routine finishes with a check and brisk clean of each toilet.

On the way to the lift at the end of the short corridor, Archibald can't resist diving into the ground floor toilets to assess the scale of work for later. Venturing inside, he notes with satisfaction that each space shows no obvious signs of major effort required. In fact, each of the toilets still feels clean, suggesting that the number of people using them that day has been small.

By instinct, Archibald flushes each toilet anyway, then stops in front of a modest circular wall-mounted mirror. He smiles and nods at himself, brushing down his coat and adjusting a long and still damp fringe to one side. In his head, a clock now ticks with relief as he removes his phone, holding it out in front to take a selfie.

Stepping back into the corridor, Archibald opens his favourite messaging app and adds a new layer to the Jess conversation thread, attaching the latest selfie. "Ground floor toilets good. Should be OK for 8. Show selfie to Jacey X."

Slipping the phone back into a trouser pocket, he moves the cart towards a dull metal door at the end and calls the lift.

"Gallery C tonight, Waspy."

Pushing the cart into the tight confines of the lift, Archibald leans across to press the round backlit number two button. With a gentle rumble and bounce, the metal door closes. Archibald watches the illuminated display above the door flicker, slowly moving from one to two.

Archibald pushes the cart out onto carpet, parking it at the side before briefly investigating the smaller second floor toilets near the lift door. Reassured they require even less attention than those on the first floor, he continues along the landing, passing the large double door to an area marked Gallery B, then turning past the top of a flight of stairs towards Gallery C.

Swiping the card at the side, the large single glass door opens slowly then stalls halfway. Archibald swipes the card again, the door clicking, engaging, shuddering, but remaining stuck. Stepping round, he nudges the glass slightly and the door suddenly stirs as if from sleep, opening wider with a mechanical gasp.

"When they going to get this fixed? It's only been like forever…"

Beyond the cantankerous glass door, old Gallery C rushes to greet Archibald with all its history. A more traditional atmosphere, refined still but completely different to the modern, totally reconfigured, airy space of the gallery downstairs. Here, the large paintings don't float in oceans of stark and clinical white space. Instead, they sit together, fixed in permanent positions on dull green walls, edged in white panelling and coving. Perhaps the positions they have existed in for years, leaving outlines on the walls behind. Near the top of each wall, ornate golden light fittings, all sparking into warm life when Archibald flicks several switches on a metal panel just inside the door.

Sniffing the air. "Hmm, smells a bit funny in here."

He rolls the cart forward into the gallery hallway on the left. Plastic wheels noisy over the joins in the heavily waxed dark wooden flooring. Clickety clack. Clickety clack. Large oil paintings passing either side, a mix of moody landscapes and austere, grim portraits of local historical figures of note. Each surrounded with an intricately carved frame, most golden, others a deep mix of dark red and brown.

Archibald walks further along, sniffing and whispering. "Think someone's been smoking in here Waspy..."

Parking the cart in the corner, Archibald quickly walks along the shorter wall at the bottom and checks back along the right-hand corridor. He pauses for a moment, as if waiting for something to happen, then turns away when nothing does. Just two rows of older paintings staring miserably back at him and a thin cylindrical litter bin, close to the entrance.

Archibald removes his phone. A flicker of a smile as he brushes past his lock screen wallpaper of Jess and Jacey smiling at the camera in close-up. Tapping through the new notifications, he navigates to and taps one of several drum'n'bass playlists. The urgent sound of 180bpm spits and hisses from the small speaker, as he places the phone on top of the cart.

He lifts the large bucket and places it on the floor, then removes the mop and drops it into the water, swirling it around before squeezing the excess in the wringer. He starts from the far-left corner, the mop moving easily and neatly across. After a few seconds, he cleans in ragged spirals, hungrily grasping more of the floor, spurred on by rasping electronic beats.

Moving briskly backwards, Archibald removes that top layer of light, almost invisible, surface dirt. Stopping every so often to check and reload the mop, he nods and dances as he goes, acknowledging the shining floor.

With the small end hallway section nearly done, he suddenly shoots upright. Frowning. Sniffing. Cutting through the pine wash; a distinct smell of tobacco.

Archibald leans the mop against the cart and taps the pause icon on his phone. He walks further along the right hallway, peering briefly out the windows to the car park below. Then looks towards the glass door, still closed, with no indication that anyone has entered.

"Fletcher? Anyone there?"

Nothing. No-one.

Archibald steps back to the large patch of shining floor and instantly chokes, staggering and reaching out a hand towards the cart. A thick cloud of blue-grey smoke appearing around him.

"Wha? Fuck…"

Coughing gently, he steps away from the low cloud which gradually dissipates. Thick spirals fading, becoming invisible, leaving only a heavy tobacco smell. Then it hits him. He looks ahead to one of the portraits, noticing a soft plume of blue smoke escaping from underneath one corner.

"Shit! Fire..."

He leaps forward, gently lifting the corner of the painting. Thicker blue-grey smoke escapes, as though being blown through from underneath.

"Oh shit, must be a fire behind the wall…"

As he leans closer, bending down to investigate behind the frame, his blood freezes when he hears a distinct, gravelly voice.

"Good lad, it's coming away now!"

Archibald recoils in confusion, letting go of the edge instantly, mind and heart racing.

"Don't walk away, lad! Lift the painting up again. Lift it off."

"What?" Archibald clears his throat. "What the… Who are you?"

"It's me…"

Pause.

"Edward?"

"Edward… Eddie…Ed…?" Archibald shakes his head, trying to recall staff names.

"The glassmaker. Edward Johnson Baker? I'm stuck behind here…"

"What the fuck…" Archibald rubs his eyes. "There's a fire there? What are you doing? How did you get in there?"

Pause.

"There's no fire, lad. Now, are you going to lift the painting off the wall or not?"

"How did you get in there?" Stepping closer to the wall, as though listening. "Can't you just walk out the same way you got in?"

Pause.

"Edward?"

Sighing. "I'm asking you politely, lad. Are you going to help me or not?"

Archibald lifts his head away, frowning in part-confusion and part-relief there is no fire.

"Still there, lad?"

"I'm… thinking. I'm not allowed to touch the paintings. Nobody is."

Pause.

"No need to touch the painting, lad, just lift the frame."

Archibald glances at his watch, seeing time creep away from him before finally shaking his head in resignation. "Alright, wait a minute…"

Grabbing either side of the large golden-framed portrait, Archibald pushes gently, shifting the painting upwards.

"Woah, hold on, lad, let me sort this on the back here. Right, there you are, should come away now."

Archibald lifts the painting away from the wall entirely, carefully lowering the canvas to the floor. Propping it against the wall at the side and revealing a strange window-shaped hole behind.

A tall, thickset man wearing a stained dull red shirt and dirty long black apron stands behind the wall, peering out. His face grimy, craggy, with untidy dark grey hair, a thick moustache and piercing narrow eyes that shine strangely, just for a moment. Archibald watches as the man leans out into the available light, lifting a thick cigar to his lips and puffing several times in a strange, impatient manner.

"It's you?"

"What would that be, lad?"

"The smell?" Archibald points at the cigar. "Thought something was on fire."

Edward makes a heaving sound, as though about to laugh then stopping short. "Don't have these often. A gift you see. From an old business acquaintance."

Archibald stares at the cigar as Edward inhales deeply and blows a cloud of thick smoke in his direction. While Archibald coughs, slicing the air several times with his hands, Edward leans over the edge of the wall chuckling.

"Don't have another one I'm afraid, lad."

"Aw, it stinks. Don't smoke anyway. I quit. Years ago." Archibald shakes his head, still wafting the fumes away. "Anyway, what's going on here? What are you doing in there?"

A strict voice bellows from somewhere behind. "It's time, Edward!"

Edward rolls his eyes, shouting over his shoulder. "I'm resting, woman, just for a minute. Taking a break, you hear!"

"Wait, wait, there's more of you in there?"

"Of course, where've you been, lad?"

Archibald steps closer, attempting to peer into the dim space behind Edwards large frame, seeing a drab ceiling with two ornate hanging lights flickering. Sometimes casting a doleful ghostly glow, sometimes fading to near darkness.

Whispering almost. "What's your name, lad?"

"Archibald, Archibald Crane."

Edward smiles coldly. "Crane, you say?"

Archibald nods. "Yeah…"

"I see. Family?"

"Yeah, a wife, one child."

Edward sniffs quietly. "Boy? Girl?"

"Girl."

"Oh. What's her name?"

"Jacey."

"Jacey? J-C?"

"Uh? Nah, Jacey. J-a-c-e-y."

Slightly perplexed, Edward lifts the cigar to his mouth and reflects. He blows a thick blue cloud that smothers Archibald, forcing him to step back briefly.

Edward shouts over his shoulder. "Rosemary? The lad has a lass of his own, Jacey her name. Heard that before?"

Ignoring. "The lights, Edward, the lights!"

"Let me settle things here, woman, didn't I say I'd sort it out for all for us?"

As if responding to an inner notification, Archibald glances down at his watch and straightens. "Look, I have to report this to security. If you're not going to explain what's going on? None of you should be here at this time."

"Time?" Edward flinches. "And what time is this, Mr Crane?"

"Late. Gallery is closed. So, unless you've all got a legitimate reason for being here? And I've got work to do..."

Edward narrows his eyes, puffing out his chest and fixing a stern expression. "You think we're trespassing, lad? How would that be? I helped build this place. That's my glass in some of those frames over there."

"What are you talking about?" Archibald screws up his face. "Nah, you need to all come with me, to security."

Behind Edward, the lights in the room flicker and fade entirely, turning the whole space inside black. Twisted, terrible voices wail in a chorus of screaming disappointment from the shadow, startling Archibald.

"I told you the lights would go out, Edward Baker!" Irate. Seething. Scolding. "Listen to the children…"

"I'm not deaf, woman, I can hear them!" Leaning out the hole, Edward rubs a sweaty, dirty hand across his jaw and sighs wearily. "No need to go on about it."

"What?" Confused, increasingly exasperated. "You have children in there?"

Edward nods, eyeing Archibald suspiciously. "What's it to you, lad? We do our best by them."

Shocked, Archibald stumbles over his words. "How many children are in there?"

"Just the two." Edward narrows his eyes. "What of it? You ever spoken to Mary Thomas in the next room? She has six with her."

Bewildered. "Does the gallery manager know you're all here? You're working on some exhibit?"

Edward laughs. Two pieces of sandpaper rubbing together.

Archibald shrugs. "Look, I can't waste any more time on this. You all need to come with me right now."

"Actually…" Edward puffs on the cigar and coughs, thinking for a few moments. "You're right. You're right. I should have said. Been working on a new exhibition, just setting up…"

The voice cries out again but the tone is distorted, giving each word a terrible, tortured sound. "Don't you start on him, Edward Baker. A young man with family of his own!"

"What's happened?" Whispering. "What's wrong with her voice?"

Edward avoids the questions, shouting over his shoulder into darkness. "I'm not starting anything, Rosemary, just having a conversation with the lad!"

Archibald glances at his watch again, precious minutes slipping away.

"I've only just started the cleaning. I'm already behind." Archibald rubs his chest nervously. "I need to go and see Fletcher, he'll know what's going on."

"I can show you, lad? I'll show you exactly what's going on, then you can get back to your work." Edward leans out further, gesturing for Archibald to step forward. "You can see what we've done so far."

"Edward Baker!" The strange, distorted voice in the background continues to scold and snap.

"Hold your tongue, Rosemary! Don't want the lad to replace the painting just yet."

Archibald shakes his head. "I have no idea what the fuck you're talking about."

Edward holds an index finger to his mouth, gesturing to be quiet.

Archibald looks over towards his phone, sitting on the top tray of the cleaning cart. "Why did they never tell me about this, Edward? Fletcher should have said something…"

Edward shrugs his large shoulders. "Fletcher?"

"The security guard, in the office downstairs."

"Don't know anyone by the name of Fletcher." Edward scratches his head then shouts. "Rosemary, know anyone by the name Fletcher?"

No answer. Only groaning, wailing, snarling from the shadows.

"Been the main guard on the site for years."

"Well, I've been busy, lad." Rubbing a grimy forehead. "You think it's easy keeping the lights on in a place like this?"

Archibald steps across to his phone and lifts it up, glancing at the time and the new notifications. Still nothing important. "Need to send a message to Jess."

"Jess?"

"My wife."

Laughing roughly. "Let her know you might be late, lad."

"Nah, I won't be late."

"Oh…"

Fingers move quickly across a backlit screen as the words 'everything OK here, looking at a secret exhibition, see you at 8' appear. Signing off with a small red heart, Archibald taps the send icon and locks the screen, placing the phone back on the cart.

"Be able to see what we've done so far." Edward gestures for Archibald to step up and through the hole in the wall. "Something to tell the family eh, lad?"

"Maybe." Archibald tilts his head, reflecting for a moment on final doubts. He makes some random noises with his mouth, before capitulating and shrugging. "Ah, whatever."

"Good lad, I'll get some light on for you."

Edward disappears completely into the blackness and an odd, whirring noise cuts through several seconds later.

Archibald grips the bottom of the hole in the wall and jumps up slightly, leaning forward over the surprisingly thick bottom edge, letting his midriff take the brunt of the pressure. He brings a leg up and round, balancing slightly, then swings it inside and lowers himself down gently. Reaching out through poor light towards a rubble-strewn section of floor.

He looks towards the dim ceiling, watching the energy build and build in the two ornate ceiling lights.

Brightening then dipping, over and over, before finally strengthening, becoming more consistent. As the lighting steadies, a tall woman and two children are revealed at the other end of the room, cheering wildly.

But Archibald's half-smile disappears when his gaze is drawn to the other side, seeing an illuminated Edward sitting atop a dirty, ugly metal contraption. His long, sturdy legs moving in an exaggerated swinging fashion, not quite pedalling but close, moving a tall grimy flywheel at the front of a litter of grubby antique machinery. Part bicycle, part engine, part electrical, gears and flat belts rotating, small rows of bulbs sparking and burning. Thick cables connected to four cannisters, as big as oil barrels, sitting stretched out in an untidy line on the floor. With generous coils of thinner cabling spiralling from each, heading in different directions and having the appearance of a web. Some disappearing into the floor, others reaching up and disappearing into holes in the walls and ceiling.

"What the fuck is that?"

The woman shouts out in a normal voice. "Didn't I tell you, Edward Baker? A young man. With family. Have you no shame?"

"Wheesht, Rosemary, it's all under control!" Stepping down from the contraption and wiping his brow with a dirty rag. "Now you watch your step in here, lad."

"It's old, dirty. Looks like it hasn't been decorated for years."

"Put a lot of work in to get it looking like this." Edward grunts, the sound gruff and harsh. "For the exhibition? Although some of the mess in here – the children, you see? A pair of messy buggers."

"Hush your words, Edward Baker!"

Edward waves an arm in disapproval.

"What kind of exhibition is this? And what is that?" Archibald points at the litter of dirty machinery occupying one side of the huge room.

"An invention, lad." Edward fixes Archibald with an intense stare. "My invention."

"Everything's so old?" Archibald looks around the room, absorbing the pale and crumbling décor, touching various surfaces. "How did you get all this in here?"

But Archibald doesn't wait for an answer. Instead, he brushes himself down and walks across to where a wiry, ill-looking woman is sitting and studying him through small semi-circular spectacles. Perched uncomfortably in the middle of a dark green sofa, long hair matted and unkempt, wearing a dirty white pleated blouse and a black skirt reaching all the way to her ankles. Archibald notices a rip in her blouse at the shoulder, the delicate ruffled material hanging down, revealing unhealthy grey skin underneath. Either side, two children, pale and barefoot, dressed only in cheeky, inquisitive expressions and simple grubby clothing. Both stare at him coldly, as if suspicious.

"You must be Rosemary then?"

"Aye, that's me." The woman squirms with a suggestion of pain, before indicating the girl standing beside her. "This is Muriel."

"And this is Henry," announces Edward gruffly, now standing directly behind.

"Pleased to meet you." Biting his lip, feeling strangely tense at the odd appearance of the family. "I'm Archibald. Archibald Crane."

Rosemary stops shifting in her seat, the mere mention of the name making her freeze. "Archibald… Crane?"

Muriel screws her face up. "Like Uncle Archibald?"

"Ssh, Muriel..."

"Doesn't look like him." Muriel, perches on the edge of the seat and screws up her face. "Did he take his name?"

"Muriel, sshh…"

Something invisible passes between Edward and Rosemary. Some message in silence, an acknowledgement.

"Well, Edward Baker, you're a terrible, terrible man but…" Rosemary studies Archibald closely.

"Told you I'd sort it out." Edward makes a tutting sound.

"Do I know you, Rosemary?" Archibald clears his throat uneasily, glancing at her sickly, gaunt face. "Have you been to this gallery before?"

"Oh, I've been here a long time, Archibald Crane. A long time. We all have."

Edward nods. "Some might say, we never left."

"Right, right, I've not been working here that long myself." Archibald glances at his watch, feeling a slight chill, swallowing nervously. "You, eh, want to show me the exhibition stuff then? Because I've got cleaning to do—"

The lights flicker briefly overhead, everyone looks up.

An inquisitive Muriel slips forward from the sofa and reaches out, feeling the smooth material of the blue work coat. "I like this colour, it's shiny. Do you like it, Henry?"

Henry shakes his head in an exaggerated fashion and drops back on the sofa. Lifting his legs up and rolling sideways, staring at the ceiling as though thoroughly bored.

"It's my uniform, Muriel. It protects my clothes. Like…" Archibald points to Edward's apron. "I use some cleaning products they… in case they splash on me, y'know?"

The lights dim further. The room remaining bright but darkness now gathering along every side, every edge.

Archibald rubs his face nervously. "Looks like they haven't finished setting everything up?"

"That's right lad. Only just started getting the main exhibit here." Edward gestures to the machinery across the room. "And that took a terribly long time."

"What else is there?"

"You can look at some of the furniture over there, a few pieces."

Underwhelmed, Archibald glances briefly towards the various bulky shapes huddled together before glancing at his watch. He clears his throat and straightens. "It's getting late, I really need to crack on."

The lights flicker again. Everyone glances up once more.

Edward casually removes the stub of the cigar from a large pocket on the front of his apron.

"Don't you light that cigar again, Edward Baker."

Archibald walks back across the dusty floor to the far wall, examining a collection of tall furnishings part-draped in a light, grubby material. "I really need to talk to Fletcher, you sure all this is for an exhibition?"

Striking a match and holding it to the end of the cigar, puffing firmly. "That's right, lad. Just started collecting things. Isn't that right, Rosemary?"

Silence.

Whispering. "Just it, all looks like it's been here for years… Ages."

Archibald examines the gloomy far wall, featureless except for two large boards that might be covering windows behind. Then he returns his gaze to the collection of dirty machinery across the floor nearby. The available light dimming, forcing him to move closer to see more clearly. Examining each metal line, straight and curved, each different-sized gear, each thick winding cable. As he follows one of the cables towards the wall, Archibald notices several large portrait paintings lying discarded on the floor, only partially covered in a dusty white sheet.

"There are other paintings here?" Turning round, silent faces. "These should be part of the collection. They belong to the gallery."

"Not those ones, lad."

Archibald steps around a large waist-high canister and kneels, throwing back the sheet and holding up one of the portraits to catch it in the fading light. A tall, severe looking man in a dark overcoat, staring coldly from the canvas. He places the portrait down carefully, quickly examining some of the others stacked behind, all featuring the same subject.

"Well loved in these parts so he was. If only they knew…"

Archibald recoils when he hears a sharp, splintering sound. Eyes shift suddenly to the nearby wall, watching a jagged crack appear and snake towards the ceiling.

Bolting up, Archibald looks across the room, eyes adjusting to the sight of Rosemary clambering to her feet and swaying, her height unnaturally tall, her gait awkward and clumsy. Guided forward carefully by Muriel and Henry, both crying and wailing, disturbed by the flickering darkness.

Rosemary fixes Archibald, staring straight ahead, eyes glinting in strange glimmers of green that appear when the light disappears briefly to black and back again.

In growing panic, Archibald whirls around to find Edward standing beside him in the shadow, narrow eyes shining like two emeralds. Holding the cigar to his mouth, inhaling deeply, blowing thick blue smoke.

Coughing. "What kind of exhibition is this? Who are you?"

The crack in the wall widens, continuing to run upwards and overhead, moving across the ceiling. Choking on the heavy cigar fumes, Archibald quietly backs away but stops when a hand like an iron talon shoots out, grabbing the front of his coat.

"Where you going, lad?" Edward's voice now distorted, twisted, strange. "Look at the walls? Even the reserves are failing."

"You can't leave!" Rosemary screeches in flickering, dim light. Steadily moving closer with both children wailing at her side. "You have to keep the lights on now, Archibald!"

"Get the fuck off me, Fletcher!" Panicking, Archibald struggles against the vice-like grip holding onto the front of his coat. "Get off me!"

Pulling closer. Voice loud, evil, terrible. "Don't curse at me, Archibald Crane. Not after what your blood did to us all those years ago. Ruining our livelihood and forcing us out. After everything I did to help build this place."

Light fades completely overhead, leaving only a dim pool near the hole in the wall.

"Now, *you* pay *us*, blood of Crane. For everything he took…"

"What the fuck are you talking about?" Archibald coughs and screams in the darkness. "Fletcher, help!"

Muriel shouts, a shrill bark spiralling, distorting. "Keep the lights on, Uncle Archibald, I don't want it to be dark!"

Frantic. Feverish. "I don't have any money, Edward, you can take my phone, it's new. I don't know who you are, what you want."

"Don't want your money, lad. Just your time. All those years I've wasted pedalling this damn contraption, keeping the lights on. Waiting and hoping for one day where his blood would return."

Archibald shakes and screams. "I don't have a fucking clue what you're talking about!"

Edward drops the cigar in the darkness and hauls Archibald to the large machine, throwing him roughly on top, something approaching a saddle. "Now *you'll* pedal to lift our curse!"

"Edward, I can't, I don't have the time."

"Oh, you have the time, Archibald Crane." A cackling Rosemary reaches out like a tall spider in darkness, forcing his legs to a long pedal either side of the bulky machine. "That's all you have… And we'll take it, just like he took ours."

Muriel screams. "Pedal, Uncle Archibald, you need to pedal!"

Archibald wails in fear as several strong, clammy hands massage the shiny material of his work coat. Like thick tentacles moving across, forcing him down, holding him in place.

"And pedal good, Archibald Crane, lest the walls collapse around your ears."

Rosemary and the children scream in the cold darkness, horrible, twisting sounds that rip and tear. In abject fear, Archibald instantly starts pedalling, legs moving slowly at first, the initial movements difficult. Tears flow from each eye as he stands to force the tough pedals to move, groaning loudly with the effort. Gradually, they begin to shift, with a strange clanking at first, then reducing to a persistent whirring after several revolutions, becoming easier to move. He lowers himself to the curved saddle, reaching out in the blackness and holding onto a straight bar in front. In utter despair he pushes on, wailing, weeping, screaming in fear and anger at the cold hands like claws caressing him.

Archibald glances to his side, seeing his only salvation in a large and ragged square of light and the familiar gallery outside. "Help!"

Voices hiss. "Pedal, Archibald Crane! Keep the lights on. Archibald Crane!"

"Stay the fuck away from me!"

Archibald closes his eyes tightly and shrieks, a terrible sound escaping from deep inside. In his mind, a flickering backlit screen shows Jacey in her child seat, her face animated, smiling, playing. Then Jess, her expression moving from happiness, through concern, to eventual anger. Checking her phone once, twice, three times. Calling again and again, leaving a final brutal message. The idling car in a darkening car park, eventually pulling away.

Wailing. "Jess… Jacey…"

Legs turning over and over, Archibald glances across to the hole in the wall again and sees a silhouette there, shining a small flashlight inside.

"Fletcher, help me!"

Archibald feels heavy, clammy hands pressing down on his shoulders and a dreadful whispering in his ear. "We'll be going now. You're doing a good job, lad!"

"Fuck… Fletcher, over here!" Anxiously staring at the hole in the wall. "Help me!"

But from the gallery, Fletcher sees nothing. The small pencil of light scanning a room strewn only with rubble and dust. A room hidden in the gallery by a single large, gold-framed portrait.

Suddenly, the beam of light flicks off and the silhouette disappears.

"No, don't go. Fletcher… Here! In here!"

Archibald screams. Legs and heart pumping. As the straight edge of the portrait slides across the hole in the wall, plunging everything into unbroken darkness.

"No! The lights… When do the lights come on! When?"

# Ashes

Mitchell T coughs roughly, rubbing his forehead and flicking cigarette ash into a misshapen ashtray on the table.

Lawson K sits quietly opposite with an air of satisfaction, a lion that just caught dinner. "Quite a story Mitchell…"

"Mm-hm…"

"So that was it? How it all finished?"

"Yeah, after the last tour. It just got to a point where I said to them, I had enough. That…"

"You couldn't do it anymore?"

Mitchell nods softly, staring through the tall window behind Lawson. Driving rain swarming the glass, creating a blurry, impressionistic view of the garden outside.

"It felt the right time. With all the changes, I could see the way things were going to go, how it was going to be… I wasn't happy with it. Also, the new material, we were going in different directions. I didn't like the new sound."

Lawson narrows his eyes and leans forward, nodding his head faintly. "So… the end of the road?"

Smiling. Drawing on the cigarette. "Yeah, the end of the road."

Silence.

Nothing but smoky air hanging over a square wooden table and a twitching row of tiny green lights on the portable digital recorder. Thin black wire twisting outwards, reaching in opposite directions, stretching over to a lapel microphone clipped to each shirt.

"But hey, look, it's been good to me. I don't have any complaints. Life has been good, life is good, right? I can afford to take a few risks now, follow my own path."

"You have the money, family…"

"Sure, all those things. It's good. And I didn't leave in a bad way. I mean there was no real fight, no fallout. We can still speak to each other, I think." Mitchell laughs nervously, the prospect briefly flashing in front of his eyes.

"A door open for the future then?"

"Look, in this business you can never rule anything out. Leaving the band was just, well, a feeling that we were never going to capture what we had before. You have to be honest, y'know? With yourself, with the others… Things were changing, we were all changing and it comes back to the music. The rest of the band, I mean, musically our influences weren't the same anyway. But in the past, it had always kind of ironed itself out, gave us a strange energy, but towards the end it was starting to tear us up, tear me up, creating a kind of tension that's more resentful, y'know? The recording on the last album, people wanting their own thing all the time, got really difficult and I'm just not into that…"

Mitchell tips the cigarette into the ashtray and presses down, extinguishing it immediately. Crushing it on the hard, curved light grey surface, adding to an already messy pile of cigarette carcasses.

Lawson settles back, rubbing and scratching his three-day-old stubble while contemplating the next line of enquiry. "So, it's been a while since you left…"

"Yeah, about eight or nine months…"

"Alright. So, with the benefit of hindsight, looking back at it, how do you feel now? You still think it was the right decision, leaving and going solo?"

"Well, it's always a risk, isn't it? But it's working out. I'm happier."

"And the new music?"

"Yeah, been putting some stuff together, released a couple of things online. Working with a few people I've met over the years. I'd been writing some new stuff anyway, already had some of the ideas down. Things I wouldn't have been able to develop in the band so, yeah, it's good to focus again..."

"And you had some holiday time after the split?"

Mitchell nods softly. "Yeah, kind of a break, I guess. Taking a couple of months. Space to think, reflect... Look I *was* a bit mixed up, maybe still am a little bit. I needed the time, y'know? Where I could close off for a while and just, I don't know, just go inward. Just be with family and friends, no demands. In the band I was away a hell of a lot, so it was good to spend time with my family again, see people I hadn't seen for ages..."

"A few reports crept out...?" Lawson bites his lip, choosing his words carefully.

Mitchell sniffs, scratching his chest uncomfortably, making a dismissive sound. "Oh that shit. People like to write anything. They've got deadlines, space to fill, mouths to feed..."

"So, there was no truth to any of it? It was just down time, recharging? Figuring things out?"

Mitchell leans back, lighting another cigarette and waving the match in the air before dropping it into the ashtray. He pauses, as though carefully considering what to say in response.

"Yeah, down time. You could say that."

Lawson shoots an attentive glance, waiting for any twitch, any flicker of a new thread to pull on.

Mitchell smiles wryly, picking up the tone again. "Look, you just have to do some clearing out from time to time. It felt like the right time to do it, to get my head together again…"

"For the new direction?"

"Yeah. That's it. Figure out who I am again. Y'know, to move on in every way. I'm different now. It's a healing thing…"

Silence.

Mitchell exhales, shaking his head after a pause. "And…"

Lawson raises his eyebrows slightly. "*And?*"

"To come to terms with things, y'know?"

"Like the split?"

Mitchell squirms slightly in his seat, becoming strangely animated for a second. "Yeah, kind of, I mean the band has been a huge part of my life for over ten years now. But, also, other things too. Stuff from way back, y'know?"

Mitchell runs one hand through his long hair, gathering it loosely at the nape of his neck and breaking eye contact. He draws sharply on the cigarette and exhales, flicking a generous amount of ash into the ashtray. Then he leans into the table, shooting a nervous glance towards Lawson but, just as he is about to form words, shaking his head and breaking away. Gazing instead through a tear-stained window once again. Studying the myriad raindrops that crawl haphazardly down the glass, blurring into each other.

"When things get quiet. I mean, very quiet. Shit comes up, doesn't it?" Mitchell slowly returns his focus to Lawson.

In response, Lawson shifts uncomfortably in his seat. Raising his eyebrows and tilting his head slightly, as though listening to an invisible voice.

Mitchell takes another drag and scratches his forehead. "I started to recall some things, from way back. Weird things. Stuff from much earlier."

Lawson carefully inches forward, the air in the room becoming strangely heavy, thicker, colder. "Before the band?"

"Oh yeah, yeah. I mean way back. Things from when I was small."

Intrigued, Lawson strikes an even softer tone. "What kind of things?"

Mitchell swallows hard and looks down at the table, the ashtray, the recorder. His expression flickering with uncertainty. "I mean, what family doesn't have a strange story to tell, right?"

"Mine…?"

Mitchell laughs out loud. "It's funny. The way things work out…"

Lawson whispers. "You want to share the story?"

Mitchell studies Lawson briefly then shifts back in his seat, smiling slightly. He takes another long drag on the cigarette and clears his throat, scratching the side of his neck.

"It was a day like this, y'know, dull, raining. We were all playing in our bedroom, as kids do. Mum was downstairs doing whatever, probably trying to ignore the noise – I was always the noisiest. I mean, I was the youngest right? The three of us were just doing our thing, which in my case was jumping up and down on my sister's bed, which she hated by the way. But it was next to the window, so I'd jump up and down, kind of, y'know, hands on the windowsill like?" Mitchell holds his hands out as though hanging on an invisible wall. "I'd use the bed like a trampoline a lot of the time. I couldn't jump on my own as my older brother and I, we had bunk beds. And I remember my sister and my brother, they were just playing on the floor."

Lawson laughs softly. "Normal rainy day, bored in the house…"

"Yeah, we were all back from school, letting off some steam because we couldn't go out. And I remember, one time when I was bouncing up and down, looking out across the main road past the bottom of the garden. I remember seeing some old guy standing there, like he just appeared? I don't know, maybe he was there all the time and I just didn't see him, but…"

"Okay…"

Mitchell points somewhere ahead. "He was just there. Standing on the pavement across the road. The street was deserted and he was, I don't know, waiting for something."

"You knew him? A neighbour?"

Mitchell shakes his head. "No. No, never seen him before. But he looked old, I mean, *really* old. It's still a bit away from the house but I could see, he had this long white beard that came down to his stomach almost. And he was a bit hunched over. But what struck me, he wasn't wearing a coat. He was just standing in the rain and it didn't seem to bother him. He had his hands folded in front, kind of peaceful like? After a few seconds he lifted his head a little bit. That freaked me out because he looked right at me…"

Mitchell shivers, taking a long drag on the cigarette, tipping a good amount of ash into the ashtray.

"Y'know when something happens and you just freeze, right? Well, I yelled out to my brother and sister. They weren't sure at first. Didn't know what I was saying but they climbed onto the bed to look. My brother was quite tall, so he was kneeling and peering over the windowsill."

"They all saw him?"

"Yeah. Yeah, they all saw him. I'm trying to remember if my sister waved at him. Not sure, she might have done…"

Confused slightly, Lawson scratches his forehead. "Okay, so?"

"We just watched him for a bit, standing in the rain, like he was waiting at a bus stop, y'know? He just kept looking up at us and we were looking at him. Then I remember some shouting from downstairs and we all turned away for a brief second, staring at the bedroom door. When we turned back, he was gone."

"Completely?"

"Gone. I mean, he wasn't anywhere. And we could see a reasonable distance up and down the street. We had the upstairs bedroom at the front of the house."

"Maybe you just didn't catch him moving away?"

Mitchell shakes his head, his own instinct revealing itself. "Maybe. I mean, we were kids."

Lawson raises his eyebrows briefly. "So…?"

"We didn't think much more about it. I think we all decided he just ran away. Comical really, but it seemed right at the time. I mean, I was small, I thought it was okay that he just disappeared but my brother, he just kept saying to both of us that he must have run away."

"And that was it?"

Mitchell draws on the cigarette then leans back, exhaling a soft blue plume of smoke. "No. Just the beginning. Sometime later, I don't know, maybe a week or two weeks, we all saw him again."

"Sure? The same man?"

"Yeah, as far as I could tell. Mum saw him first, she was downstairs in the front room. My brother was there too, probably watching the television. He called up the stairs, my sister and I, we were in the bedroom playing. We ran down and joined them, all of us just staring out the window."

"He was in the same place?"

"No, he was closer. On our side of the road. He might even have been at the bottom of the garden, I can't recall exactly. In the front, we had a straight driveway up to the garage at the side and everything else was just lawn. He was there, at the bottom. Standing in the rain exactly like last time, just closer."

Mitchell leans forward and crushes the cigarette in the ashtray, rubbing his hands together nervously.

"Then I just remember crying, I started to get really upset, which was strange. I don't know why. I just couldn't look any more, couldn't look at him…"

Mitchell scratches the naked skin on his forearm and frowns. He breaks the seconds' long trance and stares at the cigarette box on the edge of the table. Picking it up gently, he turns it over in his hand and flips open the lid, slowly pulling out another cigarette. He lights it quickly and takes a long drag, the effect instantly calming, reassuring.

"Everyone started trying to comfort me, asking what was wrong and… And the strange thing is, when we all looked again, he was gone."

"Just like last time…"

"Yeah, like, he was nowhere."

"He might have ducked behind the wall?"

Mitchell shrugs. "Maybe. But what would the point of that be?"

"Not sure. A joke or something?"

"Don't think so." Mitchell narrows his eyes, dismissing the idea instantly.

Lawson clears his throat. "You're okay with this being recorded?"

Mitchell shrugs again, studying Lawson carefully. "Alright."

"After that, things got even stranger. My parents were, well, I didn't know at the time but, they were going through a rough patch. A lot of arguments in the house, y'know? We'd listen from upstairs, crowding behind a bedroom door… It would normally end with the front door slamming, all that stuff. But one night we were sitting at the table in the front room eating. All of us. And it was quiet, y'know? Frosty quiet. Just the sound of chewing, knives scraping. Like they'd been arguing but were trying to make it seem like everything was okay. Anyway, there was a couple of sharp knocks at the door." Mitchell knocks twice on the table. "I remember my sister turning to me and whispering, that it was probably him."

Lawson nods. "The man?"

"Yeah. So, Mum gets up, but Dad says to sit down. That it's probably someone selling something and to just leave it because we're all eating here. Mum ignores him and goes anyway. I remember looking at my dad from the corner of my eye and I could tell he was pissed about it. But I suppose that, as we were all there, he kept it together and didn't want to make a scene."

Mitchell flicks a small amount of ash into the ashtray and smiles. "Mum walks back into the front room, face white as a sheet. She just looks at all of us and says he's back. It's him, the old man. At that point I just remember my brother, my sister, all of us pushing our chairs back and running into the hallway. But by the time we got to the door he'd gone – just dark outside."

"Maybe he was round the side of the house, confused?"

Mitchell coughs, shaking his head. "Mum went out to check, round the house, the garage. Nothing. If he was there, he was hiding somewhere else."

"Strange…"

"It was kind of scary but, I don't know, also kind of exciting? We were starting to wonder when he'd show up next. It was like our family secret – our own private gang thing, y'know? Something the three of us could share and talk about."

"But didn't you report any of this? Ask any neighbours?"

Mitchell glances up. "No, never. I mean who do you report stuff like this to? Maybe my parents asked around, I don't remember."

"So, did he come back? Did you see him again?"

Mitchell takes a deep breath and waves his hands in the air, creating a brief blue cigarette cloud above his head. "Oh yeah, yeah. Soon after this, coming back from school one day and walking into the kitchen, he was there, just sitting at the table. We had this typical round pine kitchen table, y'know? We used to call it the painting table. It was always a bit messy. I remember walking into the kitchen and he was just sitting there, smiling, calm as anything. Didn't even look up at me when I walked in, just kept looking straight ahead. I could see his clothes were damp and they had that kind of smell, like a musty smell. And I remember thinking that was a bit weird because it hadn't been raining that day. But…" Mitchell holds his hands up and out. "There he was, inside the house, sitting at our kitchen table, hands folded over and just looking into space. I mean, he was…"

"Weird?"

Mitchell sighs. "Yeah, kind of… old and weird. I don't know, serene?"

Lawson smiles, scratching his head. "So, your mother let him into the house? She knew him?"

Mitchell shakes his head, blowing smoke sideways. "Don't think so, I didn't ask at the time. I was a little bit freaked. I mean, he looked really old, ancient like? I mean, his face…" Mitchell makes an odd swirling gesture with his spare hand. "He did creep me out a little bit. But, at the same time, he seemed alright, he was so calm. I just said hello and nodded at him, keeping my distance."

Lawson scratches his head in confusion. "So, did you find out anything about him? His name? Where he was from?"

"No. He wasn't around all the time. Well, he might have been, but I didn't always see him. And when he was around, he never said anything. Didn't make a sound."

Lawson laughs. "You're kidding me, right?"

Mitchell stares at him. "What do you mean?"

"This is a joke, tell me it's a joke Mitchell?"

Mitchell pulls the putty-coloured ashtray closer to his side of the table and taps his cigarette over it several times. He runs his finger around the clumsy raised edges before pushing the hard grey material away.

"No. It isn't a joke. I'm serious."

Lawson rubs his eyes. "Your parents must have known him?"

"Uh, no, don't think so. If they did, they kept it a secret…"

"They must have, Mitchell. To trust him like that? To let him in the house?"

"You don't believe me?"

The two of them inhale deeply and break away. Reflecting.

"So, what about your father? How did he respond?"

"Well, he'd started working late about this time. I remember him coming home and it was always dark – and this was Spring now. Things weren't great, but at the time, you don't realise, do you? One night, think it was a Friday, I remember walking downstairs and hearing Mum and Dad whispering angrily in the kitchen doorway. Dad was really upset, just saying hello all the time, like he was trying to figure it all out, he couldn't get his mind round it. Mum was calm, really calm, just trying to reassure him that it was all okay. I remember she had her hands on his chest like this…" Mitchell holds his hands up, palms facing Lawson. "When Dad saw me at the end of the hallway he tried to compose himself and smile. Like he was pretending being pleased to see me."

"He wasn't angry about it? The old man in the kitchen all the time? Hanging round the house so much?"

"Not that time. He might have been angry some other times, I don't know. I just remember him being late, felt like every night after a while. Some nights I didn't even see him at all. But that time in the hallway I felt a bit weird because I had a drawing in my hand. I'd started showing some of my drawings to the old man when I knew he was around. Y'know, spaceships and things, all that stuff. But I felt kind of bad about it because Dad was there. I remember feeling that I wanted to run back upstairs, like I'd picked the wrong moment, y'know?"

"So, what did the old man say about your pictures when you used to show them to him?"

"Never said anything. I just used to put them in front of him on the painting table, see if I could get a response."

Mitchell draws deeply on the cigarette and exhales, breaking into small laughter. "Nothing. Not one fucking word. Maybe they weren't good enough, I don't know."

"This is pretty hard to believe…"

Mitchell shrugs. "I get it. But it happened. All real."

"Wow…"

Mitchell lifts the red and white cigarette box, playing with it briefly then placing it back on the table.

"That's how it all went for a while. We started getting used to him being around the house, in the kitchen mostly where Mum would just talk to him, over and over. But sometimes he'd be sitting in different places. I remember a few times he was upstairs in our rooms. My brother was always a bit wary of him but my sister and I, maybe 'cause we're a bit closer in age, we used to make him part of our games. He'd always be the driver or something because he never moved or said anything. Sometimes we'd just put toys in his lap, y'know? Like the plastic figures we were playing with, we'd say you need to hold onto these for us. And he'd just sit there, in this old white wicker chair, staring straight ahead and smiling. Same way as always, like he was there and not there at the same time."

Mitchell laughs then stretches across the table, extinguishing another cigarette in the ashtray. "My sister had this jewellery set, where you could make bracelets and necklaces, y'know with strings, plastic beads, all that stuff. Sometimes she'd try to make jewellery and she'd ask him questions. 'What's your favourite colour?' 'What jewels do you like?' Do you want a necklace or a bracelet?'" She tried, really tried. But after a while, she just gave up. He never said anything, so she just got bored. Even at that age, when you're trying to get a response, eventually you just think, y'know, fuck it…"

Lawson tries to laugh but succeeds only in coughing nervously. He glances at his watch.

"From what I remember it went all the way through that summer. Mum eventually put a folding bed out for him in the spare room. It was this small room at the back of the house, like a storeroom, we only had a few boxes in there, mainly stuff we didn't want to put in the garage. I don't know if he ever slept there, I don't remember seeing him in his bed at all. Until the end anyway."

"Incredible. I'm having a hard time understanding. So, you don't know anything about this old man, but he turns up one day and just, becomes part of the house? Nobody questions it, even your parents? I just find it really strange, Mitchell."

"Well, it's weird but, he almost became a sort of strange surrogate grandfather to us. We never knew our actual grandparents. On one side they both died before any of us were born and, the other ones, they were in New Zealand. It was only phone calls and cards at Christmas, just voices on a phone."

Lawson narrows his eyes, watching from across the table as Mitchell lights yet another cigarette and takes that first, deep drag. "It's possible your parents knew him, they just didn't tell you anything? You were all young."

Mitchell bites his lip. "I'm just telling it as I remember. Maybe if my parents were around now, I'd sit them down and get their side but it's too late for that. Thing is, this only happened one summer. I mean everything else, it was typical stuff, y'know? All normal. We were children, we weren't bothered where he came from or how he got there. What mattered to us, well, to my sister and me, is that he was there – we even started missing him when we couldn't find him. If he wasn't upstairs or in the kitchen, we'd go looking."

"You said your brother wasn't sure?"

Mitchell nods. "Yeah, Ollie, but he was older. He was okay with it all, it didn't freak him out or anything, but after a while he just kept more of a distance. Like ignoring that he was there, that it didn't affect him kind of thing. At that age, a gap of a few years feels huge, y'know? And he had his own things going on by then anyway…"

"And the old man, he never moved?"

"Well, he must have moved around but I never actually saw him walking anywhere. Like I never saw him walking up the stairs or walking in the hallway. He was always standing or sitting."

"And never spoke? No name?"

Mitchell shakes his head. "Nope, nothing. I think once I caught him nearly moving his head."

"Really?"

"Yeah, one time. In the kitchen. I was putting a few drawings in front of him on the painting table. I swear I saw him move his head, just a bit, but it was corner of the eye stuff so I can't be sure."

"Can you remember the drawing?"

Mitchell puffs out his cheeks and exhales. "I seem to remember it was people in a big car, moving along a road with trees. Like driving through a forest? Pretty normal. No dragons."

Lawson laughs. "No dragons… No flying saucers, no super heroes?"

Mitchell laughs too. "No, not that time."

"So, you were saying this went on for the rest of summer?"

"Yes. I remember the sun in the afternoon, the evening. As I've said, Dad was never around much then so, when he was there – and we'd be eating together – I remember those times vividly. Often the old man would be on the back lawn staring at us through the patio doors. He was always sitting on one of the old wooden deckchairs we used to store at the back of the garage. He'd just be sitting there on the grass, like he was enjoying the sunshine, staring back at us through the glass. Well, maybe at us, but probably through us, just staring off somewhere."

"Unbelievable…"

"At the table Becky, my sister, she'd keep prodding me, whispering, trying to get me to look at him. I had to keep chewing and ignoring her, just to stifle my laughter, there was something funny about it then. And when Dad was there, he was moody, y'know? Kind of pissed off. Like he didn't want to be there with us and hated every fucking mouthful. The small moments at that time and all the strange stuff, it must have been unbearable for him. At some point during those meals, it struck me, even at that age, Mum was handling it all much better than he was, whatever was going on. She was usually the one who'd break the silence, always making polite conversation or trying to. But even Mum would give up eventually and then it would just be trying to ignore the sound of cutlery. Like a weird, clumsy comedy, y'know? Just trying not to make Dad even more angry."

Mitchell leans back and turns his head, a soft plume of blue smoke thickening the air. As he exhales, he catches Lawson glancing at his watch and tapping his fingers several times on the table.

"So, how did all this…"

"End?"

"Right."

"Just a normal day…"

Lawson nods, lowering his elbows to the table, folded hands underneath his chin.

"A weekend I think, I know we weren't at school so it might have been a holiday or something, don't remember exactly. I was upstairs, playing in my room alone, think my brother and sister were outside. It was a nice day – sunny, y'know, late summer so not really hot, but warm enough. T-shirt weather. And then…"

Mitchell swallows hard, his expression tightening. He draws from the cigarette deeply as though needing reassurance.

"Then my dad, he started screaming, shouting, from downstairs. It was a horrible noise. I was upstairs and I remember just freezing instantly, I'd never heard that kind of sound before. Y'know, Dad got angry a lot, but this was different. I remember my skin just tightening up and going really cold."

Mitchell tips a generous amount of ash into the ashtray and brushes his mouth with the back of his hand.

"He started shouting, loud, really loud. Like, everyone, drop whatever you're doing and get here right now loud. Then it turned into a kind of wailing – I didn't have a clue what was going on. I dropped the stuff I was playing with and went to the bedroom door, listening. I was a bit scared at first, I wasn't sure what was happening. Maybe Mum and Dad arguing again but it didn't sound the same. So, I was standing there for a few seconds, kind of wishing my sister or my brother were there to take the lead and make my mind up for me."

Mitchell draws on the cigarette and rubs his forehead.

"Anyway, I crept out onto the landing and just listened. I heard the others downstairs y'know? Running into the kitchen, rushing around, shouting too. When I heard all of them, I rushed down the stairs. I remember running along the hallway and they were all in the room at the back."

"The storeroom? Where your mother placed the bed?"

Mitchell nods. "Yeah, there wasn't much space in there, so I just tagged onto the end next to everyone. I remember looking up at my dad. He was at the bottom of the low bed and his face was pure white. I mean scared, really scared, probably just holding it together. Everyone else was confused like, scared and confused."

"What was happening?"

"The old man was in the bed, the same look on his face, just staring up at the ceiling with a thick blanket tucked under his chin and that long white beard trailing over the top. And there was that smell, the same musty, damp smell…"

"Dad was shouting out, telling everyone to look. We were all just standing there next to the bed. Mum was really upset, I kept looking at her, she had her hand up at her mouth and was holding onto Becky. I didn't understand why Dad kept shouting, I remember thinking that the old man was probably just asleep? I mean, he never responded to anything right? So, all the screaming and shouting wasn't going to make any difference."

Mitchell coughs loudly, a deep hacking cough that clears his throat. "I remember stepping a bit closer and that's when I started to see it. This light green mist, twisting out from under the blanket around his neck."

"What?"

"Yeah. I remember Mum saying, 'what's happening?' or 'what's wrong with him?' something like that. I don't know if she saw it too."

Mitchell rubs his eyes with the palm of each hand and sniffs. "Then Dad pulled the blanket back quickly and I couldn't believe what I was seeing. This massive green mist, like fog almost, just drifted in all directions. I remember everyone looking away and crying, like really disgusted, repulsed by it all. The smell got really overpowering, that same mustiness, but much thicker. Like you could choke on it? I just couldn't look away..."

"He was dead?"

Mitchell stumbles over his words. "Well, I mean, he wasn't there anymore. He was gone, missing, nothing left. It was just his head on the pillow with his spine still attached, lying there on the sheet. But everything else? Gone."

Mitchell holds his hands up to his mouth, as though tasting the smell all over again. "Dad kind of crumpled to the floor and Mum just kept saying, 'oh God, oh God' over and over. I don't know if my sister ever looked at his remains on the bed, but I do remember my brother just running out. I mean, he was just out of there. I wanted to follow him but couldn't, my feet were stuck, like part fear, disgust, but also part curiosity, y'know? Like morbid curiosity, that kid thing."

"Jesus, I can't imagine what that must have been like."

"I remember looking at his face. It was still the same. Eyes open and staring straight ahead, all peaceful. We must have just stood there for a couple of minutes, looking at him, breathing in all that shit or whatever it was, filling the room. I try not to think about that. I mean, what would you do in that situation? I didn't know. I didn't know whether to be sad and cry, or to be scared, or whatever."

"So, what did you do?"

"I remember my dad, he's practically sitting on the floor by this point and just thinking aloud, saying 'what do we do now?' I don't think anyone answered, we're all just staring at what's left on the bed. Watching this green fog gradually disappear and trying not to be sick right there. Mum unlocked the door to the garage to try and help with the smell but mostly it was all of us just standing there in shock."

"That's horrible, Mitchell. You reported it? Did you call the police?"

Mitchell shakes his head, as though the mere suggestion was ludicrous. "The police? What could we tell them?"

"But the old man? Whatever happened to him, it's tragic, someone must have known he was missing?"

"Maybe, I don't know for sure. I never asked. The last thing I remember is Mum dragging Becky and I away, going out to find my brother. He had gone outside, round the front. He didn't say anything about what had happened, instead he just asked if we wanted to kick the ball around a bit at the park along the road. So that's what we did."

"When we came back, I didn't say anything to Mum. I remember sneaking into the storeroom and there was nothing. Just the same old boxes and household stuff. The bed was gone, maybe a slight smell but nothing more than that. I asked what had happened, Mum just told me to be quiet and to never mention him – or any of it – ever again."

"So, what happened to the body? What was left?"

Mitchell trembles, eyes misting slightly. He pulls the misshapen oval ashtray even closer and topples a generous column of ash inside. Then he looks over at Lawson, his face drawn, serious, before stubbing the cigarette out with the others. Rubbing the edge of the rough grey ashtray he exhales deeply and settles back in his chair, looking out the nearby window.

"No idea." Mitchell swallows. "I don't know. Maybe Dad did something? But he was gone and…"

"And?"

"I never saw him again."

# The Barton Doghouse

A red car snakes through a grey industrial estate. Passing monotonous lines of bland factory units, broken only by large painted signs and colourful names. Each unit exactly as the one before, desperate to punch out from the straight-line concrete swamp. Sprinkled casually between, looking down like dour parents, several taller buildings rise. Blank and silent, hiding behind rows of dark reflective glass.

Kaylee rides shotgun. Checking a row of dull red spots at the side of her nose with a small circular mirror. She moves both mirror and head around, studying the last-minute application of concealer and foundation. Just enough to cover the blooming clouds of small sharp lumps dotted across her face. She opens her mouth wide and the mirror fills with off-white teeth, a long silver brace and a twitching pale tongue.

The mirror snaps shut. Kaylee opens the glove compartment and drops the emergency make-up kit back inside. She tries to settle in the seat but can't help glancing at her reflection one more time. Checking in the wing mirror, adjusting her long hair, teasing a healthy mix of blonde and brown.

"Maybe I should have tied it back?"

"Probably have to do that anyway."

Kaylee exhales, scratching her leg. "I'm nervous, Mum."

"It's okay to be nervous, Kaylee." Lindsay glances at her from the corner of her eyes. "At least, you've been there before. You know what to expect."

"Still nervous though."

"Well, they seemed like nice people when we visited."

Kaylee shrugs, brushing the plain maroon T-shirt and removing a long blonde hair from her shapeless black cardigan.

Slightly tongue in cheek. "You did always say you wanted to work with animals?"

"Mum…" Kaylee sniggers uncomfortably, slightly embarrassed by the childhood recollection. "That was years ago!"

"You haven't changed *that* much Kaylee. You still feel that way, don't you?"

"Not really, just didn't know what else to pick from the list." Kaylee becomes more animated. "I don't want to work in an office..."

"It'll be fine. Ms Barton seemed quite a character. She took a shine to you." Lindsay laughs.

"Mum, stop it."

The car trundles forward to another junction, turning left and following a long circular road round. Sitting back from the edge, a line of shabby, nondescript factory and business units. All drab brick and old concrete, worn wooden cladding and modest panes of bar or mesh-covered glass. Everything quiet except for one forecourt, a few people in high visibility jackets, milling around at the rear of a large white van parked in front.

Kaylee stares at the buildings, reading the large digits on the front of some, pointing and guessing at the others. Number one, number two, number three, that must be number four, number five, six, seven, I think that must be eight. All the way up to…

"Number 13…"

"What?"

Kaylee laughs uncomfortably. "Mum, it's number 13."

"Really?"

"That's number eleven there. This one must be twelve... Number 13."

"So it is. Funny how we didn't pick up on it last time, Kaylee."

Lindsay tucks the car near a wall outside the plain unit, the building distinguished from the others in the row only by two distinctive signs. One long and fixed to the outside wall, the other tall and fixed at eye level at the side of the door. Each a weather-beaten bright yellow panel, covered in various sizes of red text complemented by a multitude of dog silhouettes.

Lindsay switches off the engine and peers through the windscreen, watching as a young man in overalls bursts through the reinforced glass door, carrying an A-board. She waves as he looks in their direction, his expression hard and tired. He nods, barely in acknowledgement before lifting the board again and placing it near the edge of the road.

"That must be Brian Doltrice. Ms Barton said I'd be working with him this week. Michael's older brother, Mum. Y'know, Michael, in my class?"

"From primary?"

"No, Jane's old boyfriend." Kaylee breathes quickly. "Oh God, Mum, I'm getting nervous now. What if he starts talking about her?"

"It'll be fine."

Kaylee deflates. Stretching thin arms in front, trembling white hands poking out from each sleeve. "Look, Mum."

"It's alright to be nervous, Kaylee." Lindsay reaches around her neck, lifting a long gold necklace up and over her head. "Here. This will help you."

"No, Mum."

"Take it."

Kaylee holds the necklace, studying the golden tear-shaped locket. She carefully clicks the tiny clasp and opens the door, revealing a worn sepia portrait of a woman smiling calmly, intense eyes behind small round spectacles and hair scraped back tightly. A thick dark shawl draped over her shoulders.

"Your grandmother wore it all the time. Whenever Mum felt nervous or things were difficult for her, she'd rub the locket and ask the spirit of her own grandmother, Maria, for help. Some power apparently. I don't know."

Kaylee stares at the portrait, rubbing her fingers over the surface of the dull gold locket. "Maria? Huh, she was old here."

"That's eleven children for you, Kaylee." Lindsay laughs. "Mum swore by it, said it always brought her good luck. That's why she passed it to me a few years ago. I've never had to use it. Been in our family a long time. It's yours for the week. Put it on, just… don't lose it."

Kaylee closes the locket and lifts it over her head, slipping the gold pendant down and under her maroon cotton T-shirt. "Thanks, Mum."

"No-one will see it or know about it. When you need, she'll be there for you."

Suddenly, a fist bounces rapidly several times on glass. Startled, Lindsay lowers the window.

"Can't park there. You need to move the car? Delivery, yeah? Big truck usually, need the space."

"Oh, fine, I'll only be a minute. You must be Brian? I'm Lindsay Morris. I've brought my daughter Kaylee? Just dropping her off for the work experience?"

"Awright."

Lindsay removes the keys and opens the door, stepping onto concrete. She studies Brian from top to bottom, examining the bold Barton Doghouse logo on one side of his dark overall.

"You'll have to see Ms Barton. I don't know anything about that stuff, the work experience."

"Oh, okay. She's available? It's okay to go in?"

Brian shrugs. "She's in there somewhere. Going out soon, I think. Still need to move your car though."

Lindsay nods and leans down to look at Kaylee, gesturing to leave the car. Kaylee quickly steps out, hoisting a modest backpack over her shoulder, nervously glancing at her mother across the roof of the car. They both watch Brian wearily drag himself back to the main door.

"I need to move the car, Kaylee, just wait at the front there and we'll sort it all out with Ms Barton."

Timidly, Kaylee approaches the front of the business unit. Brian, keeping the red-framed, reinforced glass door open with his back, barely acknowledges her standing nearby.

Lindsay turns the keys and the car purrs once more into life. Looking in the rear-view mirror, she releases the handbrake slowly, gently reversing the car. Engaging first gear, she glances through the windscreen at Kaylee then at Brian, now gesticulating with his hand to keep moving to the side.

Turning away from the small red car crawling forward slowly, Brian studies Kaylee intensely. "Y'know my brother Michael, don't you?"

"Mm-hm."

"Went out with Jane Wilkinson? One of your friends, right?"

"Uh huh."

"Yeah, he knows all about you."

Kaylee swallows uncomfortably, biting her lip.

Brian pauses for a few moments, then shakes himself from top to bottom. "If you want to work here proper, you need to be in earlier. Work starts at seven."

A cloud of uneasiness rapidly descends, only broken when Lindsay strolls back across the forecourt. "That's out of the way now I hope, Brian."

"Should be awright." Brian nods, pushing the door wider. "The people in the next unit usually complain when we park there. Not seen anyone this morning though."

"Won't be long, I just need to have a quick chat with Ms Barton. Go on, Kaylee."

Brian forces the door open fully, frowning at Kaylee as she steps through into the bland reception area with Lindsay behind. Closing the door sharply, Brian peers through the metal grille-covered glass briefly, checking the position of the A-board one last time.

"Awright, I'll see if Ms Barton is available…"

Words tail away as he shuffles through a grubby plain door, directly opposite the main entrance. As he vanishes, a storm of barking floods reception. Every shade bursting forth, from strangled yelps to deeper, throatier barks. On hearing the boisterous noise, Kaylee looks towards her mother with a grudgingly warm half-smile.

Lindsay whispers. "See? Told you it'll be fun."

Kaylee looks around reception, the thrill of the animal noise unable to stop her heart sinking a little at the worn, utilitarian feel of the room.

A high grey counter splits the floor in two, the front surface covered in posters of different sizes: dog food and treats, flea and worm treatments, local dog-walking services. On top, an old-style logbook sits open with several cheap ink pens scattered next to it. Further along, a branded 'Barton Doghouse' A4 notepad, sits next to a grubby, motionless Maneki-neko. At the other end of the counter, a card box of fluffy blue pom-poms, each one with a long white ribbon label, two bug eyes placed haphazardly and small paper wings, sits next to a scabby charity collection box. Bold, comic sans lettering recommends a £1 donation to help abandoned dogs across the region.

Intrigued, Kaylee can't help herself leaning over the counter to examine the desk behind. In the corner next to the wall, a typical desktop computer sits gloomily, dusty monitor angled away from prying eyes. A large blotter pad with a multitude of messages scrawled across it, covers the main working area. Situated behind this, several old mustard-coloured plastic trays with various papers stacked inside. Dotted across the whole desk, the usual assortment of office stalwarts – a heavy-duty stapler, random pens and pencils, a tape dispenser and an old hole punch.

Along the back wall, a couple of tall bookcases with a messy arrangement of books, leaflets and various folders sit next to a large floor-standing wire basket. A hastily scrawled sign with the word 'donations' is attached to the front and a few tins of food languish within.

In the other corner, near the window, a modest dirty photocopier stands silently, all powered down.

Lindsay glances at her watch impatiently, looking out through the main door towards the car. No sooner has she done this than the door behind swings open and a short woman with messy hair ploughs through.

"Sort it out please, Brian! Ah, good morning, Kaylee, wonderful to see you again!"

Kaylee smiles awkwardly. "Hi, Ms Barton."

"I'm so glad you're here dear!"

"Oh?"

"Remember Anita, the nice lady on reception? I'm afraid she's signed off for the whole week."

"Really?" Lindsay chimes in, concerned.

"I'm afraid so, Kaylee's mum. Not a great start to Monday morning."

"Is the work experience still convenient then, Ms Barton?"

"Oh yes, I mean, it's always a little chaotic here." Ms Barton throws her arms in the air and circles them wildly. "We had a new kennel system installed last week and Anita was the only one who had proper training but… Well, we'll manage."

"You're sure?"

"Yes. Yes of course. Brian is here and though I'll be out for a little while today, I'm onsite the rest of the week."

Kaylee flashes an uncertain glance at Lindsay.

"Anyway, you're both here now. It's lovely to see you all again. I hope Brian has been looking after you? I really don't know where we'd be without him sometimes."

Lindsay points outside. "I moved the car, a delivery?"

"Deliveries are usually tomorrow, dear but, yes, whatever." Brushing past Lindsay and Kaylee and moving behind the counter. "Now, Kaylee's mum. I'm sorry dear, I can't remember your name?"

"Lindsay."

Laughing brightly. "Oh, that's lovely. I'm sorry, Lindsay, haven't had my second coffee of the morning yet.

Now, Kaylee, do you have the forms I asked you to complete and bring with you?"

"Ah, yes, Ms Barton." Kaylee lowers her backpack to the floor, rummaging inside and removing two sheets of paper hastily folded into uneven quarters. "Here they are."

"That's it dear, thank you. Have you brought some ID?"

Kaylee retrieves her passport, placing it on the counter.

"Excellent."

Ms Barton tucks paper and passport away at the side of the computer, before rattling the spacebar on the keyboard. She lets out a muted shriek when nothing happens, stamping a playful foot on the floor.

"Brian, it's not even booted up yet! I'll have to do the registration later, Kaylee. Sorry, with Anita off everything is…"

Kaylee drops her eyes to the floor, stifling mild laughter.

"Oh dear…" Ms Barton tips the keyboard upside down and shakes it, wiping away the various crumbs that tumble out. "Disgusting, Anita…"

"If everything is okay, Ms Barton, I need to take my son to the nursery? He's with a neighbour right now."

Ms Barton walks to the end of the counter. "Yes, dear, I understand. Do you have any questions before you go?"

"No. No, I don't think so."

"We'll start Kaylee with the basic duties as discussed. Preparing the food, some grooming, play time in the yard..."

"You'll enjoy that, Kaylee?" Lindsay glances at her, no doubt catching her sarcastic smile. "Oh, I did pack a few lunch things, Ms Barton."

"Good, yes, not much round here I'm afraid. One of those all-day breakfast vans around lunchtime. Brian usually grabs something there. Anita tends to bring her own lunch."

"You've got some money if you need it, haven't you, Kaylee?"

"Ah, yes." Kaylee smiles at her mother, all enamel and metal.

"Right, I'll leave you to it. Have fun, Kaylee." Lindsay reaches out a reassuring hand. "Take care of the dogs and I'll see you at… Did we say a finish time today, Ms Barton?"

"About five o'clock, dear…"

"Five o'clock then. Okay, see you later."

Lindsay exits with a wave and a nearly invisible double thumbs up gesture. In response, Kaylee waves her hands nervously, without raising either arm.

Returning to the screen. "At last! Let me log in, Kaylee, then I'll be with you."

Kaylee picks up her backpack from the floor, swinging it over one shoulder. Instinctively, she touches the gold pendant through her cotton T-shirt.

"Unfortunately, it won't be dog time all week, Kaylee. With Anita being off, I need you to sit in the front office for a while, the mornings mainly."

"That's okay, Ms Barton…"

Leaning over the desk and whispering. "I try and keep Brian away from the front office, he's usually terrible with people."

Unsure whether to smile or not. "Oh, okay."

"I think you'll be perfect on the phone, dear. Just a simple 'good morning, thank you for calling the Barton Doghouse, how can I help?'"

"Mm-hm, I can do that." Kaylee mouths the greeting several times under her breath.

"Thankfully, it's a quiet week with bookings. Some of our regulars will drop in as we have the Pamper Pod, every Monday and Thursday. You'll meet Linda, a lovely girl, she runs the grooming station."

"Great." Kaylee nods. "Sounds nice."

"And you'll meet Mrs Atkins. She'll be in later with Baby Belle." Ms Barton smiles broadly. "Her poodle? A lovely dog but, oh dear, horribly spoiled."

Kaylee laughs. "Baby Belle, that's cute."

"Right, let me add you to the database." Exhaling impatiently. "Oh, it's so slow. I really must get Martin to have a look at this again."

"He works here too?"

"Oh no, dear! He built the system years ago. An old neighbour, a friend of my ex-husband. It still does the job, just getting a bit slow these days. Might need to find him again…"

"Ah."

Ms Barton leans across the desk and chuckles. "Assuming he's still alive of course."

Kaylee laughs, studying Ms Barton standing next to the slightly ripped swivel chair. A stout woman, probably late fifties or early sixties, wearing a worn branded polo shirt. An earlier version of the company logo boldly displayed in comic sans over one ample breast. A mess of spiky short brown hair with large gold earrings drooping down. Each hand, thick and strong, decorated with several large gold rings. One upper arm revealing hints of a large tattoo, just peeking out from under cotton. A kindly, expressive face – rough but not unattractive – with generous layers of make-up filling hard-earned laughter lines.

Handing the paper and passport back. "Right, that's you in the team database, dear."

"Great."

"Later in the week, you can help with the ordering, but let's get you settled in because I need to be heading off shortly. Brian should be finishing the observations. Might even have a couple of the dogs out. We don't have many staying with us right now."

Grabbing a pen from the desk and placing it in a solitary pocket, Ms Barton glides past Kaylee and heads to the heavy inner door. Opening it slowly, a symphony of barking strikes up from within.

"Let's go, dear!"

Feeling a thin sliver of excitement, Kaylee skips nervously into a room that separates the front and main sections of the building. Nothing more than dirty white walls, worn carpet tiles and a pair of doors with reinforced vision panels Ms Barton is holding open.

"Now, Kaylee, remember the team room?"

"I think so." Raising her voice over the babble of animal noise.

"I left a polo shirt on the table. Only have an XXL left, but it's just for the week, isn't it?"

Kaylee nods meekly, walking into a broad corridor. She steals a glance into a tiny office on the left, casting her eyes across a busy and disorganised interior.

"Oh, there he is." Ms Barton waves briskly through large, toughened glass windows running along one side. "Brian!"

Kaylee steps beside her, staring into a large concrete space like a small warehouse, dominated by several rows of generous-sized kennels. In the middle of the floor stands

Brian, pulling forcefully on a lead attached to a large Doberman Pinscher, snarling and barking viciously.

"Oh dear, that dog is a menace." Ms Barton shakes her head. "One of our regulars, owner always away on business."

"What's his name?"

"Pacer. He can be a sweetie but, oh, he can change in an instant. And he's always a handful the first few days." Ms Barton leans forward to the glass and screws up her face. "We have to keep him away from all the others."

Kaylee rubs her cheek on the shoulder of her cardigan then stretches each sleeve over pale hands, briefly raising a nervous cotton-covered stump to acknowledge Brian looking at her through the window. He attempts a grim smile then breaks away, clumsily stepping forward then back, as Pacer tries to force him towards the other dogs in their kennels nearby.

Moving along the wall, Ms Barton points to the far end of the large kennel area. "See the shutter door? That leads out to the yard, remember? There's a gazebo out there today. It's where Linda runs the Pamper Pod."

Ms Barton moves back along, pointing in the totally opposite direction. "The storeroom is the other side. No doubt Brian or Linda will ask you to get things for them."

"Okay."

"Right, dear, you go and get yourself sorted, I need to prepare for my visit. I arranged to meet some suppliers a while ago and just can't let them down at such short notice. If you shadow Brian, he'll make sure you're okay."

"Right, thanks." Kaylee pokes her hands back out from her sleeves.

"Well, isn't this fine, dear?" Ms Barton excitedly holds out a hand, "Welcome to the Barton Doghouse."

Kaylee extends a limp, pale hand, quickly swamped in a strong, brisk handshake.

"Ms Barton, where can I put my backpack?"

Pointing at an open door along the hallway. "You'll have to find a space for it in the team room, dear."

"Okay."

The team room is small and bright, resplendent in years old pastel yellow paint complemented with several random and nondescript MDF units. Two metal sinks with grubby mixer taps sit near a mesh-covered window, affording only a bland view of damaged wooden fencing in the final stages of returning to nature. Dotted across the work surfaces: boxes of tea bags, packets of instant soup, a few empty jars, discarded mugs and bowls and a cheap plastic jug-style cordless kettle. Parked on the floor, a modest refrigerator makes a barely noticeable hum while, on the opposite side, a circular table with four wooden chairs all sit crammed together. Sitting on the tabletop, a navy-blue polo shirt with a bright yellow Barton Doghouse logo.

Kaylee drops her backpack on the wooden chair closest to the wall, removing her phone from one of the additional pockets on the side. She messages her mum quickly, telling her that everything is fine and that she is about to start work. Then she locks the screen, dropping the phone back in the pocket and zipping it securely.

A charge of electricity runs through Kaylee as she removes the folded polo shirt. Holding it up at the shoulders, she is part-amused and part-appalled as the dark material reveals its generous proportions. No problem fitting two of her inside – maybe three even. But at least there's no-one other than Brian to see her wearing it across the whole week.

Ms Barton peers around the edge of the doorway, a bunch of keys in one hand and a crash helmet in the other. "Toilet is next door, dear, you can change in there. I'm picking a few things up from the office then I'm off. Tell Brian to be nice to Mrs Atkins and Baby Belle. I'll be back sometime this afternoon."

"Great, thank you, Ms Barton."

"Any questions, ask Brian. I've told him to look after you." Ms Barton taps the set of keys on the door frame and smiles. "See you later, dear."

Kaylee removes her cardigan, wrapping it around the back of one of the wooden chairs. She grabs the polo shirt and heads into the tiny toilet cubicle next door, fixing the simple lock behind her.

The room is cold and grey, decorated only with a plastic air freshener and a synthetic approximation of warm spice. A small white vase sits on a narrow windowsill behind the only toilet, two sprigs of artificial flowers within. On the wall, a scabby square mirror panel at roughly eye height, above a small washbasin.

Shivering, Kaylee slips off her top quickly, touching the golden pendant resting between small polka-dot patterned breasts. She clasps it tightly in one hand, mouthing invisible words, hoping for an enjoyable or, at least, an easy day.

She lowers the large polo shirt over her thin frame and smooths it out, brushing two generous navy-blue wings billowing out either side. Before opening the door, Kaylee quickly runs a hand over the side of her face, touching a series of small, concealed bumps.

Placing her T-shirt with her cardigan in the team room, Kaylee skips to the long window in the hallway and checks to see if Brian is still there. Unable to locate him,

Kaylee pulls the handle attached to the heavy door in the middle. With a grunt, she opens it just enough to let her exit from carpet to concrete.

The barking is overpowering, forcing Kaylee to stand still for a few seconds and acclimatise. A desperate sound, ferocious and demanding. Harsh, deep yaps and yelps, swirling and echoing into each other. Each dog calling out: friendly, curious, frustrated, bored, angry.

Kaylee casts her eyes over the drab yet spacious cages, arranged in four rows of four. Unable to see clearly end to end, she steps forward slowly, calling out several times and looking either way.

"Hello? Brian?"

Moving closer, Kaylee acknowledges two of the nearby dogs. One yelping and spinning in circles, the other lying quietly to the side, utterly disinterested. As she approaches, the noisy dog moves towards the front, standing on its hind legs briefly and clawing at thick wire, eager to make an impression.

Kaylee examines the laser printed notice on the side of the kennel. "And your name is… Georgie, an English Springer Spaniel. Oh, hi Georgie…"

Still excited, Georgie runs across his kennel before bouncing back to the front, tail wagging and yelping constantly, enjoying the attention.

"And who is this…" Kaylee slides to the next cage. "You're… Chester, oh, that's a sweet name. And you're a Border Collie. Do you know how I know that, Chester? Because Auntie Cheryl has a dog just like you."

Hearing his name, Chester gets to his feet and strolls forward, collapsing close to where Kaylee is kneeling. "You look so bored, Chester. I'll ask Brian if we can play in the yard. When I'm finished."

Suddenly, a loud buzzer smothers the barking. Kaylee shoots up immediately, uncertain what it means, glancing round but unable to find the source.

"Delivery…?"

Stepping away from the kennels quickly, Kaylee jogs back to a sturdy workbench situated near the hallway door. A new laptop, powered on but with a black screen, sits beside two bulky units resembling small mixing desks, with several lights flashing on top. A litter of power and data cables connect everything together, trailing off to a handful of wall sockets.

Mumbling. Whispering. "Must be the new system?"

Kaylee nudges the mouse, the black screen disappearing, replaced with a typical password required message box.

"Where is Brian…?"

The buzzer alarm stops instantly. From the far side of the kennel area, a firing sound of metal on metal, like heavy bolts snapping. One. Two. Three. Four.

"Brian…!" Startled, Kaylee looks around, nervous and bewildered. Unsure what is happening, what to do next. "Where the fuck is he?"

Kaylee sprints forward to the kennel row at the end, seemingly the source of the metallic noises. She holds her hands to her mouth in horror, realising the gates to the entire row are now unlocked.

"Shit!"

Checking each of the kennels quickly, Kaylee smiles and exhales in relief when she realises all the cubicles in the row are empty. Except for a typical assortment of rugs, blankets, toys and bowls, clean and ready for the next lodger.

Pulling one of the kennel gates further open, Kaylee examines the heavy-duty lock on the front and softly swings it back. After a second, the gate slowly creeps open again, remaining ajar.

"Brian!"

Kaylee runs across the bare concrete floor, moving to the dirty window near the large shutter door on the other side and peering through. Expecting to see Brian there, perhaps checking or cleaning the various climbing walls and frames. But no, still no sign.

Whispering. "Fucker's probably leaving me on my own deliberately. Is this what it's going to be for the week?"

Irritated, Kaylee walks briskly across the open area, passing the laptop on the table and the middle kennel rows with Georgie and Chester and a few others. Then the top row, all empty except for Pacer. Animated and troubled, barking ferociously as she walks by, a thick leash still attached to his collar.

Just as Kaylee is about to open the white door to the storeroom, Brian stumbles through without warning, arms laden with large tins of dog food.

"Brian!"

Surprised, then adopting his usual gruff demeanour. "Here already…"

"Brian, the kennels at the end?" Kaylee points to the laptop on the workbench. "Something happened. An alarm. They're open now."

Face hardening, accusing. "What did you do?"

"I didn't do anything," Feeling her cheeks flush at the abrupt accusation. "Just happened. There was an alarm, didn't you hear it?"

Brian barges past, heading towards the laptop on the workbench. He drops the tins carefully, wiping each palm on the front of his branded overall, studying the lock screen intensely.

"I thought something was wrong." Kaylee continues to unload. "I didn't know what to do. It's just, like, the kennels unlocked."

Clearly flustered, Brian gestures to Kaylee to calm down, shaking his head dismissively and flapping his hands. Studying the screen, he rubs his scalp through dark and slightly greasy unkempt hair.

"Aw no."

Kaylee moves closer. "What is it?"

"Stay back." Brian rubs his work-clothes covered torso in frustration. "It's the new system."

"What about it?"

"Nuthin, awright? Just stay back. It's new. It's how it works."

"So, it's all okay? It's meant to do that?"

Brian exhales deeply. "Are you going to spend all week asking stupid questions?"

In her head, Kaylee flashes the words 'fuck you', each letter lit spectacularly in bright pulsing neon. She closes her eyes and bites her lip, content to watch the huge burning letters fade away, all to a soundtrack of barking dogs.

Brian returns his gaze to the monitor, gripping the mouse and moving the pointer aimlessly around the screen.

"What's wrong? Brian?"

"Nuthin' Kaylee, nothin's wrong. It's fine."

Kaylee twists the generous cotton material billowing either side. "The password? Can I…"

"You can start with some cleaning." Without looking up, Brian points to the side. "The block at the end of the wall. The ones that are open now. Clean 'em. Floor. Bowls."

"The—"

"All there, everything you need." Brian swivels the same arm, pointing over his shoulder to the far corner, towards an area occupied by a long metal sink and several chest high storage units. "Mops, buckets, all the cleaning stuff. In the cupboards."

"So, I just…"

Looking sideways and increasingly exasperated, avoiding eye contact. "Y'know how to clean right?"

"No." Although not confident, Kaylee manages to roll her eyes sarcastically.

"Get on with it then." Brian exhales wearily, grumbling. "I need to sort the food out."

Kaylee takes several steps back. Her suspicion that working with Brian Doltrice for a whole week was going to be a challenge already coming true. But, during the previous night while lying in bed with her mind racing, she'd reckoned on at least a couple of days before things became toxic. So far, it's taken less than an hour on her very first day.

Although wanting to respond in kind. To give all that offended and bubbling nervous energy some even muted expression, Kaylee acknowledges that now is a time to just walk away in silence.

And that's exactly what she does, leaving Brian without another word. Leaving him to stare at the dancing mouse pointer and large digital numbers changing on his watch.

***

Kaylee drags the mop back and forth. Surface dirt lifting easily, leaving a wet shine that evaporates quickly. As she sweeps left and right, a cloying smell of pine wash evokes fuzzy primary school memories. Images from her past firing and flickering, mainly young, clumsy faces. Some still known to Kaylee, but many having moved on to different secondary schools.

The mop squelches in the wringer and plops to the floor, swinging left and right as Kaylee moves slowly back towards the gate of the fourth kennel.

It hadn't taken her long to figure out that none of the kennels really needed cleaning. At the most, a little bit of dirt in the corners, but nothing more than that. Even so, she was pleased to have something to lose herself in. Something where she could switch off her mind and take the sting out of the day so far.

She quickly recalled her last image of Brian, the one she snapped while looking over her shoulder as she assembled her cleaning kit. Watching him get frustrated near the computer, rocking back and forth, scratching his head, punching the air. The recollection makes her grin, perhaps a little wickedly, and she bites her lips to halt the smile spreading further. She glances over her shoulder, no-one there now, just the melee of several dogs yelping at each other.

Tipping the content of the bucket into the sink, Kaylee rinses the inside with a torrent of cold water and places the old metal on the floor nearby, mop propped up inside. Then, gathering the food and water bowls from each kennel, she drops them into the large sink and fills it with warm, soapy water.

After several minutes of washing and rinsing bowls that were hardly dirty in the first place, Kaylee watches the water drain away and shakes her hands. Unable to locate a towel, she finishes the drying process with the help of the generous cotton of her polo shirt.

Brian has disappeared again, so Kaylee skips across the concrete and heads through the door to the inner hallway. In the team room, she removes her phone and unlocks the screen, tapping letters quickly and without error. *Working with Brian. Just finished cleaning some kennels. Doing OK.* Adding a small heart to the text, Kaylee taps the send icon and returns the phone to her backpack.

Tempted slightly to sit at the table and study the latest notifications from her circle of friends, Kaylee glances at the clock on the wall and decides instead to find Brian. Still driven by a need to see whether she can take Chester out to play in the yard.

Back through the door to the main section, Kaylee can't help nudging the mouse as she passes the workbench. The black screen flashes, transforming still into the password required message box.

"Hey, Chester…" Looking in the cage, watching as the dog inside moves wearily forward. "I haven't forgotten. I'm going to ask Brian now."

Opening the storeroom door gently, Kaylee is immediately confronted with tall and busy racks of boxes and packets. Creeping round the side, she is startled to see Brian standing in the gloomy light, running his hands over the head of a woman in a bright yellow top on her knees in front of him.

After a second his eyes flicker, opening wide. "Shit!"

"Brian?" Kaylee gasps and looks away immediately. "What the—"

Frenziedly adjusting his clothes, Brian stumbles sideways. "Linda! Fuck…"

Instinctively, Kaylee holds her hands up, pale skin crawling, flushing, burning with embarrassment. "Oh f— What are you doing?"

The thin, wiry woman on the ground spits and wipes her mouth. "Fucking obvious, isn't it? Or haven't you got that far yet? Who are you anyway?"

Kaylee staggers back against a large shelving unit, tins and packets trembling with the impact. Hurt now cutting through the embarrassment, words stumbling. "I've… I've finished cleaning, the kennels…"

Mortified, Brian is unable to look at Kaylee, moving random packets around on a nearby shelf. "Awright, that's good. I'll be out soon."

"I'll wait outside."

"Morning." Linda steps forward, confronting Kaylee with a sarcastic, caustic expression. Popping a couple of chewing gum pieces in her mouth and redoing her hairband, pulling long brown hair back tightly. "I'm Linda. I run the Pamper Pod."

"Hi…" Kaylee holds out a hand nervously to no avail. "I'm Kaylee. I'm here on work experience."

Linda glances over her shoulder, taking some delight in watching Brian fumble around with various packets for no reason, before returning her gaze to Kaylee. "Best not to mention it eh? To Ms Barton? To anyone?"

Kaylee nods meekly, her mouth drying from the withering stare. If only the ground could open, swallow her whole.

Linda leans forward, a heady smell of peppermint invading personal space. Whispering softly. "Actually, I hate him."

Kaylee meets Linda's gaze briefly, seeing her expression turn from stone to a knowing cruel smile and back again.

Linda glances at her watch and taps it loudly with her finger. "Brian, I'm going to set up. Mrs Atkins will be here any minute. Can you bring Belle outside as usual?"

Brian shuffles, nodding uncomfortably. "Awright. Yeah."

When Linda departs, Kaylee returns her gaze to the floor. Grounding her body by holding onto the cold metal frames of the racks directly behind.

Uneasily clearing her throat. "What else, Brian?"

Hands wringing together, Brian steps to the small space in the middle. "Eh, Kaylee. Don't say anything, awright? I'm sorry. It's nuthin serious. I—"

"I'm not going to say anything. Just, is there anything else I need to do?" Kaylee puffs out her cheeks, trying to forget. "I want to take Chester outside. He looks so bored."

"Awright. Yeah. Yeah, maybe later?" Brian clears his throat. "Um, I need you to sit in reception for a bit. Mrs Atkins… She'll be here soon. I'll be there in minute."

Kaylee runs her tongue across metal braces, the familiarity of the sensation offering some slight reassurance. After a moment of uncomfortable silence, she brushes the front of her polo shirt and walks round to the white door, ignoring Brian completely. Opening it gently, she steps out into a louder cloud of barks and yelps.

On the other side, Kaylee gulps and exhales, as though purging rotten air from her chest. Taking moments to recover, she notices Pacer standing at the gate of his kennel. Impassive now, staring ahead with lips drawn back to reveal a set of fearsome teeth. Tensing then relaxing, softly whining then growling, as though becoming increasingly agitated. Kaylee follows his stare across the main area, on towards the large shutter door now rolled up. High enough for an adult to bend down and pass underneath.

"Ah, you're clever, Pacer. You want to play out there, don't you?"

A shrill bell, like a large alarm clock, rings twice and stops.

"Mrs Atkins..."

Responding immediately, Kaylee rushes forward. Firing through the hallway and the blank room before opening the door to the front office.

"Huh, there is someone here then? Been waiting at least five minutes."

"Sorry."

"I've never had to ring the bell before. Where's Anita? Valerie? She would never leave us standing here like this."

Several sharp, impatient, high-pitched yelps burst from a small poodle wrapped in two tracksuit covered arms.

"And you are? I don't think I've ever seen you before. Are you a volunteer?"

Quiet. Apologetic. "I'm Kaylee. I'm here on work experience."

"Huh. Work experience. That's what they call it these days."

Changing tone. "You must be Mrs Atkins?"

"That's right, dear."

Reaching out to stroke the poodle. "And this must be Belle?"

"Yes, this is Baby Belle." Smiling, focusing lavish attention on the poodle in her arms. "See Belle, everyone knows all about you."

Kaylee smiles as Belle licks her hand enthusiastically. "You're here for Linda, the Pamper Pod, right?"

Mrs Atkins nods, then leans over slowly and somewhat painfully, lowering the yelping poodle down to worn carpet tiles. Baby Belle skips nonchalantly across the floor, trailing a thin pink lead behind her and sniffing eagerly round the edge of the tall grey counter.

"Brian should be here shortly. He's in charge this morning."

Mrs Atkins makes a dismissive tutting sound. "Well, I might have known."

Nervously brushing the generous cotton wings either side. "I can try and sign you in, Mrs Atkins?"

"Oh, I don't sign in normally, dear. I won't be staying. Where's Anita? I swear this place falls to pieces when she isn't here."

"Anita is off today."

"Really? My, she's never off."

"Ms Barton said she's been signed off the whole week."

"Oh gosh." Mrs Atkins changes her tone immediately. "I hope it's nothing serious?"

"I don't know, Mrs Atkins."

"And Valerie?"

"Valerie?"

"Ms Barton?"

"She's away right now. Back this afternoon."

"Oh, that's a shame. I won't see her then. Remember to let her know I'm asking for her and that I'll see her next week?"

Kaylee nods in acknowledgement, stepping round the counter awkwardly, caught between the desire to rush everything or maintain a veneer of composure.

She grabs a pen from the desk and drops down into the worn swivel chair at the computer, nudging the mouse in front. A typical lock screen flashes to life.

"Sorry, what was your name, dear?"

Staring at the monitor screen. "Kaylee."

Mrs Atkins smiles. "It's your first day, Kaylee?"

"Mm-hm."

Kaylee starts with the obvious: *password.* She taps the keys and confirms. A short message appears and disappears then the lock screen refreshes. That's one unsuccessful attempt. Kaylee brushes her hands down the side of her top, small sweat seeping across each.

"You must like dogs then?" Mrs Atkins raises two sharply defined painted eyebrows.

Without looking from the screen. "Yeah…"

Glancing at her watch, Mrs Atkins lifts a small plastic carrier bag from the floor and places it on the counter. "I've brought half a tin of food for Belle as usual. It's her special food. She likes to have a bite to eat after pamper time."

Second attempt. *Barton…*

Kaylee winces. Strike number two. Fearful of locking the computer completely, she turns away from the desk. "That's fine, Mrs Atkins."

"Linda knows all about it. But can you make sure she uses it, dear? Sometimes Linda forgets and Belle gets a horribly upset stomach."

"Leave it there, Mrs Atkins. Brian will be here in a minute. If not, I'll go and find him."

"That's good, about time. I need to be going." Mrs Atkins pretends to jog on the spot. "Keep fit class at lunchtime, you see?"

"Ah…"

"Oh yes, Mondays run like clockwork. Drop Peter in town, leave Belle here, keep fit class, pick up Belle then rendezvous with Peter and drive home." Leaning forward, speaking softly. "I don't go out of the house dressed like this normally."

"Why not?" Kaylee looks at Mrs Atkins, taking in the full splendour of the purple track suit. "I like the colour."

"I do like to dress up, when I meet the girls for lunch that is. A coffee and a slice of cake, y'know? The new garden centre on Daley Way, have you been there? Lovely new café."

Kaylee reaches down, clapping an increasingly excited Baby Belle, having now completed her perimeter exploration of the front office. Belle yelps and dances, circling the seat and swinging her stubby tail excitedly.

"Oh, that's wonderful! I think she likes you, dear. Need to watch her though, she can be a strong-minded so-and-so." Mrs Atkins taps her forehead. "More like a person than a dog, aren't you, Belle?"

A flustered Brian Doltrice bursts through the door, wiping his hands on his overall.

"Where on Earth have you been?"

Brian gestures vaguely, somewhere over his shoulder.

"Huh." Mrs Atkins raises her painted eyebrows dismissively, lines forming upon lines. "At least we've had a lovely chat, haven't we, Kaylee?"

Kaylee shifts a little uncomfortably. "Yes, Mrs Atkins."

"I hope you're looking after Kaylee, Brian?"

Brian pauses, switching his gaze between both, bristling slightly. "Linda's ready. I'll take Belle now."

Mrs Atkins claps her hands together excitedly. "Ohhh Belle, pamper time! C'mon girl. Over here…"

Kaylee smiles and makes several "aww" sounds as Baby Belle trundles round the edge of the counter, dragging the short pink lead across the floor. Stubby white tail waving excitedly from side to side, gait eager and expectant.

Brian bends down, patting Baby Belle on the head once and picking the lead up from the floor. Belle yelps continuously, dancing up his lower leg before returning to Mrs Atkins again. Excited. Perhaps a shade confused.

"Oh, she loves it. Don't you, Belle? Right, I'll be back to pick her up later. The usual time, after lunch?"

Swivelling in the seat, Kaylee waits on Brian confirming.

"Yeah. After two. It's only Belle today." He steps into the doorway. "This way."

"Now you be a good girl, Belle!" Mrs Atkins waves a gnarled and wrinkled fist in the air playfully. "Don't cause any trouble for Kaylee."

As the door closes, Mrs Atkins shouts. "Oh, oh, Brian, the food?"

Kaylee leaps up, moving quickly round the counter. "Don't worry about it, Mrs Atkins. I'll make sure Linda gets it."

Walking to the entrance. "Oh, you are a dear. I'll be off then. Got to work up an appetite, Peter *always* buys cakes!"

"Ah…" Laughing awkwardly. Metal and off-white enamel shining.

Kaylee struggles with the heavy door, moving it eventually with a grunt. She leans back against the reinforced glass as Mrs Atkins steps onto the forecourt.

"Thank you, dear. Make sure they look after her, will you? Linda always makes her smell like a dream."

"I will Mrs Atkins. We'll see you later."

"Yes, goodbye."

Kaylee withdraws her foot and the door swings back, closing with a satisfying clunk. A nervous wave follows through reinforced glass, but Mrs Atkins has already disappeared inside a small white car.

For the first time that morning, Kaylee feels a sliver of positivity, happiness even. At last, an indication that the week ahead might not be as intolerable as she had previously thought. In spite of Brian and Linda. In spite, of everything.

Kaylee returns to the worn swivel chair, spinning side to side, taking a moment to reflect. A smile creeps across her face when she imagines a post-pamper, sweet-smelling and coiffured Baby Belle, yelping and staring back at her from the lock screen in front.

***

"Linda?" Kaylee steps into the yard, carrying the plastic bag containing the special food for Baby Belle.

In the near corner, underneath a sloping red painted roof, stands Linda. A cigarette hanging limply from the corner of her mouth, one hand brandishing a spray gun, the other rubbing a small pitiful creature in a thick plastic bathtub. All soaking fur and covered in warm sweet-smelling soapy froth, Baby Belle notices Kaylee and yelps three times sharply.

"Aww, she looks so thin!"

Linda tips her head, smoke escaping from inside. Mouth forming shapes as she tries to speak without the cigarette – dangling precariously from thin lips – dropping into the water.

Unable to decipher the sounds, Kaylee gestures with the bag in her hand. "Put it down here?"

Blowing smoke, Linda nods for Kaylee to place the carrier bag on the ground, next to a raised wooden tray with several large grey plastic bowls arranged in a row.

"She looks so cute."

Linda relaxes the trigger on the yellow and green spray gun, clipping it to the side of the large grooming unit and pulling the cigarette from her mouth. "Bitch. Proper little princess, aren't you, Belle?"

"Ah, you wash here…" Kaylee steps closer. "And groom there."

Linda takes a drag on the cigarette. "Yeah. All the drying and styling. Used to do it on the ground, put a few mats down but, nah. Better for the smaller dogs, they don't move around as much up here."

Scanning various lines of products. "Wow, I didn't realise there was so much just for dogs."

"Loads. Cruelty free too. Most of it."

"All the files. Wow, you file their claws?"

"Oh yeah." Linda snuffs out her cigarette on the concrete and speaks in a lighter, mocking tone of voice. "Won't need that today though will you, Belle? In here every week, aren't you, Belle? Spoiled and self-entitled little bitch, aren't you?"

Kaylee smiles nervously, continuing to glance at the various bottles, containers, brushes and assorted grooming tools on two small folding tables.

"Got everything these days. Waste of money a lot of it but most customers don't mind paying, they expect it. Look at this." Linda points to a row of small vials in a long black case. "Even got their own aromatherapy oils. For dogs."

"Can I smell them?"

Linda shrugs, wrapping a large blue towel around Baby Belle and lifting her from the bathtub. "Yeah. They smell just like the normal ones."

Kaylee picks up one of the vials, opening and sniffing carefully. "Hmm, Bergamot?"

Linda makes a series of sharp, sighing sounds as she rubs Baby Belle briskly, still wrapped up tightly in the towel. "It's all about making the owners feel good. Mind, some of the dogs I see? They do stink, I mean they really stink."

"It's a nice smell. I like it." Kaylee unscrews another one of the vials. "Lavender. Oh, that's nice. I use it at home."

"What for?"

"To sleep. When I have tests."

Linda shrugs.

"Which one do you like most, Linda?"

Gently lowering Baby Belle to the large platform on the other side of the unit. "Rose is nice. Bloody expensive though. Have to charge a bit more when I use it."

Kaylee nods softly, glancing at Linda now wrestling with a long hose connected to a large, dull chrome pet dryer. Beside it, Baby Belle shakes off a modest cloud of excess water.

Linda activates the dryer and shouts over the noise. "Can you sort out a couple of bowls please?"

Kaylee nods, leaning down and removing two of the grey bowls from the raised wooden tray, situated next to the large shutter door. Heading inside, she notices Brian hovering around the workbench. When he notices her, he moves away quickly.

Scrubbing and rinsing the bowls, Kaylee fills one with cold water before returning to the yard and replacing both in the raised wooden tray.

Melting at the sight of a fluffier Baby Belle. "Oh, Linda. She's *so* cute!"

"Yeah, little bitch scrubs up well, doesn't she? And that's just a wash. You should see her on a day where she gets the Full Monty." Linda steps back, admiring her work as she powers off the dryer. "Some smellies then she's done. Sorry, princess, just the standard wash and go for you today."

"Can I take a picture? Put it on Instagram?"

"Suppose so." Linda shrugs.

Energised. Excited. "I'll get my phone."

"Maybe you can give a shout out for my business."

But Kaylee doesn't hear, already sprinting back to the team room to retrieve her smartphone. Unlocking the screen and checking her notifications on an equally fast return trip.

"Aw, that little face." Kaylee pulls a cuteness overload expression.

"Yeah, precious little bitch." Linda puffs out slightly drawn cheeks and rolls her eyes.

Lining up the camera app for a vertical shot of Belle, Kaylee encourages. "Here, Belle, this way. Ah, that's nice."

While Kaylee hungrily adds several images, Linda surveys the contents of the nearby folding tables and picks a few of the items.

"You done?"

Kaylee flicks the screen back and forth. "Think so, just checking."

"Right…" Linda bites her lip. "Can you sort some of her food out as well please?"

A distracted Kaylee nods meekly. Eventually drawing her attention away from the phone long enough to open the carrier bag Mrs Atkins brought with her.

"Not *too* much." Rubbing more perfumed wax on her hands. "We don't want to spoil that lovely moustache, do we Belle?"

Kaylee lifts the lid on the plastic tub, revealing a modest amount of dry food inside. She tips in just enough to cover the bottom of the grey bowl in a thin layer of mis-shapen brown biscuit. "That enough, Linda?"

"Bit more. Leave the rest in the bag, I'll bring it through."

Aware of the scent of food, a now waxed and perfumed Baby Belle becomes more animated.

"Not yet, Belle, let's finish here." Linda replaces the bottles on the table and finishes her modest sculpting, before grabbing the lead from nearby. "That's it, all sorted."

Kaylee returns the tub to the carrier bag and folds it over, lowering it near the side of the large shutter doorway. Retrieving her phone from a pocket quickly, she hungrily resumes her checking of every image. Left and right. Pinching and zooming. Checking every small detail in her exhaustive search for that elusive rightness.

Fingers dance across the screen as Kaylee makes her way back through a cloud of barking dogs and into the hallway. Returning to the team room and crashing down on one of the wooden chairs. With an elbow resting on the tabletop and a hand cradling her face, Kaylee studies each image even more carefully. Now applying and tweaking filters here and there, undoing and redoing, cancelling every change and starting all over again. Finally, Kaylee is happy with two fully polished images, colours altered just enough for effect and fur suitably blurred around the edges.

Excited, Kaylee opens various social media apps and starts posting. Her fingers stopping suddenly when a loud buzzer alarm sounds. That same urgent, rasping noise from earlier. Smothering the muffled background of barking dogs, making her skin crawl with a dreadful electricity.

Kaylee turns to stone as a nightmare of terror-filled shouting and screaming rises behind. Dogs barking and yelping like wild beasts. Brian and Linda running and screaming. Sounds of intense panic. Shrieking. Desperate. Struggling. Louder now. Suffocatingly loud. Louder even than the alarm. Terrible, distorted wailing. A furious, painful cacophony that disables Kaylee entirely.

Shaking hand at her mouth. Chair scraping violently across the floor. "Shit, what?"

Kaylee bolts from the team room into the hallway, heart beating intensely, pounding through her dark brand-wear-covered chest. Thin pale arms reach to the line of windows, palms drenched in sweat. Cold, trembling skin touches glass, sticking and peeling. Nervous eyes glance through as the alarm abruptly stops.

"Oh fuck…"

A voice from somewhere inside. "Kaylee!"

Lying spreadeagled on the concrete beside the large workbench is Brian. His expression fearful, far-removed from the indifference of earlier, now anxious, scared, etched with pain. He slowly pushes himself into a sitting position, each laboured movement making him wince, one leg bloody, barely moving.

"Brian, what the fuck happened?"

"Stay in there, Kaylee!" A thick, quivering hand stretches out, pleading. "It's a breakout."

Instantly, a vicious dark shape bounds in from under the shutter door and charges furiously but clumsily across the concrete, slamming towards the kennels and storeroom. Circling back and forth, howling, barking, snarling angrily at the other dogs cowering inside their kennels. Eventually, after several terrible circuits, bolting back across the concrete and out to the yard.

"Pacer? How the…?"

Brian takes the opportunity to crawl to the side of the door, which Kaylee opens ajar and crouches down behind. "He got out. He attacked Belle, went straight for her when she was eating. Then he attacked me."

"Oh fuck…" Terrible ice seeps down Kaylee's back as she already fears the worst.

"I think… Think he's killed her…"

Cold. Quivering. "I'll call the police, Brian!"

"No! No. Not now. Give him time awright? He'll calm down." Grimacing. Groaning. "Just need to ignore him. It's happened before, just not this bad."

Stealing another look inside the open area. "Brian, where's Linda?"

"Dunno." Brian shakes his head. "She'll be hiding, there's storage out there. It's in the drill…"

Kaylee grabs the door handle, readying to open wider and help Brian.

"No! Kaylee, no." Brian screws his face up in pain, waving his hands frantically. "He doesn't know you. It's too dangerous for you in here."

"You need to get out?" Pleading. Frantic.

"I need to stay here. Ignore him. I'll bring him round."

"You can't stay in there, Brian, look at your leg."

Brian grimaces, trying to rise and look at the bloody mess. "Aw, fuckin' hurts."

"You need an ambulance!"

"Fucking kennels. Just opened."

Kaylee quietly releases her grip on the door as Pacer skips back inside, slower now, less agitated. His bloodlust fury seemingly ebbing away. His anger – no, his duty – largely played out. The job done. The work complete. Pacer fixes Brian and pads closer to the workbench, each step measured, careful.

Kaylee moves away from the door, avoiding eye contact. She doesn't look at the large shadow standing there, doesn't stare into imagined red eyes burning. Instead, her eyes see only the abject sight dangling from those crimson stained, dreadful dark jaws. A torn, bloody white, dripping half-object, hanging limp and lifeless. One rear leg missing entirely, the head dragging and dripping, torso mangled and ripped.

Pacer stops and sniffs, his expression shifting in a moment, before sauntering forward again and dropping the bleeding remains on the concrete. He drops down only a couple of metres away from Brian. Paws extended. Panting.

"Belle!"

Kaylee lifts her hands to her mouth, stifling either a scream of pain, or fear or disgust. Her face crumples with upset, the image of ruin on the concrete just metres beyond the wall unable to be unseen, seared forever. Her chest heaves miserably as sickness rises but can't release, the necessary muscles throttled by sheer visceral shock. Uncontrollable warm tears form and flow, trailing down each cheek.

Kaylee steps further away, flattening her hands on her chest, trying vainly to soothe sharply rising and falling cotton. To pacify the stabbing pain, somehow. And then, as she presses down, she feels it underneath. The pendant. Through the flowing, quaking tears an insane idea grips her, something that could only make sense in this very moment.

Trembling, Kaylee runs to the toilet, wailing and gasping as she slams the door and latches it behind her. In a frenzy, she lifts the chain out from under the billowing polo shirt and grips the locket tightly.

She catches her reflection in the mirror, the image initially making her unsure as a voice rises and scolds, trying one last time to make her see reason. To make her feel the apparent lunacy, the shame even, of what she is about to do.

But the shame doesn't win.

Instead, she snaps open the locket and glances at the bespectacled old face staring back. Then she clasps her eyes together and takes several deep, troubling breaths, trying to find a sliver of calm focus in the centre of all the horror. A tiny window, just enough, to reveal the words, to believe.

"Maria? Maria, I don't know if you can hear me." Stumbling. Unsure. "It's me. Kaylee. You don't know me. No, you must know me… I don't know you. But. You're family? Mum said… Lindsay said. If I ever got in trouble, if things went wrong… I could ask you for help?"

Eyes closed with tears still escaping. Forced calming breaths, over and over. Pale fingers wrapped tightly around the golden locket.

"There's been an accident. I need help. I don't know who to turn to. I can't… couldn't… save one of the dogs. Belle… She's… she's dead."

Kaylee sobs again, body shaking with emotion under dark and damp cotton as she recalls the terrible sight. "Maria, I need your help, I need to save her. Can you save her, please? Please! I don't know what else to do. I never thought I'd have to ask anything. There's nothing I can do… Please, Maria? If you can hear me, if you can see this. Put everything back the way it was? Save her, bring her back? She didn't deserve …Please…"

Desperate tears stream as Kaylee slides down to cold floor, feverishly kissing the locket in her hand before snapping it shut and burying her head in folded arms.

"Can you hear me? Please, Maria… Please listen…"

Three heavy tears drop one after another to the material of her trousers. After the third soaks in, Kaylee takes a deep healing breath, trying to stifle her sobbing.

"Please…"

Kaylee rubs the palm of each hand across her eyes, pulling the shoulders of the polo shirt across to finish mopping her tears. She leans back against cold wall, rendered even colder by damp cotton.

"Mum…"

Swallowing painfully, she tries to find an empty moment, the space underneath. The inner space where she continues to plead and echo. Crying out to Maria, or any other mysterious invisible agency caring to listen. Imploring. Begging.

Moments pass and Kaylee slowly gets to her feet, glancing briefly at her thin, sad visage in the mirror before reaching out to unlock the door. She takes a deep breath before widening the gap in the doorway, peering around the edge with one eye. Hands trembling, face quivering.

Quiet greets her outside. No screaming. No barking. And through the long window, no movement even. Carefully, Kaylee steps across the hallway, moving towards glass and gazing into the kennels area. Anxious. Trembling.

There's no sign of Brian near the door, the workbench or anywhere else. And no sign of Pacer either. No longer lying on the concrete floor with the remains of his quarry beside him.

Pressing her face to the glass, Kaylee tracks along the long window then stops instantly. There is something else. Someone else.

Sitting on the concrete at the other end, near the large sink, Kaylee notices a short dark figure hunched over. Wearing a dull, plain dress, head and shoulders covered in a large black patterned shawl. Kaylee stares in part terror, part fascination, as short, shadowy arms pull and move in strange rhythmic motions. Gracefully lifting and swooping over a ragged white bundle on the floor.

"Maria?"

As though hearing the whisper, the pale hand stops in the air. A large shining needle held aloft with glistening silver thread trailing, stretching all the way to the ground. Back to the ruined body there, where it tugs and pulls at ripped skin.

The head turns slowly, a kindly face staring through small spectacles, much younger than Kaylee expected, much younger than the portrait. No expression at first, then soothing with a gentle smile of acknowledgement before turning back. Focusing on Belle once again, looping and stitching quickly, the white body now twitching strangely. Needle and thread moving easily and magically through once dead skin. Sewing together the last of the terrible wounds, binding the small body together.

Kaylee turns away, her body folding in weary gratitude, one hand grasping the pendant and the other covering her mouth. "Thank you. Maria, thank you…"

A fresh flow of warm tears falls. But no longer tears of hurt or despair. Only joy. Somehow, it's done. It came true.

Slowly, Kaylee opens the door to the main area and steps inside. As she does, Baby Belle runs across the bare concrete, yelping and circling, demanding attention.

"Belle…" Lifting the excited poodle into her arms, Kaylee laughs as the now sweet-smelling dog licks her face.

With Belle in her arms, Kaylee walks across to the kennels, the poodle squirming and yelping excitedly when she sees the other dogs. But there's no response from any, each one lying silent, all fast asleep inside. Even Pacer, his bulky and powerful frame moving only slightly with each breath, lies stretched behind the gate of his kennel.

"I have no idea what just happened here, Belle." Then glancing over to the yard. "Linda…"

Kaylee walks swiftly towards the large shutter and creeps underneath. Scanning the yard, she breaks into a smile as she notices a trail of blue cigarette smoke, creeping skyward from the roof of a large wooden doghouse off to the side.

"Hello?" Linda calls out sarcastically from within, as though expecting no-one to answer. "Anyone there? Is it safe to come out now?"

Walking over, following the scent of cheap tobacco. "Linda…"

"Kaylee?" A hand with a cigarette pushes the edge of the roof. "What the fuck happened?"

Kaylee shakes her head when Linda's confused face appears, unable to express anything of the last few minutes in words.

From under the shutter door, Brian appears quickly, slightly out of breath. "Linda! Kaylee!"

"What's wrong, Brian?"

"You're not goin' to believe this…"

With everything that has happened, Kaylee can't help the words 'try me' flashing in front of her eyes. Behind, standing in the middle of the doghouse with the flat roof pushed across, Linda draws long and deep on her cigarette.

"It's Ms Barton. She's had an accident!" Brian swallows in shock, unable to register the news. "She's dead…"

# The Tunnels of St Mary's

Billy Craven turns off the road, pulling his silver Ford Focus into the layby and rolling towards the solitary rubbish bin at the side. As he nears, he makes a disapproving sound at the dismal sight. The bin overflowing, a flurry of a few spilled items already swirling over concrete, skipping on a light breeze.

Turning off the engine, he removes the keys and scoops up the triangular box of sandwiches and can of Cola resting in the passenger seat.

Exiting the car, Billy steps into the grey of his common stopping point. This and the other layby across the road, depending on whether he's travelling to, or from, the city. Today, a busy afternoon shift ahead sees him chasing leads in the suburb of Monktown. The next few addresses clustered together across the same three estates.

Billy takes a moment to drink the loneliness of the place, feeling an odd sense of relief as he watches a plastic cup and crumpled fast-food wrapper move over the ground. No other drivers parked alongside means he won't need to have the same conversation he's had a hundred times before. The whole "who are you, what's your name?" routine. Today, Billy isn't in the mood for casual chat. His morning head already loud and bursting, pulling on various threads of stress. That never-ending pressure cocktail of work, money, family…

Today it's lunch for one and that suits Billy just fine. Time to loiter round the edge of the car, bolt down whatever food he's been able to grab on the way and try to blot out the pressures of the work phone with the trivialities of the personal one. There must be one new message in there, one new meme that can ride the dodgy signal and lift his mood. To set him up for what is likely to be a tough, thankless afternoon.

SNAP! Fizz…

Billy opens the Cola, takes a sip and burps. Placing the can on the roof of the car, he tears open the sandwich box, lifting out one half of the BLT and taking a large bite from the middle. He tucks the lid of the box under the Cola, then slowly saunters to the rear, spending a few seconds walking in tight circles, loosening his neck and shoulders. He takes another bite of the sandwich, chewing quickly while trying desperately to clear his head. To think about nothing much. Or, at least, to dwell on going home later, or what might happen tomorrow night. Tomorrow being Friday, after all.

Another long sip of Cola is disturbed by the spritely work phone melody. Billy places the remains of the sandwich back in the box and rubs his hands together briskly. Then he quickly removes the smartphone from his suit jacket and swipes to answer.

"Walker White Insurance, Billy Craven?"

"Billy?"

"Mm-hm… Alan," Billy coughs, clearing his throat, "sorry, just having a bite tae eat."

The voice on the phone is curt. "Awright. Ah thought yid be on yir lunch. That's why am callin'? I'll keep it brief."

A sound of inhaling and exhaling deeply.

"Jist been goin' through the figures again, fir the last few months…"

Billy screws his face up in mock pain, bringing his other hand to his mouth, biting playfully on it.

"Doesnae make fir good readin' Billy. Ken what am saying?"

"Right." Billy coughs. Instinctively nodding.

"Aye, doesnae make gid reading at aw…"

Billy pushes the phone away briefly, nervously clearing his throat. "Summer was pretty slow Alan, and—"

"Aye, ah thought you'd start coming out wi' aw that, Billy, but let's no go there, eh? Aw that summer is slow crap. Wasnae the case last year was it? And ah'll tell ye another thing, it wasnae slow this year either because the south had one o' their best ever quarters."

"Right."

"Aye, so… Here's what we're doin'. I've called the whole team now, you're the last. I'm putting aw of ye back on the standard training programme. Another monthly report like this and it goes on yir file, permanently like, for aw o' ye. And if we dinny turn this roond in a couple o' months, aw o' ye will be on notice."

Billy rolls his eyes, punching with his free arm in disgust.

"Yir aw goin' tae have tae work extra hours, there's no other way. I cannae keep reporting on new business like the last few months, ken what am sayin'?"

"Ah know it's no' been great, Alan, but it's tough out there. The areas we're operating in. People are, struggling."

"No. It's no tough, Billy." Another deep exhalation unfurls from the smartphone. "But ah'll tell ye what it is. Fuckin' embarrassing. That's what it is."

Billy moves the phone away from his ear again and shakes his head, his expression hardening. "Alright, well. I'll do what ah can, Alan. I'm not making any excuses but it's no easy."

"Ye'll get the email later oan about the training. Enrol straight away, I dinny want te hear any excuses. The whole teams oan it, so no complaints from any o' yis. Let's get busy and turn this ship roond. Awright?"

"Aye." Billy stares at the ground. Precious lunchtime minutes soiled and stained with one call. "Aye, alright."

"Gid. That was aw—"

Billy bites his lip, stopping what he really wants to say dead in its tracks.

"Gid luck this afternoon, Billy."

"Aye, thanks, Alan."

Having delivered the good punch, Alan cuts the call.

Shaking his head, Billy locks the work phone and drops it back into his jacket pocket. He drags his hands across his face then looks left and right, letting out a loud shriek as a car zips past. He grabs the Cola and the half-eaten sandwich from the roof and marches across the concrete, swigging and chewing in part-fury, part-disbelief.

In the empty layby, Billy allows himself the luxury of letting his frustration boil over completely. And when the little energy he has ebbs away, he stands still with face frozen, looking up through layers of grey clouds. Lowering his head, he fixes a point in the distance, across the surrounding drab fields and takes several long, deep healing breaths. Washing down the last of the sandwich with some Cola, he reminds himself that everything should be better than this. That everything can be better than this.

Yet in between the anger and the cursing, what frustrates Billy the most is his own sales instinct, that nagging pride that once drove him to salesperson of the year, twice in a row. Now that same pride goads him, inwardly teasing that he, Billy Craven, *should* be doing better than the results of the last nine months.

More than this, that prideful sting stokes a fire deep inside. Reminding him that it only takes one hit to start a roll. Just one catch. So why not this afternoon? One breakthrough to take the heat away. And then, from there, a whole new run. A new streak to remind everyone that the Billy Craven magic is still there, just lying dormant. Waiting.

Spitting the last mouthful of Cola on the concrete, Billy crams the empty can into the bin, pushing it deep into a corner, underneath tightly packed plastic and paper. Then Billy retrieves the sandwich box from the car roof, one BLT triangle still inside, and swings the driver door open. Placing the sandwich on the passenger seat, he studies his face briefly in the rear-view mirror and manages a grim half-smile before turning the key.

***

Afternoon sunshine finally breaks through as Billy leaves the main dual carriageway, taking the slip road marked for Monktown and Garston. He follows the signs for Monktown across several large roundabouts. Passing, yet barely noticing, a scattering of small green spaces, fast-food outlets, worn local shops and one modest petrol station as he travels deeper into the suburb.

Further down the now single carriageway, concrete rises and closes in. Large faceless blocks so typical of the area rise upwards, all patterns of brown, grey and sickly white combining to blot out the sun with bland, strictly functional façades. From the road, all appear identical, the straight lines broken only by scattered balcony additions hiding behind railings. Perhaps a large houseplant or some laundry, maybe an old rug or carpet draped over the side.

As Billy slows and takes the slip road up towards a smaller roundabout, he can't help comparing the concrete honeycombs either side, with the cream walls and neat painted surfaces of his own relatively new family home. The comparison is stark, sending a tiny shuddering chill across his neck and shoulders.

Once upon a time, Billy called a flat similar to any one of these his home. But that was then. And those early years seem a whole world away now. That memory distance creating an odd sense of escape, but also giving rise to a strange insecurity, a sensation that he no longer belongs in such places. Perhaps, somewhere deep inside, even a modest sense of betrayal.

Although never comfortable here, Billy is familiar with some of the streets, Monktown having been a successful hunting ground some years back. Just not now.

He turns again and slips down a single road punctuated only by a handful of largely deserted car parks. The shadow of several large tower blocks wash across the windscreen.

"Jeez, aw looks the same..."

Pulling into one of the smaller car parks occupied only with a large skip, Billy applies the handbrake and takes a moment to unlock the work phone.

"Think it's down here... Beechgate... Beechgate..." Billy examines the street map, making a mental note of the route ahead. "Alright, yeah, got it. At the bottom here. Ah remember."

Looking up from the screen, Billy stares down the road towards the last few tower blocks. Suddenly, the emptiness in the purring car feels overwhelming and he instinctively lowers his window to inhale fresh air. Before releasing the handbrake and reversing, he listens and watches for any sign of life.

Muffled and distant, dance music plays as a few children suddenly dart from the edge of a building, chasing an older boy pedalling furiously on a bike that appears two sizes too small for him. He rides across one of the other car parks and disappears again, the crowd of children running angrily behind. Billy smiles, glancing up at the nearby flats and noticing a couple of faces peering back at him from behind glass.

Crawling along the road, he turns right onto Beechgate, a dead-end street that runs along the back edge of the estate.

Passing several blocks of rundown terraced houses, he drives into a much wider space dominated by three large tower blocks. Just ahead, a small group of children play football on one of the generous swathes of rough over-grown grass. As Billy passes, one of the boys quickly picks up the football and stares at the car.

Billy parks in one of the many empty spaces near the flats and raises the window. Turning off the engine, he checks the notifications on his work mobile then drops it into his jacket pocket. Glancing in the mirror, he watches as the group of children shuffle across the car park towards him. Billy frowns, noticing how bedraggled and painfully thin they all look.

Suddenly, a small face and two hands lash and squeak against the passenger window.

Shocked, Billy waves slightly at the young girl outside. "Hi!"

She doesn't meet his gaze, her eyes fixed on the sandwich still languishing in the box on the passenger seat.

Billy opens the door and steps out, turning to address the small group now gathered on the other side of the car. An older boy in front, wearing a dirty blue T-shirt with several rips in the bottom, watches him closely, bouncing the ball a couple of times and catching it.

Adopting a broader accent. "Okay then. Which one o' ye is going tae look after the car fir me?"

Silence. Just the ball hitting the concrete one more time.

"One o' ye surely?" Billy places a hand in his pocket, feeling no more than small change. While it should be enough, it's hardly going to be a convincing windfall. "I'll pay ye?"

Silence. Billy looks at the girl staring through the passenger window.

"Tell ye what, ye aw think about it while I get my bag."

Billy moves to the rear of the car and retrieves a small rucksack containing his laptop and a few company leaflets and brochures. Lifting it out and swinging it over a shoulder, he locks the car again and steps back towards the ragged group.

"That's enough, Katie!" The boy shouts towards the girl staring in through the car window.

Katie glances miserably over her shoulder before reluctantly moving away from the car. She returns to the group, whispering something to the ringleader.

Looking at Billy. "Mister? She wants tae know if you're goin' tae eat it?"

"The sandwich?"

"Aye."

"Maybe." Billy nods. "Might be mah dinner."

Katie frowns, casting her eyes downward. She fidgets with the two grubby yellow strings drooping at the front of her dirty track suit.

Another voice from the group, one of the youngest. "Ye got anything else tae eat, mister?"

"No…" Billy scratches his head, casting his eyes back across a line of dirty, dishevelled, hungry faces. "Right, ah tell ye what. If one o' ye looks after mah car, one of ye can have it."

A slight ripple of anticipation passes across the group.

"And, lissen, if mah business goes well here, ah'll get ye a box each from the store up the road. How does that sound?"

The older boy steps forward excitedly. "What do you need tae do, mister?"

"Talk to someone here." Billy points somewhere off to the side. "One o' these is St Mary's, aye?"

Katie pipes up, pointing across to a small fair-haired boy in shorts and T-shirt on the edge of the group. "Gregor lives in St Mary's."

"Is that right, Gregor? Which one is St Mary's Tower then?"

Gregor screws up his freckle-covered face, pointing firmly at the block off to the right.

"Good. Alright." Billy adjusts the rucksack, looping it over both shoulders. "So, aw o' ye, ye keep yir fingers crossed that things go well, eh?"

Billy steps away from the car, moving no more than a few metres before hearing the children scuffling and arguing. He turns round but keeps walking backwards, watching them congregating and jostling at the passenger window.

"We got a deal, right? Not a scratch?"

Stepping across a large patch of worn, litter-strewn grass, Billy glances towards a grubby painted sign fixed over the main door, white letters on dark brown: St Mary's Tower. He takes a second to glance skyward, examining the patterned concrete face stretching up in front.

"Twelfth floor then…"

The heavy dark brown door moves only slightly, making a terrible scraping sound as Billy edges it wider, creating just enough of a gap to slip through with his rucksack.

The space inside is dull and grim, littered with several abandoned possessions, a modest notice area with several dirty posters and a handful of large graffiti tags all sprayed in different colours. Off to one corner, a supermarket trolley lies awkwardly near the bottom of a flight of concrete steps. In another corner, the ashen remains of an armchair with an accompanying soot shadow on the concrete wall behind. The scene explains the slightly acrid tinge to the stale, oppressive air inside the building. A smell that sticks at the back of Billy's throat, making him gag.

Billy looks across at one of the doors to the nearby ground floor flat, all broken and splintered down one side. He removes and unzips his rucksack, delving inside to retrieve a leaflet and a business card. Stepping forward, he pushes the materials through the letterbox, causing the door to swing open a little more. He can't resist peering round the edge of the broken door, one eye checking the dark litter-strewn hallway inside.

"Jesus, does anyone still live here?"

He removes another leaflet and card then slips the rucksack back over one shoulder. Moving quickly, Billy stuffs another leaflet and card through the letterbox to the other ground floor flat.

Walking round the walls in the centre, Billy notices the lift. Unlike the rest of the ground floor area, the metal surfaces of the lift appear to be undamaged, in good order, clean even. Stopping in front, Billy glances up at the bright number 5 in the horizontal panel above the lift doors.

"Alright, lift it is then…"

He reaches out and taps one of the arrow buttons on the side panel. Instantly, the sound of the lift machinery whirs into life above. Billy watches the numbers steadily decrease.

The letter G lights up and the lift makes a soft pinging sound. Featureless metal doors slide sideways, revealing an empty modest space within. Billy steps inside and presses the button to number twelve.

"Going up…"

The doors shuffle back into place and the whole lift judders briefly. Billy clears his throat and watches the first number change before removing his mobile from his jacket and checking the screen. Ignoring several new notifications, he unlocks the device and swipes to confirm once again the details of his next lead.

"Mr… D… Bilton… Floor 12, second… St Mary's…"

Billy's words stop instantly as the lift grinds and lurches to a halt. Glancing at the numbers above the door, Billy sees number ten illuminated. He quickly presses the button labelled with a twelve several times. No response.

"Aw fuck…"

He lowers his rucksack to the floor and bends down at the control panel. Noticing a button marked with a bell, he presses it several times. Nothing appears to happen, at least nothing that Billy can hear from the inside.

"Aw shit…"

Switching attention to the silver button and speaker grille positioned underneath, Billy leans in closer. "Hi, eh, am no sure how this works but I'm stuck in the lift in St Mary's Tower? Can someone help me out please?"

No response.

Billy glances at his watch, hanging on for a few moments more before his impatience overflows and he presses the silver button again. "Hello? Can anyone hear me? Am in a broken lift in St Mary's Tower, ah need some help tae get me out o' here."

Exhaling deeply in frustration and growing stress, Billy unlocks his mobile phone and grabs the contact number for Mr Bilton. Tapping it, he attempts to connect, but quickly gives up when he realises there's no signal inside the lift.

He drops the work smartphone into a jacket pocket and retrieves his personal device. Checking the screen, he deflates further seeing the same message: no service.

"What? What the fuck…?"

Suddenly, the speaker emits several soft tones. Billy moves quickly towards it, pressing the button several times and shouting, but there's no response.

Punching the nearby metal wall . "Fuck, what do ah do now? Ah've no got time fir this."

Out of ideas, Billy opts for the obvious and starts banging loudly on the lift doors. "Help, someone! Am stuck in the lift here. Help!"

But no sooner does he start making noise, the power in the lift drops before fading out completely, plunging him into virtual darkness.

"Fuck!"

With a mix of nervous comedy and stress, Billy removes his personal phone again and unlocks it, swiping and tapping to his trusty torch app. The LED sparks into bright life, offering some reassurance. Billy batters the lift doors and shouts again in desperation. Still nothing.

Exhaling loudly. "Fuck!"

He taps the app and drops his shoulders in the darkness of the lift. The only option seemingly to wait, to ride it out. To bang on the doors and call out every so often, hoping that someone will hear and report the breakdown.

Wearily, he drags his rucksack closer and slides to the floor. Shaking his head miserably, he can't stop the raw perception building inside. That feeling he gets from time to time, where the entire world appears to be conspiring against him.

In the mash of stress and frustration now steaming and circling inside, Billy knows only too well that even a short delay to the numbers game can be deadly. He can ill afford this episode with such a heavy diary over the next few days, the current low total for new business this month and, especially, after that lunchtime call.

Lifting his smartphone, he swipes and taps the torch app once more. The LED bursts into powerful life and Billy brandishes the device, waving it in a circle around him, perhaps more for reassurance than any other reason. He taps the screen and changes a few settings, the white light transforming into a repeating pattern of blue and red.

Holding the phone above his head and smiling grimly. "Emergency!"

A harsh grinding and clanging immediately saps any humour from his predicament. Billy bolts to his feet and turns off the app. He moves across to the lift doors, banging on them several times.

"Hey! Someone? Am stuck in the lift! Ah need help here!"

Nothing.

As Billy gathers his thoughts, contemplating further shouting and banging, he hears a faint adult female voice. "Hello? Hello in there?"

"Hey?"

"Can you hear me?"

"Aye. Am in the lift, I need help? It's broken."

"Can ye hear?"

"Ah can hear ye! Where are ye?"

"The lift's broken down…"

"Aye, ah know, I'm inside… Can you help me? I need tae get out, I'm runnin' late."

A sound of metal groaning, like old hinges.

"Can you hear me better now?"

"Aye, that's better, I can hear ye better."

"Ah've reported it. But they dinny have a spare engineer to send oot. Thirs nae-one available. Said it might take up tae eight hours fir someone tae get here."

"Eight hours? Fucking hell…"

"Hello? Ye in there?"

"Aye. Am just thinking what tae do. Ah cannae wait eight hours!"

"Well, if ye dinny want tae wait. Ye can climb oot?"

"Eh?"

"Aye, ye can get oot…"

"How? I'm no sure if am near a floor? Think it broke down around floor ten. Can you get the doors open?"

"No. Ye climb up. Through one o' the safety tunnels. Ladder on each side o' the lift shaft. It's aw happened before son. I've telt them tae fix the lift so many times but they never dae anything, ye ken?"

Billy snaps the torch app on again and talks softly to himself. "I dinny see anything here… Where am ah meant tae be looking for the way out?"

"Should be a narrow panel."

"In the ceiling?"

"Naw. Oan the sides. Just push one o'them, doesnae matter which one. Should spring open towards ye, now the power's off."

Billy holds the smartphone up to one side of the lift and studies the metal walls closely. Several seams run top to bottom across the wall, but only two appear to cut through a horizontal metal panel that runs across the middle. Billy examines one of the edges, feeling a slight coolness from it.

"Think I've got it."

"Gid. It's a big gap when ye climb out mind, so be careful. There'll be a ladder ye can climb up, tae get ti the wee tunnel. Ye cannae miss it."

"Ah jist push it, aye?"

"Aye, push it. Should work 'cause the power's off. It's a safety thing. It's happened tae others."

"Okay…Thank you eh… By the way, what's yir name?"

"Am Viv. Ye can call me Viv anyway. I live on the eleventh floor."

"Ah well, thanks Viv. Hey, Viv, do ye know a D Bilton?"

"Aye, aye, Derek? Deek Bilton? Aye, he's a neighbour, lives upstairs."

"Ah, that's good. That's who am here tae see."

"Aye? Oh, that's mah phone ringing. Ye climb oot then?"

"Thanks fir yir help, Viv."

Billy taps and prods the narrow metal panel but nothing happens. Then he stretches up, placing his hand next to one of the edges at the top and presses down. The panel dips and springs, revealing a thin opening along the entire edge. Billy swings the thin metal panel door towards him, pushing it to one side.

He flashes the smartphone out into the lift shaft, revealing a sturdy metal ladder fixed to the wall in front, appearing to run all the way from top to bottom, at least as far as the app can illuminate. Further up, Billy notices a small rectangular tunnel, seemingly all metal.

Glancing upwards and exhaling wearily. "You'd better be fuckin' worth aw this Derek Bilton."

Billy checks his rucksack is secure before slipping it over both shoulders. He steps carefully to the side of the lift and shines the light into the shaft again, checking the gap. Enough of a space to be trouble if he's clumsy. But nothing that his gangly stretching legs can't accommodate.

Billy flashes the light one more time, fixing the distances and next steps in his head before placing the device in his jacket pocket. Stretching out a leg from the lip edge of the lift, he locates a rung with a foot. Pushing over the gap, he quickly grabs another rung at chest height. Exhaling sharply, he takes a moment to gather himself in the cooler air of the lift shaft before moving up the ladder briskly, stopping a short way up beside a metal tunnel in the wall.

Peering inside, Billy detects a dim light source from some way further along. With a groan of exertion, he clambers carefully from the ladder to the tunnel, taking a moment to gather himself before pushing forward on the metal surface. The tunnel height isn't high enough for Billy to crouch and walk, so he has no choice other than to crawl forward on his hands and knees.

"Suits goin' tae be fucking ruined at this rate."

Moving along steadily if not quickly, Billy drops and gags from a sharp, pungent smell that drifts past him in the tunnel.

"Jesus, smells like gas, the fuck?"

Taking a moment to cough and clear his nose and throat, Billy looks ahead, using the available light reflecting off each surface in the tunnel. He starts crawling forward again, reaching a section that curves off sharply to the right.

As he changes direction, Billy hears a harsh squeal and bang that stops him immediately. A sound of metal on metal, similar to the sound he heard before in the lift. As the harsh grating washes over him, the available light in the tunnel fades, evaporating quickly, completely.

"Hey! Hey! Am in here!"

Frantically, Billy reaches into his jacket pocket and withdraws his smartphone. Tapping and swiping, he activates the torch app quickly, pointing it forward.

"Anyone hear me? Viv! Derek!"

Silence. Only the sound of his own quick breathing in the darkness.

"Fuck, I've got tae get out of here!"

Billy contemplates his two choices. To crawl back the way he came, or to continue. The rising stress insists that going back is best, that maybe waiting eight hours for an engineer to arrive is at least marginally better than being stuck in a small, now pitch-black tunnel. On the other hand, the end of the tunnel must be near. It's probably a lot quicker to press on than it is to go back. Billy slumps a little, pondering both options in the darkness for several moments before a loud voice rings out.

"Hello? Ye no oot yet?"

"Viv?"

"Aye."

"Viv, am in the tunnel. There's no light?"

"What ye day-in? What's taken ye so long?"

"I cannae see anythin'."

"It's jist a tunnel. Ye need tae crawl tae the end. Ye roond the corner yet?"

"Just about."

"It's no far fae there, gets a bit low. Ah thought ye'd be oot by noo."

Billy sighs. "Right. Right, am on mah way."

Checking his phone in vain for a signal, Billy wipes his forehead wearily before placing it back in his jacket. He crawls forward, any scraps of tolerance or novelty now gone, replaced with a single over-riding desire to just get out.

The curve seems to go on for longer than Billy anticipated. After a few seconds he hits another straight, the ceiling quickly sloping down, exactly as Viv indicated.

Now very low, Billy resorts to dragging himself forward. "Viv? Fucking hell, I need some help here?"

Billy sinks further, arms ahead, practically dragging himself along the floor. He winces from a terrible grating sound that fills the tunnel but is relieved when grey natural light mysteriously spills inside once again. He lifts, looking forward. Eyes adjusting, seeing the outline of several heads all backlit and peering at him.

Reaching out a hand. "Viv? Can you pull me out? It's getting tight."

But there's no movement. No attempt to help.

"Viv? Can ye help me?"

The tunnel plunges into complete darkness as a heavy door slams and grinds back into place.

"Fuck, let me out!"

Panic grips Billy entirely and he bashes at every side. Punching and kicking with all his remaining strength. Screaming. Howling. Shrieking.

As he twists and turns, a flurry of small footsteps runs across the top of the tunnel, causing him to pause his panic just for an instant. But no sooner has Billy heard this, a metal panel – exactly like the walls of the tunnel – drops down behind him, cutting off any escape.

"Fuck!" Clambering forward and pushing up against what must be a door. "Let me out of here! Let me out! Fucking hell, Viv!"

And then a smell. Like before. Like gas? It invades his nose, his lungs…

Inside the dark cramped space, Billy squirms and lashes out, punching the walls as flames instantly fan and light along every single edge. He bangs on the rough metal door just in front, but there's something heavy holding it perfectly in place. Something on the outside.

"Help! Oh fuck! Help!"

The terrible flames reach out towards Billy, quickly building to an inferno, lighting up the metal space fiercely. Blazing easily through clothes, hungrily licking every inch of skin, burning and cooking Billy Craven who screams, writhes and twists in terrible agony before eventually falling silent.

In those final moments as Billy succumbs to fume and flame, he may just have heard a sound of cutlery. Held in the many hands from across the estate. Hands big and small, arranging their knives and forks. All crowding impatiently in the modest kitchen just outside.

# Mia Cartwright and The Beginning of Her End and The End of Her Beginning

Uneven, hard floor underneath. A gentle, miserable sound, drifting overhead.

The quiet weeping rouses Mia Cartwright, motionless and spreadeagled. Waking from strange sleep, as if to be reminded that she is indeed still waiting. Still, *somewhere* after the shock of what happened that night. The unexpected, terrible instant. The hollow pain of it. What she left behind; playful voices upstairs.

Flickering eyes reveal changing shadows and fades of light, seeping through countless fractures in four skeletal wooden walls. Two large windows either side, both poorly boarded, with unknown muted light pulsing through from somewhere outside.

*What house is this?*

Throbbing. Moving. Groaning quietly. Something attached to her back, Mia winces. Mouth painful and dry. She turns her head slightly, managing to look up, seeing a dream of an old familiar room. Flashes of colour, the noise of a television and a lingering burning smell combine briefly.

The vision quickly fades to a ball of light directly above. Mia narrows her eyes, seeing a naked lightbulb and a cloud of several small insects dancing. She watches them tap the surface continuously. Over and over. Confused. Disorientated. Determined.

As she stirs slowly towards full consciousness, so too does the despair. Dormant before, it finally breaks through mercilessly, as though waiting on the very moment of her awakening in this nowhere place. For a handful of initial seconds, Mia traps wretched sounds in her throat. But only for seconds. One anguished wail of injustice followed by another eventually escapes. A purging of sorts, transforming to a sad and twisted sobbing, ending as an abject whimpering. A why-me-ness, soft and tragic.

"I'm sorry." Weeping warm, miserable tears. "I'm sorry."

Amidst the sorrow of the floor, Mia tries to recall what happened. To piece fragments of memory together, now turning like broken gears. Everything had seemed so normal and then, in one moment like a stone through water, she was sinking inward. A violent emptiness. Down she fell, straight down. The feel of carpet sharp and awkward underneath. One moment alive, the next?

Gone.

Perhaps a small sparkle of light before that catastrophic implosion. Perhaps some lashing outwards in vain, some last instinctive flurry of resistance from useless limbs. But only a slight burning smell, a terrible sensation of falling, a feeling of space melting and time disappearing for sure.

Clouds of colour follow immediately after, descending like slow motion rain. Small items of clothing chasing her collapse, arriving for the final image. Soft, familiar material landing on and around, reaching out as if to say:

*"Don't forget us…"*

Mia bolts upright in the strange room, chest rising and falling, skin and plain loungewear sticking with cold sweat. She coughs horribly, pulling her legs closer, cradling her face in a cage of fingers.

Tense eyes navigate the periphery of both sockets, seeking clues. Seeing the splintered walls, fading lights meandering through cracks, boarded windows. *What is this grey space?*

Hands slowly lower to chest, trembling fingers running across cotton, the simple top unchanged since that night. Touching thick strapping across each breast, following tight canvas loops round and over each shoulder.

Bewildered, Mia touches soft, thick plumage draping down behind. Running her hands through feathers, she turns her head painfully, examining the top and bottom of two large dappled grey wings seemingly clipped together.

Bringing a hand to her mouth, choking back a mix of emotions. Dark brown eyes glistening with fresh tears. "Jesus, what is this?"

Suddenly, Mia holds her breath, conscious she is not alone. Crawling forward then turning, sensing another presence in flickering shadow behind.

On a low bench along the wall, two older women sit huddled together in the corner. Bloody wounds glisten at the front of each cranium, several dry trails of red sprouting and crawling down weary skin. Both are dressed casually, bright pastel colours spattered with lines of red. Bloody expressions kindly and sad, one noticeably more upset than the other, the source of the earlier weeping. Both women have the same style of wings fixed to their back.

"Fuck…" Mia recoils, unable to stop her expression registering vague horror. "Who are you?"

One stares ahead, looking through Mia, lost in some imagined reverie. The other crumples forward again, sobbing at the question. Shaking her head from side to side, unable or unwilling to answer.

In the opposite corner behind, Mia senses another quivering body lying in the shadows. A male figure, clothes burned to mere shards, revealing terrible marble swirls of black, purple and pink underneath. Only slight patches of skin and hair remain, an entire body blackened. All curling limbs and clipped grey wings.

"Oh my God…" Holding her hands up at the sight, whispering. "What happened to you?"

Interrupted by the sound of sharp giggling, Mia turns swiftly. Her gaze drawn towards a door that was not there before, open just enough for two children to peer round the edge. Laughing faces oddly indistinct, staring at Mia then running away while she tries to focus. Grey wings open, flashing briefly at their side.

"Boys? Is that you?" Mia instinctively scratches the wooden floor with her fingernails. "Don't go, please…"

"A phone…" The woman taps her sobbing friend on the shoulder, pointing across the room. "A phone, Iris. Look, there! It just appeared, on the wall. Do you see it too, dear, maybe you can call?"

Trembling, Mia nods at the woman in acknowledgement before staggering towards an old push-button payphone fixed to the wall. Grabbing the handset and wedging it between face and shoulder, she frantically searches each trouser pocket.

"I don't have any money…" Looking at the women sitting on the bench. "Do you have any?"

"Oh, I'm sorry, dear. Iris and I, we don't appear to have anything at all."

"I need money for the phone."

"I lost my handbag in the struggle. I think that's why we're still waiting here." The two women confer quietly for a moment. "Iris believes that if you remember the number, they'll hear you. If they're listening."

Unconvinced but resigned, Mia taps the numbered buttons methodically. Eerie tones pulse as the line crackles, strange interference sweeping in and out.

"Can you hear me?"

Mia winces when she hears her words echoing, swirling several times before submerging in background noise.

"Jaden? AJ…?" Mia bites her lip, letting the echo fade. "If you can hear me, I need you to do something. Go next door and talk to Angela's mum. Tell her to call an ambulance right away, you got that? Tell her it's an emergency."

The echo of each word lays clumsily on top of the other, twisting into a sudden and unexpected cacophony before fading in every direction, sinking to faint crackle.

The message delivered, Mia's voice and hands tremble, raw emotion rising unchecked. "Please hurry… I love you both."

The sound of weeping echoes down the line. From inside one of the spirals a tiny voice whimpers, strangely distorted and drawn-out.

"Mommy?"

"AJ, is that you?" Mia wipes the tears streaming down her cheek. "Can you hear me?"

"Mommy's lying on the floor..."

"AJ? No. It's okay, it's okay… Mummy's here. Did you hear what I said? Did you get the message?"

Louder. "Wake up, Mommy… Why won't Mommy wake up?"

"AJ?" Mia's face collapses, pressing the back of her hand against her mouth. "I love you, tell your brother…"

Mia drops the handset which clatters against the wall, swinging back and forth, spilling static.

Turning to the old woman still watching from the corner. "I don't think they heard me?"

Lowering her head, visibly upset. "I'm sorry, dear."

The door pushes open once more, laughter shining from beyond like a signal. Bewildered, Mia wipes her eyes and instinctively moves forward. Stepping through the doorway into thick, unbroken darkness.

"Hello?"

A sound of large metal equipment dragging and scraping across hard floor followed by several sharp clicks. A single spotlight to one side temporarily blinds.

Mia instantly shields her eyes. "Where am I? Who are you?"

Stepping forward, away from the ferocity of the beam, using an edge of the illumination to check her surroundings. Noticing a man in a knitted cap and overalls standing there, studying her closely.

"Hello?"

Ignoring her cries, the man turns to the large studio light. Making small adjustments to height, direction, intensity.

"Who are you?"

No acknowledgement, not even a flicker.

Mia glances down, able to discern dark wooden flooring and ornate edging. A stage perhaps?

"Um, my apologies." A voice from the shadows somewhere in front, speaking in a tone of voice as though pre-occupied with other matters. "We'll be with you in a minute."

"What is this?" Calling into the darkness beyond. "Who are you?"

The beam of light points directly into her face again, blinding temporarily.

"Um, if you can stand still, that would be extremely helpful."

Exhaling in irritation. The light already disorientating, warm on the side of her face. "Can someone just tell me what's going on?"

Mia flinches suddenly, a small object hitting her chest and falling to the floor. She crouches down, reaching out in all directions. Hands feverish, desperate, eventually locating. Stretching up, Mia holds her fingers in the beam of light to reveal a small green grape.

Whispering. "They don't like grapes…" before dropping it to the floor.

Movement in the shadow on the other side of the stage. The same sound of equipment scraping across hard floor, followed by several loud clicks and a second beam of light. The two sharp diagonal beams now splitting the darkness, creating a small pool of intense illumination where they cross.

Mia holds her hands up to her face again. "It's too bright. Please! Can you point it away from my face?"

From the shadows behind the lighting, the sound of a throat clearing and murmuring.

"Hello?"

Mia edges forward slowly, seeing a flickering outline of several rows of ornate seats, as though in a theatre. Sitting huddled together, a litter of shadowy grey faces there, tips of wings rising behind. A few of them are standing, scattered across the aisles, holding what appears to be some type of clipboard, from which long rolls of paper droop down messily.

"Please stop moving on the stage. For your own safety, you must remain in the pool of light."

"Then tell me where I am?" Mia edges back and forth, shielding her eyes, trying to find an optimal space. "Are my children okay?"

No sooner has Mia spoken, three children appear from the side, running and laughing hysterically. Each wearing colourful pyjamas with large grey wings open behind, their faces indistinct, blurry. They move noisily across the empty space between the studio lights and the first row of seats, throwing more grapes as they pass. Several of the figures voice their frustration, their reactions causing Mia to break into a quiet, guilty smile.

"Mommy!"

The children disappear into deep shadow at the side, the sound of a door opening and closing.

"Wait…"

Weary, slightly exasperated. "Will you please remain in the light. Ms…?"

"Where am I?"

Metal scrapes across the floor as another light is dragged into place.

"Walker? Carrie Walker, is that right?"

Mia shakes her head in confusion. "Me?"

"Cassandra… Walker? Claire? Kyra Walker?"

Staring to the gloom beyond the lights. "I don't know who you're talking about. I don't know anyone called Carrie or Kyra… Don't know anyone called Walker."

The murmuring increases, the group consulting with each other, sounds of gentle bickering even. But Mia is still unable to hear any of the words clearly, focusing on the man in the overalls instead, busy positioning and adjusting the heavy studio light.

"You are Carrie Walker, age twenty-six or not?"

"No..." Confused. "No, I'm thirty-six."

Murmuring. "It sounds similar, don't you agree?"

"I..." Mia breaks slightly, stepping to one side and rubbing weary eyes with the heel of each palm. "Where am I? I want to see my children..."

"So, Carrie Walker. Twenty-six..."

Interrupting. Irritated. "I told you. I'm not telling you again."

Tailing off. "Claire... Walker...?"

The third beam switches on with several loud clicks, drowning Mia in ever increasing light.

"Cassandra Walker then? Um, it must be one of them?"

"Stop, stop please..." Shaking. Quiet. Mia screws her eyes shut, both to blot out the light and the rising upset. "I don't know these people, the names you mention..."

Taking several moments to gather herself, Mia is shocked when she opens her eyes to see several tall pale figures now standing at the stage. All wearing thin, ragged cloth tunics with grey wings open and rising behind. Eyes shining like bright pearl, skin all shades, healthy and strong. Each figure holding and referring to a clipboard from which trails of paper stretch back across the floor.

The voice in the darkness scolds. "Stay in the pool of light please, Clara?"

"I want to see my children..." Mia sighs wearily at the stupidity of it, the pity of whatever game it is.

"Um, children?"

Indignant. "My children. They were here a moment ago."

"You have children?"

"Who are you?"

"Thomas, I believe? And his sister, Jacqueline? No, maybe just Thomas…"

"You're not listening to anything I'm saying. Why don't you listen?"

The sound of metal scraping. Another light dragging across, arranged like the others, forming a line in front.

"Um, born in London?"

"No." Holding up her hands, trying to shield her eyes. "Bristol. Not London."

With a harsh snap the light fires into life. The strong beam converging with the others, the intense light even more suffocating.

"No more lights, please."

"Um, are you sure? Our records indicate… London."

Bathed in the light, increasingly unable to see beyond the cloud of it, Mia drops wearily to her knees. Several of the strange faces near the stage lifting their heads from their clipboards in anxious response.

"We don't seem to be getting far, Ms Walker…"

Two further lights snap on. The pool deepening, consuming.

"I don't know…" Mumbling. Confused.

Mia rubs and closes her eyes, leaning forward gently and slipping downwards on the stage.

"London. Good. Did we say twenty-six? I don't remember."

Mia wraps her arms, consoling herself on stage. There's no point continuing to answer, the voice is clearly ignoring everything she says. Or, perhaps worse, is either incorrect or doesn't know.

As Mia drifts underneath the intense cloud of bright light filling the middle of the stage, small hands prod behind.

Pushing and pulling at the straps binding the wings together, eventually unclipping them.

Mia cries out wearily. "Please, leave me alone."

Whispering. "Mommy?"

Eyes flicker open, turning in the direction of the quiet, wistful voice whispering in her ear. Mia sees three children on their knees around her, two girls and one boy, all dressed in bright pyjamas with grey feather wings fanning out behind.

"We heard the message. We're here now."

Astonished, Mia reaches towards each of them in turn. Holding and touching each face, feeling the soft, smooth skin, proving to herself that all three are real.

"Who are you?"

All three stare at each other blankly, the girl who spoke earlier leans closer. "What did the voice say?"

"I don't remember everything." Mia frowns. "Carrie, Kyra? Thomas? London, twenty-six…?"

The children laugh. "Who are *you?*"

Mia pauses, smiling tearfully. After a moment of reflection, she wraps her arms around them, the large grey wings on her back unfolding and stretching out as she gets to her feet. They leave the stage quickly and quietly, exiting through a door on the other side.

Behind them the lights switch off one by one and the voice from the darkness continues to speak, asking questions and shouting random names.

# Ewan's Fortune

"Jesus..." Ewan Fortune stares in frustration at a narrow, brightly lit screen embedded in the middle of his forearm. "C'mon, c'mon..."

He swipes the screen impatiently. Right to left. Left to right. Rows of shining digits and icons, tiny pulse charts and heat graphs flashing by. Rising and falling. Most of the information cycling quickly, impossible to track. Other data static or transforming slowly. Hearing a voice nearby, he lowers his shirt sleeve quickly.

"Excuse me. Do you mind...?"

A young woman and child holding hands appear right in front. Sullen, pale faces stepping out from the bustling swarm of people crowding the main concourse. The small boy, silent, dirty, eyes to the ground, dressed in a thickly padded and stained jacket, a simple blue woollen hat on top. The woman, thin and dishevelled, spiky, untidy hair cut clumsily, ragged clothes swamped in a long brown ex-military overcoat with several gold buttons missing.

"The machine?" Lifting a slender hand, two fingers wrapped in bandages, pointing forward. "For my son?"

Glancing round, acknowledging the tall vending machine directly behind. "Sorry, of course. Let me move these."

Ewan moves the two bulky cases so they are no longer barricading the vending machine and steps to the side, giving access to a large, multi-coloured oval glass panel with rows of candy behind.

"Thank you." Pushing the boy gently forward. "There you go, Regan."

Slightly apprehensive, Regan looks for further approval.

"It's okay. Go…"

He steps forward slowly, fixing the brightly lit confectionary behind the glass. His eyes eventually widen, pale fingers poking and dancing, smearing from one choice to the next.

"We don't have all day, Regan."

Ewan disguises his grin, glancing at the woman from the corner of his eyes, wondering. Her gaze never once leaving that small blue woollen hat in front of the vending machine. Her manner impatient, anxious, pre-occupied. Watching Regan make his choice and stare into a thin sliver of bright white light.

The machine stirs into life. Ewan watches closely as the boy leans down, eagerly awaiting the chocolate reward dropping into the metal trough at the bottom. While he waits, patterns like dancing soundwaves, spiral and pulse on a long, narrow screen. Moments pass in anticipation before Regan gets to his feet upon hearing a dull buzzing sound, turning to look at his mother in confusion.

Smile evaporating, Ewan checks the screen. Dancing patterns gone, replaced instead with the bold words 'Authorisation Denied. Transaction Void'.

"No, that can't be right." The woman steps forward, frustration clear. "He hasn't… he saved his allowance."

"Sometimes it happens, the…" Ewan bites his lip and pauses, holding out a hand. "It's okay. I'll get it for him."

"But he didn't spend his allowance." Becoming more agitated. "We knew we were making the trip."

Holding out both hands. "It's okay…"

"No, it's not right. Can't be right. The machine, it's lying." The woman reaches out firmly, smacking the front of the vending machine.

"No, don't get angry. Let me get it for him." Ewan scans the ceiling warily, checking over the heads of the large crowd. "Hey, Regan. The machine wasn't working properly. You have to pick again."

After some reassurance, Regan steps forward again and presses his finger on the glass. Ewan stares into another line of thin white scanning light, this one set higher on the side of the unit.

Clunk…

With relief, Ewan notes the shining words 'Approved. Transaction Complete.'

Regan crouches down eagerly, gathering up the brightly coloured confectionary from the metal tray and returning quickly to his mother.

"Salted Stardust Crunch." Ewan raises his eyebrows. "Good choice."

Uncomfortable, unable to look Ewan in the eyes. "Thank you."

"It's okay."

Gripping and shaking a small hand. "What do you say, Regan?"

Ewan smiles. "Happens sometimes. I know."

The woman continues to study Regan. Her expression warming, watching the boy take a bite from the chocolate bar.

"You're sailing today? Work? Family?"

Shooting a suspicious glance at Ewan. "Both. Maybe…"

"Right. I'm sailing to Godwin 3. The station near Dunvega. Are you—"

"We should be going, thank you for your kindness." Changing tone instantly to complete disinterest, the woman places one hand on blue wool, gently persuading the boy to move away. "Let's go, Regan..."

"Maybe eh, see you... later..." Ewan watches them move away quickly and whispers rhetorically, "Wonder what Salted Stardust Crunch actually tastes like."

Ewan glances round the edges of the busy area, then resumes tracking the pair as they submerge into the bustling throng. Glimpses of blue in the crowd, bobbing and disappearing several times. Ewan sees them resurface further along a narrow corridor, moving towards the main departure dock.

He rolls up his sleeve and taps the narrow screen in his arm, waking the display. The image brightens quickly, revealing different account figures than before, fresh digits partially hidden by a notification window in the middle. The text is small, causing Ewan to lift his arm closer to skim through several long paragraphs of tiny shining letters.

"Yeah, yeah. Whatever..."

An index finger hovers above the screen, wavering for a moment then activating an 'Accept' button. Dropping his arm, Ewan exhales with relief and rubs the back of his neck, looking over to the huge, ever-shifting departure and arrival board. Confirming the voyage operator, he brings his left hand to the side of his face and speaks.

"Call Reese at West Office."

A bright, short tone followed by a soothing synthetic voice inside his head. "Calling Reece. West Office number."

The voice that answers is warm and bright. "Division Four, Hygiene."

"Reese? It's Ewan."

"Boss! Thought you'd be on your way by now? Tracker says you're… still dockside."

"Yeah, running late. Been waiting on a couple of transactions going through."

Confused silence. "Okay."

Quietly, matter of fact. "Mm-hm, yeah, been a little tough lately."

"Right." Sighing loudly. "Shit happens huh?"

"Could say that. Anyway, look, Reese, just had an advance for the trip hit the account but, seems like there's a penalty attached. It's less than expected. Just wondering if you can raise an enquiry with Central, get them to confirm any policy changes I might have missed?"

"There's no penalty code on the drop?"

"No. Nothing. Just the usual terms."

"Alright."

"And eh, Reese, can you keep it discreet? Y'know, don't mention…"

"Maybe you should call direct, boss?"

"Yeah, but I'm heading to the dock now. It's all last minute and… I don't know what the connection is going to be like when I'm sailing."

"Should be fine. You're expecting problems?"

"I don't know…" Ewan rubs his forehead awkwardly. "Look, Reese, I'm… I'm sailing on a budget clipper. I can't guarantee reliable comms for a couple of days."

"What?"

"It's fine, it'll be okay. Don't worry. It's all checked out."

"You'll get there on time, they got security for the stock?"

"All good. The stock will be fine. Even budget corps have secure cabins, Reese."

Ewan grins nervously, glancing at the two cases on the ground. "Don't worry. Really, it's okay. I figure the boredom might be good for a few days. Less distractions."

"Least you can catch up on your sleep." Laughing. "As long as the prototypes are safe. Uh, boss, I need to go. Calls backing up here. You need anything else?"

"No, nothing, just that. Whisper any response, I'll pick it up when I disembark."

"No problem. Seems strange though?"

"Might be an error, I don't know. Something I've overlooked."

"Yeah, I mean, you're going to need every single credit for all that late-night partying in your budget cabin."

Ewan laughs. "It's the way it is right now. And it gives me extra time to recharge and plan. Need to stay sharp on this one. I have to land it."

"Yeah, big contract. If we get it, opens the zone up."

"Oh, Reese, before you go…"

"Ya."

"Looks like I'm sailing Starbird."

"The budget corp that bought the old combat clippers?"

"Mm-hm."

"Oh right, wow. Your trip just got more interesting. Y'know, that fleet is all end of line military hardware?"

"Seems so."

"Haven't been on one yet. Can you take some shots inside?"

Laughing. "You're in luck, I've got a spare card. I'll fill it with shots of bunkbeds and bulkheads."

Reese laughs. "They're still getting established. Early ratings seem… okay. I'll have to see if I can sail a short haul with them myself. Right, really gotta go now, boss, it's just me in the office. Eh, if you need help, call the personal line, right?"

"Don't worry, Reese, it'll be fine. I'll be in touch."

"Bon voyage!"

"Thanks."

Two bright tones signal the end of the call. Ewan drops his hand and swipes the narrow screen on his arm before lifting each case at the front and rolling them forward. He stands gazing at the huge departure board again, scanning shifting rows of glowing letters and numbers, waiting on the gate number appearing.

Silent words like a mantra. "Godwin 3, Dunvega, Starbird…"

Minutes pass in anticipation. Rows of information transform across the board.

"Okay, there it is. Gate 5."

Large swathes of the assembled crowd take their cue, moving instantly towards a corridor leading off to one side. The initial burst of speed falters quickly, slowing to a mere shuffling pace as a thick snake of hats, hair and luggage, forms. Ewan sticks to the rear edge of the ragged mass, rolling his cases forward as information bulletins and advertisements drift overhead.

*"We regret to inform you that inclement weather on Lundstrom IV is affecting all Radiant Corp services to and from MacKenzie Parkway. Will passengers travelling to Lundstrom IV please ensure they have the correct payment, travel and security details ready, to ensure swift departure."*

An irritated face turns and glares angrily from inside a worn balaclava. "Hey, watch it with those cases!"

"Oh, sorry."

Ewan swerves the bulky case away from the old legs in torn grey trousers that stopped without warning. Instinctively shaking his head, irritated at the abrupt rudeness. Unable to stop silent words rising within: *the equipment inside these cases is worth a hundred of your old legs.*

After several sweeping curved sections, the corridor opens into a spacious departure hall. Lone travellers and families of all sizes spill out across a sparsely decorated, polished white atrium. Haphazardly congregating at various numbered zones situated along three sides. Tall display boards and security cameras dominate each gated area, screens flickering wildly with endless travel information, safety messages and product advertisements.

Two sleekly curved desks stretch back from either side of these imposing, complex gated sections. Wave-shaped barriers stand in front, arranged like a tiny maze, while several tall masts of cameras, spotlights and various other sensors intimidate. A few of the units beam light towards the floor, strange blue sensor clouds that hover off the ground with sharply defined edges. At the front and rear of each section, several security guards in dark uniforms with yellow flashes and hard white hats, all stand motionless. In contrast to the flurries of activity behind a few of the desks, where figures wearing yellow overalls ready those gates about to go online.

Ewan walks across the middle of the hall area, mumbling as he rolls the two cases either side. "Okay. Gate 5. Gate 5."

As he strolls towards the departure gate, the penultimate dock on the far wall, he acknowledges a tall, cylindrical, calm-bot standing silently. The clear plastic head turning ninety degrees one way then the other, emitting beams of flashing and pulsing light, but producing no calming music and dispersing no calming aerosol. A hastily erected fence of drooping tape hangs around each side of the stationary silver machine. A handwritten notice informing passengers that internal services are aware of the malfunctioning unit and are very sorry for the inconvenience.

Small wheels stop on polished floor. Ewan lingers at the edge of the large crowd, gathering at Gate 5. He gazes to the front, seeing the woman and boy from earlier at the very tip of the queue. He lingers for a moment, trying to watch them casually, before the impatient noise of various advertisements and other messages draw his attention away.

He taps his arm and the screen bursts into life. Flicking through, Ewan notices a whisper message from Reese, confirming he's made an enquiry. Then he flicks to a different page, another list of messages, tapping the row containing his booking details and scanning codes.

Ahead of the assembled crowd, an older man and woman, both dressed formally in dark green uniforms with silver piping, appear from a door that blends in seamlessly with the wall. The staff in the yellow suits disappear back through the same door, as the new arrivals take their respective positions behind the curved desks, positioned either side of the gates.

Immediately, both work through an instinctive routine of powering up, logging in, rearranging mounds of physical and digital paper and testing the thin headsets that curve from ear to mouth. Ewan watches as they unfold a green pointed cloth cap at precisely the same time, carefully positioning it on their head and nodding at each other. Each brings a right arm up sharply, in a military style salute. After this, several red lights appear on one of the masts and a buzzer sounds. A couple of the sensors on the camera mast rise and turn slightly, as though refocusing on specific areas close to the gate.

*"We regret to inform you that the Niebieski Kula galactic service to Garov Central is currently delayed dockside due to a technical malfunction. Passengers for this service are advised to remain on the main concourse and await further updates."*

Languishing at the rear, Ewan scans the long weary line that snakes around the various barriers, towards the main desk. Seconds pass, then minutes. Each one faceless. Nothing but changing voice announcements and a stream of loud advertisements. The crowd impatient, mostly bored. Many visibly tired and a few strangely anxious.

Ewan pays only modest attention to the line ahead, with most progressing quickly through the various checks. Their luggage inspected and removed, voyage agreements in order, account already settled, required information and security details all checking out. Each individual pausing briefly in a strange blue light just beyond the desk, before moving through several heavy silver bars that retract and extend. From there, brisk strides along a more dimly lit tunnel ahead, on towards dockside and any final barrier checks.

But others are not so swift to pass and an even unluckier few do not pass at all. That's when Ewan does pay attention. When the flight details are incorrect, when the luggage sparks an alert, when a balance is outstanding with no means to pay, when the medical declarations are incomplete or, in two specific cases, where restricted metals are smuggled inside coat linings.

At best, individuals and families are turned back from the front desk, forced away to rectify whatever needs to be done. At worst, as with the smugglers, the security teams spring to life, pulling the always struggling, protesting passengers behind the desk and through the seamless white door in the wall. As they complain and struggle, Ewan notes that no-one ever tries to run. There's an immediate sense of the game already up, an overwhelming resignation.

Ewan half-smiles at his own tired reflections. "Budget corps…"

Nearing the front of the queue, towing both cases slightly behind, he thinks once more about the woman and the boy in the blue woollen hat. Both must surely be dockside by now, perhaps already onboard the ship. Although seemingly random, Ewan takes some solace knowing that everything worked out okay for them both. No hold-ups. No trouble.

"Good day, sir, thank you for sailing Starbird. I am Land Officer Taylor, your full name please?"

The spritely standard greeting flashes by completely unnoticed by Ewan, his mind initially elsewhere.

"Sir? Your full name please?" Smiling politely, a slight tone of exasperation noticeable.

The reverie breaking, Ewan steps forward to the desk, dropping the cases either side. A petite, sharp middle-aged face in smart green military attire, peers impatiently back at him.

"Sorry, world away there. Ewan Fortune, I have my passes here – it was a provisional booking."

Ewan taps the narrow screen on his arm, showing the various voyage references and sales code markers. Land Officer Taylor shines a handheld scanning device over several of the codes and settles back.

"That's okay, sir, we can confirm the booking and take payment now for you."

"Good." Ewan relaxes.

"Travelling to the Dunvega system, Mr Fortune?"

"Yes, the first stop. Godwin 3."

Land Officer Taylor looks up, breaking into a half-smile. "Business or pleasure?"

"Business."

"That's good." Land Officer Taylor grins, focusing her system again. "Have you sailed with us before, Mr Fortune?"

"Eh, no."

"That's interesting. You're being flagged on our system." Land Officer Taylor stares closely at one of the monitors in front, looking briefly bemused.

Ewan swallows nervously. "Flagged? Is there something wrong?"

"No, nothing wrong."

Ewan breathes a sigh of relief.

"Can I check your company name, Mr Fortune?"

"BCB Hygiene."

Land Officer Taylor taps further details. "Ah yes, we've had other travellers from your corp."

"Really?"

"I can't reveal details, Mr Fortune. But it does mean you qualify for an upgrade so, good news for you."

Ewan frowns. Confused. "Okay, I wasn't expecting—"

"As an employee of BCB, we can offer you a discounted upgrade to your standard pass?"

Ewan clears his throat, turning briefly to glance at the short line of sullen faces behind.

Quietly. "So, what's the difference here?"

"In cost?"

"No, the upgrade."

"A more spacious cabin on the restricted upper decks, Mr Fortune. Several other perks such as cabin service."

Ewan glances at his cases and rubs his jaw, reflecting on the offer. "And the cost difference?"

"The standard pass to the Godwin 3 station in Dunvega is 1089 credits including taxes. Your discounted upgrade with two large cases makes for a total of... 1479 credits, inclusive of tax."

Ewan rubs his forehead. "The cabins are more secure?"

A flicker of a frown flashes across Land Officer Taylor. "Security is paramount across the whole Starbird fleet, Mr Fortune, we take it very seriously. What I can tell you is that the upper decks are usually much quieter. All your meals are included. You have an old Officers cabin and you'll likely be travelling with other corporate passengers. Would you like to go ahead with the upgrade to your standard pass, Mr Fortune?"

Although more credits, Ewan can't resist the guarantee of increased peace and quiet, perfect planning conditions for the huge meeting ahead. "Yes, might as well. Thank you. I'd like to go ahead."

"Excellent. Let me confirm and get your cabin number... Right, you are in cabin number 6. Now we just need to settle the new balance." Land Officer Taylor gets to her feet and holds out a hand, the skin of the palm revealing the ragged shape of an embedded sensor. "That will be a total of 1479 credits, when you're ready?"

Ewan bites his lip before stretching out his hand to meet Land Officer Taylor. The narrow screen on the inside of his arm waking up instantly as the hands meet. A dull green band passing across the display.

Land Officer Taylor sits down, watching the monitor in front and breaking into a warmer smile. "Let me check that's all gone through… there it is. Now, if you can place the first case here, please?"

Ewan lifts the heaviest of the two cases onto the ground level moving platform, patting it on top as it slips away under the front desk and stops. He watches Land Officer Taylor sweep a scanner over every surface and clip a large digital security tag around the handle, attaching two pieces of digital paper each side.

"Business-related mechanical parts and clothing, Mr Fortune?"

"Yes, all pre-approved."

"Anything additional you want to declare prior to the last security checks, Mr Fortune? I must warn you, luggage is destroyed if restricted items are detected by any of our sensors on route to the ship."

Ewan shakes his head, watching as the case disappears through a section of white wall, completely indistinguishable from the rest.

"And the second case please, Mr Fortune." The next lighter case follows, Land Officer Taylor continuing with her checks and making small talk. "You'll be planning to visit the surface? Springtime on Dunvega can be beautiful, Mr Fortune. Have you ever visited the Temple of Mori Anna VII in Holst City? Oh, it's glorious. When all the spider trees are in bloom the canopy criss-crosses the sky."

"Hmm, sounds nice. Unfortunately, I don't think I'll be able to make it to the surface this time. Business meetings then straight back. Maybe, some other time."

"That's a shame. Such a beautiful sight. I must visit again soon myself."

Ewan watches the second case slide away along the track, escaping through the wall.

"Right, Mr Fortune, providing your luggage meets dockside security checks everything is all in order for your voyage. Your pass has been upgraded and the details should now be with you so please check before passing through the gate. Oh, one thing, I assume you only have the usual standard commercial corp enhancements?"

"Yeah, standard managers kit."

"Good. I'll add a temporary note to your voyage information as some of your records aren't fully available right now. Sensors may trigger when you pass along the tunnel. If this happens, please show your upgraded pass to security."

"Oh, right."

"Have your pass ready for inspection at dockside and use the red pathway gate A for the upper deck, Mr Fortune."

"Great."

"Any further enquiries, please talk to the Starbird staff dockside. Now, is there anything else I can help you with this evening?"

"No. Thank you."

"In that case, Mr Fortune, please follow the arrows on the floor and pause in the blue zone. When the red light turns green, please head straight through the main gate to dockside. From everyone at Starbird, we welcome you onboard and thank you for sailing with us. We hope you have a comfortable, enjoyable voyage."

***

Turning one way, then the other. Pulling several thin blankets over, wrapping and unwrapping, repeating. Eyes eventually opening. Groaning softly. Cold. Certainly uncomfortable.

"Jesus…" Muttering in the darkness. "And this is an upgrade?"

One arm reaching out to the near wall, hand feeling its way across the surface and locating a small switch. A narrow bar of light slowly fades in from the ceiling, illuminating the small, utilitarian cabin space.

Ewan swings his legs round and sits on the edge of the bed, staring at the floor and rubbing his arms. To open the other case and grab something warmer or simply pick from the untidy pile he left on the floor earlier? For the time being, that decision can wait. Nature calls.

Ewan grabs the thin cotton fabric of the BCB-Hygiene-branded dressing gown from a nearby moulded bench, situated beside a small square table that also juts out from the cabin wall. Pulling it over his matching night vest and shorts, he shuffles into light slippers and steps to the cabin door. Lifting a small cover to reveal a thin stripe of white, he stares with tired eyes. The cabin door slides silently to one side.

The corridor is quiet and clean but has a gloomy atmosphere. Curved buff metal surfaces all poorly lit by a miserable line of emergency lights overhead. Large, exposed support struts, thick cabling and railings fixed either side, broken only by cabin doors with embossed room numbers. No attempts made to disguise the functional, industrial guts of the ex-military clipper, except maybe the middle of the raised floor. A wide stripe of dark wine carpet there, soft underfoot and seemingly the only nod to comfort. As Ewan walks along towards the washroom at the end of the section, he imagines the fun Reese would be having, studying every seam, every fixture.

Overhead lights and a large fan in the wall immediately spark to life when Ewan enters, illuminating the modest, functional cold space. He shivers, skin tightening slightly under the thin dressing gown as even cooler air wraps around him. He moves to one of the small urinals and pees, noticing that the health monitors set in the wall above are all offline, the screens dark and lifeless.

"Must turn everything off at night."

Moving past a small communal shower area to a row of three wash hand basins, Ewan discovers that two of the soap dispensers aren't working. He waves a hand in front of the taps and water runs, relieved when the temperature finally reaches lukewarm but goes no further.

He questions his own reflection in the long wall mirror, whispering. "Wonder who has the contract here?"

Facing the nearby hand dryer, Ewan stops for a moment before walking away from the lifeless unit, exiting the washroom wiping his hands on the fabric of his gown.

Pausing outside, in no rush to head back to one of the most uncomfortable beds he's ever slept in, Ewan decides to return along a different corridor. Except for the different numbers etched on the cabin doors, the low curved corridor looks and feels the same. The same lack of decor, the same naked metal structures, the same dim emergency lighting and deep wine carpet underfoot.

But stop.

Ewan holds his breath. A wry smile slowly creeping across his face. Loud, rhythmic moaning, skin meeting skin in almost violence. And woven between those scattered and snatched sounds, slowly revealing themselves while Ewan listens, cries of struggle. A morbid, painful wailing and weeping, causing his smile to drain quickly.

"Hold him properly."

Hearing the sharp voice, Ewan steps closer to the cabin door, tracing the aggressive gasps and cries from inside. The latter rising in urgency, becoming more intense, more desperate, perhaps more frustrated, as seconds pass.

He places his ear on the cold metal, hearing other voices now. Not just two, maybe three or four. All encouraging at random times, excited cries and soft cheers barely restrained. He lifts his head away from the door when a voice shrieks and wails loudly, met with small laughter and one slap then another.

More cries and cheering. Everything faster. Rougher.

Whispering. "Who are you?"

Ewan flicks his head to the side, noticing a suspicious young face staring round the edge of the next cabin doorway.

"What are you doing?"

"Nothing." Ewan shakes his head instinctively. "Couldn't sleep."

An uncomfortable silence hangs heavy, enhanced by the background of painful cries and shouts all gaining in intensity.

Ewan wraps his gown tighter, gesturing clumsily then forcing a smile. "Just, heading back to my cabin."

He walks past, avoiding the challenging, questioning gaze. Opting for brisk steps, but not so quick as to indicate any sense of fear or intimidation. He doesn't look back, doesn't have to, the weight of the hard stare still burning from behind, real or imagined.

A shiver passes through him. That chill of stumbling into the middle and knowing neither the good nor the bad of it. Wondering whether you should remember and investigate or forget and ignore. Wondering whether it even matters, either way.

The path eventually loops back to the first corridor. Finding the door to cabin 6, Ewan lifts the cover on the sensor and stares into it. The door moves sideways and, after glancing along the corridor each way, he steps inside. As the door slides behind him, he exhales deeply, finding some weird relief in the sparsely decorated, cold, poorly lit cabin space.

Keeping the gown on, he clambers into the hard bed and reaches out to the light switch, the room immediately plunging into darkness. After a second, he instinctively lifts his arm from under the blanket and taps the narrow screen there. He studies the static glowing figures, all frozen hours ago, then taps the screen again to restore the darkness. He slips his arm back under the blanket and tries to find a sliver of comfort. Eyes heavy, staring into inky space, mind restless and uneasy.

***

The greeting is flat and emotionless. "Good morning, Starbird coffee to start the day?"

Ewan stifles another yawn, smiling wearily at the face under the green cloth cap. "What gave it away? Yes, thank you."

"Table just for you, sir? This way please."

They navigate a modest canteen space, moving across tough plastic flooring and between several seated parties, all eating from small plates of food. Heading to a section where the moulded tables and accompanying benches are smaller, suitable only for two people maximum.

"Here?"

"Thanks, Officer…?" Ewan cranes his neck, trying to read the dark lettering on the combat fatigues.

The young woman glances down, pulling the material out slightly and pointing to the letters. "Albright."

Sliding onto the bench. "Thank you, Officer Albright."

"Standard breakfast with coffee?"

Ewan looks up, noticing eyes as weary as his own. "What's on the menu?"

"Two pieces of lightly toasted bread, with a selection of cold meats and a side of beans. A bowl of Starbird gumbo is optional, our speciality dish on this route, made with fresh Dunvegan Okra. It's always popular."

Ewan pauses, giving his still foggy brain extra time to fire. "OK, yeah. I'm starving. Haven't eaten much since yesterday. I'll take the coffee, standard breakfast and the…"

"Gumbo."

Ewan nods.

"Everything fine last night, sir, in your cabin?"

Ewan flinches slightly, clearing his throat nervously. "Yeah. Yes, great. Thank you."

"That's excellent, sir. I'll bring your food when it's ready."

With a closing smile of cold duty, Officer Albright walks away. Ewan watches her passing through two white swing doors at the rear of the canteen to the kitchen behind. He rubs his eyes briskly, clearing mild morning blur, looking through the long narrow hatch in the wall and seeing the arms of several random people in white, now joined by Officer Albright.

Turning back, he taps the screen on his arm and the display glows immediately, letting him swipe through several pages of information quickly. Everything still frozen. No signals. No updates.

"Won't be much use here friend."

Ewan swings round, seeing a couple sitting at a table behind, studying him intensely. An older man, his face open and smiling, healthy tanned skin covered in a smart light-blue shirt with dark embroidery patterns curving across. The woman sitting opposite, many years younger, wearing a single grey tone formal business suit and a sleek silver communications collar around her neck. Several other smaller silver shards peer out from the dark skin of her hands, all suggesting a level of technology far removed from stock BCB Hygiene manager issue.

The older man continues. "Not much use on these older clippers. All the shielding? Well, I think it's the shielding. Knowing Starbird, they probably just turn all the comms off."

Smiling knowingly, the woman places her cup down on the table and picks up the thread, voice warm and bright. "You'll reconnect from time to time. Depends on the route – if we run close to a mining station or a satellite. And it depends on your network."

"It's okay. I expected the disruption anyway. Just waiting on a few messages."

The man slices some of the cold meat and bread on his plate, chewing thoughtfully and sipping from his coffee cup. "Hope it isn't urgent, I sure wouldn't hold your breath."

"No, not urgent. Um, I'm Ewan."

The woman breaks into a broad smile. "Very pleased to meet you Ewan. I'm Camila and this is my colleague, Lawrence."

Lawrence tips his head, chewing quickly. "Business trip, Ewan?"

"Yes, new business." Ewan crosses his fingers in a good luck gesture and waves them in the air.

"Oh good. Good. What's your line?"

"Hygiene."

Camila makes an exaggerated, approving sound. "Ah not so far away then. You might know our corporation, Calder Arkwright?"

"Recycling? CAI?"

"That's the one. Lawrence and I, we manage several processing plants across Lundstrom."

Lawrence lowers his knife and fork to the plate, pushing it slightly forward. "So much opportunity now, Ewan, all the new colonies and stations coming online."

Camila smiles, qualifying his words. "About to come online, it's still… delicate, in certain sectors."

"Okay some of it isn't there just yet but it's going to happen. So much potential."

"I know CAI. Massive corporation. A few of our techs, they mention your research a lot. I'm in Field Sales so, eh, they lose me y'know?"

Camila grins warmly, pleased with the feedback. "Yes, we have experienced massive growth and transformation recently. But what about you?"

"Oh, we're nothing like your scale. Tiny in comparison. BCB Hygiene?"

Camila and Lawrence glance at each other before the latter says, "Can't say I've heard of it, Ewan."

"We're fairly new. A couple of the main techs left Trojan Mobile Cleaning years back, decided they could do things better. They started their own corp and it became BCB. Been going a few years. We're doing okay."

Perhaps out of kindness, Camila takes a sip of coffee, disguising any further reaction as worlds of entirely different scales clash across the tables. As she drinks, double doors swing open and Officer Albright steps through, carrying a white plastic tray in front. She walks across the floor carefully, lowering the tray and lifting the items off, arranging them on the table surface in front of Ewan. She lifts the coffee pot and swirls it slightly, before steadily pouring the deep brown liquid into the white cup.

"Standard breakfast. With extra Starbird Gumbo as requested."

"Thanks."

"If you need a coffee refill, please raise your hand."

Ewan looks at the table, pushing down any flickers of disappointment. By any stretch, the standard breakfast is hardly a feast. The white plate has a modest range of processed pale meat, all placed on top of two thick slices of toasted bread. To the side, occupying most of the plate, a generous thick paste mountain of dark red bean. In a separate bowl, a hearty, bright red gumbo, consisting of generous meaty chunks and various green vegetables, acceptable enough to quell the hunger for a short while.

"This'll be fine. Thank you."

Placing the white tray under a shoulder, Officer Albright withdraws a small square-shaped, printed paper pad and a short plastic pen from one of her pockets. "Sir, when you have finished your meal. If you can complete our breakfast evaluation and either hand it back to me directly or just leave it on the table when you leave?"

Ewan glances at the paper to the side, a typical short survey about the standard of service and whether he'd recommend Starbird to a friend. "Thanks, just leave it there."

"Officer Albright? We're finished here." Camila and Lawrence both rise from the table, the former lifting a large digital paper satchel from the floor and slipping it over a shoulder. "We've completed the form."

"Thank you, these comments are really important. Have a good day."

Stepping forward, Lawrence stops briefly beside the table. "See you in the lounge deck this afternoon for a drink, Ewan?"

Ewan chews quickly, trying to shuffle a mushy bolus of bread and cold meat to one side of his mouth. "Ah maybe, Lawrence. I have a lot of background reading to do, things to prepare. Important meetings coming up, I have to get it right."

"I see, maybe tomorrow then?" Lawrence nods his head meekly. "Well, good to meet you anyway, Ewan."

Camila beams a farewell smile across the canteen floor, which Ewan acknowledges by lifting a hand, metal knife clasped within. He watches them walk slowly through the main door and into the dim corridor, both exuding a smooth, serene professional air.

When they depart, Ewan chews the cold meat and bread thoughtfully, glancing round the canteen at the scattering of other travellers. A strange reflection flickers, how Camila, Lawrence and most of the others here are not what he expected. All formal, polite manners, sharp attire and fully upgraded sleek personal tech. As Ewan stirs and lifts a heavy spoonful of Starbird gumbo, he wonders how many of the others sailing on this budget flight belong to huge corporations like Calder Arkwright Industries.

Hearing a raised mumbling voice from behind, Ewan looks over his shoulder. Seeing Officer Albright standing close by, hurriedly checking and re-checking the survey paper that Camila and Lawrence left on the table.

Speaking quietly, noticing a shade of anxiety. "Everything okay there, Officer Albright?"

She looks across, gaze weary and shaking her head softly, instinctively, then regaining her composure. "I don't know. I think so."

Ewan turns back and lifts his cup, carefully watching over the rim of the thick white plastic as Officer Albright brushes past the table, stopping at the small podium situated just inside the main door. She quickly slips the survey paper into a uniform pocket, before removing a second sheet from a different pocket and feeding that into a silver unit on top. Ewan watches her remove the cloth cap and straighten her hair quickly, taking a mere second to compose herself.

Ewan drops his gaze to the next spoonful of gumbo when Officer Albright unexpectedly looks in his direction. As he chews thoughtfully, the man that challenged Ewan in the corridor the previous night enters the canteen. After the standard greeting at the podium, Officer Albright leads him towards a table close by, where he sits and nods almost imperceptibly at Ewan.

***

Sitting quietly on the edge of the bed, Ewan studies the production prototype move slowly back and forth along the same strip of carpet. Inspecting fluctuating lines of data dancing across the domed black pearl surface, comparing the figures with the readings fixed on the digital paper in his hand.

"Build seems okay." Whispering rhetorically. "Got to be an improvement over that aging Trojan fleet…"

He breaks off from his observations and rifles through the melee of real and digital paper, scattered across most of the lower bed. Unfolding one of the digital shards, it springs into backlit life, displaying a wall of dense text which

Ewan spends the next few minutes mumbling through. Then he lifts and unfolds another, opening and scrolling through the first of the technical white papers.

Having already dedicated most of the afternoon to amendments, Ewan reasons that another few hours of edits in the evening won't make any difference. As he scrolls slowly through, he breaks his silence with a groan, stumbling upon an error still lurking in a solitary appendix full of performance statistics. He places his finger gently on the screen and speaks the correction.

The synthetic speech confirmation is immediately interrupted by a flurry of loud, frantic wailing from the corridor outside. Shocked, Ewan lowers his hand and drops the digital paper to the bed, stepping quickly to where the cleaning robot tirelessly follows its invisible line. He presses a circular button at the rear of the unit and the robot initiates its shutdown protocols with a low melody.

Pulling the sleeves of his corporate sweatshirt down, Ewan stares into the sensor and the cabin door slides open. Glancing left and right in the corridor, he sees one of the other passengers, a much older man wearing a lavish dressing gown, standing further back towards the main deck entrance. Another cabin door opens, two younger women appearing in the doorway, their expressions disturbed, concerned.

"You hear that? What was it?"

"I don't know..." The door closes behind as Ewan creeps forward.

Suddenly, three figures in dark combat uniforms burst through the main deck entrance at the bottom of the corridor. One of them stopping briefly and shouting, gesturing fiercely with thick gloved hands and a large baton, attempting to usher a growing number of people back to their cabins. But as the soldier jogs away to regroup, most continue forward, even more curious.

The soldiers rush past Ewan, moving swiftly to the washroom corridor, eliciting terrible screams and shrieks from whoever is already there. Disturbed by the sound, Ewan hastens each stride, now skipping along the crimson carpet, until an outstretched uniformed black arm and glove stop him in his tracks.

"Return to your cabin please."

"Is something wrong?"

"Nothing wrong. Just a breakout."

"A breakout?"

"Yes, a breakout. The situation is under control."

"I might be able to help?"

"You can help by returning to your cabin, Mr Fortune."

Ewan stops, startled slightly that the soldier has addressed him specifically. Before his attention is drawn to three more soldiers bursting through the main door and sprinting forward. Ewan notices the rifles over their backs as they pass, all dark metal with small panels of dull silver and orange.

Somewhere ahead, a door slams. Limbs lash against metal. Screams of pain, rage, frustration.

"My baby!"

The soldier spins round immediately and runs into the washroom corridor. Leaving Ewan free to follow behind with a few other concerned passengers, all unsettled by the commotion.

"Where is he? What have you done with him?"

The soldier who spoke to Ewan moments before now faces him again, effectively sealing off one side of the washroom corridor from the small group of onlookers. Cold eyes set behind a clear visor in a dark combat mask and helmet, heavy suited arms stretched out left and right. To the other side, another soldier standing in a similar position.

"Stay back!"

In the middle, Ewan watches a woman standing near one of the washroom doors, brandishing a knife. Four soldiers stand in a semi-circle around her, leaving no option other than to fight or disappear into the washroom behind.

Ewan watches through the black uniforms, seeing her swing back and forth. Shouting. Confused and uncertain. Waving the knife violently in front of each of the masked faces. Expression pulsing from anger to fear and back again.

"Put the knife down, crewman…"

"Montrose, sir, Lynell Montrose."

"Ms Montrose, you need to co-operate with us. That way, we can help you."

"No!"

"The upper deck is a restricted zone. You're disturbing your fellow passengers. You don't want to cause any more of a scene, do you?"

Upset. "No… No…"

"Good." A dark, gloved hand gestures to calm down. "I need you to put the knife on the floor, now."

"It's not, not my knife…" Nervous muttering, only just audible. "Someone gave it to me."

"That's fine, Ms Montrose, we can clear this all up quickly, but first I need you to put the knife on the floor. That way we can conduct our business and let these good passengers, people who have done nothing wrong, carry on with their pleasant evening."

Pausing as though confused, then brandishing the knife again, "Where is he? What have you done with him?"

"Ms Montrose…"

"You've taken him. Must be here somewhere. Where is he? He wouldn't just disappear like that."

Ewan watches as Lynell lifts her head, staring left and right at the scattering of passengers. Her face shaking, expression desperate, eyes wide and fearful, pale skin dirty and tear stained. A small line of blood trailing from scalp to forehead. Everything framed with light, untidy long hair.

Addressing the passengers either side. "Which one of you?"

"Okay, Ms Montrose, I'm going to ask one more time."

"You've taken him. I know you have."

Instantly a soldier springs forward and grabs Lynell from behind, focusing on the arm with the knife, which soon clatters to the floor. One of them picks it up immediately and withdraws, leaving the other two to add their weight to pulling Lynell back into the washroom. As a screaming Lynell is dragged inside, the soldier with the knife stands in front of the door, barring the way.

Uneasy, Ewan glances at the passengers on the other side. Eyes locking with the young man from last night, staring straight towards him, expression blank and unmoved. A connection only broken when the soldier there begins ordering and moving everyone back towards the cabins.

The soldier nearest to Ewan addresses the passengers. "We apologise for the disturbance. It's important that you now return to your cabin immediately so that we can secure the deck and ensure your full safety."

Ewan stutters, addressing the masked face as other passengers drift away. "What about the woman, what was she talking about?"

"Back, Mr Fortune. Clear the corridor. Lockdown status."

"Lockdown?"

"Only temporary, Mr Fortune. We need to clear the corridor as quickly as possible so we can transport the felon. And we can't rule out the possibility there may be others. We need to secure the area. Cabin 6, isn't it?"

"Yes…" Ewan shivers.

"Everybody back, return to your cabins!"

Ewan moves to the side, hesitating and looking back towards the washroom. Sounds of screaming, of struggle, no longer bleeding from within.

"Ewan!"

Further along the corridor, Lawrence holds up a hand. Ewan tips his head and returns the gesture, stepping over carpet quickly.

"Terrible business."

Ewan nods. "She was looking for someone. Standard class?"

"Maybe." Lawrence looks perplexed as he starts walking back. "Not sure. Might be from the lower decks."

"Lower deck?"

"Shhhh, don't let them hear." Lawrence nods ruefully, taking a moment, expression sober, reflective. "I heard that, sometimes, they transport special passengers."

"What? Like criminals? On a budget passenger clipper?"

Lawrence sniffs then stops walking, standing in the area where the three main corridors meet. He watches the last few passengers drift by.

"It's what I heard. They do it sometimes, y'know, special jobs. This is all military hardware, right?"

Ewan frowns.

Lawrence raises an eyebrow. "Come on, Ewan, think about it. You think Starbird breaks even selling standard travel passes?"

"I don't know."

"Course, it's only a rumour." Whispering then making a swirling gesture with a finger, pointing at all the walls. "Best not to speak about it."

A soldier catches up behind, shouting at the last few stragglers. "Move! We need to clear the corridors now!"

"Alright, alright!" Lawrence holds up his hands in mock surrender. "We're going. I was thinking we can meet up tonight, Ewan? Have a drink in the lounge and put this all behind us?"

"Ah, no, not tonight, Lawrence."

"Let me guess. More work, right?"

"Yeah, sorry. Still have a load of construction tests to run and check."

Lawrence looks deep into Ewan's eyes and taps a slightly scolding index finger on his chest. "Look, I know what it's like. But don't burn yourself out. Take some time, join us."

"Return to your cabins please!"

Noticeably disappointed, Lawrence slowly moves away, heading towards the corridor that curves back along the other side. "Well, maybe tomorrow night?"

"Yeah, maybe." Ewan approaches his cabin door sensor and glances back. "Lawrence?"

Lawrence peers around the edge of the corridor wall.

"Does this happen all the time on a budget voyage?"

"Sometimes."

"You put up with it? You, and Camila, you both work for a huge corporation…"

"It's all down to cost, Ewan." Lawrence breaks into a wide grin before tapping the side of his nose. "And a few other benefits, right?"

Ewan smiles uncertainly, rubbing his face with his hand. Turning briefly to look down the corridor towards the main door, seeing two other soldiers standing guard there.

Lawrence shouts, "Night, Ewan. Let's have that drink tomorrow before it's too late."

Staring into the thin white strip, the large cabin door slides open. Stepping inside, Ewan closes his eyes and exhales wearily, attempting to purge the uneasiness flowing through him. But the peace of the cabin simply encourages his mind to replay everything over and over. All the images. All the shouting. All the screaming.

His eyes flicker open. Drawn immediately to the cleaning robot, noiselessly moving across a different section of carpet near the bed. The dark translucent dome littered with changing sensor output.

Muttering. "I turned you off."

Ewan fires across to the bed, checking the litter of actual and digital paper. Sifting through quickly, confirming each file by unfolding several pages and scanning each one. Everything seemingly in order, no obvious changes, nothing missing.

Reaching over to the floor at the end of the bed, he checks the two large cases. One lying open, with only a few additional garments remaining inside. The other standing, tucked away at the wall. An outside examination of each revealing no foul play, no signs of any tampering.

Ewan stares at the robot, still following its new invisible routine across the smooth carpet. Lost in a reflective daze, he lets it trundle back and forth a few times before reaching out to power it down.

Small paranoia crawls like shadow across his shoulders as he sits on the edge of the bed, staring aimlessly across the dim room. His expression troubled, no longer concealing his growing anxiety. Could it be that whoever stole into the cabin was somehow connected to the incident? Should he report it to passenger services, just in case?

Ewan breaks off his troubled reverie, quickly tapping the screen in his arm which springs to life. The normally rolling information there still frozen in time, the figures unchanged since he boarded the clipper the day before. Pausing for a moment in vain hope, he taps the screen once more, turning it dark. The inability to whisper message the BCB office and file a report, hardly mitigating his increasing sense of isolation.

Then, another voice inside. Bad enough that one of the passengers on the clipper might be a petty thief, but what if the intruder is so much more? What if a fellow passenger on the upper deck already knows about the prototype? What if that person used the incident as cover to break in? Didn't Lynell say that the knife wasn't even hers, that someone had given it to her?

Ewan glances at the cleaning robot now motionless on the floor. Nothing seemingly damaged, but could something have been added, during those few minutes instead? Perhaps some sabotage routine that, at the appropriate time and signal, will trigger one malfunction after another?

Ewan shakes his head, the internal clamour to work through all the tests from the start becoming louder. This is the main demo unit after all which, if agreed, will be staying on Godwin 3 for a trial period. Success or failure rests on this cleaning robot right here and there's only the finest of margins. One unforeseen malfunction might tip the delicate scale, spoiling any opportunity. One error might offer the potential buyers on Godwin 3 just enough time to stall and rethink. Enough time to hold renewal meetings with Trojan Mobile, to explore what they can offer to extend their existing contract.

"Thank you for the demonstrations, Mr Fortune. We're very interested in the new models but… we don't believe they're quite ready for production and certainly not robust enough for deployment in such a high-demand environment. Maybe next year?"

Ewan brushes his hands over his head and slowly gets to his feet. A once confident, relaxed evening now smothered in a harried redo haze of even more tests and routine checking. As Ewan paces uneasily in imaginary circles and lines, another vision intrudes, taunting him further. Lawrence and Camila in full evening wear, drinking, joking, laughing with the other passengers in the deck lounge.

"I wonder…"

Knock. Knock.

Ewan steps to the sensor and stares briefly into the light. The large door slips to the side, revealing Officer Albright standing there silently. Khaki-covered arms dropped behind the heads of a young boy and girl either side. Both children shifting on the spot nervously, grubby elfin faces tattooed lightly, their expressions concerned and sad. Each dressed in loose shirts, ragged, stained trousers and wearing several pieces of simple tribal jewellery. They glance at Ewan warily then drop their gaze to the floor.

"Officer Albright?"

Instantly, she holds a finger to her mouth, quickly nudging the children forward into the cabin. The door closes silently behind.

Whispering. Tense and fearful. "Are you one of them?"

Confused, Ewan nervously half-smiles.

"I need to know..."

"What?"

Even closer. Head shaking, expression folding, becoming upset. "*Are you one of them?*"

"I, don't know what you mean?"

"*Are you one of those people?*"

Albright talks with her eyes, glancing at the two children either side. Ewan follows her gesture, looking from face to face while young, weary blue eyes stare somewhat fearfully back.

"No, what is this?"

"You don't know?" Albright narrows her eyes. "Can I trust you?"

Ewan barely hears the words.

"*Can I trust you, Ewan Fortune?*"

Eyes meet in confusion. Ewan steps back, slowly.

"One of the passengers on the upper deck. Made a complaint already. He won't be the last. The disruption, all the noise..."

"About Lynell?" Ewan points somewhere to the side. "The woman in the corridor?"

"Yes."

"The guards took her away. She escaped... A criminal? I don't know."

"No... Not a criminal." Officer Albright glances down, her expression crumpling. "It doesn't matter, *can I trust you?*"

"Yes... Of course."

"These children, here..." Officer Albright glances down at them, trying to compose herself, "...they're given as payment – complimentaries for the evening. *On the house.* They're the first, but they won't be the last. It's how it always goes…"

Ewan wavers, reaching out for the moulded table behind.

"I have to escort them to the passengers and sometimes… but, I can't do it any more, can't be a part of this. It's not right. Too many now." Officer Albright chokes, holding up a hand to stifle tears, her breathing suddenly sharp, upset. "Can't do it… And that's why. I need to know if I can trust you?"

Shaken. Increasingly anxious. "Haven't you reported this? There must be some procedure."

Albright steps closer and glares into his eyes, her expression incredulous, frustrated. "*Are you crazy?* Haven't you been paying any attention since you came onboard?"

"I've been working…" Ewan stares at her, watching as several tears escape, only to be wiped away briskly. "I don't want any trouble. Just want to get to my destination. What is all this? What do you want me to do?"

"I need you to play along. Someone needs to do the right thing…" Officer Albright tries to compose herself. "I need to leave them here for a minute, pretend I've got it wrong. The wrong cabin – an admin error."

"You're coming back? What are you going to do?"

"I'm going to switch them in the confusion…" Officer Albright pauses, as if her mouth is suddenly dry and she needs to summon the courage to unburden further. "Look, there are more than three decks on the ship…"

"More?"

"I work all the passageways. It's a military clipper, there are rat runs everywhere. The lower decks are all hidden, secret, nobody knows about them. Except for the guards and a few trusted crew – the few allowed to roam the tunnels – like me. It's all hidden, that's how it's done. How they do everything so quietly."

"There's people there?"

"So many…" Albright sighs, voice cracking with emotion. "You wouldn't believe. All kept in huge cages."

"Why? What are they doing?"

"Grey world. Trade… processing. And entertainment, during the voyage." Albright shakes her head instinctively. "Maybe it's best you don't know."

Ewan crouches down, staring at the children, their expressions now more bemused than frightened.

"I'm sorry. Sorry it's you. The system said you've never sailed with the company before. I recognise other passengers… I can't trust anyone else. I had to take the chance, on you. I can't keep doing this, I can't… I have to find a way. Even to save one of them…Somehow…"

Ewan stands up, awkwardly holding out a reassuring hand that stops short of contact. "The people down there? How?"

"All ages. Families. People who've lost everything. Hidden cargo, shipped from nowhere and going nowhere. Most will end up dying a few months from now, starving to death in some Dunvegan mine. A lucky handful might make it, maybe slaves on some large estate. A lot won't even make it off the ship. They'll murder each other or… worse."

"Worse? And the children?"

"The younger ones are normally separated. They have, other uses. For the clients, right? They pay a lot of credits. It's how the corp survives, you understand?"

"I, I can't believe this."

"Hasn't it struck you as odd that so many powerful people are sailing on a budget clipper? Haven't you stopped to wonder why?"

Ewan stares at the floor, the walls of the cabin seemingly closer and closer as words repeat inside his head. No, he hadn't stopped. No, he hadn't wondered why.

"I'm sorry, I have to go, other passengers will be complaining by now and some of the guards will be getting suspicious. I need you to listen."

Instinctively, Ewan reaches out. "Okay. I'll help you."

"At the bottom of the main stairwell, there are racks of grey power boards on the wall. Behind one is a small tunnel with a ladder that leads all the way down to the lower decks. When I leave, I'll leave the hatch open, just enough. If I'm not back after a few minutes to collect them… somethings happened, gone wrong. You'll have to bring them."

"But what do I do if a guard catches us?"

"The lower decks are only lightly patrolled. But if one of them catches you, just stop. Be polite. Explain you're from the upper deck. Nothing will happen. You're the priority customer, you're paying their wages and in on the game, right? Besides, it'll be my fault, I was clumsy. You saw the hatch left open… You weren't happy with the complimentaries."

"This is insane." Ewan stares at Officer Albright. "How long have you known all this?"

"Not long, just long enough. But now, tonight, it hurts again. These are my people. Please, just get to the holding sections, I'll do my best to clear a way. You'll see them all. I'll come and find you."

"And then?"

A flash of insecurity, of desperation, flickers across Officer Albright. "I can open the cages. The children can go back and take their chances on another night. If they can make it to Dunvega at least… Then I'll escort you back to your cabin, try and calm everything down, correct my mistakes."

"But this will make things worse? Won't they bring more people, more children?"

"Please…" Officer Albright says, sobbing and pointing at the boy and girl. "I need you to help me save *them*, do you understand? *Them*... They're…"

"You know them…" Ewan slumps down wearily on the bottom of the bed, staring at the faces in front. "I'm just trying to get to Godwin 3 to land a new contract. It's difficult enough. I thought, maybe an uncomfortable journey. Small cabin, bad food…"

"The longer I wait here, the less time I have." Whispering softly. "I can't trust anyone else. When you get to Godwin 3 or when you get home you can tell people. The right people. Tell them what's really going on…"

Ewan places the palms of each hand over his face and lowers them.

"I'm sorry, I need to go. Please, let me out."

Lifting slowly from the bed. "I don't know what to do."

"Just help me, please? No one will know. Give me twenty minutes, that's all I ask."

Officer Albright leans towards the children and whispers in an unknown language, the words strange and musical. Both children slowly turn to face Ewan, their expressions lightening instantly.

"Okay, I'll keep them here." Ewan steps to the door sensor. "If you're not back, I'll find the way down."

"Thank you." Officer Albright replies with a gesture, one hand wrapping around a fist. "Remember, find the hatch."

"Got it."

Officer Albright steps into the corridor and turns immediately, facing Ewan and saluting sharply. "We sincerely apologise for the disruption to your evening, sir. We trust this settles our business. Please be reassured that we have increased our security patrols to ensure there are no further interruptions to your pleasant evening."

As Officer Albright marches away, Ewan glances up and down the corridor several times, eventually withdrawing inside.

Checking the time on the screen in his arm first, he walks over towards pale, grubby faces and places a hand on his chest. "Um, my name is Ewan. What are your names?"

Narrowing eyes glisten with worry, scanning Ewan carefully then shifting to look around the cabin.

Ewan clears his throat, pointing a finger at his chest. "Ewan. Ew-an."

After uncomfortable moments, the girl breaks into a brief smile before shooting a puzzled expression sideways.

"Alright…" Ewan glances again at the time on his arm. "How about we… watch the robot?"

The two remain silent, examining his every move as he crouches down beside the cleaning robot.

Ewan presses one of the buttons on the rear of the unit and pats it reassuringly on top. "Now this is one very special machine. Brand new. Best in class."

The cleaning robot lights up and chirps a short melody. Finishing the last of its initial routines and moving slowly across the carpet, pulsing layers of brightly lit data over its curved pearl surface.

Initially wary, both children take a step back as the robot moves slowly between them. Each expression a mix of caution succumbing to fascination.

"It has many different modes you can combine. This one, it's how it checks." Ewan lowers onto his knees and hovers a hand over the carpet. "It's testing the material, the carpet, the floor underneath? It's working out what it can do. It's thinking, what it needs to clean –even whether it needs to clean at all. And the hook on the back, that's for the reservoirs. A tank."

Ewan holds up his hands, approximating a rectangular shape in the air. But the two children ignore him, studying the robot closely as it passes back and forth. He continues speaking, knowing full well that they must be understanding nothing of what he is saying.

"One of the special features, it can call on its friends. Y'know, maybe there's a spillage somewhere in a priority area – a popular area, loads of people. If this unit is pulling a dirty tank, it can call others, other cleaning and drying bots."

As the robot tracks back, the girl looks towards Ewan and grins, revealing two rows of blunt, discoloured teeth. She points at the machine and the lights on top, tracing invisible lines into the air with an outstretched finger. Excitedly, she mumbles several musical words that collapse and merge into each other.

"Kerrin-bah, sorro-oshtana-kineca-doo-emish!"

The boy shrugs in response, leaning over the robot, walking alongside it and chuckling. "Laka-ban, moh-shasko-bdesha-doo-emish."

Perplexed yet curious, Ewan listens to the continuing chatter and places his modified hand on the side of his head. "What language is this?"

The synthetic response is quick and typically soothing. "Warning offline data only. Appears to be a dialect of Lokeeshan. One of several languages spoken widely by indigenous inhabitants across Numinossium, a binary star system in the outer rim."

"Can you translate?"

"Translation services are unavailable offline. Outer rim language translation available to premium issue tier managers only."

Ewan drops his hand. Looking at the two children chattering and moving with the robot, trailing back and forth.

Whispering. "How did you get here…?"

Minutes pass in quiet reflection, the peace of the cabin disturbed only by the chatter of some alien tongue and a compulsion towards ever-more time checking. But that remaining peace gradually submerges into a growing anxiety, becoming more desperate as the moments pass, with still no knock on the cabin door.

Now on the edge of the bed, flipping open various digital papers randomly, Ewan is unable to focus on anything else except the remaining time. Eventually, at no more than a few seconds after the twenty-minute deadline, he takes several deep breaths and gets to his feet.

"We need to go. Now."

Heads turn. Blank expressions cover each face.

Quickly, Ewan tries a different approach, pointing to everyone first then over to the door, finishing with a gesture of making two fingers walk like legs. This appears to work, the children immediately stepping away from the robot still trailing across the carpet. Ewan steps over to power off the unit.

"Good. Let's go…"

The cabin door silently opens and Ewan glances outside, checking both ways. He gestures to the children and they follow, one either side, stepping onto soft crimson. Ewan pushes both gently forward, encouraging them along the corridor while the cabin door closes softly behind.

"This way…"

They slip quietly along the empty passageway. Attention drawn briefly to the door of cabin number two, behind which a cacophony of several seemingly drunken voices rage and weep.

Slipping through the upper deck door they hit the top of the stairwell, plunging into a warm semi-darkness. The carpet stops just in front, meeting a flight of wide, punctured metal steps heading down with sturdy bannisters either side. Across the walls and ceiling run a melee of cables, each one pinned to dim, blank surfaces by huge metal brackets bolted at regular intervals. No attempt at decoration, no attempt to hide the strictly functional. The only nods to colour are two signs. One a modest golden rectangle situated above the door, displaying deck level and cabin numbers. The other a long, multi-coloured plastic sign, containing rows of passenger safety information fixed to the near wall. The whole stairwell has a smell to it, something Ewan can't quite place, something acrid, electrical, a slight burning.

Pausing. Listening. Hearing only a modest background hum that seems to seep from the walls themselves. "Let's go."

The children watch as he climbs down the steps, glancing at each other blankly then following. Much to his relief and surprise, Ewan senses that neither appears to be particularly concerned, no strange words or panic. Nothing. Unlike Ewan, his skin turning increasingly cold under the soft material of the BCB sweatshirt. His ears burning for the slightest stray sound. His eyes scanning the gloom for the merest of movements ahead.

Ewan reaches the small metal landing halfway and turns to face the next flight of steps. At the bottom, another patch of carpet and a solitary door, exactly like the one above. This one leading to the lounge deck, containing several more cabins, the Starbird canteen and the spacious lounge itself.

Ewan moves closer to the door and listens carefully, praying for no sound. Hearing nothing, he gestures for the children to hurry past. They skip forward, moving out of sight in the gloom, further down the metal stairs.

More steps follow, over and over. Gentle feet tap on metal, creating a soft, persistent rhythm. A rhythm that pauses only once more when they hear voices talking far above, a party of people moving to, or from, the lounge deck.

Finally, they reach a fenced-off utility area at the bottom, a sturdy metal door barring any further progress along that level. Around the walls, exactly as Officer Albright indicated, large dirty grey panels covered in various switches and gauges, with huge power cables passing overhead. Ewan examines the panels nestled closest to the ground, feeling around the lower edges, finding one at a slight angle.

Waving a hand. "Here."

Although appearing heavy, the large panel moves surprisingly easily as Ewan pulls it towards him. It swings gently from the wall to reveal a modest space behind, a sturdy metal ladder curving down inside.

"Is this the one? Where we'll find Officer Albright?"

Hearing the name, they launch into a burst of excited chatter. Ewan watches helplessly as the girl climbs into the hidden space, manoeuvring quickly at the top of the ladder and starting her descent. She stops briefly, staring at the boy in front, voicing words of encouragement.

"Kerrin-bah... Vikonosh-doo! Vikonosh-doo-omish."

The boy moves quickly, swinging his legs over and down, reaching the top rungs. His movements hasty, harassed, as though nervous at being alone.

"Careful."

Ewan watches the boy move further away as doubts rise from within. Intensifying as he steps towards an imaginary line, the one beyond which the luxury of choice no longer exists. Perhaps, it's better to turn back? To let them move on ahead without him and take their chances finding Officer Albright. Just secure the panel, return to the cabin and deny anything when asked. Besides, there's still so much work to be done, so many tests to complete.

And yet, Ewan instinctively leans forward to peer inside the secret hatch and check the surprisingly well-illuminated route down. Between two bands of curved light, he watches the top of a head becoming ever smaller, while curious invisible forces hold him fast. Any thought of escape, of abandoning the children to whatever is down there, feels impossible, wrong even. He exhales wearily, head clouded with doubts but his heart already inside the hatch, climbing down the ladder, responding to something greater.

Feet latch onto sturdy metal rungs before one hand reaches out, grasping a large circular handle on the rear of the door. Ewan carefully draws the heavy panel towards him, pulling it closer, the handle turning slightly as it travels. When the hatch door closes it removes any remaining thoughts of escape. Instead, Ewan glances warily downwards, seeing the children far below.

"Wait..."

He follows quickly but quietly, unsure of what lies behind the curved walls. On the way, he passes several doors. Sturdy metal panels studded with thick bolts, a large wheel handle fixed in the middle and small viewing panels all obscured. Some of the doors are grimy, dirty, as though never used in years, others clean and polished. This juxtaposition of the old and the new, the burnished and the neglected, intrigues Ewan only slightly on his descent. His mind fixed on catching the children, some way below.

As the end of the ladder nears, Ewan watches the girl step off and jog away, disappearing instantly from his limited field of view. The boy follows just behind, leaving Ewan alone to continue his hurried descent. For a moment, he considers calling out, but channels his dismay into ever quicker steps.

Not long after, Ewan reaches the dark floor below and scans the modestly lit, seemingly featureless curved section of corridor for the merest sound of activity. But the only thing he can hear is the children somewhere in the shadows ahead, their running steps echoing back and forth.

"What are they doing...?"

Staying close to the side and glancing at the edges of the ceiling for cameras, Ewan moves forward quietly. The dull, blank walls now punctuated by imposing metal doors. All new, polished metal surfaces with bulky reinforced hinges and heavy locking mechanisms. On each door, a rectangular display switches between two screens. One showing a large keypad and the other various lines of status information.

Ewan continues warily, passing each identical vault door, eyes and ears straining, burning. As he edges closer, he hears a wash of despair seeping from the background, all dark and shapeless. Every so often, a louder cry, brief and shrill, like a spark leaping from fire. The sounds muddied and distant, yet enough to cool his skin, to make him shiver and glance over his shoulder. Perhaps, it isn't too late to return to the barely illuminated ladder? To climb up to the panel and return to the cabin. To check that everything is as it should be, just as he remembers it, as he needs it to be.

Nervous spit forms, spilling out slightly, causing Ewan to wipe it away with the back of a cold hand. He looks forward again, furiously waving at the two silhouettes further ahead, gesturing wildly for them to stop. But the children continue to ignore him, apparently oblivious to any danger.

"Wait… Don't go on…" Ewan mutters under increasingly frantic breath. "What is this place?"

Ahead, Ewan sees the children stop and examine one of the doors. Instantly, he raises his arms and gestures in desperation, pleading in vain for them both to move away. Likely each surface will be rigged with sensors, detecting any change in temperature, movement, sound.

The girl waves an arm in response, her gesture calm and fluid yet causing urgent words to fire inside Ewan's head. Hurry! Hurry, Ewan! Surely that's what those strange words mean?

When Ewan reaches them, both are trying to move the large circular handle on the front which stubbornly refuses to shift. As they struggle, Ewan glances at the nearby display, noticing a circle of red light on the modest dark screen, moving from big to small and back again. Pulsing, like a heartbeat. Nervously, he looks across to the other displays, seeing the familiar keypad and status screens. Every single one the same.

Except, this one.

Just this one. Different.

"It's already open," Ewan mutters, staring into glistening, confused eyes. "You knew? You both knew."

A cacophony of musical words floods, yet something still snaps inside Ewan Fortune. All the nervous energy stored, from the cabin to this door here, bursts through the surface. A silent terror, an instinctive acknowledgement that the point of no return for him is already gone. The wire already tripped. There can be no return now, not without some reckoning, for better or worse.

As if led by an invisible force, Ewan grips the circular handle tightly and pulls. The curved metal moving painfully slowly at first, then spinning easily as it gains its own momentum. As the wheel turns, over and over, the edge of the unlocked heavy door rises like a hidden vertical step in the wall and slowly, steadily, glides open.

And as it opens, scattered shouts and surprised cries rush to greet them in the corridor. Crying that quickly transforms to something more ferocious. Rising to become a horrible, tortured clamouring, a brutal frenzy of screaming, wailing. The howling anguish of despair, desperation, futility, drowning the air itself in a wash of utter misery.

The children are already inside, fitting through the merest gap, seemingly unconcerned for their own safety and unperturbed by the dreadful, violent noise and odour that pours from within. Ewan tentatively follows behind. Uncertain, frightened, cold skin becoming ice. He briefly holds his hands to his ears, as he staggers further into the clean, brightly lit room.

He stands shaking, almost rooted, gazing in horror at what he sees. A plague of tear-stained faces, jammed thickly behind bars from ceiling to floor. Large, crowded cage sections across each wall, with bodies animated and motionless behind. Those who can, climb and press forward, creating a loud, writhing, dismal chaos. They press against the bars, trampling dead or tired bodies below, calling out. Screaming at Ewan in every voice, every colour.

Arms ending in claws clutch at spaces through the bars. Thin clothed and naked limbs tearing, ripping at the air, howling at this unexpected visitor. Exhausting any last scraps of energy, of hope. All striving to reach out, begging to touch the intruder. To hold onto him and never let go. As though the precious moments of that mere touch can silence all the screaming, heal all the pain, soothe every terrible cry.

"No!" Ewan flinches and turns away from the hand gripping his top, the material ripping slightly as he recoils.

He stumbles further forward, adrift in the ferocious cacophony, saturating him with fearful, paralysing electricity. Slowly, he slips to his knees, glancing over his shoulder at the exit behind. The route still clear, inviting him to run, to get away. And yet, he is powerless to move. As though the nightmarish sound itself holds him there, disabling him, gripping like a terrible vice.

Through the dreadful fog Ewan sees the children, crouching in a far corner, next to a large cage at the rear. Small arms disappear inside, two longer pale arms reach outside, wrapping all together. Not even the bars can separate that quiet embrace, those reassuring touches. Ewan sees the mothers thin face briefly. Weeping. Holding on. Shining still with tiny hope.

As he watches them, he doesn't see the guards arrive behind or the heavy baton whip the rear of his head until it's too late. The sound of the solid, sickening blow lost amidst the multitude of despairing cries and screams. His body slumps forward awkwardly over hard, white polished floor before everything goes dark.

***

A taste of blood. A sharp, futile scream. A sound of ripping fabric. Ewan rouses from darkness as though drowning.

"Remove her clothes."

Blurry shadows of dark boots fill his view from the floor. He shudders briefly and winces. Body hot and aching, a patchwork of new bruises.

The boots move away. "He's coming round, Captain."

"Watch him." The voice sharp, calm, authoritative.

"Get off me!" Sounds of struggle. Another scream. "Leave me alone! I haven't done anything! I did everything you said!"

"I know what I said, Albright. We're not going through it again."

"Bastard!"

Ewan blinks several times upon hearing the name. Gingerly, he lifts his head, trying to clear the blur and push through the pain in his limbs. Eventually, his vision clears enough to see a large and warmly lit meeting space, with several uniformed guards standing around dark, wooden-panelled walls. In the middle of the floor is a wide table, from which a holographic display ripples and stretches towards the ceiling like a digital fountain.

From his position at the rear, Ewan can only discern the head and shoulders of a man in a peaked hat sitting at the table. Apparently watching and interrogating the pale, semi-naked figure of Officer Albright standing nearby. A guard either side restrains restless arms, while a third struggles to remove the simple khaki uniform.

Furious. Frustrated. "I said get off me!"

"Enough!" The figure in the peaked cap settles back, sighing loudly as though exasperated. The chair creaks underneath. "Off! Now!"

"Bastards!"

Ewan flinches when he hears a gloved hand slap Officer Albright hard on the side of her face. With the angry energy temporarily lowered, a guard tears violently at the khaki fatigues. Removing them roughly and dropping the bundle on the table.

"And the rest. None of it belongs to her now."

Pleading. "No! No!"

The guard continues, quickly pulling the simple under-garments away and throwing them with the other items of clothing. They push her closer to the figure sitting at the table.

"And I thought we could trust you… Are the vows unclear? The reward insufficient? You've made a complete fool of your Recruitment Officer. Brought him a lot of shame. Cost him valuable credits."

"I don't care. I hate you, all of you…" Albright lowers her gaze.

"You think I enjoy these punishments? On the contrary. But your behaviour… it shows such a lack of respect. For our company, our investors. I run a clean ship, Albright!"

"Fuck…" Officer Albright finds just enough energy. "You…"

"Such a shame… Still such pride when there are so many down there just waiting to take your place." Turning to address the guards in the room. "It appears we need to find a new Officer Albright."

Ewan shivers as small laughter rises, filtered through dark combat masks.

The chair scrapes on hard wooden floor as the figure rises. Tall, imposing, all dark uniform and ornate gold trim. Leaning forward, the Captain reaches out a strong, firm hand, gripping Officer Albright tightly around the jaw.

"You people. You're all the same. Never enough, is it?"

Albright squirms, but the gloved hands of the guards holding her naked body don't yield.

"You think I should care? You think I have time for your stupid games? You have no idea, no idea what it takes to run a successful ship."

Ewan shuffles on the floor, rising slowly so as not to provoke the guard standing nearby. Watching as Albright tries to form spit, her mouth dry and jaw held tight.

"I gave you an incredible opportunity. All you had to is fulfil your duties and you'd be safe, along with those dear to you. But it's not enough for people like you, is it? There always must be more. So, it'll never be enough, will it, Officer Albright?"

"Bastard!" Albright releases her face from the hand and finds a new seam of energy, thin limbs squirming. "My family…"

One finger held in front. "You repay all our faith, all our investment… with betrayal."

"I hate you!" Albright bursts into tears, as though the violent futility of her struggle, her vulnerability, bursts though. "You… I fucking hate you."

"There, there." A glove caresses smooth pale skin. "You really think you can save them all? Do you realise that if we don't process some of those people then the ship doesn't sail? Your record shows several voyages, I thought this would have been abundantly clear to you by now. Haven't some of those people survived? Perhaps many more than if they stayed on their own war-and famine-ravaged worlds in the outer rim?"

"How can you… Monsters!" Weeping.

"Maybe we over-estimated your intelligence, Officer Albright. I must mention this to the recruitment team. Perhaps some alterations to our training, the medication…"

"All of you, fucking monsters."

The guard who removed the clothes steps forward again and lands a single, ferocious blow to the body. Albright doubles over, gasping and heaving in pain, the guards either side preventing her from collapsing entirely.

"It's simple economics. Sadly, if even that is beyond you then our business is done here. Take her away!"

"No!" Albright screams, violently pushing against a trio of dark uniforms holding tightly.

"To the holding section, Captain?"

"Oh no. Processing is much too good for her now. Take the felon to the guard quarters and do what you want. Just get rid of her. Inform any remaining family on the outside of the tragic accident. Waive any rights to standard compensation on the grounds of sedition and other criminal activity. I'll complete her file later."

"Yes, Captain."

"You can't do this!" Albright struggles violently. "No, get off me!"

Several guards join the small melee, eventually restraining each kicking and flailing limb. After several more blows, flurries of gloved hands lift the young woman from the ground and carry her away. As they leave, she continues to shout in ever more weary desperation. Cries of anger no longer sharp or vicious, more wails of realisation, of failure, of despair.

The captain scoops the garments from the table and throws the messy bundle into the arms of another guard. "Pass the order. Recruit another family as soon as possible. And tell them to get it right this time."

The soldier salutes and exits the room quickly.

"Captain, what do we do with him?"

Creeping back to his seat, the captain stops, before raising his hands and making a sequence of quick gestures in the air above. The hologram over the table responds by flashing several times, bright colours swirling upwards. Then, with a calling out gesture of each arm, several rows of shining text begin to form.

Still quivering, body hot with pain, Ewan looks at the words now suspended in the air over the table and recognises them.

"Bring him."

Two of the remaining three guards move towards Ewan and reach down, hauling him up to unsteady feet. One leg gives way almost instantly, the pain shooting like fire, causing Ewan to wince and crumple. Regardless, they drag him across the hard floor quickly, supporting him at the side of the table beside the captain.

"Ewan Fortune… Unusual."

Ewan shudders. Traces of blood in every mouthful of spit, sliding with difficulty down his throat. His body aching, flushed with hot discomfort.

"Unusual for criminals to use their real name."

"I'm not… a criminal."

The captain sinks lower in the chair, staring intensely at the words suspended above the table. "Ewan Fortune. Single. Thirty-four years old. Birthplace and biological parents unknown."

Groaning. Whispering. "What is this?"

"You have a small apartment in Garton Bay, a nondescript suburb of New Boston. Your elderly foster parents helped you purchase the property, given your history of… poor personal decisions. They have two older children, but you care for your parents routinely and, largely, on your own. They live much further away, don't they?"

"Why are you doing this…?"

"The information is correct, is it not?" The captain focuses on Ewan, who drops his head in response. "You work in field sales for a new corporation called BCB, specialising in experimental hygiene technologies. You are carrying a new production prototype onboard this clipper and, if all goes well, you'll agree a temporary contract to leave it on Godwin 3. Assuming the trial is successful, BCB will secure a permanent supply and maintenance contract and gain a foothold, in a potentially lucrative system. You have a good closing record – not great – but good enough that you should feel somewhat confident in being able to achieve this."

Ewan glances nervously at the captain. Unsure how to respond, what to say.

"In all other aspects you appear to have an excellent report record in BCB. No history of poor behaviour, disobedience, or any other difficulties resulting in disciplinary action. You are seemingly well-liked by your colleagues. We might even say, something of a company man."

Ewan stares at the captain wearily. "Why…?"

"According to our records, you placed a call a couple of days ago, to a colleague. Reese Paulson?"

Ewan swallows hard. The taste of blood suddenly colder.

"What was the reason for the call, Mr Fortune?"

Ewan pauses, as though to make sense of a flurry of anxious inner voices drowning in parallel. "Business."

"I see." The captain assumes a nonchalant tone. "And what kind of *business* might that be?"

Unable to meet the stare. "Personal… business…"

Ewan drops his head to his chest, eyes studying lines of crusted blood stains splattered across the light corporate top. He glances at the BCB logo on one side then notices the tear further down. Suddenly, he sees them all again. He remembers the sound, their faces, the hands reaching out…

The captain taps his fingers on the rich surface of the table. "You see, Mr Fortune, we have something of a delicate situation here. And as a manager yourself, I'm sure you can appreciate that delicate situations require a specific understanding. A sensitivity."

Ewan puffs his cheeks, trying to deflect. "What will happen to her?"

"Officer Albright? I'm surprised you care, given her willingness and the ease in which she led you astray." The captain shakes his head. "We'll replace her. There are so many Officer Albrights in waiting, Mr Fortune. You wouldn't believe how many."

Ewan stares into the deep brown eyes hidden in the vague shadow of the peaked hat. They stare back calmly. Dark, cold steel.

"Actually, you're rather lucky, Mr Fortune. I suspect we can settle our business here very quickly. You've made some friends on this voyage. Important people. Powerful people. Because of this it's vital that we keep our onboard matters as private as possible. Especially so, given your own… financial irregularities."

Ignoring. "What about all the people down there? What happens on this ship – your ship?"

A heavy gloved hand lashes the side of Ewan's face in response.

"Not the face." The captain holds up a hand. "I suggest you start listening, Mr Fortune."

Ewan slumps forward. Twisting. Grimacing.

"The cargo people… are not your concern."

Wearily. Painfully. "This is wrong. What are you running here?"

"A good service I think you'll find." The captain smiles coldly and clears his throat. "The only thing that matters at this time, the only thing you should be concerned about right now, is the safety and wellbeing of your fellow travellers."

"But the people there…"

The captain rises from the seat and moves closer, perching on the edge of the table. "Let me tell you about the people you seem so fond of, Mr Fortune. Officer Albright was one of them. And she led you on a merry dance, didn't she? She knew she could trust you. Knew that you'd do what she asked. She knew that you'd fall for her crusade, no matter how insane. After all, she has access to much of the same information as I… It wasn't enough to save her own skin and her family down there, by keeping her mouth shut and delivering a good service. No, she thought she might save more of them. Maybe, that she could save them all…"

Ewan frowns, his expression crumpling in confusion, uncertainty.

"Oh, apart from your life of course, Mr Fortune. She didn't really care so much about saving that. You were just the unlucky means to the end and… here you are. Paying the price."

Mumbling. "No. The children, she—"

"They kill each other in those cells, y'know? They're all so desperate many of them turn on each other. This is a great help to us. On my ship at least, we process the lifeless bodies first."

"What is this… processing…?"

"Best not to know, Mr Fortune." The captain taps a black gloved finger on the side of his nose. "It might spoil your appetite."

"And the children, on the upper deck. What goes on there?"

"Ah the children. Yes, unsavoury I agree, but our primary aim in Starbird is to ensure our frequent travellers have an enjoyable voyage. As I already mentioned, the safety and happiness of our elite customers is the highest priority. I think you'll find we maintain very high satisfaction ratings – no other sailing corporation comes even remotely close to our level of repeat business."

"It's disgusting." Ewan shakes his head miserably.

"It's not your place to judge, Mr Fortune. It may surprise you but many of the parents need only the slightest hint of a reward to push their child forward for selection. Still, you'd do well to remain quiet on the matter. Forever. Especially so as we count several of your BCB colleagues among our most valued travellers."

"I can't believe it."

The captain stares coldly into Ewan's weary eyes. "And I'm assuming you want to walk off this ship alive when we dock? With your adopted family still breathing? Your work career and prospects still intact?"

Ewan suffocates growing sobs.

"Sometimes, all it takes is to pull on a single thread and the whole picture is revealed. Don't you think, Mr Fortune?"

The pain, the worry and the anxiety break free and Ewan weeps. Several warm tears flow over cold, marked skin.

"These last few months have clearly been a difficult time for you. Sometimes we all make decisions that we think are for the best but, ultimately, turn out to be… unfortunate. Things that we… come to regret."

Ewan bites his lip deliberately, using the extra pain to sharpen.

"Look…" The captain reaches out and touches the BCB logo. "You're a good company man. Working for a new corporation that's just starting to make their presence felt in the market. Do you know how much shame this can bring if it leaks out? How dirty this can get? It will taint everyone and everything you know."

Ewan shakes his head weakly, instinctively. "I've done nothing wrong. Nothing…"

"You and I both know that isn't strictly true." The captain places a reassuring hand on Ewan's shoulder. "Besides, it doesn't matter. We have all the circumstantial evidence we need to shatter your life into a thousand painful pieces, Mr Fortune."

"I've…" Ewan wails, his voice breaking again. Fresh tears.

"It's fine. I understand. Please, take a moment."

The captain slips off the edge of the table and adjusts his jacket before settling back in his chair.

Seconds of tear-stained inner torture finally pass. Upset yet resigned, Ewan fixes the captain with glistening eyes drenched in hurt. "What do you need me to do?"

"Nothing, Mr Fortune. Absolutely nothing. Spend your remaining time forgetting everything you have seen and everything that has happened. Stay in your cabin. Do your tests. Work in peace. Make appearances for breakfast and dinner. Be civil with your fellow passengers but maintain a respectful distance, should some of them ask any awkward questions. And then, when we dock at Godwin 3, leave immediately and never ever breathe a word of this – any of this – to anyone."

Ewan stares at the floor, his chest heaving with ragged breath. The pain in his legs and side burning, insisting.

"If you do… Well, I'm sure I don't have to remind you what will happen. To you and those around you." The captain removes the sharp peaked hat briefly, running a gloved hand across neatly clipped silver hair. "And one final thing. Perhaps you will be so kind as to leave a positive score and review of your voyage?"

Ewan sinks inside. A terrible, all-consuming, emptiness that seeps from every cold pore.

"Clean him up… Escort him back to his cabin when it's safe to do so." The captain gestures to the guards to move Ewan away then smiles ruefully. "I run a clean ship, Ewan Fortune, and I'm a more merciful captain than some. In time, you may even come to thank me."

Then he returns to the hologram, arms swiping and gesturing in the air, the suspended text slowly fading and transforming into a complex star map.

The guards half-lift, half-drag a weeping Ewan away, over towards a large wooden door with distinctive golden fittings.

From behind, the captain calls out. "We'll be watching, Mr Fortune. Let this be the end of it."

Ewan glances over his shoulder as the guards escort him from the room. Somehow, even among the emptiness, the wreckage of all the tears, the pain and the anger, a strange, calm warmth begins to unfurl. Some dark bloom of relief, just there inside.

As they carry him along the corridor, he consoles himself with the only thought left. Somehow, he made it out with his life, and his future, intact.

***

Ewan stares through dark shades at the bowl of thick gumbo and the modest plate of sliced meats and beans nearby.

"Everything okay with your breakfast this morning, crewman?"

He looks up. Piercing eyes and a broad smile study him from a cloud of freckles. An olive cap hides deep red hair, most of it tied back but a few thick strands escaping to the shoulders.

"I'm, sorry, Officer Albright. I don't appear to have much of an appetite this morning."

"Is there something wrong with the food? Do you want me to take it away?"

Ewan nods softly. "Sorry."

Officer Albright reaches down and lifts the plate and the bowl. As she does, Ewan notices the anxious expression.

Whispering. "It's okay. Don't worry. It won't affect my feedback. It'll be fine."

Officer Albright smiles uneasily then quietly walks away, through the white doors at the end of the canteen.

Ewan winces briefly as he lifts the cup of coffee, scanning the other faces at the various tables, the busiest he has ever seen the canteen for breakfast. As he glances casually around the space, he finally notices the curious lack of children and families present. Only working adults. Small groups and singles dotted across the plastic tables, each enjoying or enduring their last simple meal before docking at Godwin 3.

A familiar voice breaks through the background chatter. "No appetite, huh?"

Lawrence again, sitting at a table on his own diagonally behind. The words catch Ewan in mid-sip and he turns slowly, trying to disguise the pain in his side.

"Lawrence, I didn't see you there. Yeah, I just… I can't face any more Starbird Gumbo."

Smiling and nodding. "I hate the stuff too. An acquired taste. Never really got used to it."

Ewan clears his throat.

"Busy this morning…" Lawrence gestures with a knife in the air.

Ewan nods. "How's Camila?"

"Business…" Swallowing a piece of bread, impatient to answer. "Personal business."

"Oh." Ewan senses his face flush slightly at the words and fights to keep his expression cool and indifferent.

"Yeah, with the captain." Lawrence changes tone. "Hey, we never did have that drink, did we?"

"I've just been so wrapped up in work, Lawrence. I really need to land this one."

"Sure, I was like you years ago. You remind me a lot of myself. Real company man when I was younger. Still am but, not quite as hungry these days. It's natural. Oh, you'll be good, you'll do well. It'll happen for you, sooner or later." He starts to chuckle. "Was beginning to think that maybe I'd said something or done something. Offended you in some way?"

Ewan laughs as earnestly as he can without pulling myriad bruised ribs. "Oh no, just… I've been so focused. Glad you understand. I'm not always such poor company."

Laughing. "That's good to hear, Ewan!"

Officer Albright arrives at the side of the table again, placing the paper survey on the surface.

"Oh, thank you, Officer Albright, I'll sort it out."

She nods softly and moves away.

"Well, at least you're okay. Camila will be pleased. When we didn't see you yesterday, we thought… Y'know, the business from the other night? Maybe that had affected you. We were going to come round to your cabin but decided against it. Thought it best to just, give you some space."

Ewan nods, quickly weighing up an adequate cover story. "Some of my tests from the previous day… I realised a lot of the configuration was wrong. Had to run another soak test for twenty-four hours in the cabin."

"Ouch!" Lawrence pulls a painful expression. "And there we were enjoying ourselves all night."

Ewan smiles on the outside only, disguising the pain. "Going to make a start on packing. Disembarking soon."

"Sure, yeah, Godwin 3. Your stop."

Ewan nods, grabbing the paper from the table and reading it. The same survey as every morning.

"Need a pen? Here."

Ewan takes the pen from Lawrence and scrawls a maximum score for all the categories. He hands it back to Lawrence, who drops it into his shirt pocket then continues to arrange a new sandwich.

"I guess this is it then?" Ewan gets up from his seat and holds out his hand.

Lawrence wipes his sensor hand on his trousers before holding it out. "Let's stay in touch?"

The screen wakes in his arm, business contact information passing from sensor to sensor.

"Say goodbye to Camila for me."

Lawrence chews thoughtfully and nods. "Maybe we'll catch up on another voyage Ewan? Us good people, we need to stick together, right? And that drink…"

Ewan feels the inside of his mouth dry slightly but nods his head and smiles in return. "Maybe Lawrence. Maybe…"

He walks away slowly, navigating between several busy tables and moving to the front where Officer Albright is standing beside the podium, staring into space.

"Here you are, Officer Albright. All done."

A shade apprehensive, nervous. "Thank you, was everything."

Ewan holds up a hand to interrupt and whispers. "All fine."

Officer Albright smiles, forcing a lighter expression. "Have a good day, crewman!"

Ewan walks through the main door and into the corridor, one side of his body still burning underneath the thin BCB shirt. He moves towards the far door then the stairwell behind, ignoring or barely acknowledging the few passengers he passes. The dark shades make it easy to avoid almost all eye contact.

Ewan ascends the metal steps slowly, each movement uncomfortable, involving a small amount of disguised pain. When he reaches the upper deck, he passes cabin six and follows the corridor all the way round to the empty calm of the restroom.

A gentle fan whirrs on arrival and a slight perfume fades in across the air inside. He moves to a dispenser and lifts the shades onto his forehead, spraying cold water on his face. He shakes off the excess water and studies the weary, marked reflection staring back at him from the mirror. After a few moments, he drops the shades back into place, and lifts one side of the pristine light blue BCB shirt to reveal patches of bruised skin underneath. He touches the injured areas lightly and winces, then drops the soft material quickly back in place.

***

Ewan grips the handles of both cases tightly, as mechanical sounds clang and groan from outside. Meanwhile, a loud synthetic voice coolly announces overhead.

*"We have docked at… Godwin 3. Disembark here for all local services to... Dunvegan colonies. Next stop is… Holst Terminus. Passengers disembarking here please ensure you have all your belongings and travel passes ready. Thank you for sailing Starbird."*

Ewan opens eyes still hidden behind dark shades. Haunted by the pain in his side, he watches the solitary large red-light spin above the main hull door ahead. With growing impatience, he wills the light to change to amber and, from there, to green. Eager to be as far away as possible from this seemingly damned clipper and the events of the last few days.

Tense minutes pass and the light finally switches to a steady amber. At this signal, the guards either side of the door spring into action, manipulating several switches on two long vertical panels fixed to the inner wall. In response, door locks release one after the other, the sounds sharp and violent. Then a heavy, curved section of wall slowly moves outwards, before gliding gently to the left. The loud bustle of Godwin 3 dockside activity floods inside.

A towering, high-sided metal ramp structure moves forward, the edge of the tough rubber platform on top in near perfect alignment with the floor of the clipper. A young man in army fatigues and cap stands to the side, arm raised in a sharp salute.

Grinning. The tone bright and proud. "Good afternoon, crew! I am Land Officer Reynolds. I trust you've all had an enjoyable voyage with Starbird? I want to thank every one of you for choosing to travel with us and I hope we see you again soon. Those of you continuing to the next stage of your journey, I wish you well. And for those of you remaining on Godwin 3, let me take this opportunity to wish you a very pleasant stay."

Ewan sighs inwardly. Not much longer to wait, to hold on.

Land Officer Reynolds swings a small grey digital survey board over his shoulder and rests it on his chest. "When you disembark, please rate your happiness with Starbird by tapping on a rating here. From one to ten, where ten is the top rating."

As Land Officer Reynolds steps to the side of the door, the short line begins to move. Ewan rolls the two large cases forward and watches carefully, studying the few passengers ahead, all leaving a high rating.

Land Officer Reynolds straightens, his expression one of bemusement when he notices Ewan, next in line and wearing sunglasses. "Expecting sunshine on the station, sir?"

Ewan places one foot on the ramp outside and stares at Land Officer Reynolds. "Every day Officer. Every day."

"Good."

Ewan reaches a finger out and taps the circle with the number ten inside.

"Another top rating. Thank you indeed, crew member. I expect we'll be seeing you again soon?"

Ewan forces the muscles in his face to move. "Absolutely. And… Thank you for helping to make this journey one of my best ever."

Land Officer Reynolds nods and smiles approvingly, a gesture accompanied by a sharp salute.

And with that simple lie, Ewan Fortune slowly rolls the two cases forward and begins to descend the huge ramp that zig zags down the side of the clipper to the busy dockside below. Painful step after painful step, one way then the other, hobbling towards the combination of toughened rubber and polished metal floor of the Godwin 3 station.

Halfway down Ewan stops, both to give his leg a rest and to tap the narrow screen embedded in his forearm, to confirm that all internal systems are back online. Reassured by the shifting numbers and small pulsing line charts, Ewan's skin turns immediately cold when he notices a considerably larger balance in his personal account. Shocked, he taps into the recent transactions, noticing a transfer of one hundred thousand credits with no accompanying reference.

Muttering quietly. "What… is that?"

Ewan glances warily over his shoulder, smiling uneasily as several passengers walk past. Concerned and anxious, he rolls his shirt sleeve down and pulls the two cases forward, eventually reaching dockside.

He steps across the wide platform and finds a space at the rear, away from the remaining bustle of lingering groups of first-class passengers. Now mainly gathering at the security area, towards the docking bay exit.

For a moment, Ewan attempts to distract himself, studying the immense size of the old military clipper. A monstrous hulk even with the lower third of the ship hidden below the bay platform. The curved hull smooth and dark, as though constructed from a single mould. The rear of the huge ship tapers slightly, curving up and over, like a scorpion. No doubt where a substantial portion of the offensive capability might once have been stored. And perhaps, Ewan conjectures, might still be.

Yet he is unable to distract himself for long and lifts the sleeve of his shirt, revealing the narrow screen. He focuses on the digits again, the most he has ever seen. The figures real, no matter how much he disbelieves.

"Let's move please!"

A woman in yellow overalls gestures to catch up with the other passengers. Ewan raises an uncertain arm in acknowledgement and pulls the cases forward, wincing slightly as he shuffles. The smooth floor causing less pain at least as he eventually stops at the rear of the small group, close to a short maze of impenetrable security barriers. Around the barricades, a swarm of bright blue station uniform and Starbird khaki.

Troubled, Ewan lifts his left hand to the side of his face. "Open whisper messages."

A sharp tone sounds, followed by a familiar synthetic voice. "Ready."

"Anything from Reese, limit three days?"

"Checking…" Cool and formal. "Negative."

Ewan frowns, edging closer to the barrier. "Anything new?"

"One. New whisper message."

"Play."

A familiar old voice. "Ewan… Camila was disappointed she didn't get a chance to say goodbye. All that personal business, y'know? Anyway, thought we'd drop you a little something. Enjoy yourself on Godwin 3, eh? You're a good man, we'll see…"

"Stop…" Ewan drops his arm to his side. "Delete."

A terrible flush of anguish, shame and sadness rises within. Ewan gasps audibly then glances over both shoulders, feeling oddly vulnerable under the cold gaze of barrier cameras and armed security. With eyes tightly closed and head bowed, Ewan attempts to find some strange solace in the clamour of dockside. Enough to blot out that voice, to unhear the message. But it's too late. Instead, warm tears gather and glisten behind dark plastic.

Ewan fumbles clumsily with the narrow screen, eventually focusing the Starbird travel pass.

"Sir? Head up please!"

The last of the first group, Ewan steps towards a section of high barricades and cameras. Streams of blue light circle and pulse.

"Travel pass?"

Trembling, pre-occupied, Ewan holds out his arm while a figure in blue uniform scans the narrow screen.

"When the light changes, move through the barriers and along the corridor to the main gates. Thank you."

Ewan barely acknowledges the instruction. Instead, he stares straight ahead, willing the blue light and heavy intersecting metal bars criss-crossing in front to shift. Uncomfortable moments pass and skin begins to cool and tighten. *Does the light usually take this long? Why aren't the bars withdrawing?* Uneasy seconds follow before blue changes to dull yellow and the heavy bars retract immediately.

Not far beyond, he shuffles to the side and pauses near the wall. Wearily, he sits down on one of the cases, precious moments to rest. To compose himself. To focus ahead. To wipe away these troublesome stray tears before he meets his station contacts.

*Oh, those first few seconds, how important they are…*

Ewan exhales deeply and stares along the platform as standard-class passengers filter through. He pushes his shades onto his head, rubbing tired eyes with the palm of each hand.

When he removes them, he notices the boy in the blue woollen hat walking briskly by. The small dirty face recognises him instantly and breaks into a smile. One arm stretches out in a quiet wave. A gesture of happy recognition and farewell.

Ewan smiles in reply. Gingerly, he lifts an arm slightly and waves too, his side bruised and burning.

# Happy Birthday, Love Alice

Gabi Jenkins scratches a reddening scalp. "I told you I don't want her to come!"

"Calm down. Please?"

Gabi groans. The kind of groan that tells you an entire world is collapsing. She lashes the air angrily with her arms and pulls at the sides of her sky-blue 'Lex and Pup' T-shirt.

"I hate her! She's not even a friend. Everyone that's coming hates her."

"How do you know that?"

"'Cause they do."

"If you keep this up, I'm going to cancel the whole party."

Gabi stamps the floor.

"Did you hear me?"

"But why did you invite *her*?"

Mary Jenkins throws the dish towel from her shoulder onto the small circular kitchen table nearby. She leans down, staring into two narrow and frustrated blue eyes.

Gabi screws her face up further. "Why?"

"Because."

Sullen. Bitter. "Because what?"

"Because she's a lovely girl and…"

"She is not, she is not…"

"And she spends way too much time on her own…And…"

"Because no-one likes her." Gabi bristles. "'Cause no-one likes her!"

Holding up a finger. "And… And… because I spoke to her mum yesterday."

"Her granny?"

Mary bites her lip. "Her mother…"

"So what?" Gabi changes her tone instantly from pure frustration to frustration laced with mild disbelief. "How does that change anything?"

"I mentioned the party and thought it would be a good idea for Alice to come."

Gabi groans, the picture becoming clearer. "Why? None of my friends like her, everyone hates her! She's going to ruin everything!"

"Everything?" Mary tuts loudly, indicating her complete disapproval. "No, she isn't Gabi. Poor girl. Anyway, if you're all going to be mean and horrible, I'll talk to her. She can spend her time talking to me. Or Amy."

"She won't."

"What do you mean?"

"She won't talk to you. She doesn't talk to anyone, Mummy! She never says anything. Even when the teacher asks her a question."

Mary bites her lip. "I had a good chat with her mother…"

"Call her. Tell her not to come?"

"I don't have her number."

"I can't believe she's coming to *my* party with *my* friends."

"Well…"

Exasperated, Gabi winds up further, stamping her feet and hyperventilating on the way to a full sobbing breakdown. "I'm going to answer the door and tell her to go away because no-one's going to play with her and we won't let her play any games with us because she'll be on her own and it'll be horrible for her because no-one wants to be her friend and it'll all be your fault, Mummy, because you invited her!"

"Right, that's it! Go!" Mary holds out an arm and points at the door to the hallway. "Go!"

Gabi bursts into tears and storms from the kitchen. Wailing and stamping her way up the stairs, she clatters her bedroom door behind her.

Trembling, Mary exhales and rubs her forehead along a thin arm. Closing her eyes, she shakes her head, forcing them open to gaze at the wall clock and the surrounding party preparation chaos.

Several baking trays dot the kitchen battlefield with packets of party snacks defrosting on top. A few small pyramids of sausage rolls and biscuits, assembled and covered in cling film, sit wherever there is a space for them. Scattered here and there, piles of multi-coloured napkins, paper plates, disposable knives and forks. Short towers of paper cups poke upwards, breaking free between two large multi-pack crisp bags that smother everything else underneath. And there, sitting on the table in the corner of the modest kitchen, the point of all the careful chaos. Gabi's large birthday cake still under wraps, hiding the edible 'Lex and Pup' photo icing on top.

Taking a moment, Mary stares into the beams of bright midday sun streaming in through the window. She focuses on the large collapsible table outside, standing proudly in the middle of the lawn, resplendent with colourful bunting and spiralling paper streamers. Her hard expression softens. Healing breaths. One. Two. Three.

"I'm doing my best here... You're doing your best Mary."

A sharp rhythmic knocking on the front door disturbs her reverie. Mary fixes a smile on her face, brushing hands across the front of jeans. She moves briskly along new hard-wearing carpet and unlocks the front door. Swinging it open, she's delighted to see her good friend Amy and daughter Cassie.

"Hello!" Mary throws out her hands. "Oh, wow, Cassie, I love your hair!"

Cassie looks up, deep ebony eyes tinged with indifference.

"Love it, Amy. The beads, the colours…"

"Hmm, it's okay." Cassie sighs. "But she didn't really do it the way I wanted."

"Right…" Mary laughs uncomfortably.

Amy flashes a wide-eyed, knowing glance at her friend as they step into the hallway. Just enough of an indicator for Mary to pick up on the warning wrapped within – don't push the hair conversation any further.

Amy registers the hallway decoration, sniffing the vague smell of new paint. "Hey, Mary, you made some improvements already. Nice."

Mary rubs her simple wine-coloured top and nods. "Mm-hmm, I keep forgetting you've not been back since the move."

"I like it."

"Yeah, I'm getting there. Slowly. Still getting used to the new area."

"Least Gabi hasn't had to change school."

"That helps. A bit further to walk but… She walks to school with one of the girls who lives nearby. Paulina? She's coming today."

Cassie, already looking bored as the dull adult conversation starts, flicks her micro-braids and plays with the small blue and white beads. "Is Gabi upstairs?"

"Yes, you can go straight up, Cassie. Oh, Cassie?" Mary leans forward, whispering. "Gabi might be in a bad mood…"

Cassie drapes her arms over the simple white handrail, looking down. "Why? Didn't she get what she wanted for her birthday?"

"Cassie…" Amy cringes quietly, softly shaking her head.

"No, I…" Mary bites her lip. "Actually, it doesn't really matter. Go on. If her door is closed, it's the room just along from the bathroom."

Cassie disappears upstairs. Mary and Amy glance at each other when they hear the bedroom door open and close, listening carefully to the all-important initial few seconds.

Amy smiles. "I think they're okay."

Mary nods. "Coffee?"

"Got her present here, hope she likes it." Walking into the bright kitchen, Amy places the large supermarket carrier bag she's carrying on a nearby chair and grins at the chaos. "Oh God, why do we do this, Mary?"

"I've been asking myself that all morning, Amy." Mary pulls a weary, exaggerated sad face. "I could use a hug right about now."

"Oh dear…" Mary and Amy hug each other, laughing.

"Thanks for helping me out with the move. You and Bruno. And thanks for coming today, it really helps."

"Ah, no problem, Mary. You've always helped us in the past and… And we've both had a lot going on. We haven't seen each other since the move, we got plenty catching up to do, girl."

"True. We are definitely due a pizza and prosecco night." Mary moves over to the oven and holds up her hands. "But first, we've got cheese twists and sausage rolls to take care off."

Amy makes an exaggerated rueful expression, pulls up the sleeves on her bright yellow top and quietly says, "Think I'm going to need that coffee."

***

Mary shouts up to the bedroom from the front doorway. "Gabi? Paulina's here! Thanks, Elena. I can drop her back if you want?"

Elena removes her hands from her pockets and holds them up. "Uh no. I will walk, Mary. It is five o'clock finish?"

"Yeah, around that time, any time."

"Good. I see you then." Elena stretches into the hallway. "Bye, Paulina, be good please?"

Paulina completely ignores her mother leaning through the doorway, already running up the stairs to see her friend, clutching a thin birthday present in her hands.

"Careful." Elena raises her eyebrows and laughs nervously at Mary. "I see you later. Call me if you need. If anything happens, y'know?"

Mary replies with a gesture, forming the shape of a heart with her hands.

A small car pulls up at the front, next to a modest square of yellowing laid to lawn and concrete space.

"Is that Magda?" Shouting upstairs. "Gabi, can you be here for your friends please, I think Dora's here?"

Amy pops her head round the side of the kitchen doorway. "Mary, all the foods ready and cooling down. Gonna start putting a few bits outside and sort all the game stuff."

"That's great, Amy, thanks."

Mary steps out onto warm concrete paving, waving at Magda as she exits her car and lifts her sunglasses onto her forehead. Dora has already escaped from the vehicle and is walking swiftly along the side of the dry grass, clutching a tiny present.

Dora shouts across. "Gabi's mum, do I need to take my shoes off?"

"Call me Mary, Dora and no, you can go straight in. They're all upstairs. We'll play some games in a while."

Barely waiting for the answer, Dora vanishes inside the house.

Magda lifts her arms in mock celebration and laughs, adjusting her patterned summer dress and speaking in a thick Eastern European accent. "Freedom. Two hours, yes!"

Mary smiles. "Lovely to see you again, Magda. New car?"

"No. Second hand."

"Very nice."

"I don't like the colour so much. But, it was a very good deal, so I start to like it better now." Magda laughs quietly. "We should have a coffee sometime. You can show me the new house?"

Mary nods. "Stay now if you want?"

Magda glances at the expensive jewelled watch on her wrist. "I can't today. But another time? I am meant to be meeting Stefan for coffee." Magda leans in closer and grins. "He is bringing his new girlfriend."

"Oh." Laughing. "I hope that goes okay, first time?"

"Yes. It will be good." Magda smiles, perhaps a little wickedly. "Anyway, I need to go. I hope it is a good party, Mary? I will see you later, you said five o'clock?"

Mary nods.

"You have my number?"

"Yes." Mary gives a thumbs up. "All good."

Opening the car door then remembering. "Oh, also, Mary, we didn't know what to get, so we got her a gift card. She'll have to use online?"

"That's perfect, Magda, thank you."

"Good. See you later, have fun!" Magda raises her eyebrows before dropping her sunglasses into place, closing the door. After a second, the car sparks into life and moves away quickly.

A small, thin child holding a present out in front sprints towards the house from somewhere along the street.

"Hi, Mary!"

"Oh, hi, Lottie!"

A pale, sweating, freckled and grinning face looks up. Slightly breathless. "It's just me. My mum had to stay with my brother because he got angry."

"Really? Why did your brother get angry?"

"'cause he knew I was coming to Gabi's party."

"Oh, I should have said to your mum that Christopher could come as well."

Lottie screws up her face and adopts an indignant tone. "I'm glad you didn't. I don't want my brother here, he's not very nice. Anyway, he hates Gabi and Gabi hates him. He'd just eat all the sweets…"

"I see, well there's a lot of sweets."

"Maybe I can take a party bag for him, are there going to be party bags?"

Mary smiles, looking further up the road, expecting to see Karen, Lottie's mother, standing watching from the front garden but no. "Yes, don't worry, Lottie, we've got plenty of party bags. Go on inside, they're all upstairs."

"Can I give you the present?"

"No, it's okay. Just hand it to Gabi when you see her."

"But it's sweets. Is Gabi allowed them now?"

"Mm-hmm, I think Gabi is keeping all her presents together."

Lottie grins excitedly and skips into the house, squeezing past Amy now standing in the front doorway.

"Hey sister, the piñata is up, and I've chalked the donkey on the wall. Think we're good to go. You want another coffee?"

Smiling, giving her friend a heart gesture. "Love you, Amy."

Mary steps back along the modest pathway, noting the few slightly parched plants sitting in the narrow and dry border channels nearby. She studies the photinia, the brachyglottis, the euonymus with vague interest. Modest lines of tough young plants, their only job seemingly to interrupt the street curse of poorly maintained turf.

Her attention is drawn back to the road, focusing on a car slowly meandering by. She watches it perform a three-point turn further up then crawl back along the street, towards the house.

Mary returns to where the simple paving meets the narrow pavement. A tall woman, hair a mix of brown and silver, slowly and carefully exits the car, straightening out a long red patterned summer dress.

"Hi again." Thinking, screwing up her face slightly. "Rosemary, isn't it?"

"Rosemary-Anne, yes." Nervously reaching out a slim and slightly trembling manicured hand. "Lovely to see you again… Mary?"

"Yeah. Just Mary."

Both laugh briefly.

Rosemary-Anne looks up and down the street. "I've never been here before. This area. All new, isn't it?"

Mary nods. "Mm-hmm, last few years. This is one of the new roads."

"Social housing?"

Mary casts her eyes down briefly, letting the words slide to the ground. "A mix, yes."

"Mm, I see. It's nice. The streets are quite small perhaps. But nice."

Mary shrugs uncomfortably.

"Anyway, thank you for the invitation. Alice has been really looking forward to the party. She is very excited about it."

Mary glances at the car, trying to peer through the shadows inside. "Great."

Loudly. "Alice?"

Silence.

Rosemary-Anne steps to the rear, wincing. Seeing her poor mobility, a concerned Mary leans forward with an arm outstretched.

"Are you okay?"

"Oh, I'm fine, I'm fine. My right hip, it stiffens up in the car sometimes, even on a small journey. Alice? Are you coming out, dear?"

Rosemary-Anne taps the window and opens the passenger door. She peers inside, leaning further in, talking to Alice in the back seat. Mary steps back, letting the exchange happen out of earshot.

Rosemary-Anne tilts her head. "I'm afraid we didn't have time to buy a present for your daughter, Mary. Alice is worried about it."

"I'm sure Gabi won't mind." Inwardly, Mary congratulates herself at sounding so earnest while speaking such a bare-faced lie. "Is Alice okay? It's past three, we need to start the party?"

"Always takes a little time." Rosemary-Anne smiles uneasily, exaggerating the whispered words before returning to her normal tone. "Come on, Alice, we're here now. You can go and play with—"

"Gabi?"

"Yes, Gabi."

After an uncomfortable silence, Alice Cartwright shuffles along the rear seat. Her small elfin face fixed on some invisible point straight ahead. Her expression one of cold boredom, framed by two long curtains of dead straight reddish-brown hair.

Mary interjects. "Hi, Alice. Nice to see you. The other girls are inside, do you want to go and join them?"

No response.

Rosemary-Anne bristles, clearly beginning to lose her patience with the continuing silence. Her words stay bright and chirpy, but underneath each sound, cracks of exasperation appearing.

"Come along, Alice, remember the discussion we had at home? I thought we sorted all of this out, didn't we?"

Silence.

Snappy. Irritated. "Now you're just being rude, what would your mother say?"

Alice flicks her eyes at Rosemary-Anne. Staring at her coldly as she swings pale legs round to the side and slips off the seat, placing a pair of neat shining black sandals on the ground.

Rosemary-Anne grins with barely disguised relief, closing the door quickly behind. "There you are."

"Oh, I love that dress, Alice."

The olive branch gesture is entirely wasted on ten-year-old Alice Cartwright. Standing in her black and white dress, long straight hair reaching down to her chest, she remains silent, staring through Mary to some invisible distant point far behind her.

So, *this* is what Gabi had meant. Suddenly, Mary senses her inner tension dial moving several notches further. The next couple of hours now assuming a more ominous shape. Promising to be even more tiring, even more stressful.

"Say hello then? This is Gabi's mum."

Alice flicks her eyes upwards, staring through Mary.

Mary smiles. "Hi!"

Alice frowns then moves to the edge of the garden, stopping at the top of the path and staring up at the windows. Several faces peer back through the glass.

"Oh, I don't know what to do."

"It'll be fine. We'll keep encouraging her."

Rosemary-Anne places a hand in a hidden pocket at the side of her dress, removing a yellow paper square. "My number, Mary. Just in case things become a little argumentative. They're all getting older."

Mary accepts the note and slips it into a tight jeans pocket. "It'll be fine, Rosemary-Anne. If anything happens, I'll call. But I'm sure they'll all play together. They know each other from school…"

"Yes." Rosemary-Anne reflects, seemingly unconvinced. "Around five did you say?"

"Perfect." Mary turns to look at Alice, firing the words in her direction. "That'll give us plenty time to have some fun won't it, Alice?"

Silence.

Rosemary-Anne walks slowly to where Alice is standing on the edge of the garden and straightens a couple of the red ribbons on the front of the black and white dress, before gently waving a finger.

"Now be good. Remember that Mary will tell me everything that happens. Try and play along nicely with everyone. Please."

Rosemary-Anne slowly returns to the car, carefully slipping behind the steering wheel and wincing several times. She closes the door and starts the engine, lowering the window to speak.

"If I get a chance I'll try and pick something up for your daughter later."

Mary holds up her hands. "Don't worry about that, Rosemary-Anne."

"No, I'll get something sorted. I apologise." Then Rosemary-Anne projects her words over to Alice, standing quietly in the garden. "Now you be good, Alice. Don't cause any trouble. I'll be here at five, Mary."

Mary smiles and waves, watching the car slowly drift along the road. She turns to stare at Alice and frowns. Inside, a growing concern, a sense of pity even. Then, glancing up, Mary notices the other children looking through the window. She makes a swatting gesture with one hand, causing the spectators to move away.

Walking along the path to the front door. "Let's go, Alice. Gabi is upstairs so you can go straight up if you want. I don't know who you know and who you don't, but I can introduce you?"

Silence.

Mary grabs the golden effect door handle and looks back across the path. "Alice?"

Behind Mary a troop of girls led by Cassie and Gabi trample down the stairs and run into the hallway. They disappear noisily through the kitchen door, running straight into the back garden.

Mary continues. "We're going to play some games? And we have a piñata?"

Alice switches her gaze from the window and stares straight at Mary, her expression blank and unsure. After a few short seconds, she places one foot in front of the other and walks slowly into the house.

***

"Make a circle, everyone!"

Amy points and guides, cajoling the girls into imagined right spaces and guiding them as they sit cross-legged on the tightly clipped lawn. "That's it. Ah come on, you can make it bigger than that."

Paulina complains quietly. "We can't make it too big, there's only a few of us…"

Amy holds out her arms. "Sure, but you can make it bigger than that."

Everyone wearily pulls themselves backwards on the grass, expanding the rough circle further.

"Y'all need to make a space for Alice now…"

No-one moves.

Amy turns and stares at the doorway into the kitchen, waving at Alice standing there, silently. "We're going to play pass the parcel, Alice, come on. Let's go?"

Behind Amy, a tangle of irritated voices rises like disgruntled fog. A thick murmur cloud of complaints, all forming from the displeasure that they might be the one Alice is sitting next to.

"C'mon, all." Amy claps briskly. "Gabi, make a space."

Gabi shakes her head. "I don't want to. I don't want her next to me. Mummy invited her. She didn't even bring me a present."

Catching the words hanging in the air, Cassie gasps loudly. Her face a mask of faux shock and astonishment. "She didn't bring you anything?"

"Mm-hmm." Gabi nods. "Nothing."

Cassie drops her jaw and looks disapprovingly at Alice, the latter now standing outside, at the top of the garden.

Dora breaks the silence with a tone of voice suggesting she doesn't care either way. "But did you like my present, Gabi?"

Nodding. "Mm-hmm, I just don't know what I'll get with it yet."

Lottie rubs her hands on the bottom of her T-shirt. "What about my present, Gabi?"

Gabi raises her eyebrows. "Yours was just sweets, Lottie."

Lottie casts her eyes downward.

"I like them though. At least you got me something."

Amy deflates on the spot, feeling as though her feet are sinking into the lawn, as though standing in quicksand. She looks over at Mary, hoping for a lifeline, but Mary is still engrossed in pairing the mobile phone with the modest Bluetooth speaker, balanced on the edge of the party table. Every so often a small burst of 'Mambo No. 5' teases the warm air.

"A little bit of…"

Amy exhales then eyes Paulina, the quietest in the group. "Can you move over please, Paulina? Alice needs to sit somewhere."

Paulina seems to think carefully, biting her lip and glancing warily at her friends.

"If y'all make a bit of space here, between you and this girl?" Amy looks at Dora, her face sullen, seemingly irritated that she's also been picked to give way. As Amy encourages, Dora shrugs her shoulders sharply before grudgingly moving to the side to create a bigger gap.

"That's it. Thank you, girls. Here you go, Alice, there's a space for you."

Amy gasps loudly when she finds Alice already standing behind her. "Oh, there you are, Alice, I didn't see you. Right, you can sit here."

Alice steps to the side quietly and sits down, in the space between Paulina and Dora. As she sits down the two girls eye her up and down cautiously then slowly move further away, creating an even bigger space each side.

"One. Two. Three, four, five…"

Amy steps into the circle and drops a modest parcel in the middle.

Seeing the present, Lottie breaks the ice excitedly. "I think Gabi should start, it's her birthday."

Cassie nods, approving. "Yeah, you're right, Lottie. You should start, Gabi"

Gabi crawls forward into the middle, staring at Alice coldly while grabbing the present. She drags it back across the grass and starts inspecting it, trying to feel what's inside.

"Little bit of Sandra in the sun, a little bit of Mary all night long…"

Amy smiles and points at her friend. "Yeah…"

Mary laughs, tapping the pause icon, now dancing as she walks towards Amy. "Are we all ready?"

Everyone except Alice cheers.

"Let's play."

Mary dances next to Amy and makes an exaggerated press of the play icon on her phone. The music sparks, bursting into life again.

Everyone except Alice erupts, shouting excitedly at Gabi to hurry up. But Gabi is in no mood to hurry and hangs onto the present a little longer than might be expected. Eventually, she throws it across the more generous gap, then Cassie does the same. Driven forward by the infectious rhythm, the stabs of brass, the hands waving, crossed legs that transform to an excited kneeling, the kneeling that turns to a barely controlled bouncing on the spot.

Amy dances around the perimeter of the circle. "Keep the speed up, girls, no cheating now."

"Mambo number five…"

"C'mon, Paulina!"

Excited and nervous, Paulina adjusts her glasses and throws the present to the side. Alice makes no attempt to catch it, watching as it bounces off her legs and lands on the grass in front of her.

"C'mon, Alice!" Mary and Amy, both dancing to the music, shout out. "Keep it going!"

Alice simply looks down at the present lying on the grass.

Gabi lifts herself up slightly and shouts. "Alice!"

Looking at her friend first, Cassie stretches out her arms in front of her, as though pleading, asking what it's all about, as though she can't believe Alice isn't picking up the present.

Dora sighs and makes a dismissive gesture with her hand, shaking her head in an exaggerated and violent fashion. She crawls quickly over the grass and picks up the present, sitting back in her space then laughing suddenly as she disguises her throw to Lottie. The latter, not expecting such a quick throw, fumbles the catch. Everyone laughs.

Everyone except Alice.

And then the music stops. The girls cheer.

"Yay, Lottie!"

Lottie blushes and grins, a wide and toothy grin. She glances at Mary, as though asking for permission.

"C'mon, Lottie, open it!"

Needing no further approval, Lottie tears hungrily into the first layer of gift wrapping.

As Lottie unwraps the paper, Gabi pipes up reassuringly, "Don't worry, it's not the main prize."

Amy reaches down and picks up the discarded paper. "What ya got there, Lottie?"

Lottie holds up a small purple and orange packet, showing it excitedly to everyone but drawing nothing more than a few muted responses. "A bag of fizzy crystals."

Without warning the music starts again.

"A little bit of…"

Lottie lifts the parcel and flings it towards Gabi, who snatches it from the air with a firm grip. Turning it over, inspecting it, moving it from hand to hand. The other girls start shouting, increasingly unhappy with the time-wasting, even if it is her birthday party.

Spiralling across the grass, Mary reminds her daughter. "Music hasn't stopped Gabi."

Gabi rolls her eyes, throwing it to the side without even as much as a glance at Cassie.

Cassie screams, as though the parcel has transformed into a brightly coloured rattlesnake landing right in front of her. Picking it up, she rolls it in her hands briefly, laughing at everyone before launching it sideways.

Unprepared for the violence of the throw, a slightly flustered Paulina adjusts her glasses before quickly recovering the parcel from the grass.

Paulina glances nervously to her side. "Please catch it this time, Alice."

Carefully, Paulina aims and throws the parcel towards Alice. The package landing perfectly in her lap.

Caught in the excitement, the entire group shouts out. "Alice!"

But Alice doesn't respond. Doesn't even look at the parcel resting on her crossed legs. She stares ahead, as though looking through all the garden fences, gazing at some far away point.

Gabi expresses her frustration straight away, scampering across and taking the parcel.

Mary interrupts her dancing to lift her hands sharply. "Gabi!"

"Why? She's not going to throw it." Gabi shakes her head in frustration. "Don't throw it to her, Paulina, just throw it to Dora next time."

Paulina looks uncomfortable, as though uncertain about what to do. She looks to the side, staring at Alice. "Why don't you just play, Alice?"

Gabi sits back in her space and throws the parcel across the circle towards Dora, smiling wickedly before Mary bends down, whispering angrily in one ear. Just in time, the parcel arrives from Lottie, causing Gabi to launch herself away from her mother who steps back, expression taut, unhappy.

Amy rolls her eyes instinctively as Mary approaches, smiling grimly at her friend and trying not to let her own growing exasperation show.

"A little bit of Mary…"

No longer dancing or even pretending to, Mary and Amy look on in silence, watching as the parcel passes quickly round the circle. A long, looping throw from Paulina to Dora, enough to bypass Alice completely on every turn.

***

"I'm getting dizzy…" Gabi complains over the beat of the background party music. "And the sunglasses are hurting."

Mary keeps spinning. "Maybe I should keep going, what do you think, Amy?"

"I hear ya, Mary…"

Gabi explores the thick black material stretching across the top of her face and tied behind her head.

"No cheating, Gabi!"

"But it's too tight, I can't see anything!"

Amy laughs and clasps her hands together. "That's the idea, Gabi!"

Mary checks to ensure the blindfold is properly in place and smiles quietly at Amy. "I need to spin you again now, just for luck. Remember, one arm in front. One behind your back."

"Go on Gabi, you can do it!" Cassie claps and punches the air.

Everyone except Alice forms into a small group, cheering and encouraging. Gabi finally stops spinning and lifts her hand out in front, gripping a generous ball of Blu Tack, stuck with a few long and stringy pieces of multi-coloured ribbon. She quickly takes several steps forward, drifting sideways with every step, then pauses, instinctively trying to assess her position.

The group chants, "Gabi! Gabi!"

Edging onto the small slab area at the rear of the house, Gabi shouts out in distress. "I can't see anything!"

Cassie shouts over the cheering. "You're nearly there, Gabi!"

"Am I?"

She moves forward again, stepping carefully but incorrectly, reaching the thick chalk outline of a large donkey scrawled over brick.

Mary encourages further. "Go on, Gabi, pin the tail!"

Gabi shouts, exasperated. "Am I there? Is it the right place?"

Everyone in the group shouts. A mix of yes, no, maybe…

"You're not helping, none of you."

"Pin it, Gabi!"

Gabi presses the Blu Tack onto the brick, ensuring that it doesn't fall off before stepping away and hurriedly removing the blindfold and the dark plastic shades underneath. She looks at where she's pinned the tail, drooping from the middle of the torso, the skin on her face reddening and prickling with the sting of abject failure.

Pulling the side of her T-shirt in frustration, the group laughing and joking behind her. "It's not easy, you'll see."

Amy claps warmly and holds out the consolation prize, a small packet of gummies. "Was a good effort, Gabi. Well done."

Gabi ignores the sweets, holding the shades and blindfold out instead. "Don't want them."

"Oh, Gabi…" Mary tuts at her daughter, taking the blindfold and shades. "Right, who's next?"

Hands shoot skyward.

Turning to everyone in the group, Cassie makes a dampening-down gesture with her hands. "I'm still Gabi's best friend, I should go next."

Amy smiles ruefully before interrupting. "Let someone else go first this time, Cassie?"

Crestfallen, Cassie looks across at her mother and quietens immediately. She continues staring, her expression one of disbelief, astonished that her mother would even think – never mind say – such a thing.

Paulina soothes. "It's okay, Cassie's mum. Cassie can go next."

Dora nods, shrugging. "Yeah, I'm not bothered either way."

With a painful expression, as though sucking on a very sour lemon, Amy shrugs. "Okay, you go for it…"

"Right Cassie, let's see how you do."

Mary walks forward and hands the shades to an all-smiling Cassie who quickly loops them over her ears. Then Mary wraps the blindfold around her head, tying the material securely at the back.

Languishing at the rear of the group, watching intently, stands Gabi. Her ears ringing from yet another hushed and seething private chat with her own mother. Disconsolate, she stares at the Blu Tack and ribbons hanging from the wall. Miserable face hardening, caught in that tension between pretending to be unaffected and bursting into tears.

Mary retrieves the tail from the wall and places it in Cassie's right hand. "Remember, Cassie, your other arm stays behind your back."

"Uh huh." Cassie giggles as Mary starts spinning her round quickly.

"Cassie! Cassie!"

"Ugh… I'm getting dizzy!"

"Go, Cassie, go!"

The girls cheer as Cassie lurches forward and to the side, nearly losing her footing.

"Ugh, it's weird!"

Seeing Cassie struggle, Gabi re-joins the group, laughing and cheering.

Both clapping, Mary looks at the girls and suddenly notices Alice is no longer there standing off to the side. She looks around the garden, checking under the table, but there's no sign of her.

"Amy, have you seen Alice?"

Amy stops clapping, glancing round. "No."

"You carry on here, I'll go and find her. Can't have gone far, front door's locked."

Mary strides into the messy kitchen, checking under the table laden with additional snacks and discarded packaging.

"Alice?"

Silence.

Stepping into the quiet hallway, Mary looks at the bottom of the staircase, half-expecting to see Alice sitting there on the steps, staring at the wall but no. She opens the cupboard door that leads to the small utility storage space under the stairs and peers inside. Nothing.

A different tone. "Alice?"

Silence still.

Mary glances around the doorway to the modest lounge. The settee and chairs all empty, with no space behind them to hide anyway. She scans around the perimeter, checking behind the large television. Still nothing.

Stepping back along the short hallway, one foot on the bottom step. "Alice, are you upstairs?"

Mary sighs before quickly shuffling her way up the staircase. Noticing the closed bathroom door, she raps lightly on the surface.

"Are you in the bathroom, Alice?"

No response. She pushes the door and quickly glances inside, the small bathroom concealing no-one, with nowhere to hide.

"Alice?" Mary pushes the door to Gabi's bedroom.

And there, in the middle of the room, is Alice in her tidy black and white dress with the drooping red ribbons. Standing with her back to the door, as though studying the full, messy splendour of Gabi's poster-covered bedroom. The toys and games discarded on the carpet, mixing with the shards of wrapping paper strewn all over. Ripped envelopes, birthday cards and bags of sweets. The latter all open and spilling out their bright insides, splashes of colourful rain.

"There you are." Mary closes her eyes and exhales with relief. "I've been looking everywhere for you…"

***

Grunting with the exertion, Dora ferociously swings the short wooden pole. The baton misses the multi-coloured piñata completely, scraping viciously over brick.

Surprised and laughing, Amy gestures at the group. "Woah, careful! Everyone, take a step back. Okay, Dora, second swing…"

Dora inhales, her shoulders rising and falling, summing up her energy reserves and unleashing them with a fearsome hacking sound. This time the baton meets the pretty cardboard with a dull thud.

Lottie cheers the loudest. "You got it, Dora, you got it!"

Hanging from a flower basket holder, the brightly coloured unicorn reels and swings awkwardly. But as it slows, the group audibly moves from excitement to disappointment. No cardboard disembowelment occurs. No candy inner organs rain down.

Mary claps her hands together in time with the latest party track on the playlist. "Come on, Paulina, you're turn again."

Paulina nervously steps forward, smiling and holding two thin, pale arms in the air. She receives lukewarm support, reflecting her efforts in the previous round.

A disgruntled Dora hands the baton and blindfold over. "Try and hit it this time, Paulina."

"Dora…"

Mary looks at Amy and raises her eyebrows, disappointed and surprised that Dora would say such a thing.

Amy chides. "Let's be there for each other, yeah?"

Cassie glances at her mother briefly, picking up her supportive vibe on round two of the piñata game. She changes her manner from commiseration to enthusiasm and rallies everyone in the group with impromptu fist pumps.

"Wait a minute, Paulina." Mary steps forward, checking the blindfold is properly in place while encouraging her into a better position. "Okay. Go for it!"

Cassie encourages further. "Go, Paulina. Just one hit! It must be getting weak by now…"

Pausing in anticipation and small nerves, Paulina lifts the baton with the streamers attached, holding it skyward like some fabulous magical artifact. "I don't know if I can even hit it. Maybe I should hold the stick differently?"

Amy smiles. "You can do it, Paulina. Try and give it a good whack this time."

Mary laughs, wrapping her arms around her own body and dancing, mouthing the words to 'Men in Black' playing in the background. "Aw, Will Smith, huh, Amy?"

Amy grins wickedly and raises her eyebrows, laughing and leaning across to high-five her friend.

Dora half-encourages, half-scolds. "Paulina? Do something?"

Paulina shuffles back and forth on the spot uncomfortably, dropping the baton then lifting it back up. "It's okay, I'm just getting ready, trying to think what's best."

Dora shakes her head. "Don't take all night about it. We might have to go round again."

Seeing her apprehension, Cassie starts circling her hands in the air excitedly, motivating her team to play their part and start chanting her name. Lottie joins in enthusiastically, Dora and Gabi less so.

"My glasses are hurting."

"Paulina! Paulina!"

The baton swings downward lightly, innocently. Missing both piñata and wall.

"Oh close, close. Try again, Paulina."

Mary scans back across the garden, seeing Alice standing in the middle of the lawn, staring straight over the fence to some point in the distance. She walks over, Alice turning her head to the side briefly on hearing her approach.

"Alice, sure you don't want a turn?"

Silence.

"Alice?"

Mary sniffs and crouches down, looking up at the small elfin face framed in straight, tidy reddish-brown hair. Narrow clear eyes set on some faraway point, staring into unbroken blue sky, somewhere far beyond the end of the street.

"Do you want to talk, Alice? Y'know, since you've been here, you haven't said a word. Haven't spoken with any of the others. You haven't joined in with the party."

Silence.

"Are you hungry? Do you want me to call your mum… your gran? To come and pick you up, take you home?"

Silence.

Mary exhales softly and glances down at her watch, noting with some relief the beautiful last hour approaching. The last hour where the games are replaced by eating and celebrating with birthday cake. She pulls herself to her feet and briefly considers reaching out to a small shoulder but doesn't.

"We're going to eat soon. At least have some cake. And if you don't want to sit with everyone, it's okay. You can stay here or sit inside. Just, I don't know, just try and enjoy… something."

Alice appears to sigh, then leans her head to one side, as though listening for something. Her shoulders sink slightly as she lifts her hands to stare at them intensely for a moment, then drops them again to her side. Completely ignoring Mary, she turns and walks quietly over the grass towards the house.

Mary watches her go, disappearing through the back door into the kitchen. Completely oblivious to the group of girls now encouraging Paulina to have a bonus third swing, because all her previous efforts have been so poor.

Having watched Alice disappear inside the house, Amy looks over towards Mary, holding her hands out in an exaggerated gesture of helplessness. Mary returns the gesture and shakes her head, walking back to the group just in time to see Paulina finally hit the piñata.

"Wow, you actually hit it, Paulina!"

Everyone cheers.

Paulina excitedly removes the blindfold, adjusting her glasses quickly to watch the piñata spin only slightly from her shot. She grins broadly, although there's no additional damage, a hit is a hit.

Cassie reaches out and grips Paulina firmly by the shoulders, like a sports coach demanding that extra five per cent. "Good shot, Paulina, we got it next time."

Amy claps her hands together. "Alrighty then, let's go round again."

"Wait a minute!" Mary holds up a hand and everyone turns to listen. "Who thinks we should let Amy have a go?"

Amy laughs at the flurry of thin arms, cheering and giggling. "Mary…"

Mary leans closer, whispering. "You can pretend it's Ronnie. You'll smash it in one shot."

"Sold." Amy winks and grins cruelly. "Give me the baton."

Mary holds an arm out to each side, like a steward at a large outdoor event trying to contain an eager crowd. "Right, girls, we all need to step further back for this one because it's going to get *messy*."

Cassie laughs excitedly. "Go, Mummy, go!"

Amy nods in response, stepping close to the piñata then wrapping the folded black material over her eyes and tying it behind her head. Without drawing any attention, she adjusts the blindfold carefully, ensuring her visibility is the best it can be without any obvious signs of cheating. Mary drops the baton, covered in weary tinsel and multi-coloured streamers, into her outstretched hand.

"Okay, back everyone."

"Mary, you know what to do, yeah?"

Mary takes a moment to connect. "Ah yes, of course, the song!"

"It's alright, girls, don't you worry," Amy says, "just need to play a special song to bring out my best."

Mary unlocks the screen on her phone and the party playlist stops, the sudden silence hanging strange over the garden.

"Okay, here we go!"

Cassie shouts out her agreement when the opening beats of the Montell Jordan classic 'This Is How We Do It' blasts through the speaker.

Amy rolls her head and limbers up, taking several deep healing breaths. She winds her right arm slowly in the air, building her power, waiting on the right moment to unleash. Soaking in the beat, the music, the lyrics, she smashes the baton on the side of the piñata, making a violent, vicious connection.

Gabi and Cassie turn to each other, wide-eyed and laughing at the sheer ferocity on display.

"Wow, your mum!"

"Go, Mum, go!"

The group watches the piñata spinning wildly out of control, jangling horribly on the short string. As it slows, everyone except Amy can see the damage, the side bashed and caved in slightly, but not ripped.

"Come on, girls!" Mary claps in time with the beat. "I'm feeling this, Amy. It's personal."

"You betcha…"

Amy adjusts the blindfold quietly, just enough to see the bottom of the piñata again. She lifts her arm, drawing energy from the music looping around her. The song that never fails. Their song. Once upon a time.

Another vicious blow follows, landing directly at a join, immediately causing the decorated cardboard to buckle and twist. Everyone cheers.

"Think you got it, Amy!"

"Go on, Mum!"

Another blow lands in the same place and the neck of the piñata begins to droop to one side.

Sensing that success is near, the girls chant. "Amy! Amy!"

The baton lashes into the cardboard again. Everyone now seduced by the increasing damage, never stopping to wonder how Amy can be so precise.

"Phew, this revenge is hard work, Mary!"

Mary laughs, dancing on the spot, arms in the air. "Oh yeah…"

Amy composes herself in the chaos once more. Knowing exactly where the piñata is, knowing exactly the place to hit.

That place.

Right. There…

WHACK.

The cardboard rips horribly at the neck, causing several packets of gummies to drop to the ground. Sensing blood, Amy goes in for the kill, lashing the piñata continuously, ferociously. The cardboard tearing further with every blow, eventually collapsing and opening completely. A cornucopia of brightly coloured candy, with and without packaging, spills out. Immediately, the girls scamper forward like ravenous birds gathering rainbow worms.

Amy drops the baton on the paving and lifts the blindfold fully, taking huge satisfaction in her work.

Avoiding a crawling Lottie and Paulina, Mary steps forward and smiles at her good friend. Nodding softly, reflecting on the carnage, she slowly holds out a fist which Amy meets with one of her own.

"Told you."

***

"Alice, we're doing the cake now?" Mary shouts into the hallway from the kitchen doorway. "Come and eat something?"

Both listen quietly, hoping for the sound of enthusiastic steps, but hearing only a deathly silence.

"You okay up there, Alice?"

Mary steps onto the hallway carpet. Noticing the cupboard door slightly open, she nudges it closed again, hearing a satisfying click.

"Alice?"

Sharp. Instant. Irritated. "What!"

Mary is taken aback with the ferocity of the voice howling out from somewhere upstairs.

Slightly garbled. "I'm not hungry. I just want to be left alone to play!"

"Are you okay up there?"

"Yes!"

"I can bring some cake up?"

"I said, I'm not hungry!"

Mary looks back at Amy through the kitchen doorway, a half-amazed half-bemused expression etched on her face. Staying silent, Mary points to herself then points straight up. Amy replies in silence, shrugging and pointing at the birthday cake, now sitting uncovered on the busy kitchen table.

Mary weighs up the options then shrugs her shoulders, returning to the kitchen. "She doesn't sound happy."

"Well…" Amy rolls her eyes "if you walk under a raincloud all the time."

"No, it's my fault. I didn't realise, Amy. I made a big mistake inviting her." Mary bites her lip and sighs deeply. "That's why Gabi was in such a bad mood earlier on. I thought I was doing the right thing."

Amy nods, the picture becoming clearer. She leans back against the sink, sipping from a mug of coffee. "Aw don't worry about it. It's not like they're going to be friends anyway. Cass has mentioned her a few times in the past, school stuff. It's never been good – yeah, she's got something going on there for sure but…"

Mary raises her eyes. "But…?"

"You got her to say something?"

"Right…" Mary giggles, checking her watch. "It's only taken two hours."

Amy places her mug on the side. "That's tough. Wish I could stay quiet that long."

Mary grins in response, removing a small one and zero candle from a clear plastic box and carefully pressing the pointed sticks through a skin of thick icing. "Never…"

"Wow, Mary, double figures now..."

Mary giggles.

"Gonna get a whole lot worse from here on in…"

"Ye-ah… We were there, remember? Not *that* long ago."

"Mm-hm."

Mary retrieves a cheap plastic lighter from one of the kitchen drawers. "What do you think?"

"Am sure she'll like it."

"It's Gabi we're talking about. She's already seen it. She picked the photo."

"Typical." Amy looks down at the image printed in icing. "It's pretty good for a photo. What is this anyway, all this 'Lex and Pup' stuff?"

"It's online, some animation she's started watching."

"Oh."

"They're detectives."

"Alright."

"They switch characters, but they don't know when it's going to happen. Lex acts like pup and pup becomes Lex, y'know?"

Amy nods in vague understanding. "Gotcha."

"And they swear…"

"Ah, I see…"

"Yeah, they swear a lot… And there's a *lot* of jokes. Bums and poo especially."

Amy laughs, holding up her arms in mock surrender. "Alright, alright, I got you."

Mary looks at the cake fondly, flicking the lighter to test the flame which responds weakly but good enough. Then she glances through the kitchen window, seeing everyone sitting at the table outside, laughing, eating, drinking, gesticulating wildly.

"I wanted to do something a bit more special this time, y'know? New house, new start?"

"It's been good fun, Mary. Don't let Mrs Misery up there spoil it."

Mary looks at Amy, pondering, reflecting then breaking into a smile. "Yeah, I think I've earned a glass of wine tonight."

Taking a final sip from the nearby coffee mug, Amy nods enthusiastically. "Right, let me see how they're doing out there so we can do the cake thing."

While Amy steps into the garden, Mary moves back to the doorway and shouts along the short hallway. "Alice? We're going to light the cake?"

Silence.

Turning, Mary sees Amy already peering back inside the kitchen, giving the thumbs up. "They're all finished so I've cleared a space in the middle of the table. Let's light up."

"Okay." Mary leans over the cake, lighting the two candles carefully, before turning the cake-board round and lifting it gently.

Stepping towards the back door, the singing begins. "Happy birthday to you…"

On cue, everyone outside starts cheering and singing, bolting to their feet excitedly. Everyone except Gabi, who remains in her chair, vaguely horrified by the clapping and loud singing, covering her face with her hands as a smiling Mary and Amy approach.

Cassie shakes Gabi by the shoulder. "Oh wow, Lex and Pup! Look at the cake Gabi…"

Hands stay fixed in place.

"Happy birthday dear Gabi, happy birthday to you!"

Everyone cheers as Mary carefully places the cake in the middle of the table. Nestling amidst a melee of party food scraps and paper cups with varying dregs of cola and lemonade.

Lottie bursts out laughing, clapping her hands. "Look at the candles melting, blow them out, Gabi!"

Gabi instantly moves her hands away, pointing and laughing at the melting candles.

Amy encourages. "C'mon, Gabi, before they melt all over your cake."

Gabi leans forward and inhales deeply before unleashing it fully on the two rapidly distorting wax numbers. Both extinguish instantly. Everyone cheers and claps.

Paulina exclaims, "Lex and Pup Gabi, it's your favourite?"

Cassie answers for her friend. "Yes, Gabi loves Lex and Pup."

Dora examines the picture closely. "How did they do that, they put a photo on the cake?"

"That's it, Dora. Oh, Amy can you grab a knife from inside?"

Amy disappears into the kitchen, reappearing quickly with a long knife which she hands to Mary.

"Right, Gabi, I need you to stand here with the knife, like this. Everybody, move to each side, there, that's it."

The group huddle and giggle around Gabi, holding the knife uncomfortably above the centre of the cake, watching Mary as she retrieves her smartphone and focuses the camera.

"Okay, everyone smile." Just as Gabi is about to complain, Mary taps the screen. "One more, one more, one more..."

"Mum…!"

"Let's go!"

Everyone laughs and complains in faux exasperation.

"Come on…" Mary cajoles.

After a brief moment of tutting, everyone turns again to the camera and poses in the perfect birthday group photo.

"Great shot. Right, Amy, can you help Gabi cut the cake if I record it?"

Amy leans through the group, steadying the knife and pointing it diagonally down, cutting the icing slightly.

Gabi howls comically. "No, don't cut there, it's going to split them up."

"Alright then, Gabi, where about?"

Amy lifts the knife and lowers it again in several different places. Each time Gabi disagrees, finding some excuse relative to the design of the icing on top.

"C'mon, Gabi, make up your mind."

"Oh, okay, there, there…"

"Fine. Ya ready, Mary?"

Mary signals that she is and starts recording, focusing the knife as it sinks down easily through the soft icing and sponge before stepping back to include everyone in the film. Lottie and Paulina clap excitedly as Amy takes control, removing the malformed candles and carefully cutting the cake into generous slices.

"Perfect." Mary taps the stop recording icon and places her phone in a rear jeans pocket. "Cake time everyone!"

Lottie cheers.

A slightly miserable Gabi enquires, "Mum, did you take a photo of the icing?"

"Don't worry. Don't worry. I took some earlier in the kitchen."

Cassie turns to her friend. "It's okay, Gabi. You can post one of those?"

Amy leans across towards a now happier Gabi, lowering a paper plate with the first slice of chocolate sponge cake and a plastic fork on top. "There you go, birthday girl."

Amy distributes the other slices, with everyone returning to their seats to focus solely on cake. The sounds of singing, clapping, cheering, all absent. Hushed words only, struggling to be heard over loud chewing and the scraping of plastic forks across paper plates.

Sitting further back, Amy helps herself to a slice, taking a moment to savour the taste. "Hmm, nice. Good cake, Mary."

Resting on the grass nearby, Mary agrees. "Not bad. A little on the dry side but…"

A horrible scream from inside the house.

Suddenly, Alice Cartwright bolts from the kitchen into the garden. Howling and wailing, she storms across the lawn to the table, a terrible bloody patch splattered down the front of her dress. Outstretched hands and arms stained with bloody trails, some dry, others fresh and running. From her gaping, spitting mouth, blood spills freely from injured gums, pulsing down her chin and neck in thick trails, soaking into cotton and pale skin.

Amy and Mary both cry out, shaking. "Oh my God! Alice!"

The children scream hysterically, recoiling but unable to move swiftly. All frozen with shock as Alice crashes forward across the grass, a bloody mess howling in pain and rage.

Stained hands slam the table surface in front of Gabi, scattering paper plates and cups, leaving a horrible confusion of spiralling red trails. Dropping a soaking black elastic line with several bloody teeth attached at intervals along it. Each tooth hanging down, clumsily attached with small shards of brightly patterned sticky tape.

"I didn't forget, I didn't forget!" Screaming and gurgling. "Happy Birthday, Gabi!"

And as Amy and Mary scramble across the grass in terror to grab her. And as the girls scream and run, diving and weeping. Alice stands with red hands in her hair at the edge of the table, howling and screaming in an endless, terrible cacophony. Covering the birthday table, and everything on it, in a fine bloody mist.

# David Crominous

"It's out there again…"

Lena Kowalski drops wearily to her pillow, covering her face with the duvet and sighing in frustration. Her partner, Jack Bartley, frowns gently in the darkness of the bedroom, crouching at the side of the window, watching.

"Weird…"

Lena grunts in disapproval.

"Hey…" Jack gestures through the darkness. "Come here. Why don't you want to see?"

Irritated, Lena pulls the duvet from her face. "Because it's quarter past three in the morning, Jack, and I have to get ready for work at half six?"

"It's funny though. Strange…"

Another sigh. This one more exasperated. The 'it's the sixth night straight Jack, so definitely *not* funny' sigh.

The darkness suddenly chills to an unsettling crowing sound from outside. Rough, guttural, unnatural, rising slowly but falling off quickly to leave only a faint echo.

"He's calling out again?" Jack stifles nervous laughter from the other side of the room. "He's got to be on something… Lena?"

Frustrated, but aware that without showing further interest her chances of returning to sleep are even more remote, Lena props herself up in the bed. She looks over to where Jack is crouching at the window, holding out the curtain just enough to enable him to peer through. He drops the curtain suddenly.

"Jack?" Lena slides across the bed, concerned, whispering. "What is it?"

"Ssshhhh, he might have seen me." Jack raises a hand Lena can only barely see. "He looked up. He's staring at our window…"

"Oh, I can't stand this, Jack. Feels like it's all the time. I'm going to call the police…"

"Lena…" Jack whispers. "It's probably just some prank. He isn't harming anyone."

Both stop whispering when they hear another haunting crowing sound rise and fade. Then another noise, a low harsh murmur, musical almost, strange and pleading.

"Jack, he's disturbing the whole square, every night now. We've only been living here a week. Is this what it's going to be?"

Jack holds an arm out in the darkness. "Don't stress about it."

"I'm tired. You think we're the only ones sitting here like this? What about all the families here, all the children? Probably all freaking out right now."

Jack lowers his arm and bites his lip, gestures hidden in gloom.

"It just needs to stop. Whoever he is, whatever he's doing. This… this weird nocturnal thing going on." Lena crashes back to the bed. "Oh, I'm so tired Jack."

"I'm tired too Lena. But it's, weird. He's probably not well. Medication or something."

Sitting up in the bed again, Lena brushes her long messy hair in frustration, adopting a slightly mocking whispering tone. "Oh really? Great, Jack. Who made you Sherlock Holmes?"

Both hold their hands to their faces, stifling laughter.

Jack returns to the edge of the curtain, gently pushing it to the side and peering out to the square again, unable to check his curiosity. Still there, standing in broken moonlight, a tall ungainly figure dressed as a bird.

Lena crawls back to her side of the bed, wrapping the duvet tightly around. "Well, whatever, I'm going to try and get some sleep. Only got another couple of hours."

Jack nods but doesn't break away, continuing to peer at the figure outside, illuminated only in flickering moonlight. Each arm seemingly covered in what appears to be large panels of feathers, moving up and down slowly, in a poor imitation of flying. Feet set as large talons, some ugly rubber covering, moving round and round in a tight circle. The body covered in a similar material, a repeating feather pattern daubed across, arranged in clumsy rows from top to bottom. A long dark beak and two large circular eyes poke out from a clumsy painted head covering. The rough, misshapen face twitching one way and another, as though mimicking a bird calling.

The unsettling figure turns and turns, wings beating slowly, inconsistently. Head moving sharply left and right, as though scanning the surrounding houses, blank and lifeless. Sometimes, a haunting crowing sound, as though trying to draw attention.

Jack continues watching with a frown and a soft barely audible whisper. "What the fuck…"

***

Lena watches her colleague Tracey Lawson closely, moving a steaming mug away from her mouth.

"So, you're getting woken up in the middle of the night again and it isn't Jack?"

Lena pulls a weary expression. "I'm serious, Tracey. It's getting out of hand."

Maria Sanna peers round the edge of her monitor. "I don't like it, Lena, it's freaky. Makes my skin crawl. I'd have reported it by now."

Lena nods. "I'm going to, Maria. I can't believe someone hasn't already. I think it's getting worse but, it might just be me. After six nights of broken sleep, I'm exhausted."

Tracey sips from her mug and swings her chair round, the cable from the headset tightening. "What about Jack? What does he think?"

Lena rolls her eyes. "He thinks it's funny."

"Typical." Maria puffs out her cheeks and shakes her head in dismay.

"It doesn't affect him as much. He can sleep in. He's working from home most of the time now."

"And there's nothing weird happens during the day. It's only at night?"

"Mm-hmm."

Tracey continues her questioning, increasingly concerned. "What about the neighbours, have you asked any of them? They might know something?"

Lena shakes her head. "We don't really know the neighbours yet. We've been busy getting the house sorted. It's a quiet place."

"But if it's been going on for a long time?" Tracey leans forward, seemingly shocked her colleague hasn't acted in a more decisive manner. "Other people must be affected by it too?"

"I know, Tracey, but I feel a bit weird having a conversation after we've just moved in. I don't know them yet. What if they've never heard anything?" Lena smiles. "Hi, my name is Lena, your new neighbour. Oh, I am wondering, do you see a strange person dressed as a bird in the middle of the night?"

"But it's bothering you? So, ask them." Tracey frowns at Lena and Maria. "I can ask, I can come round if you want? Stay over one night and see what happens? Hey, maybe we can all go out? Make it a girls' night?"

Maria makes a heart sign with her hands from across the desk.

"Maybe. Yes, that will be good. You haven't been round yet – you can see the house."

"Yeah, let's do it. Oh wait, got a call…" Tracey pushes her chair and taps a couple of keys, opening with a bright and energetic rendition of the standard company greeting.

Lena whispers. "Maria? You on a call?"

Maria peers around the edge of the monitor, shaking her head and leaning across.

"What would you do?"

"I don't know. It would make me nervous. It might be dangerous?"

Lena frowns. "Dangerous?"

Maria lifts the thin headset from her head and plays with it. "You don't know what it's about. And happening every night? Six nights and no-one has done anything? Probably drugs or something."

Lena sighs. "Yes, Jack said something similar."

"Or, y'know…" Maria makes a swirling motion with an index finger at the side of her forehead.

"Or both, right?" Lena sniggers.

Maria nods ruefully in agreement. "It's pretty creepy. I bet if you were on your own, you'd have reported it by now."

Reflecting. "Probably. You're right, Maria, if it happens again tonight, I'll phone the police."

A distinctive metallic melody interrupts.

"Ah, my phone…"

Lena quickly removes her headset and reaches down into the pocket at the side of the large handbag, parked under her desk. She removes the sleek device and checks the incoming caller, a local number, but not one she recognises. She swipes to answer, asking the caller to wait a moment, before tapping her keyboard to switch her status and apply the screen lock. Then she skips quickly across the modest open-plan area, passing through the double doors to the small landing at the top of the empty stairs.

"Sorry about that, thank you for holding…"

No voice. Merely a rising mush of static.

"Hello?"

Nothing.

"Hello…?"

A sudden harsh whistling sound, then an angry, distorted female voice rasps from the small speaker. "Did you see him?"

"Who are you? Who is this?"

Another blast of noise screeches from the speaker followed by the voice again. "Do you want to watch David Crominous die?"

Lena moves the phone away, dropping the call instantly and staring at the screen in fear.

She lifts her head and recoils in shock when the doors open unexpectedly. Smiling uneasily at Paulina, one of the account managers, walking briskly towards the nearby toilet.

Lena exhales deeply, trying in vain to dispel her distress, rubbing her cold skin, shivering. She glances at her phone and swipes the screen several times, navigating the call log, unable to find any details about the last caller.

Shaking her head, she opens the ongoing conversation thread with Jack and starts a new message. Explaining what just happened, pleading with him not to answer his phone. Then she switches the device to aeroplane mode and takes several deep breaths, staring through the large windows in front of the staircase. Gazing across the car park, taking precious moments to calm down and pretend that nothing happened.

***

Lena shrieks, rising suddenly in her bed, gasping. Sweating. Breathless. "Oh God…"

Jack, sitting quietly in a folding chair at the window, turns and whispers. "Ssshhh."

Lena rubs her eyes. "Jack?"

"Mm-hmm."

"What are you doing?"

"Waiting."

"Waiting?"

"Mm-hmm."

Lena drags her hands through long hair and peers through the gloom, eyes slowly adjusting to the darkness. She pauses, sifting through a bunch of responses for the right one but decides to stay silent. She slips across the duvet and sits on the bottom of the bed.

"You need to sleep too. Have you been awake, all this time?"

"Yeah."

Disapproving. "Jack…"

"It's okay. I might have dosed off in the chair a couple of times."

"I'm sweating." Lena paws at her nightshirt. "I was dreaming…"

Jack reaches across and touches her knee reassuringly, then returns to the edge of the curtain, maintaining his watch on the square outside. "Should be here soon. It's nearly three."

"It's the same time every night?" Lena chuckles quietly. "Wow, you really are Sherlock Holmes."

Whispering. "What were you dreaming about?"

"I don't know. A busy street. In the middle of a crowd of people, all pushing me along. All of us, we were heading to some vans at the end of the road. There were people on top, they were handing out food, supplies…"

"Was I there? Was I with you?"

"I don't think so… I don't know. I didn't see you."

"Then I was on a raft I think, drifting on water. Something tipped me into the sea. And someone else was watching, from a beach in the distance. That was when I heard it?"

Jack turns his head, staring at Lena through the darkness. "What do you mean?"

"I was in the water, trying to swim and… I heard it. The noise. The bird sound, the call we hear every night." Lena points to the dark window. "Maybe it was him on the shore, but I couldn't see. I was drowning. Kicking. Trying to move towards it because it was all I could hear. I started to get more desperate… That's when I woke up."

Lena exhales deeply, as though blowing her dream back into shadow.

"Oh. Weird..." Jack shifts loudly in the folding chair, returning his attention to the view from the edge of the window.

"God, I need to have one night where I can sleep through. At least it's Friday."

Jack sniffs, holding up an arm and tapping his watch, checking the time in a tiny glow of illumination.

Lena lifts herself from the bed and walks round to the door. She navigates two modest cardboard boxes stacked nearby, each one containing a few low priority bedroom items still to find a home.

She crosses the small upstairs landing and steps onto cool bathroom tiling. Slipping down her panties and sitting on the toilet quietly, listening for any sound from the other room.

"Lena?" Whispering. "He's back."

Lena lowers her head then flushes the toilet, staring wearily at her dark shadow in the mirror as she walks past.

Straining. "Lena?"

Stepping quietly back into the bedroom, dropping onto the bed near Jack. "I'm here."

Whispering. Apprehensive. "I looked away. Then it was there, in that instant. I swear he just appeared, Lena."

"Maybe this is the night, Jack, let's just call the police and—"

"No. Lena, listen, just listen."

Lena drops back on the duvet, closing her eyes and covering her face with her hands. "Jack…"

"Can you hear it?"

A barely audible crowing reaches out to them. A soft, gentle enquiry. A call searching quietly for a response. Then a louder sound, rougher, harsher, but still with the same musical quality. Then faster, pleading, as though hearing that response.

"Jack… Jack?"

Lena tears her hands away and stares at the window, seeing Jack standing in front of it, in what must be full view. The curtain moving only slightly behind him.

"Jack, get away from the window!"

Lena shrieks and dives from the bed, knocking the folding chair over, trying to pull Jack away. As they struggle, the crowing from outside intensifies.

"What are you doing, it'll see you?"

Jack doesn't answer, struggling to remain upright at the window as Lena wrestles with him repeatedly, trying to haul him away.

"I'm listening. I can't hear, Lena."

"It's the middle of the fucking night, Jack!"

Lena grabs hold of his middle and pushes him to the wall at the side. Surprised by her strength, Jack shouts out, forcefully pushing Lena away and turning to the window again.

"What are you doing? Calm down!"

"What am I doing Jack? What are you doing, always staring outside like that? It's going to see you."

Lena gathers her strength and continues the struggle. Her only thought to get him away from the window, away from full view, away from that thing calling out there, whatever it is.

"Jack, move away from the window… I swear I'm going to call the police!"

Using her body weight, Lena tries desperately to push Jack across to the bed. He staggers, clattering into the over-turned folding chair, holding onto a nearby unit to quickly regain his balance. Instantly, he returns to the window, angrily swatting the curtains back along the pole.

From outside, the musical cawing becomes louder. Insistent. Pleading. Excited.

Lena struggles forward in a last attempt, but this time Jack is ready and responds fully, throwing her back to the bed where she punches the material and sobs. Crawling quickly across, Lena slips down to the floor on the other side.

"Stop, Lena, can't you hear it's louder tonight? Someone else must be hearing this?"

Weeping. "It knows you're watching."

"Maybe I should go out?"

Lena wipes several stray tears on her arm. "No, don't go out, Jack! Please!"

The crowing is almost a cacophony, with only the briefest of silences between each cry. A rough musical sound, deep and guttural, now merging with other voices. People shouting and screaming. Angrily calling out.

Confused, Jack spins round, pressing against the window; watching in horror as a thin scattering of people emerge from all sides of the surrounding shadows, converging on the strange figure and dragging it to the ground. Kicking. Punching. Battering.

Through the terrible flurries of violence, a horrible, twisted wailing replaces the call from before. Wings all dressed with feathers flap up and down uselessly, unable to protect from myriad vicious blows. Skin and costume tear easily. Bones splinter and break.

Jack winces, recoiling from the window immediately, looking across to Lena weeping in the shadows. "Oh fuck, Lena, something's happening out there."

Morbid curiosity forces him back. Staring through glass as the thin circle of shadowy limbs continue to lash mercilessly at the now silent figure rolling on the ground. He watches, helpless in horror, as someone runs into the circle and tips the contents of a bulky fuel canister over the top of the body, quickly setting it alight. Everyone moves back instantly as a tall plume of flame shoots brightly upwards, before dropping to a harsh, living shadow dance.

From the floor at the side of the bed, Lena stares into the night sky outside, seeing only the tops of dark trees now flickering with fiery light. Unlike Jack, she doesn't need to see, doesn't need to look closely. She knows what's happening out there, she can hear it. Strange light shimmering across bedroom walls.

And then a loud, angry banging on the front door downstairs.

In a panic, Jack dives to the floor, crawling around the bed. "Lena, your phone, the police?"

More knocking. Followed by a mobile phone ringing on the bedside cabinet. As though awakening from another bewildering dream, Lena reaches out, instinctively swiping to answer.

Lifting the phone to her ear. The same static. The same strange whistling sounds. The same terrible voice.

"Did you watch him? Did you watch David Crominous die?"

Lena swallows in the darkness as static washes from the small speaker and the banging continues downstairs. She looks at Jack, hunched over, hands on the side of his head, terrified.

She lifts the phone to her mouth. Her skin crawling. Hands trembling. Head shaking. "No..."

A louder wash of static and whistling responds. Then the voice again, sudden and rasping. "Do you want to watch? Do you want to watch David Crominous die?"

Shouting outside the house. The banging on the front door. Incessant. Suffocating.

She glances at Jack again. "No…"

Dreadful seconds pass with only a billowing murk of static.

Then silence. Lena moves the phone away with trembling hands, dropping it to the carpet.

"Who was that?" Shivering, Jack stretches out for it in the gloom. "Lena? The police? There's been a fucking murder…"

Lena looks at him, eyes wide and glistening. His face moving, twitching with firelight reflection. "It saw you. It must have seen you."

The heavy knocking resumes on the front door.

Grabbing hold of her shoulders. "Lena?"

"It saw you. You can't call the police now, Jack."

"What? What are you talking about?"

"They're waiting for you. All of them. They're waiting for you downstairs."

***

Warm tears trail across each cheek, rousing Lena Kowalski from troubled sleep. Formed by voices on the inside, seeping from walls real and imagined, reaching out towards her from shadow. Friends. Family. All of them shouting and soothing in equal measure, their words overlapping, deafening. She reaches out one hand, exploring the bedclothes and feeling a pristine coolness that comforts for a tiny moment, before fading to something else.

Pushing long, thick strands of hair away from her face, Lena glances at the dull digital figures on the clock perched atop the nearby cabinet. After several breaths, she swings her legs to the floor wearily, mattress groaning slightly underneath.

Lena stares into dark space, rubbing tired eyes. The troublesome silence of 2:56 AM greeting her, just as it does every night.

She crawls slowly around the edge of the bed, stepping quietly to the empty chair at the window. Sitting down carefully, a wash of terrible concern floods, her face crumpling as emotion rises. Lena holds the back of her hand to her mouth and bites it, smothering the sobs rising within.

Dim digits change, switching to three o'clock.

And in the darkness, she hears it. A soft, gentle crowing from outside.

*"I don't know... I don't know if it's him or not..."*

She holds out her arm in the gloom, grimly clinging to the edge of the coarse curtain material but unable to move it even slightly. Her entire body tense and sweating, one outstretched arm fixed, frozen in place.

The crowing sound again. Floating from outside.

"I can't watch. I know I have to but I can't, I can't..."

Lena closes her eyes and grits her teeth. She imagines him there, wings slowly beating, eyes scanning, talons endlessly circling.

"I can't look. I don't know if it's you or not...?"

Tears streaming. Sweat on shivering skin. A sound of gentle weeping. A soft crowing, almost musical.

And a phone ringing. Out of reach, on the bedside cabinet.

# The Night Shop

Ian Bolton ambles towards The Old Crow, as though on remote control. Pushing through familiar wooden double doors with thick leaded glass.

Inside, the modest bar is calm, warm, inviting. The typical, nondescript mix of dark, decades-old furnishings and mundane music. The latter pleasing no-one consistently, but quiet enough to be tolerable in general. Darkly upholstered benches and worn rectangular tables push to the edges of the space, a scattering of patrons their only adornment. The place neither busy nor empty. A typical mix of regulars with nowhere else to be and strangers who've stumbled in, likely never to visit again.

Helen Mayweather, a short, stocky woman patrols the brightly lit bar, wiping the surface briskly before attending to a fair-haired man in a padded green jacket. The man Ian is here to meet. The man he meets most Sunday evenings, especially this last year since Sandra died. His old friend, Colin Buchan.

Colin looks across, noticing Ian walking towards him, acknowledging one of the regulars on his way to the bar. He holds up his hand as a welcome and a notice that the drinks are in order.

"Awright, mate?"

"Eh, no bad, Ian. The usual?"

"Perfect."

Helen leans over the bar, turning her head so her good ear can receive the order clearly. She holds up two slightly gnarled fingers to confirm. "Golden Ship? Two?"

"Aye. That's it, Helen." Colin flicks a thumbs up as a further confirmation.

She nods to acknowledge Ian, then retrieves two clean pint glasses and tends to the first beer.

"Busy week then?"

Ian puffs out his cheeks. "Could say that."

"Same here. Had another run in with Beattie. The manager in distribution I've been telling ye about? Been having a real go the last few weeks. Dunno what his problem is."

"Aye."

"So, how's things been?"

"No bad. I mean…" Ian shrugs and exhales loudly. "Ach, y'know, the same. Back's still sore at times and head's up and down."

Colin nods ruefully, sadly he does know. He knows all too well what Ian is trying to express.

"No point complaining though, eh?"

Ian chuckles. Attempting to keep that heady mix of anxiety, pride, loss and discomfort he endures in every waking moment from bursting through. After all, it's still so early. Best not to taint the only night of the week he looks forward to straight away.

"Aye, of course, ah miss her. Some days… Ah go over it. Over and over. Every day. If I'd just taken a different route."

Helen parks the second pint of beer on the short, brightly coloured bar towel in front of Colin. "That's £8.80."

"What…?"

Retrieving the card reader. "Aye, same as it was last week, Colin…"

While Colin fumbles with his debit card, Helen rolls her eyes and shakes her head comically. "Yir awright then, Ian?"

"Nae bad, Helen. Yourself? Ye been busy?"

Helen screws up her face. "Och, no really. Usual crowd again. Back to normal now the summer fair's gone."

"Aye, we'd better keep working then, Colin. Y'know, keep the place going."

Helen glances at the card reader and confirms. "That's fine, Colin. All gone through."

"Suppose so, Ian. Way the prices are goin' here I'll need a promotion every month just tae buy a beer, eh?"

Helen rolls her eyes again, swatting the comment away with a hand and moving along the bar to serve two younger men who've just arrived.

Smiling, Ian reaches out for the glass and savours that first sip. "Cheers, Colin. Oh, that's good."

Colin crouches and picks up a large supermarket carrier bag languishing on the floor. He tips his head towards the back room. "Bit quieter over there, Ian."

"Aye, okay." Ian nods meekly, slightly surprised at the change of location and the breaking of the usual side table tradition.

Both move slowly to a more private, raised area at the back of the pub which is currently empty.

"Here, this'll do. Brought something with me tonight, Ian. Been meaning to show it to ye for a few months now. Something that's been helping me out."

Ian places his beer on a mat and removes his thick black fleece jacket, folding it and placing it on the dark wooden chair next to his own. "Aye, right."

Colin slips along the wall seating with the large carrier bag beside him. He unzips his padded green jacket but chooses to keep it on, leaning in closer with elbows on the table.

"Aye, thing is Ian, a while back now. A few months ago. I wasnae in a good place." Colin scratches several days' old stubble in reflection. "It was affecting me at work, causing some problems. Ah told you about it, some of it anyway, remember?"

Ian sips his beer quietly and whispers. "Aye…"

"But I got through it. It was tough. At times. You know yoursel', no-one to talk to or…" Colin breathes in and out sharply. "Anyway, I never really told you what helped me out…"

"Right…"

"See, I started talking to one of the women, in the office. Cannae explain it really, she must have got to know my situation somehow, knew ah wasnae happy. We started to get friendly, y'know break time, lunch, coffee…She starts opening up and we start sharing things, right? Turns out she'd lost her husband sometime back and…"

Ian grimaces.

Colin shrugs in response, adopting a pragmatic tone. "Aye but she was doing fine, right? Doing better than me. She was saying that she understood what I was going through. That it was hard but, for her it was a lot better now. She could cope."

Both pause for a long sip of beer. Ian glances at Colin, picking up on a flicker of what might be uncertainty passing quickly across his face.

"Thing is, Ian. She got help."

"Like counselling? Drugs or something?"

Colin shakes his head. "Nah. It's a place. In the old town. Helped her out. A shop."

Ian frowns. "A shop?"

"Aye, a shop."

"Like, home remedies?"

"Naw, no."

"Right. So, what is it?"

"It's a place, called MacLeod's Miscellany. They make things."

Noting the growing confusion across the table, Colin waves his hands and glances over Ian's shoulder, checking the coast is clear. He leans in further, taking several breaths, as though reflecting hard on what he is about to say.

"Aye, she went to this place. This shop. And they helped her out."

"How?"

Colin becomes slightly apprehensive, lowering his voice even further. "It's a small family business. They make… different things. For people. She, eh… They made a backscratcher."

"You serious?" Ian chuckles in disbelief. "What you talkin' about?"

Colin runs a nervous hand across his face and rushes another sip of beer. "See, Ian, they make things. To order? They take bits. Like, bits of… y'know, bodies. The people you've lost, right? Then they make stuff. Things. Whatever you need."

Shocked, Ian recoils in his chair. "What?"

Colin frowns, biting his lip. "Aye, she told me. One lunchtime. She remembered she had a couple of fingernails. That's all she had. And she went there and they suggested a few things. They made a backscratcher for her. They put the nails on the hand right?"

"You're fucking joking me, Colin? That's fucking sick…"

Colin glances everywhere. "Ssshhh…"

Ian studies his beer, somewhere between appalled and confused.

After an uneasy silence, Colin becomes visibly irritated. "Jeez, Ian, try to understand, eh? You know what's it's like. I'm telling you that's how she got through it, how she dealt with it. She'd use the backscratcher and it would feel like in some way he was still with her, you understand? Just that touch on her back, y'know? I thought you'd be able to understand that? Everything you've been through, everything *we've* been through."

"I dunno what tae think about it, Colin." Ian exhales. "It's fucking sick."

"Aye, I understand, I get it. When she told me at first I couldney get away quick enough from the canteen. Had tae excuse myself. Thankfully there was no-one in the toilet."

Ian lifts his glass quickly, taking several gulps of Golden Ship, wiping his mouth with the back of his hand. "I just don't know what to say about it, Colin."

Sensing the distaste, Colin strikes a softer, disconsolate tone. "Shit… I'm sorry mate. I shouldnae 'ave mentioned it."

"It's alright, Colin. Just a shock, y'know? I mean, how do they get away wi' it?"

"Wi' helping people?"

"Naw, wi' running a place like that? Doing what they do, y'know?"

Colin scratches his head as though surprised by the question. "It's in the old town. Only opens at night. From midnight to four, something like that."

"Just doesney sound right, Colin. She must have been on drugs or something. She's spinning ye right?"

"Naw. I saw pictures of the backscratcher. On her phone. And anyway…" Colin rubs his scalp nervously. "I've been there myself."

Ian closes his eyes in shock, trying to reconcile everything he's hearing.

"Ah was going to tell you a few months back but, how to start right? And you were going through a rough patch then, so I thought I'd leave it for a while but… Aye, they helped her. They helped me."

Ian stares at his friend. A flurry of feelings, good and bad, spiral and spill on the inside. Longing. Pity. Repulsion.

Colin reaches into the nearby carrier bag and removes a small lamp, placing it in the middle of the table. A nondescript, cheap-looking item, the central column split into three segments each edged with a brass ring. A small cream coloured shade sits on top.

Colin points to the dull grey band in the middle of the wooden column. "See this here? That's bone…"

Ian nods and looks away. Confused. "Jesus, Colin…"

"Ah ken whit you're thinking Ian – it's what ah was thinking. Maybe ah still do? But here's the thing. I've been in a shit place for a long time. Just like you. And all I know is she helped me – and so did they…." Colin touches the lamp lovingly. "It stays on the bedside cabinet. Every night, I go to bed and ah read. And ah can see the words using that light. The light from this lamp. And that gives me some comfort. Just enough, right? Just enough to get by, to make it so that I can go into work every day and get through it. So that I can breathe in the silence and no feel trapped by it. So, if you think that's all sick. I'm sorry. I'm sorry, I shouldnae have mentioned any of it. But all I know, it's helped me."

Seeing his good friend unburden and become emotional, Ian fumbles with his hands before reaching over to lightly grip and reassure a green padded shoulder.

"Am sorry, Ian, ah didney mean to put all that on ye but—"

"It's jist a lot to take in, Colin, y'know?" Ian exhales. "I'm pleased it's helped. I mean, aye, you've been a lot happier the last few weeks."

Colin nods in agreement. "It was worth it. I had to pay more, a lot more. Some of mah savings, a lot of mah savings. Ah didney have anything of Carol's, so they had to do everything. It's more expensive if they have to go and get the material themselves."

"Jeez, they do that?"

"Aye, that's why it's all word of mouth with the shop. Has ti stay all clandestine, right?"

"And this shop…"

"Aye, MacLeod's Miscellany."

"It's closed during the day?"

"Dunno. Never been. Think so. Don't know why you'd want to go there during the day anyway."

Ian settles back in the chair, which creaks with the movement. He lifts the now half-full glass to his mouth and sinks another few generous mouthfuls, the beer slowly helping to blur the sharp edges of the conversation. Precious seconds to reflect, to wonder.

"Look, we've talked about this enough. Maybe I should'ave left it a wee bit longer."

"No, Colin, I'm glad. Now ah ken, eh? Don't know what tae think of it. I mean, I'm shocked but… I'm glad you thought you could tell me."

Colin reaches into a jacket pocket, lifting out a worn square of brightly coloured paper with a few lines of handwriting. "It helped me, Ian. It might help you?"

Ian places the glass on the table and pauses before reaching out for the piece of paper. Glancing at the name and address briefly, he folds the paper carefully and places it in a trouser pocket.

"I'll think about it. Thanks, Colin." Ian sniffs. Troubled. Disturbed. Yet quietly intrigued.

Lifting the lamp and carefully lowering it into the carrier bag. "That's fine, Ian. Just thought I'd mention it."

Ian breaks into a nervous smile. "Drink up. Mah round."

***

The gloom of a bedroom wraps around two hands. One holds a small square of paper, the other a smartphone displaying a zoomed-in street map. Eventually, both those hands fall back wearily to the bed, for the third time. Always the third.

Troubled. Frowning. Bemused. Ian stares through the only window. Seeking a different view but unsure of what to find, he tries to focus simply. Watching light grey sky turn slowly darker as early evening gives way to late. A solitary bird silhouette dodges and flies; the top of the tall tree nearby sways . The only details to be picked from an expanse of billowing, dull emptiness. A view amplifying the already suffocatingly silent atmosphere in the bedroom.

Though shocked at the time, Ian had nonetheless become increasingly haunted –consumed even – by his friend's revelations. Every waking hour over the last couple of days, at work and out, his thoughts turned to a growing possibility. That maybe MacLeod's Miscellany might give him something back, something to hold onto again, just like Colin. Something solid in his rolling sea of dwindling images and imagined voices. The hellish vapours he staggers through every day since the fatal accident. When his world changed forever.

But unlike Colin, Ian does still have something. Something right here in the bedroom cabinet on the other side of the bed.

Moments in thought. Ticking, like a familiar, old clock.

Ian swings his legs round, feet earthing on the carpet as he adjusts his dressing gown carefully. Staring at the side, he glances at a modest pile of dirty dinner plates, perched somewhat precariously on the bedside cabinet. Reaching over, he gently pushes them back then focuses the cabinet on the other side. The one that still belongs to Sandra and still contains a collection of her items.

Ian rolls clumsily and slips to the floor, wincing as a sharp pain glances up and down his back. On his knees in front of the simple matching pine cabinet, he opens the larger door underneath the solitary drawer and slumps sadly at the busy sight. Untidy piles of small everyday things: a few old batteries, a couple of purses, several modest boxes of jewellery, three watches all frozen in a different time, a couple of phone chargers and cables, a handful of grubby, well-used make-up sets, random papers and cards, a small pile of photographs, one unopened pack of paracetamol and an old hairbrush. And there, buried away at the rear, a folded plain blue carrier bag that holds exactly what Ian is looking for.

He lifts the tightly wrapped package carefully from the bottom of the cabinet space, trying desperately to avoid disturbing the general layout and order of things in their arrangement. Then he empties the bag, the contents tumbling to the duvet. A clear plastic wallet folded over, containing generous swirls of long hazelnut hair and a couple of creased newspaper clippings.

Discarding the bag to the side, Ian rubs his forehead sadly and unfolds one of the articles. He can't help the bittersweet smile as Sandra stares back at him from the large image, a shocked expression on her face. Next to her stands Maria, a colleague from the salon, lifting Sandra's hair while gleefully brandishing a pair of large scissors. The headline reads 'Cutting For Charity', an event Ian remembers all too well, and a local news article he must have read over a hundred times.

Folding the clipping again, Ian turns to the large clear plastic wallet containing some of the long hair cut off that joyful Autumn morning. He unzips the pouch halfway and reaches inside, touching smooth, soft hair.

He slumps down at the end of the bed, reaching over for the bright square of paper, immediately rubbing his forehead with it. Troubled, he sits trembling for moments, paper in one hand, wallet of hair in the other.

Muttering. "Ah don't know what to do. Dunno what to do…"

As he stares through the window again, the light fades further. Darkening clouds all he can see from his position on the floor. No bird, no tree even.

Bed soon.

Tomorrow night?

***

"This'll do, mate."

The taxi driver responds with a shadowy nod of the head. Slipping the car towards the pavement at the side of the empty, dark road. He pulls gently on the hand brake.

"Ye sure?"

"Aye, this is fine."

"£8.30, mate."

"Awright." Ian fishes in his fleece jacket, retrieving his wallet and handing over one of the three £10 notes he has there. "Just gie me a pound back."

The driver nods jokingly. "It's well past last orders?"

"Aye." Ian smiles, accepting the coin and dropping it into the small change pocket. "Ah just need a bit of space tonight, that's the way it is sometimes. Aw the best, eh?"

Ian steps onto the pavement, damp with rain from earlier that evening. When the taxi pulls away, he glances at his watch, briefly lighting digital figures to confirm: 12:27 AM.

He pulls at the raised collar of his jacket, but the chill air still manages to circulate and gather around his throat. With a shiver, he looks up and down the dimly lit street, checking his bearings. Removing his phone from a trouser pocket, he studies the backlit map, reinforcing the quickest route. The one that takes him further up the street with a detour through nearby Kettle Park. If the park is closed, then a longer walk beckons, circling up towards the back of the castle. Either way, nestled amongst the snaking cobbled streets of the old town, he should find MacLeod's Miscellany.

As Ian walks on, he instinctively dwells on the change of character around him. How mere hours alone transform a world, his world. How the bustling of daylight evaporates into the solitude of night. It resonates deeply for him, as though his own outer and inner lives naturally align here on the dark, empty street. His world of day, engulfed in work, with all its associated laughter, mundane tasks and small company, now consumed by the lonely silence of night. The inescapable darkness, taunting and magnifying, creeping outward.

Every so often, he wipes the moisture that accumulates over his face like glistening webs. His only company, two cars that pass not long between each other. One quiet, the other loud, travelling well above any speed limit and braking hard somewhere in the near distance.

He hurries. A large stone wall now at his left, replacing the railings of period buildings all converted to offices. Just ahead, a narrow archway set in the wall, framing a wrought iron gate.

Ian grips and pushes heavy, ornate metal and, to his surprise, it yields. He pushes further, opening just enough to allow him to slip through. As he does, dark metal hinges choose that very moment to groan and complain, tearing still midnight air.

Closing the gate carefully behind, Ian walks briskly on, shoving his hands into his pockets, holding onto the smartphone inside one and the plastic wallet folded three times in the other. As he skips forward, he acclimatises to the drab vista of the darkly lit city park. The mix of busy flower beds past their seasonal best, scattered empty benches, curving pathways and meandering teardrop splashes of lawn that reach out from all sides. Their daylight vibrancy gone, now replaced with sullen nocturnal faces. Each a hiding place for one of Ian's thoughts, no matter how unreasonable.

The path dips and rises softly, then slopes off towards the right. Ian follows it quickly, keen to be at the end of it. He takes a moment only to acknowledge the rising shadows of the large castle ruins in the near distance. Towering up from behind a large, ragged bank of tall trees on the other side. A handful of broken light beams filter upwards from within, ensuring an eerie, miserable glow.

Wiping the moisture and sweat from his face, Ian cajoles his internal voice into creating a constant stream of reassurances. Just enough to counter the effects of the other ones now rising, the ones encouraging the first seeds of doubt. Is this really a good idea, Ian? Wouldn't you be better off at home asleep, Ian? It's not too late to have a rethink, Ian? You can still head back? No-one will ever know, Ian. Ian, how much do you really need this? Just get a cab. Get one. Now…

Under his breath, gripping the skin of the plastic wallet in the coat pocket increasingly tightly. "Quiet… Quiet…"

Finally, the path straightens, and the opportunistic inner voices sink back. Ian, now breathing heavily, slows to a more comfortable pace. Running either side, two lines of benches and small trees, leading the way from Kettle Park to Fairbanks Lane.

Suddenly, his attention is drawn towards two dark figures huddled around a park bench. Scratching his head anxiously, Ian pushes further left with each shortened stride, creating more space between. Fixing straight ahead, he swallows nervously as he approaches.

A figure in a dark brown raincoat sits hunched over, weeping and groaning, quivering hands held outstretched and covering a face wrapped in bandages. Blood appears to be seeping freely through the material on one side. The second figure, leaning over and embracing, seems determined to soothe the other. Singing in a language Ian can't even recognise, each word spoken softly with hints of random melody. Trying to look from the corner of his eyes, Ian is relieved that neither of the mysterious figures seem even remotely interested in him as he walks by.

Disturbed, he quickly jogs towards the wide break in the combination of thick hedging, short black railings and ornamental shrubs lying just ahead at the edge of the park. A solitary mournful streetlight greets him as he snakes between a handful of parked cars, all arranged haphazardly on the normally picturesque Fairbanks Lane. Rows of uneven period buildings on each side, stripped of their historical charm by the midnight hour, and the chill of nocturnal mystery and threat.

Further up, the shadowy trees and meagre streetlighting combine to greet Ian as he turns onto Mathieson Street. The strange patterns flowing across each uneven rooftop breaking only when he sees a tall figure loitering at the end of the short street. Not looking for any trouble, he crosses the cobbled street and continues, scanning each slightly irregular building either side, searching for signs of life.

With each step he tries to recall the conversation with Colin, whether his good friend had mentioned anything about the shop that might make it easy to recognise. Perhaps he should have made the journey during the day? But would it be the same, the nature of the place might be completely different at night.

Nothing other than the dead end of the street beckons, lines of cobble terminating in a rough wall that runs fully one side to the other. Unsure, Ian turns, nodding instinctively at the figure standing in dim light, wearing what appears to be a top hat and long dark overcoat.

Muttering. "Must have passed it…"

Ian surveys the street behind him. The buildings all unlit, some with shutters or blinds drawn, others with small, shadowy glass panes uncovered, all staring. The two recognisable shops, all bay windows and traditional hand-painted panelling, are silent and dark.

Unsure, Ian glances at the tall figure leaning against the final streetlight, now observing him with interest. The figure has an unsettling appearance, wearing a balaclava as a disguise underneath a top hat decorated with a tall red feather.

"Excuse me, mate. Any of the shops here open at night?"

The figure doesn't answer. Instead, it looks back along the street, straightening its coat and adjusting its hat. Ignoring. Perhaps stalling for time.

Ian exhales and rubs his eyes, caught in the space between waiting anxiously on a response or simply walking away. The figure rummages inside a coat pocket and removes a small bar. Swinging it in front, the bar clicks and transforms into a long baton.

"Woah, no trouble, mate." Ian recoils, holding up his hands. "I'm here… A friend of mine. Told me there's a shop. Just wondering if you know anything about it?"

The figure pauses again, tapping the baton in dark gloved hands, as though studying Ian. Then it softly nods its head, stepping off to the rear of the pavement, moving to a small wrought iron gate there. Ian watches from the road as gloved hands swing it open gently and beckon him forward. Lightly tapping the top of the gate, the figure points the baton down towards the basement area.

Ian swallows. Nervously crossing to the other side of the street. "Down there? MacLeod's Miscellany, aye?"

Shadowy black eyes stare from under the brim, slowly followed by a single gloved finger placed over the mouth.

"Awright, ah understand, keep it quiet."

Ian steps forward and studies the short flight of stone steps and the shadowy basement space. All he can see is a narrow heavy door next to a large window, the latter covered adequately with old wooden shutters. A mere sliver of warm light escapes at the bottom, a tiny sign of life largely invisible from the pavement above.

As Ian descends, he looks for any further signs of life but there's nothing. No boards or decorations outside, only a pile of dirty old crates stacked and tucked away in the corner closest to the front door.

Looking up at the figure in the top hat. "Ah, just go in, right?"

The figure nods and makes an odd grunting sound, then closes the small iron gate above.

Ian turns the large door handle, pushing the dirty heavy door back. It eventually gives way, opening just enough after several moments of struggle.

A fade of warm light and noise greets him in a modest candle-lit room, littered with tables and various types of display cabinets, most of which appear to be empty. A simple wooden display counter runs from side to side at the rear, with a doorway at the back through which Ian hears good-natured shouting, laughing and music. As Ian closes the front door, the boisterous sounds fade quickly, as though the people inside are instantly aware of his presence.

From the back, barely shuffling through the patterned beaded curtain, an old and painfully thin man in a bronze velvet waistcoat and cream shirt appears. Shuffling along the counter, one sickly hand on the surface as a feeble support.

"Evening… Sir."

Ian frowns, unsettled by the rough voice and almost ancient appearance. "Evenin'."

After a few moments, a shorter, younger man with slicked back greying hair follows, making final adjustments to his outfit. Straightening a neat blue tie and ensuring the ornate cufflinks on each sleeve are fastened correctly. He approaches Ian in the main area, then spins round to face the old man at the counter.

Holding arms in the air in a questioning gesture. "Grandfather? Didn't we agree?"

The speech muffled and slurred. "Yir lazy, Morton. Slow these days, since you got wi' her."

The man in the sharp blue tie and cufflinks sniffs uncomfortably, scratching his cheek and rubbing his hands together. He turns to Ian and forces a mock grin, indicating slight embarrassment.

"Myrtle?"

A thin, dreadfully pale woman with lank brown hair hanging like a hundred rat tails peers wide-eyed round the doorway. Although her expression seems friendly initially, her words spit and snap like a viper.

"Whit now, Morton? Am dressin' a body in here!"

Arm outstretched, pointing at the unsteady old man to the side. "Grandfather? It's very late for him?"

"Wha' di you need me ti dae aboot it?"

Gesturing towards Ian. "To take him away? So, I can deal with our customer?"

"Whoh do yi think I am? Am no yir skivvy. Ideas above yir station, Morton MacLeod. I'm busy here too, ken? Cannae dae everythin'… am no at yir beck and call aw the time." Myrtle disappears quickly, her anger at being interrupted obvious, now barking the same order at others to fulfil. "Tammy, Jacko, Billy, Katy, come an' get your great grandfather!"

After a moment, four small children in ragged pyjamas run through the doorway giggling. They latch onto the hands of the very old man still grumbling and protesting at the counter, carefully guiding him away. As he shuffles back to the doorway, he turns his head, trying in vain to look at Ian.

"Ye let me know now, if he doesn't take care of ye…"

Ian clears his throat nervously at the somewhat chaotic scene. Not quite what he had anticipated.

As the group disappear back through the curtain, Morton makes an exaggerated gesture, like rolling a large invisible bowling ball in their direction.

"I'm extremely sorry about all that. Family, eh? You have family Mr…?"

Ian bites his lip, his mouth becoming dry. "Aye. One son. In New Zealand. We don't eh…"

"Ah, I see…"

"This is why you're here, maybe?"

"Aye. Well, kind of."

"I'm sorry our crows let us down tonight, we weren't expecting anyone." Pausing, then holding his hands in the air. "Anyway, I'm Morton MacLeod. Welcome to Macleod's Miscellany."

A hand stretches in front, draped in several thick golden rings and a chunky golden links bracelet. Ian meets the gesture and shakes three times. Always the third.

"Am Ian, Ian Bolton." Stifling a yawn. "Least I've come to the right place. It's no' an easy place to find."

Morton nods as he moves back behind the counter, gesturing for Ian to come closer. "Yes, we prefer it that way. Our business is purely word of mouth. I take it you're familiar with our line of work already?"

Grimly. "Aye, aye…"

"Good. Then you already know the most important aspect of our business, Mr Bolton. Discretion."

"So how long have…"

"We been operating? Oh, a long, long time. You've met Grandfather? He modernised our entire network. We all owe him a great deal. That said," Morton chuckles and adopts a quieter tone, "back in his time, operating conditions were considerably easier than they are now. A small observation I like to remind him about. Continuously in fact."

Morton bends down behind the counter, pulling out a few old notebooks and a couple of homemade catalogues, laying them on top. Ian flicks casually through one, noticing the almost antique age of the document and the complete lack of photographs. Hand-drawn illustrations of various household items only, accompanied by generous pools of ornate handwriting.

"Let's cut to the chase, Mr Bolton, what brings you to MacLeod's Miscellany tonight?"

Ian withdraws the plastic wallet containing the hair, unfolding it carefully and placing it on the counter in front of Morton.

Nodding softly. "Your wife? A relative?"

"Yes, my wife. My friend told me you might be able to help, said ye helped him."

Morton stares at Ian intensely, unsettling him, piercing blue eyes glistening in warm candlelight. "I see. Wonderful. Well, we will do our best, Mr Bolton, you're thinking a wig perhaps?"

"Something like that. Aye."

"And this is all the hair you have?"

"Aye."

"I don't believe this will be enough for a wig unless..." Morton scratches the side of his face, thinking and reflecting, "...there's enough for some small extensions?"

"Extensions?"

"Yes." Morton nervously glances at Ian's thin, cropped hair. "Well, I take it the item is for your personal and private use only?"

Ian stares directly at Morton and his mind suddenly goes blank. He hadn't even thought about it. His own thinking had simply stopped at the construction stage, that deep need just to have again. He hadn't considered at all what he was going to use the finished item for. The question suddenly troubles Ian, as though somewhere deep inside a mysterious valve opens, leaking discomfort.

Morton reaches underneath and removes what appears to be a very old ledger. Then he lifts a pair of round spectacles, near a small antique bell on the counter, placing them carefully on the tip of his nose. He starts scanning several pages feverishly.

"Let me check some of our previous records. It's a shame my wife isn't here, she attends to all the weaving jobs normally. We do get a few from time to time. Used to be very popular."

After reading a few more sections, Morton places the spectacles on the counter and lifts the wallet with the hair, as though trying to roughly assess its weight.

"As I suspected, Mr Bolton, I'm afraid this is considerably less than what we require for a wig."

"Awright."

"This leaves us with two options."

A strange shiver passes through Ian.

"Now, we can still make a wig. But if we have nothing suitable in stock, we'll need to find other donors."

"Aye. Okay." Ian rubs his eyes, tentacles of tiredness creeping.

"Alternatively, as I suggested, we can make some smaller hair extensions. This will be much cheaper and, if you are considering a small memento only, likely your best choice."

"Awright." Troubled. Reflecting. "Am no' sure now."

Morton smiles calmly from behind the counter. "If I can give you a small slice of humble advice, Mr Bolton? Normally in these matters, it's best to dwell on how much the person meant to you. For some people, a mere cheap trinket is enough but for others, well, no stone is left unturned."

Frowning. Confused. "And if ah go for the wig, how much we talkin' about?"

"With human hair?"

"Aye."

Morton draws in a sharp breath and flips open the smallest notepad on the top of the counter. Quickly discarding the page full of scribbles on top, he plucks a short pencil lying next to the antique cash register and starts scrawling hasty arithmetic across the blank page.

Sucking in his pale cheeks. "Approximately somewhere in the region of £2800-£3000."

"Jesus…" Ian reels with the shock, rubbing his forehead nervously. Small sweat quickly developing. A different kind of fear now, the purely fiscal kind. "Ah knew it was going to be expensive but—"

Morton sighs. "Speaking honestly, Mr Bolton, not particularly expensive for what we usually class as a luxury item. Considering the sourcing of materials and the extensive handiwork required across the construction, this is a reasonable price. We do have a conditional first-time discount of 10% which we can apply?"

"Aye?" Ian fidgets. "What's the condition?"

"Oh, nothing sinister, Mr Bolton, we just need you to pass on our work when an opportunity arises. Someone else who might benefit from our services? We can track things that way. Our crows, you see?"

Ian sinks deeper in bewilderment, unable to follow.

Across the candlelit shop, the front door groans and shifts as the masked figure from the street steps inside. Removing the top hat and placing it on the table near the window, the figure collapses wearily on a simple wooden chair.

Shouting over Ian's shoulder. "Everything fine out there, Doric?"

Ian is astonished when the figure answers, the voice much younger than expected.

"Aye. Borin' as usual."

Morton holds up a finger, vainly attempting to stop any further disgruntlement. "Oh, that's fine, Doric. Thank you."

"Aw-ways borin'. Ah never get tae go wi' Nelson and Oscar oan excavation night."

"Well, you're a lot younger than they are, Doric." Morton glances at Ian and smiles, rolling his eyes. "We've talked about it many, many times."

"Still borin' tho' isn' it?"

"We'll have a think about your duties after your next birthday. Right now, see?" Morton gestures at Ian. "I'm trying to deal with a customer."

Doric stands up quickly, clearly irritated, swiping the top hat from the table. He moves briskly across the shop floor, removing his coat, gloves and balaclava and dumping them on the counter.

"I'm oan mah break."

He heads straight through the beaded curtain without any further words or gesture. In the background, several screams of frustration, a flurry of concerned voices and a door slamming shut.

"I do apologise, Mr Bolton." Morton exhales, thinly disguised frustration. "Children. Not even mine. Anyway, where were we…"

Ian lights up his watch, now well past one o'clock.

"Have you decided what you want to do?"

Ian knows full well that the order will empty his rainy-day account completely and make for a very lean next month. Yet, if there's any chance that this might help. The same way it helped that woman at Colin's work, the same way it helped Colin, that's good enough. It's worth the money, worth the risk.

"Yeah, I'll go for it."

"The wig? With human hair?"

"Aye."

"You are certain, Mr Bolton? Once we agree there's no turning back. We don't do refunds."

"Aye…"

"Excellent, well, let me update the order book here." Morton grabs a fountain pen from an open wooden box and scrawls something on the next blank row in the old ledger. "One wig, human hair, incorporating the sample in this wallet. Right, if you can sign just here, Mr Bolton?"

Ian nods meekly. Leaning over and signing his name where Morton is indicating.

"Wonderful. I'll need a few measurements and then you are free to go." Morton smiles warmly. "Must be getting late for you?"

Stifling another yawn. "It's okay, doesn't take too long to get home."

Lifting a square-shaped red box from under the counter and removing a measuring tape from inside. "And where is home for you, Mr Bolton?"

"Ah it's…" Ian stops suddenly, smiling ruefully as he instinctively puts on the brakes.

Morton laughs heartily, waving an index finger excitedly in approval. "Ah yes. I understand. Discretion."

Ian feels the skin on his face prickle.

"I like you, Mr Bolton." Morton slips from behind the counter brandishing the measuring tape. "I like you a lot. You are my favourite kind of customer. One who knows *exactly* what he wants."

As Morton begins to measure the circumference of Ian's head, the latter slowly ponders those few lingering words. It's possible Morton really does think that but, at this hour, Ian can't bring himself to believe it. Not in the slightest in fact.

While Morton busies and babbles various measurements about him, Ian lowers his gaze to the murky floor and hears the doubting voices once again. Those despairing words, increasingly cacophonous, encouraging strange tears. Feeling these, Ian hurries to quickly dispel them by forcing a dream. The same dream. The normal every-day dream. The one that starts with an alarm clock, with grey morning light, and the security of routine and daily inconsequence.

***

Distraught, watery eyes stare from under mixed streams of long hair. While the glow of a bedside lamp casts strange shadows across an agitated face. Sitting on the edge of the bed, Ian glances again towards the floor mirror in the corner. Unable to protect himself from a terrible growing despair, that ugly reflection staring back.

The long wig disguises his number one cropped hair entirely, thinning his own face, distorting his own appearance in strange ways. The shifting patterns of low light barely covering the bedroom conspire further, forcing him to move position, to look from all sides. To raise his head and lower it, vainly chasing the elusive picture where the wig can match the image inside his head. Or, if not match it, at least come reasonably close.

But it's impossible. No matter how hard he tries in this dim light. No matter which way he turns, which position he adopts, the image is not even remotely close. It's all mixed up. In fact, perhaps cruelly, it seems as far away now as it has ever been. As though he's been asleep, but the sheer ugliness is now rousing him to full consciousness. And the only thing that rises to fill the growing void is a certain hate, a wretchedness, a terrible self-loathing. Now he is horrified by what he sees in the mirror, appalled by what he has done. What he, Ian Bolton, has done to his own memory.

Quivering hands force upwards, meeting long swathes of dark hair falling limply over narrow, weeping eyes. They try to brush the hair back behind each ear, over the shoulders again, then they rip away, as though unable to bear the very touch of it. The mere feel of the wig confusing. Unravelling. Traumatising.

Of course, there's no mistaking the quality. Morton had taken great delight in explaining the entire construction process, how his wife had laboured over that single order for weeks, painstakingly weaving the hair all on her own. No-one else skilled enough for the job as he put it – not even his great grandmother, who, by all accounts, was the greatest weaver that ever lived but can no longer work the order book because of her deteriorating health. It was as though by explaining all the effort, all the intricacies of the weaving process, Ian would be completely reassured that he was indeed in possession of a most unique, prestigious, luxury item. A dream perhaps. One of a kind.

It was only when Ian listened to the voices and enquired about the other hair used to fulfil the order, the several lighter and red shades in the mix, that Morton had exercised discretion. Looking up from the counter, while counting the bundles of cash Ian used as payment, he had grinned like a cat and tapped the side of his nose. "I'm afraid we can't reveal that, Mr Bolton. Trade secrets you might say."

But right now, here in the suffocatingly dim bedroom in the middle of the night, it all felt a very long way from luxury. The sickening had started then, right there in the shop, in fact the very moment that Morton had placed the wig on Ian's head, checking the overall fit in case some final adjustments were required. But no, the perfect fit, he said. Not only that, the perfect look, shouting at the other members of the family to come and see. Handfuls of faces, young, old, very old, all shuffling and peering from the doorway, voicing muted approval at a job well done.

In those strangely uncomfortable seconds, Ian suddenly realised he had been biting down hard on his tongue, so hard that a dribble of blood had crept out the side of his mouth and down his chin. Noticing it, Morton had simply wiped it away with a small grubby handkerchief, then stuffed it back in one of the small pockets in his thickly striped waistcoat.

Then, when Morton removed the wig, asking if it was okay to use the same plastic wallet as before, Ian could barely nod in his direction. The taste of his own blood, the pressure on his head as though the wig was still in place, the well of upset rising and flowing freely, the strange whirling cloud of terrible voices lifting and tearing at his very soul, all conspiring to dismantle his ability to speak. To think straight even.

Thankfully, Morton had been so pre-occupied with counting the bundles of money to pay any further attention to Ian shaking and shuddering on the spot. As it was, Ian had precious seconds to breathe somehow and bolster some temporary defences, to find what little voice he could muster. And that's when he asked the question, the one that troubles him still.

"Morton..." Swallowing nervously. "The other hair, where did ye...?"

Ian shudders on the bed, weeping in sudden, abject misery. Clawing at his clothes with feverish hands, as though struggling for air, he stumbles out and into the small bathroom. Wincing from the pounding in his back and head, he grabs the light pull with a flailing hand, flooding the modest space in harsh, cold white.

Staring into the sliding mirror doors of the wall-mounted cabinet, he's immediately horrified by a painful, exhausted face framed in long hair of many shades. He steps closer, wanting to be certain, to be sure of what he already knows. Studying every strand and trying to isolate each in a frenzy, to separate Sandra from the others. His hands shaking in terrible sweat as they try to accomplish the impossible, unsure even where to start. Unable to distinguish her beautiful hair even in this sharp, white light. Every precious thread submerged in and dispersed across other shades.

As he wrestles with each hair, his mind screams at him mercilessly. How it's all too late now, already lost, that he's made the most colossal mistake, that he should never have listened to his friend, that he should have turned back when he saw the people in the park, when he saw the man standing in the street and certainly when he met him, Morton MacLeod… That he, Ian Bolton, should have left her hair alone, back there in the bedside cabinet with all her other things. Unspoiled. Where she would have been safe. Locked away to fade in time with dignity intact. But no, that selfishness, that wanting. To be helped, always to be helped, to take the pain away. And it's led to all this, this collapsing monster right here in the mirror.

A world spins. The sensation of sinking while standing. Ian stumbles backwards, nearly falling at the side of the bathtub. Tears of remorse, of anger, of despair, now flow as he rips the wig from his head, holding it in front of him. Chest rising and falling sharply, he flails and pulls at the swinging string as he exits clumsily. Anything now to turn it all off, to blot it out, to take the memory of it away, anything.

Staggering back to the bedroom, he throws the wig on the bed and recoils, standing with his back to the wall, turning his face away, unable to bring himself to look there. He slides around the wall, hyperventilating, wiping sweat and tears from cold, pale skin. He reaches his side of the bed and drops down weeping, knocking the pile of plates to the floor as he grabs his smartphone.

Weeping. Exhausted. Suffocating. Trembling fingers reach out for his contacts list, tapping on the stored number for his preferred taxi company.

"Brady cars?"

Swallowing. Deep breaths. "Ah need a taxi straight away, please…"

"Where are you travelling to?"

"The old town." Pausing. "Fairbanks Lane..."

***

Under the single streetlight, Doric removes his old silver watch from an inside pocket and studies it, reassured by the time he sees there, knowing that his nocturnal shift is nearly over. Another tedious four hours with only his embittered and ultimately pointless late teenage chatter for company. Well, that and the handful of crows that Agnes talks to, the ones that circle the city, returning with any leads.

And then there was the guy picking up the wig, the quiet one that looked like he needed the ground to open and swallow him whole. What was his name again? Ian? Yeah, that was it. Poor guy. All confused. Upset. Doric could tell that alright. Not sure if he wanted to be there or not. Maybe even a bit rude when he left. Doric had never seen someone take off so fast.

Slipping the watch into the pocket again, he lifts his top hat briefly and scratches his balaclava-covered scalp. Turning along the pavement, he finds his customary spot at the railings and leans back against them, willing the last minutes to pass even more quickly.

At the end of the street, a car slowly travels into view on Fairbanks Lane and stops. After a few moments, a short, stocky figure exits from a passenger door, standing to watch the car do a U turn and drive away. Doric narrows his eyes, watching from the shadow as the passenger now stumbles forward onto Mathieson Street. Half-jogging, half-walking.

Doric recognises him. It's the man from earlier, Ian, the man with the wig who left in such a hurry. His heart sinks, why now? Why, at the end of his shift, just when he's starting to wind down, likely trouble arrives.

Not that Doric is particularly surprised, maybe he was the only one that could tell there was something off from earlier. The hurried way in which Ian had left, how confused he appeared to be. While everyone had been congratulating Ian on the beautiful wig, Doric was standing at the back, taking it all in and paying close attention to the other signs.

Even then he realised it was going to end in one of two ways. The first option would see Ian going home, pouring himself a generous drink or two before collapsing on his bed or couch and sleeping the stress away. He'd wake up in the morning feeling lighter, more resigned, more accepting of the wig that would greet him on the kitchen table next to the whisky bottle and the empty glass.

Or he'd take the second option. He'd go home, sink quickly into crisis, have a complete meltdown, hate everything he's just done then, unsure of what else to do, he'd come all the way back here to try and make some sense of all of it, to sort it out.

Except, there's nothing to sort out. MacLeod's Miscellany doesn't do refunds. Never has. Never will.

As Ian staggers up the pavement, the clear plastic wallet underneath one arm, the other arm rubbing his clearly upset face, Doric slides a gloved hand into his coat pocket, feeling the retractable baton inside.

In a flash, Doric hears Oscar and Nelson in his head, telling him to use his height and to always watch his position. He moves quickly towards Ian, cutting off the direct route to the gate and the steps down to the basement.

Stretching out an arm, pointing and waving angrily. "Get out my fucking way. I need tae see Morton!"

"We're closed pal."

The simple reply works. Creating just enough doubt, forcing Ian to check the time in his upset.

"It's not four yet." Pointing at the watch. "Yir still open. Twenty minutes."

Without warning, Ian clumsily lunges forward, his weight more than enough to knock Doric to the side. But the sudden powerful move also pushes him off balance and he falls awkwardly, wincing as he lands beside the plastic wallet already on the ground. In the seconds that follow, younger reflexes tell, as Doric gathers himself quickest. He slips back to the gate, even gathering his top hat in the process.

"Said wir closed!"

Ian slowly straightens. "Yir no fucking closed, pal. This'll only take five minutes wi' him."

"Wir closed. There's no need for ye tae be back here."

Ian winces, grabbing the wallet from the ground and shaking it in front of Doric. "Aye, there fucking is."

Ian bristles with anger, close enough to share the same air as Doric, the same spit. Shuddering with frustration, his body awash with pain now coursing freely up and down his injured back. But the pain is nothing compared to the hurt and desperation driving him on. He has to sort it all out tonight, to finish this bad dream. It's clear now, clearer than it's ever been.

Wedged between Ian and the short iron gate, Doric tries to remain cold and calm. But inside his own head, the imagined harsh voices of Oscar and Nelson, berating him mercilessly for letting an old guy like this get the upper hand.

The opportunity adds some further pressure. Doric knows only too well that if he can deal with this incident successfully, it'll be yet another sign to Morton that he's finally ready to take on heavier duties.

Ian twists the dark coat in one hand. "I need tae see him. I fucking need to see him."

"Ye need tae leave. I've telt ye, wir closed."

Instantly, Ian grimaces as he swings an arm wildly, catching Doric on the side of the head. Doric crumples temporarily, grabbing the railings behind for support as the top hat falls into the basement below.

Standing up, adjusting his balaclava. "Am telling ye. Go hame."

Ian steps back, seething now, as though caught in the space between lashing out and collapsing entirely. "Don't you people understand? I don't have a fucking home any more!"

Gloved hands held up, gesturing to slow. "Stoap. Am telling ye. Calm doon. Ye dinny want ti dae this."

"Or what? What you gonna do, eh?" Ian steps forward aggressively. "Well, if you're no going to let me see him… then I'm going to the polis."

"Naw, dinny dae that…"

"Aye, see what they say, eh?"

Doric flinches, a gloved hand instinctively reaching into his coat pocket.

"See what else yir up tae. Am sure they'll find your wee operation here to be of some interest."

"If ye ken whit's gid fir ye, ye dinny wanna dae that."

Ian gloats. "Watch me, pal. Aye that's right. You won't let me in then I'll come back wi' them. We'll see what else has been going on in yir little family business here."

As Ian leans back to assess whether his new line of attack is working, Doric flicks the baton and whips it across the leering face in front of him in a sudden, well-rehearsed move. Ian cries out sharply, leaning and staggering forward. Unable to protect himself as Doric brings the baton down swiftly on the back of his head, silencing him instantly.

Retracting the baton and placing it in his pocket, Doric opens the gate quickly, glancing around at nearby buildings. Content that he isn't being watched, he retrieves the plastic wallet, folding then stuffing it into his other coat pocket. Lifting Ian under each arm, he drags him down the first few steps, dropping him briefly to close the gate. Then he continues slowly, struggling with the heavy unconscious body down the worn stone steps, disappearing into the shadow of the basement.

Dropping Ian near the door, Doric retrieves the top hat from the bottom of the steps and rips his balaclava and gloves off, placing them inside the hat.

Pushing open the front door and sliding into the shop, he calls out for support. "Can anyone gie me some help here? Oscar?"

A tall, powerfully built woman in a polo shirt moves across the shop floor towards the doorway. "Whit ye dun? Is he deed? Ye fuckin' killed him?"

"Naw, Oscar ah swear it, he's breathin'." Doric shakes his head frantically. "Fuckin idiot was startin' on me. Wanted ti see Morton."

"Awright." Oscar kicks the body in frustration and shouts back inside the shop. "Nelson, ye there? We got a joab on."

An even bigger figure swings round from inside. "Fucking hell, Doric, ye need to be more careful, eh?"

Leaning over the body, Oscar is shocked. "This is the guy from earlier oan?"

Doric nods. "Aye, the guy wi the wig."

"Fuck." Nelson scratches the side of his face, the scraping sound of four-day old stubble. "Had a feeling he was going tae be trouble."

"Aye." Doric nods. "Said he was goin' tae the polis, aw that crack like."

"Nae fucking respect any more is there?" Oscar shakes her head, as though disgusted that any customer would even threaten such a thing. "Ye aw-ways try tae dae the right thing and ye get this. It's awright, Doric, ye did good. C'moan, Nelson, need tae get 'im inside."

Ian stirs as Oscar and Nelson half-carry, half-drag his recovering body into the shop. Doric doesn't follow immediately, instead he turns to stare at the sky, ignoring the three crows now watching him from the railings above. A grin creeps across his young face and he shakes his fist in silent triumph. Then he returns to the shop, gently closing the front door behind him. As he does, all he can hear inside his own head is the sound of Oscar's voice, over and over.

"Ye did good. Ye did good. Ye did good..."

***

"Sshh, he's waking up now…"

The sound of a familiar voice causes Ian's eyes to flicker open. He takes a few moments to register dull, blank space somewhere in front of him as a ceiling. Wincing. Head and back throbbing. Everything hot, clammy, nauseas, tasting of blood. He closes his eyes then opens them again, the fog clearing slowly, vision adjusting.

Pain.

"I did wonder if we'd see you again, Mr Bolton? Doric here seemed convinced of it."

"Morton," Ian whispers, groaning and wincing as he tries and fails to rise quickly. "Ah just wanted tae see ye…"

Indistinct voices grumble and complain. A circle of faces encroaches, appearing from all around the edge of his vision. Ian glances about him, disturbed by the size of the crowd standing and watching his every move in warm, flickering candlelight.

Morton gestures to reassure. "It's okay. Everyone, please, let's be civil here."

Ian sits up painfully, following the voice that leads him to Morton, standing in front. Striped waistcoat and white shirt now unbuttoned, his face lined and weary at the end of the nightshift.

Grimacing, Ian slowly gets to his feet, turning every way, looking at the line of heavy candlelit faces staring back at him. Young and old. A few he remembers, but most he's never seen. So many of them. Several generations. Some dressed old and shabby, others with at least an attempt at grace.

Shocked. "You aw live here?"

Morton steps closer. "This is about you, Mr Bolton, not us. Our shop, our business, has been running far, far longer than you have been alive."

Ian glances at two of the children closest to him, perhaps their mother standing behind, her hands draped across them both. Neither meet his confused stare, instead they let their eyes wander off somewhere to the left. Anywhere but stare at the difficult man delaying lights out. This unreasonable customer in the early hours of the morning.

"Doric was telling me how threatening you were being outside? You didn't give him any choice, is that accurate, Mr Bolton?"

"Naw." Ian swallows. Shaking his head. "Threatening? No."

Doric shouts from somewhere behind. "He's lyin', he's fuckin' lyin'."

Morton rubs his forehead and exhales wearily.

"Ah just wanted to see ye. That's all."

"But your business here is finished, the order complete? Other than your end of the deal of course. To pass on our details, when appropriate."

Ian shakes his head. "Naw. No. I made a mistake. Can't be like this."

Muted laughter ripples across the audience.

"But it is." Morton smiles, his expression softening, as though finding the very idea outrageous. "Mr Bolton, you can't come back to the night shop every time you make a mistake?"

Ian places his hands on his face. "Ah was wrong, was wrong to do what ah did. Wasnae thinkin' right."

Morton reaches out a consoling arm but Ian flinches angrily, lashing out and recoiling. Reacting to the sudden violent movement, Oscar and Nelson step through the line quickly. Ian calms immediately, sensing them standing behind.

"How do you know you were wrong, Mr Bolton?"

Ian feels tears welling up. "'cause it's no fucking right is it? Aw this. Yir fucking shop. It's fucking sick, that's what it is. What yir doing here."

"Really?" Morton leans forward.

"Aye, aye." Ian spins and scowls at all the faces around him, his expression a mask of pain and upset. "And yiv got children here, mixed up in aw this? How can you do this, Morton?"

"This is our business, Mr Bolton. Our livelihood. It provides. It's always provided."

Appalled. Shocked. "What? It's disgusting."

"You're just upset. You're being unreasonable."

Ian's face twists, his words lashing out on fine sprays of spittle. "Ye took advantage of me. That time, ah didnae know what I was thinking. Earlier oan. What I was doing. But I've got it now."

"And what would that be, Mr Bolton?"

"Ah know. Ah know how tae fix this."

Ian stumbles back, the ragged circle in the shop breaking as faces young and old move out his way. All except for two, Oscar and Nelson, now standing side by side in front of the main door. Thick arms crossed in front, expressions cold and stern, eyes narrow. Hungry dogs waiting on the command to kill.

Morton appears at the side, speaking softly. "How will you fix it, Mr Bolton?"

Ian swallows nervously. "Am going to the polis…"

Whispering. "I'm afraid we can't let you do that, Mr Bolton. We can't let you jeopardise our livelihood like this. My family. Our survival. You came here freely, used our services. This is how you repay us?"

Ian bows his head, weeping softly. "Ye used me, Morton, this is no shop. Just yir sick mind wi' aw these people."

"That's right, Mr Bolton." Morton leans in closer and taps Ian on the side of his head. "That's right."

Ian screams and raises his fist viciously but is unable to connect, his arm caught by Nelson who grabs and pushes it back instantly, painfully. Ian howls in agony as Morton dives to the side, clattering against one of the empty display cabinets, hastily mopping his forehead with his handkerchief.

Oscar is already securing her prey easily, well-rehearsed moves rendering Ian's fatigued and aimless lashing completely ineffective. He struggles to no avail, tired limbs no match, Oscar soon pinning him back while Nelson lands two cruel and sickening punches to his head. Then they change positions, Nelson holding Ian's now increasingly limp body as Oscar flashes fists into his middle. Blood spitting, dribbling, as the others now crowd round and join in. Oscar stepping back, shaking the sting of the blows from her own hands.

In a panic, Morton crawls across the carpet, gesturing at two of the children. "Tammy? Billy? Put the music on, Chiquitita, remember?"

Both glance at each other and smile, skipping off quickly through the beaded curtain at the back.

"Not too loud, it's late."

Morton slowly gets to his feet, holding onto the nearest display unit for support, catching his breath and trying to tease out the small aches across his own body. He stretches up, a troubled smile as he hears the music now loud in the background, smothering the painful sounds before watching the crowd easily lift Ian aloft and carry him away. Watching open-mouthed as they lift his battered, limp body through the doorway to the rear of the building. Only when the main room is empty does he exhale, wiping his mouth and placing the handkerchief back in his pocket.

"Morton."

The young voice makes him turn, one figure moving out from the darkness in the corner.

"Ah, Doric."

In the background, a sharp scream cuts through the music. Morton winces.

Doric steps forward, his young and tired face nervous, unsure about the correct words to say. Eyes scanning anxiously, studying Morton for any sign he can pick up, any flinch he can use.

"Ah ken it's a bit soon but… Ah did gid tonight. Oscar said so. Ah think am ready, the promotion, aye?"

Another scream from the back, the final one, submerged in music.

Morton nods and smiles ruefully, placing a hand on a black shoulder. "Doric, can we talk about this tomorrow, please?"

"Ye aw-ways say that, Morton. But nuthin ever happens?"

"Doric, I'm tired." Morton stares into dark, uncertain eyes. "I'm tired."

***

Colin Buchan steers his small car into Fairbanks Lane. As he moves from concrete to cobble, navigating the meandering street, lit only by ornate and mournful lighting, he dwells on the strange disappearance of his good friend.

There were no warnings. No frantic calls. No babbling messages or updates. Nothing. Just the awkwardness of standing at the bar on Sunday evening as usual. Waiting and waiting. Ordering a solitary beer and feeling somewhat awkward when Helen eventually asked "no Ian tonight?" Smiling anxiously, admitting that "something must have come up" then sitting down. Table for one. Pulling out the smartphone to check for any reason why but no. Texting again and again. Still nothing. Then taking the last few sips in the glass and quietly leaving the pub via the rear exit. The first tentacles of deeper worry creeping, forcing yet another round of unanswered calls on the way home.

And then the knocks on the door. The empty house. Still nothing. Followed by several days of increasingly troubled thoughts. Lying in bed at night, scouring back through the previous Sunday evening conversations like a gold prospector, trying to remember any nuggets that might give some insight. Some clue to indicate what has happened, where Ian has gone. But the secrets, assuming there were any, remain locked away. When Colin recalls any of those conversations, when he flips over each stone, there's nothing there. Just the same Ian. Slightly morose at times, bemoaning his situation and his own role in the accident, but nothing new. Nothing different from the hundreds of other conversations.

But it was during one of these late-night reflections that Colin started to wonder. To wonder whether those hundreds of conversations, always saying the same thing, were in fact the clues? That the endless mentioning and climbing down, repeated ad nauseum, were the very breadcrumbs he needed to follow?

Maybe Ian had visited MacLeod's Miscellany after all? He hadn't mentioned it but maybe something had happened there. After all, it was no easy course to navigate, something that Colin knew only too well from personal experience. Perhaps it had all been a bit too much for Ian? Maybe he just needed to get away, clear off for a while, be alone. Anonymous.

Ian never had talked much about his family, his first family. Colin recalls him briefly mentioning the difficulties with his son, who lived far away, but he never mentioned anyone else. Only Sandra.

Colin turns off the engine and slips the lock through the steering wheel. He opens the door and steps out, retrieving a short blue jacket from the rear seat then closing the doors and remotely locking the car. Adjusting his jacket, he looks through the gloom, sniffing at the sight of Mathieson Street just over the road.

He's never been back here since the time he came to collect the lamp. While MacLeod's Miscellany had helped him, he could never truly wash the distaste from his mouth completely. When he passed the information on to Ian, he had hoped that would be the end of it, he'd never have to come back, night or day.

So as he walks quietly along the pavement, stepping towards a tall dark figure in a top hat and coat, he hopes and prays inside that his enquiries here lead nowhere. That he can get back in his car as quickly as possible and drive away, finally forgetting everything about this place.

A crow watches Colin suspiciously from a nearby railing as he wipes a lonely drip from his nose, acknowledging the figure in the top hat.

"Awright?"

Silence. The crow answers slightly.

"Am eh, looking fir someone. Wondering if he came here?"

The dark figure leaning against the railings stretches up, adjusting his hat.

"Aye, called Ian. Just wonderin'. If he came here?"

The figure appears to shrug his shoulders and exhales, as though bored. "Yill have tae gan in and see Morton."

"He's in?"

"Aye, aw-ways in." The dark figure steps closer, eyes narrowing in the round holes of the balaclava. "Ye been here afore? I recognise ye?"

"Aye. Months back. Got a nice lamp."

"Thought so. A lamp eh? Braw." Doric sniffs, leaning back against the railing as before. "Ye can gan in then. He's no in a gid frame ay mind tho'. Nuthin' new tho' is it?"

Doric chuckles. A little dig here. A little dig there.

Colin raises his eyebrows. "Ah winny be long."

"Aye, that's fine. Nae trouble though eh? Ye dinny look like the type tho'."

Doric swings the gate open lazily, barely moving from his slouched position. With a vaguely puzzled expression, Colin descends the stone steps, scanning several crows now sitting watching him.

Taking a deep breath, he pushes on the door and steps in, closing it firmly behind. Warm candlelight greets him as memories of when he was here last flood back. But now the display units scattered across the modest shop floor contain items, unlike the previous time where everything was empty.

From the beaded doorway at the rear, Morton Macleod appears carrying what looks like several pieces of jewellery. As he walks from the counter he is startled to see Colin standing in the middle of the shop.

Colin swallows nervously, pointing behind him, indicating the street. "He said it was okay."

"Did he now?" Morton nods, a pulse of anger fading in and out.

"Aye."

Sighing. "Well, let me put these down and—"

Morton moves quickly to one of the display cases on a table along the wall. He places the items down then lifts a large glass lid with a wooden frame up carefully. One by one, he arranges each piece in the empty case.

"So, what brings you here?"

"Just droppin' in. Wonderin' if you've seen someone. A good friend of mine. Name is Ian Bolton, here…" Colin holds out his phone, a picture of Ian on screen.

Morton lowers the lid on the case and studies the image, his face already a mask of denial.

"Can't say I've ever seen him. It's been exceptionally quiet here the last few weeks. No new business." Morton bites his lip, fixing a slightly resigned expression. "Unfortunately, I might add."

"Ye dinny recognise him?" Colin frowns. "He's no been here then?"

Morton removes his handkerchief and wipes his nose. "Nope."

"Right, well, if he does come in can you…" Colin stops, puts a hand to his mouth and shakes his head. "Och forget it. Sure he'll turn up."

"Did he say he was coming here?"

"Dunno. I passed the details on, as ye said but…" Colin shrugs. "He never said anything about actually coming."

Morton pauses. Then he narrows his eyes and rubs his chin. "Wait a minute. I recognise you."

"Aye. Colin. I came here a few months back."

"That's right. I remember. A lamp, wasn't it?"

"Aye. Use it every night. It's been a big help for me, Mr MacLeod."

Morton bursts into a broad grin. "That is wonderful to hear, Colin. You wouldn't believe how much work we put in, ensuring our customers are happy."

Colin guiltily clears his throat, his laughter a shade nervous. "Can imagine…"

"Now. Now… Wait." Morton holds up a finger as though thinking, walking purposefully across the shop, moving behind the counter and checking the shelves underneath. "We have a sale on at the moment. As you can see, we have some new items. Surplus stock, going cheap."

Colin walks over to a few of the units and peers inside. Mainly jewellery and typical household items such as cutlery, combs, brushes. All unique. Some much prettier than others.

"Nice…"

"Please, here." Morton ushers Colin forward towards the counter. "Before you go, let me show you this."

Morton bends down and pulls a small lamp from under the counter. The style almost identical to the one that Colin had picked up months ago.

"Almost the same?"

Morton nods excitedly. "Surplus stock. We need to get rid of it. As I say, going cheap."

"Cheap…?"

"Mm-hm. Very cheap in fact."

"Really?"

"Oh yes." Morton closely inspects the quality of the craftsmanship on the lamp, studying the patch of hard grey material in the middle of the column, decorated with two large brass rings. "It's a good job, shame we have to sell it all so cheaply. Now, I was thinking, as you have one similar…"

Colin glances up at him.

"You said that you have your lamp on a bedside cabinet?"

"Aye."

"And there are normally two bedside cabinets? What do you have on top of the other one?"

Colin stretches up, the plan now clear. He shakes his head dismissively. "Naw, I cannae afford another one."

Morton smiles. "Oh no, not this time, Colin. Surplus stock. We need the space. Everything's on sale right now."

Suddenly warming to the idea, Colin strikes an interested tone. "Awright then. How much?"

Morton rubs his hands together. "For you, to complete the set, a mere £6.00."

"Six quid, really?" Laughing. "Ah cannae even get a beer for that."

"Told you it was cheap. But as you can see, we haven't skimped on the quality."

Colin smiles at Morton, the smile that says it's an offer he really can't refuse. "Aye, it would make things easier to read. Wi' just the one, can still be a bit dull sometimes. Another light makes a set."

Morton raises his eyebrows and nods encouragingly from across the counter.

"Aye, okay. I'll take it."

"Wonderful."

Colin fishes into his jacket pocket and removes his wallet. "Yir lucky actually, just happens I have a tenner oan me."

As Morton lifts the lamp into a brown paper bag, Colin removes the note from the rear compartment of the wallet and places it on the counter. Morton takes the note and slips it into a trouser pocket, then rummages in each before placing several coins back on the counter.

"I hope you find your friend?"

Colin lifts the package from the counter and cradles it in one arm. "Aye, he was going through a rough time. I'm sure he'll figure it out."

Morton shrugs. "Family business can be a strange thing, Colin. Doesn't always make sense from the outside."

"Aye. Aye, ah guess yir right." Colin takes a final glance around the room. "Well, I'll eh, see ye…"

Morton narrows his eyes and smiles politely. "Good luck."

Colin leaves the shop quickly and skips up the stone steps. As he closes the wrought iron gate he stops for a moment, watching the man in the top hat dancing on the street. Brandishing a baton and swinging it like a sword in front of him, as though duelling some invisible foe across the cobbles.

Smiling at the scene, Colin walks along the pavement under the watchful eyes of several crows circling overhead, the new lamp resting carefully in his arms.

# XY and The Suicide Companion

Jack Barker shivers. That creeping itch again…

Always starting from a nowhere that must be a somewhere. Necessitating the usual blend of casual, largely invisible mitigations. All the scratching. Rubbing. Brushing. Pulling. The initial touches Jack employs as quickly as possible to dull and delay the sensation of it happening. That dreadful thing that happens to him, whatever it is, over and over.

Jack has long perfected the art of applying self-soothing mechanisms without arousing any suspicion in his workplace. (Or the club or the bar or the cinema or wherever Jack happens to be at that specific point in time.) He's mastered their disguise completely. Hiding every one of those mitigations in his toolbox, making them all seem so natural. A boredom flick here. A high energy quirk there. Or merely some random nervous gesture that, in isolation, would never strike anyone as unusual.

Unless that person was *really* paying attention of course. If anyone was looking that little bit closer, somehow picking up on the frequency of the brushing or the regularity of the scratching. Then they might pause and wonder whether Jack was really alright after all.

But this isn't the worst of it. For even Jack realises that his toolbox of well-disguised alleviations can't hold the terrible dark horses back forever. Right at the outset he knows that his well-worn catalogue of initial palliations is not a solution, not a cure for the itch which is both warm and cold. He hopes of course, he always hopes that every time will be different, but it never is. It's all merely a way to extend time and space in every direction, or something like that. Something to delay as much as humanly possible his transition from Stage One to Stage Two.

For Stage Two is when everything shifts, becoming more intense, more desperate. It's also the stage where it becomes abundantly clear to even the most removed or indifferent of onlookers that, indeed, something just isn't quite right with Jack. The brushing, the soothing, the scratching… The frequency of it all changes, becoming so desperately infused with a cold sweat frenzy that anyone in the vicinity is, usually quietly, but immediately, disturbed?

Stage Two has no use for a healthy picklist of modest behavioural salves like Stage One, spinning like a gun chamber inside Jack's head. No. Stage Two only features one word. Escape. Rising suddenly behind smashed inner glass and blaring klaxon.

At this point, the only option is for Jack to excuse himself, politely or otherwise. To extricate his now sweating and quaking body from whatever sequence in which he finds himself. To find a space, some crack in the wall he can disappear into. To vanish for a while. Melt away into the background. Perhaps a toilet cubicle? A fire exit maybe? That lonely car park or rough patch of tree and shrub that no-one ever visits. Somewhere he can gulp in the air, like a fish gasping and burning in the middle of a desert. Somewhere he can ultimately prepare for Stage Three.

Usually, if Jack hits Stage Two at work, he'll head immediately to the rear of the stock room. He might casually call out "break" to a couple of his colleagues on the shop floor, his voice twisting, straining. But most of the time, he simply melts away to try and ride it out among cluttered shelves and stacks of cardboard boxes. Where he'll dance in the farthest corner of the dim room, vainly dampening down invisible flames licking every inch of skin.

Then, further along the terrible road of Stage Two, just as the fire becomes unbearable, everything stops in a jolt of sudden clarity. An implosion you might say. A sucking of time, of distance. A collapsing inward. A light switch snapping on and harsh glow revealing…

Stage Three.

And it's getting close. Here.

Right now.

In this very hall.

Jack has already lost track of the slick new speaker, all white teeth and careful hair, grinning and gesticulating wildly on the modest, neatly lit low stage. His near continuous seat squirming, the writhing from side to side in growing discomfort, has put paid to any chance of him picking up on the results of the recent employee competition, the latest regional sales updates or the changes to company branding for next year.

Not only that, with the tentacles of late Stage One asserting their dominance, Jack's continual shuffling and restlessness is now affecting those sitting around him. Twice already, someone in the row behind has prodded him. Once on his shoulder and then a second time, sharply in the middle of his back, indicating their displeasure at the continual fidgeting.

The girl to the right has also expressed her frustration, shooting the same distasteful frown sideways at least three times. Now Jack can no longer bring himself to meet her disapproving, withering glare and twists awkwardly to the left when he senses another incoming scowl.

Thankfully, the young male trainee in the next seat appears completely oblivious, having spent the entirety of the presentation so far leaning forward with head in hands and eyes closed. A set of earphones discreetly lodged underneath long hair.

None of their irritation matters now though. It's time already. Stage Two. Glass cracks and shatters. An alarm sounds.

Escape…

Jack rises from his seat violently. Fumbling between apologies and excuses while navigating the various legs, shoes, carrier bags and rucksacks littering the row.

The audience ripples with applause – but not for Jack, now striding across dark patterned carpet to the nearest double doors and ploughing through them. Collapsing into the corridor, gasping and groaning with skin on fire. He writhes and squirms for moments, pulling at his tie and collar, releasing invisible steam.

Two thin, young men wheeling a serving cart loaded with plates of biscuits, mugs and a pair of large stainless-steel vacuum flasks, meander through nearby double doors. They stop instantly, disturbed by the sight of Jack wrestling with himself.

"Are you okay?"

Jack looks towards them, grimacing, struggling for breath. "The toilets, where?"

"Sir…?"

"It's fine, fine…" One shaking, feverish hand raised high, the other massaging and scratching chest and neck. "I need… the toilets?"

"The main toilets are back along. At the front of the building. Near reception…"

Jack shakes his head, sliding down the wall slightly, groaning. "No, I don't think that's right. There must be another one. Something quieter?"

"There's a smaller toilet in the basement, for staff only."

"That must be it." Jack grits his teeth. "Yes, that's it, thank you."

"But it's staff only, sir?"

Mumbling, almost incoherent. "Doesn't matter. That's where he'll be. I have to find… How do I?"

Both men glance at each other nervously, concern and alarm obvious.

"Quickly!"

Taken aback, one of the men stutters and points in confusion. "Go through that door, along to the end. You'll see a single door to some steps. Go right to the bottom, you'll find them there. Are you sure you…"

Jack raises trembling hands briefly in a gesture of appreciation before half-staggering through the doors. As he ploughs through, he hears one of the men shouting, asking again if he is okay.

Underneath thin soaking cotton, Jack's skin is alight with the strange invisible fire of Stage Two. Somehow, during this time, he must remain as calm as possible. To keep dampening down, to keep scratching, to keep breathing. In and out. In and out. In and out. What was it Dr LeFarge said again? Inhale for six, hold for three and exhale for?

*What was it?*

As Jack swings and staggers from one wall to the other, he tries to remember, tries to think of a number. Any number. He counts them out loud, hearing each one echo along the empty corridor. Trying to think clearly, to concentrate on each sound.

Jack staggers clumsily across patterned purple and black carpet. A sick-inducing, repetitive, angular design, forcing his eyes to focus ahead. Seeing the prize at the end, a single door marked 'Staff Only' which he eventually throws open with a victorious shout.

Stumbling into an empty stairwell, he grabs hold of the metal banister and half-steps half-slides down several flights of stairs. As he spirals down haphazardly, he lets out a delirious wail.

Barging through the only door at the bottom, Jack stumbles past a line of abandoned trolleys, each laden with stacks of fresh laundry. Passing by several other blank wooden doors, scanning each one feverishly, he finally reaches his destination.

Pausing momentarily to gulp stale corridor air, Jack holds out a quivering hand and lays it on a gold effect push-plate. With chest heaving, hyperventilating almost, Jack throws open the door and storms inside, ready to face the violence of Stage Three.

He stops and spins around in the modest, lightly perfumed space. One small wash basin. One large rectangular mirror. Two urinals. Two cubicles.

The cubicles? Yes.

Jack lets out a cry and staggers forward, pushing violently against one of the doors. Unlocked, the thin door bounces and clatters against the side, revealing only empty space within.

Jack steps back, arms and legs shaking, face twisting with invisible fumes, eyes sensing victory, glancing wickedly at the only hiding place left. The only place it can possibly be…

"Got you fucker…"

Through gritted teeth, Jack launches forward at the second door, the locked panel buckling but resisting the fierce charge. Immediately, Jack steps back and launches forward again with a loud wail. This time the simple lock behind the door splinters, pieces of it clattering to the hard floor.

Instantly, Jack is thrown back by the occupant on the other side. Someone who had been hiding there. Someone who looks exactly like Jack. Someone holding a large bottle of pills, the contents of which now spill and scatter across the floor. Someone we can call Stage Three Jack or even Jack Two.

Each Jack grapples with the other, trying to gain an upper hand, piling out the cubicle and pirouetting clumsily across the hard floor. Each holding the other in check, spinning round, first one way then another. Eventually, with hands wrapped around each throat, both clatter into the confines of the small cubicle once again.

Jack One seethes and spits, shaking body awash with Stage Three. "I knew you were here…"

Jack Two doesn't answer. His face cold, blank, expressionless. He stares at Jack One, maintaining his unwavering, vice-like grip.

With a howl, Jack One leans back to release an arm then, summing up the last dregs of strength, lashes a frenzied fist towards Jack Two.

Jack's eyes flicker open. Pitch black. Night?

The itch again, like a fire crawling across his skin.

He leaps from his bed and bolts across the short landing, snapping the light on in the bathroom and shocking the man standing there. A man that looks *exactly like him*, holding a small knife in his hand which drops immediately to the floor when Jack One lashes out. Grabbing his Stage Three intruder by the throat, throttling him, spinning round and round in the small bathroom.

"Found you..." Grimacing, shaking, straining. "Go. Away!"

"Jack?" A voice from somewhere in the darkness. "Is everything alright through there?"

Jack's eyes flicker open. Daylight now. Squirming, he takes in the whole of the meeting room. Skin burning as he glances at the line of bored faces around the square table.

"I just need to, eh... I need to have a few minutes, get some air. Won't be long..."

Jack slides his chair quietly over hard-wearing carpet and bites down on his tongue. One of his favourite alleviation techniques for dealing with the onset of Stage Two.

He glances at a couple of the faces again. Pulling his gaze away quickly when he notices one of his colleagues already studying him closely, wearing a slightly quizzical, bemused expression.

"You feeling alright, Jack?"

He exits the room slowly before running and smashing through several doors. Clambering up a stairwell. Shoes on concrete steps. Breeze block wall and naked metal banister to the side. Crawling under a large yellow chain barring the way at the top. Pressing metal behind an external door then walking out into grey and blue. Skipping past vents, assorted funnels and other outlets dotted across an expanse of flat roof. Spinning round. Searching.

And seeing *him* there. Someone who looks exactly like he does. Someone we might call Stage Three Jack or Jack Two. Someone standing on the very edge of the roof.

"No!"

Jack One sprints forward, stopping just behind. Carefully wrapping his arms around Jack Two and dragging him back from the edge of the roof, collapsing down to sharp stone.

Then the sound of a door closing?

Jack's eyes flicker open. Familiar shelves, boxes and service trolleys. The stockroom?

*Not the stockroom again...*

Him. Something clatters to the floor. *What is it now?*

Voices?

Jack's eyes fire open, inviting bright sunlight. Ahead, deep shades of calm blue sea meet lighter shades of blue sky, mixed with thin wispy trails of white. He stares at the near straight line in the far distance where they meet, looking at several small boats on the horizon.

He glances right, ragged coastline rising to cliffs, sweeping round and beyond. Then he looks to the left, with its near empty flat beach and rolling sand dunes behind.

Exhaling peacefully, Jack lets his gaze wander across a handful of strangers. Some lying semi-naked under the warm sun, others walking along the shore aimlessly. Away to the left, a solitary dog splashes and runs in a variety of circles, retrieving a bright yellow ball thrown into the water by its owner.

Jack gets to his feet. There is something strangely inviting about the water. He lifts his shades, perching them on his head, staring at the gentle movement of the waves. Watching. Absorbing. Studying. Rolling forward quickly and dissolving.

He drops the shades to the towel and kicks off his sandals. Sand slipping underfoot, he skips forward to the water. It laps around his ankles, the temperature somewhere cool at first then getting colder. He continues, the water higher now, reaching above his knees, the top of his legs, his waist.

Jack turns when he hears someone shrieking and sprinting into the water behind him. Unable to avoid the attack, he flies sideways and sinks. Throwing an arm up instantly, trying to break the surface and reach for air. But the other familiar body wrestles on top, pushing him back down into the water.

"No!" Spluttering. Struggling. "Help!"

Jack kicks and lashes in desperation, eventually managing to wriggle free, slipping from his attacker's hold. This other person who looks like Jack. The one we might call Stage Three Jack, Jack Two or even Another Jack or…

With lungs and legs now beginning to burn, Jack drags himself back towards the beach. But he is soon knocked over, landing awkwardly in shallower water. Coughing. Choking. Trying to resist his attacker with movements increasingly tired, his strength ebbing away.

"Help!"

Pinned on wet sand, Jack One watches as Jack Two raises his fists and punches hard into his torso. Another punch lands, as though seeking to burst through the skin itself, almost cutting Jack One in half. He howls and winces, gritting his teeth, able to neither protect himself or escape. Writhing in slow motion; a third massive blow. A blow that tears through skin and bone with a sickening crunch, plunging straight inside his body.

Jack One shrieks and heaves in terror, eyes wide open, looking at the huge ragged hole in his torso. Seeing part of a broad arm submerged inside, shaking with strain as it grips and pulls at something within.

Jack One watches as the quivering arm slowly – painfully slowly – pulls and forces. Something dark and glistening, shining like a huge, ragged column of thick oil.

"No!" Jack screams out. "There is no Stage Four!"

The dark, shining fluid spits and spills, forming a mess of puddles on the sand nearby, flowing like thick black mercury. Jack One shrieks in agony, horrified at the sight of the gaping wound and the frenzy of his attacker. Straining. Pulling. Hauling something outwards. Something that moves, something alive inside the strange substance.

Then, without warning, Stage Three Jack or Jack Two falls backwards. As though the last shred of connection inside the body of Jack One snaps, with no resistance left to hold the dreadful oily mass inside.

Quickly, Jack One staggers over to where Jack Two is wheezing and rolling on the sand, as though *his* entire body is now on fire. He grabs Jack Two's face, pulling the skin upwards, which stretches easily like a thick glue. As he stretches the skin, he wraps it across his own body, moving it round and round, where it mysteriously sinks beneath, as though being absorbed.

He pulls the skin further, wrapping and pushing his limbs and body inside quickly. Forcing himself on, glancing warily at the slimy, warped figure now struggling to climb from the dark puddle nearby. Watching as terrible and pathetic limbs attempt to rise, each quivering as though cold. And amidst the darkness of what might be a face, only a strange and dreadful mouth, with several rows of sharp white teeth like thin needles and a tiny light within.

In a frenzy, Jack pulls the last of the skin across, watching as it drops and fades into him. Wearing it like a costume, now indistinguishable from his own.

"I did it…" Jack howls violently as the small creature bares its sharp teeth, making a strange hissing sound. "I did it!"

Jack watches as the creature now rolls backwards wailing. It slips away slowly, down into the oily mess. Weak, quivering limbs clawing the air in vain, unable even to struggle, as the strange slimy form sinks from sight. And as it slides away, the dark shining pools scattered across the sand evaporate.

"Jack?"

Hearing the voice but not hearing, Jack rubs sand from his arms and looks down at his torso. The skin there unbroken. The terrible wound of mere seconds ago now gone.

"Jack, are you okay? I just went to get some ice cream."

Mumbling. Shaking.

"We really need to talk."

On his knees, Jack turns slowly, his expression bewildered as he stares at a smiling, happy Aisling. Her long chestnut hair tied back, wearing a bright summer top and a light cotton shawl over her shoulder. Standing with arms outstretched and both hands burning intensely, each consumed totally with fire.

"I'm pregnant Jack."

# Nestor 33 and The Uncertain Destiny of The One-Eyed Dog

Darkness.

Breathing. Irregular and shallow.

Moments…

Diffuse overhead lighting flickers. Quickly flooding a cramped, functional living space in cool, hard white. Everything – most things – pristine. Edges straight, some curved.

Four walls.

A striped glass shutter cuts into the far corner of the room. Directly beside a narrow white panel door, smooth, almost invisible except for a dark circular handle. On the far wall, a row of metal dispensers with a tiny sink positioned underneath, low units running towards a modest square table at the front of the room. On the near side, close to the single main door, several tall and narrow panels. Two of the folding doors ajar, revealing a line of neat grey overalls and other utility garments hanging inside.

A soothing artificial voice. "Good morning 33…"

Inside the sleeping alcove, two old, lined eyes open to reveal weary, yellowing eyeballs, staring ahead.

"Weather is… fair. Chance of rain… 5%."

Nestor stares at several torn images fixed haphazardly to the low ceiling above, tired eyes gradually focusing the middle picture. A large image, ragged and ripped along one side, showing a bird perched high on a branch. Plumage like fire, sparks of brilliant red and yellow. Head turned to the side revealing a graceful golden bill and one dark, keen eye. The backdrop indistinct, blurry, likely a forest somewhere, all green and lush.

"You have… one… new message 33. Playing…"

The voice changes to an abrasive but engaging masculine tone. "Nestor? It's Arlo. Drop into the office before your shift. Got some things to, eh, discuss. Won't take long…"

The female voice soothes again. "Message Ends."

Lifting his remaining human arm, Nestor attempts to trace the outline of the bird with an outstretched finger. As he moves, his hand begins to twitch, softly at first, then transforming to a stubborn trembling.

He lifts his other arm, all curved metal beam, polished plates and strong micro-gearing. Steadying the shaking limb, he guides it carefully, tracing the outline of the bird above. Metal parts quietly whirring before falling back to the bed.

No smile. Only weary eyes acknowledging another day.

"Early shift begins in… fifty-eight minutes."

Nestor inhales. Chest rattling at first, expanding only slightly. Then he carefully lowers his legs to smooth white floor and inspects each, part of his usual morning custom. Checking for any wear or damage that might have gone unnoticed from the day before. Anything that might require immediate attention from the mech staff.

He examines the arrangements of strong, curved metal shafts and the various partially covered fluid cables wrapped and clamped along each artificial limb. Using his human arm to lightly feel the patches of skin-like plastic stretched across certain areas, Nestor lifts and exercises each foot in turn. He watches mechanical ripples of movement, with a barely discernible whir, from toe to heel to ankle to lower leg. Content with their functioning, Nestor rises gently from the edge of the bed, joints clicking and exhaling softly.

Straightening, Nestor pushes one metal and one human arm under the light cloth tabard covering his torso. Lifting it over his head, he looks across all that is left. That momentary reflection, this morbid daily ritual of his, acknowledging the fusion of human and machine that has come to represent him.

More replacement than human now, his advanced age even rendering some of the technology that sustains him near obsolete too. A thought that always raises a flicker of a tired half-smile. Even his limbs, the very machinery that sustains his life, is no longer the cutting edge. No longer exemplifying the sheer boldness, the wonder, the magic of decades before.

Nestor lifts his mechanical arm to his chest, an area half-consumed in dull metal that fades into a dirty line, where metal and tough plastic meet withered skin. Several buttons and lights sit in a compact row above two clear windows buried there. One, shaped in a circle, contains a deep brown liquid with the thickness of oil. The other, a thin horizontal gauge, contains a clear fluid, like water. Nestor presses one of the buttons which fires some embedded circuitry into life. A blue light blinks and steadies while an initial monitoring process engages. The horizontal gauge shifts the tiniest of fractions, injecting a small amount of Psylinax directly into his bloodstream.

Nestor stretches his trembling human arm out, studying it coolly as the tremors instantly fade, succumbing to the effects of the drug. He clenches his fist and releases it, watching worn skin fold and tighten. His mouth shaping soundless words in approval, his malfunctioning vocal circuits having never been repaired.

"Early shift begins in… forty-eight minutes."

Dropping the nightshirt into the laundry chute in the wall, Nestor pushes a narrow panel door at the side of the glass-fronted washroom. Moving into a tiny, brightly lit utility space he attends to the waste-sac that has filled overnight. Depositing the old and replacing with new, Nestor saunters out and into the adjacent washing space. Pulling the thin glass door behind, he closes his eyes as the machinery inside makes the sound of a gentle storm, first cleaning every surface, then drying.

Stepping from the washroom, Nestor inhales the light perfume deeply, staring at his face in the strip of a mirror fixed on the wall near the dispensers. A smile flickers when he notices the thick, irregular tufts of silver and white hair sticking out comically from his blemished scalp. He lifts his machine arm and brushes with metal fingers, the unkempt hair flattening with every pass then slowly rising again.

"Early shift begins in… thirty-eight minutes."

Retrieving and slipping on a clean, two-part undergarment first, Nestor then unhooks a heavy grey overall from a hanger in the wardrobe. Sitting on the edge of the bed again, he methodically pulls on the uniform, covering each piece of metal and skin. Rising, he zips the front of the dark company overall and finishes by pressing several studs down the front. Straightening out the garment with both arms, he inhales deeply, thoughtfully. Touching the embroidered rectangular badge on one side, feeling the simple curved 'Citi-Clean' logo and 'Nestor 33' woven underneath in bold letters.

***

Nestor stands in the large lift with several other collectors, everyone silent in early morning weariness. When the doors open, they step into a cavernous, sprawling garage area. The Citi-Clean hub already bustling, loud, having the air of a busy factory. Alive with the frenzy of activity, typical of the shift change window.

Nestor walks carefully along an outlined pathway. One edge continuous, the other formed of thick white dashes. The broken lines used by the guidance systems of various patrolling utility bots, slowly moving around the entire hub circuit.

The expansive space is dominated by yellow-marked vehicle bays, each with a towering repair station to one side, always draped in a busy selection of cables, tools and safety equipment. Alongside the portable frames and racks, standing where the two parking bays meet side by side, large cylindrical charging points rise from the concrete. Dark, grubby machines covered in various gauges and lights. Long, thick, heavy cables draping down each side.

Painted in white on the concrete at the front of the bay is the section number. A reference indicating the section of the city that specific collector and 'bullet' cart is assigned to. The collectors affectionately using the term 'bullet' as a reference to the overall shape of the bulky vehicles and as an ironic dig at their slow maximum speed. As Nestor walks past each bay, he does what he always does and counts the numbers, hearing the progression in his head.

Smaller utility vehicles buzz almost manically in front of and around the parked carts. Orange lights flashing as they criss-cross with each other in the middle of the extensive space. Metal workers around a bullet cart queen, moving quickly with purpose, always hurrying to load and unload the various large cages and tanks each bullet cart carries.

A few electric engines whine as the section mechs power them up, running and recording the typical pre-shift checks and making any last-minute adjustments. Nestor catches loud fragments of the exchanges as he passes behind the bays, guessing from the words he hears whether the exchange will end in either a thumbs up or down. An outcome usually dependent on whether the mech is still mainly human or not.

Nestor follows the white line to the next section, stopping to move sideways every so often. Letting both weary night shift workers and slow-moving robot drones pass uninterrupted.

"Hey, Nestor!"

Lynette lowers herself from the cab and gestures at Nestor to come closer. She removes a pair of thin dark gloves and places them on the nearby repair station unit, revealing two shining metal hands underneath. Picking up a rag from nearby, she wipes her face and sighs, her shoulders dropping but her face smiling at Nestor as he slowly approaches. Two metal fists meet head-on gently in the usual informal collector greeting.

"Phew, am I tired…" Lynette grins comically. "Arlo got me doing 24 now. He's given 45 to Daven."

Nestor nods, retrieving a small ring-bound paper notepad and pen from a side pocket. He writes quickly, holding a few hastily scribbled words out to Lynette.

"Yeah, for sure. Arlo changed it, can you believe that? 45 wasn't bad. I mean, it's always had a rep' right?" Lynette shrugs. "But nothing ever happened. Not to me. Alright, a bit of cart damage from time to time but who doesn't have that? I mean, ah saw a lot of shit Nestor, but they keep to their own out there y'know? *You* don't mess, *they* don't mess."

Nestor scrawls another note, enquiring about 24.

"Ugh, 24 is kind of, boring. I mean it's a lot quieter, dead in fact. Didn't see a soul last night. That's the thing ain't it? You get closer to the centre, it's dead. D-E-ED."

Nestor raises silver eyebrows and tips his head, a gesture to imply this might not be a bad thing.

"Ah, maybe you're right. Maybe I should be thankful. I mean. There's less graffiti to clean off the side of the bullet now…" Lynette laughs, tapping her hand on the side of the cart. "And Arlo should be happier. My Psylinax consumption is going to go through the floor there."

A younger woman in overalls, with a pale, weary, dirt-stained face, taps Lynette on the shoulder. "Collector, we need to talk about the daily wear on your front brakes?"

"Yeah…"

"And the drop links, the daily tyre wear…?"

Lynette brushes off the interruption. "Okay, Rhoda, sure. Be there in a second when I'm done here."

Rhoda bites her lip, pulling an irritated expression as Lynette turns to face Nestor again. Pausing briefly, she returns to the front of the bay, continuing with the inspection.

"So, you still in 33 Nestor?"

Nestor nods.

"I passed the edge earlier on, scenic route, y'know?" Lynette leans forward, speaking quietly. "See they've finally opened Eden Terrace? Probably explains why there's more security along the river these days. Bet you've seen some shit down there too, eh? Along the canal?"

Nestor shrugs and scribbles one word: sometimes.

"Heh, I'll bet…" Lynette smiles knowingly. "Right, let me straighten this shit out with the mech and get my tanks unloaded. Then it's sleep time for me because I am *tired.* I've had to cover a few extra shifts recently and that's all it takes. Man, I am wiped out… Hey, aren't you running a little late this morning, Nestor 33?"

Nestor points first to himself, then all the way across to a small office, tucked away near a large concrete incline with several barriers.

"Arlo? You got to see Arlo? Huh, good luck with that!"

Nestor nods. Assuming a vaguely bemused expression.

"You take care, Nestor." Lynette steps even closer. "And hey, y'know, we all look out for you round here. You and a few of the other old-timers. You can trust us. Just watch Arlo? Heard a few things y'know? Company's watching him tight these days…" Then Lynette steps back, breaking off and adopting her previous lighter tone. "Just like I can watch you now… Now I'm here in the second wing."

The lines in Nestor's face deepen as he smiles then screws his face in mock pain and silent laughter. Lynette grins, holding out a metal fist once more. Nestor meets it slowly head-on with his own.

"Safe shift. And think about me? Sleeping!"

Holding up a metal thumb, Nestor retreats carefully from the yellow bay and continues along the route outlined by white lines. At a break in the pathway just ahead, he stops to let a small utility vehicle, complete with spinning orange light and harassed driver, pass in front. Several platform units trundle and rattle behind, each loaded with a fresh tank and cage, ready for distribution.

Finally reaching his home bay row, Nestor smiles when he hears the familiar whine of his own bullet cart winding up. To the untrained ear, all the cart engines sound identical when they start, but not to Nestor. He can easily pick out his own bullet cart from the others.

"Morning, collector. New tank is in place, routine checks are fine. Probably leave off on some of the filters until later, all that canal water you use... Oh, and that new battery we put in a while back? It's holding the charge well considering we're not using top line kit any more. You're heading out now?"

Nestor shakes his head, holding out an arm, pointing at the corner office.

"Meeting? Okay, I'll power her down then. But she's good to go when you're done."

Before Nestor turns away, he runs his human hand down one surface of the vehicle. The touch is cold, smooth, with hidden bumps and dents still detectable under the white paint, scars Nestor secretly delights in. He taps the surface of the vehicle lovingly with his human arm before returning to the path, following it round and out the section, into a much wider, open space.

Passing through a simple, short gate, Nestor walks alongside the office building as several early shift bullet carts drive past, stopping briefly at the main barriers and concrete ramp ahead.

Creeping round the edge of the office building, with most of the vertical window blinds closed, Nestor pauses when he hears Arlo's raised voice from inside. The brusque tone floating easily through the open door.

"Don't know what kind of damn miracle worker she thinks I am, Bade..."

"It'll be okay. We made some changes. We're doing alright so far?"

Arlo guffaws. "Ain't that grand, doing alright. Let me tell you something, Bade, something they probably don't teach you in that business school you came from. It's not about doing *alright*… I've been running things here for over twenty-five years. Twenty-five lousy fucking years and guess what? For every year in the last ten? I'm getting poorer year on year. Bonus gone. Margins shot. Now it's just cut this. Cut that. Yeah, doing alright… I got a fucking incinerator to run, carts to fix. I got people to keep happy… How long you been here, Bade?"

"Eight months."

"Eight months!" Arlo laughs, a distinctive, staccato cackling sound. "*That,* my young friend, is why I manage the site and you deal with the customers. Huh, doing alright…"

"You could have had a droid instead? They design them at the school."

"Ha, funny. Yeah, you got me there, Bade, you got me. Give me a light for this… Nah, she's got it in for me, I swear. All this tour the site, check the records, meet the crews stuff. Like the company actually gives a shit. As long as their backers are cared for… Nah, they just want something to pin on me. Why else is she coming back now? She was here a couple of days after you started, a whole eight months ago… Ah, Collector!"

Suddenly Nestor steps through the open doorway, causing the conversation to stop abruptly when he walks into the bright but cramped reception space.

Embarrassed, Bade holds up a thin, nervous hand as a greeting but is unable to look the visitor in the eyes. Instead, he sinks down in his seat and switches his attention immediately to the long, brightly lit curved screens on his desk. Arlo shows no such embarrassment, throwing thick welcoming arms in the air.

Slipping an arm ending in a cigar across Nestor's shoulders. "Rule number one, Bade, always treat your staff well. Nestor 33 here? One of the best, the most loyal, trustworthy... Faithful service to me and Citi-Clean for years."

Bade looks up from the screen, nodding uncertainly. His young face blank, tired, still a shade embarrassed.

"Bade, I need ten minutes with the collector here, no interruptions." Arlo opens the nearby door to his personal office, gesturing for Nestor to follow. "I won't hold you back, I know you're on earlies."

Nestor nods, stepping softly into an unlit, familiar office.

"Take a seat, Collector."

Nestor sits on one of the two swivel chairs in front of the modest, heavy wooden desk that once belonged to Arlo's grandfather. He watches Arlo systematically open each vertical blind, pausing at one of the windows, gazing out at several departing bullet carts.

"I'm proud of what I've built here, Nestor. Proud of what we do, keeping the city clean."

Nestor scans the desk in front as he always does, looking for the few framed images usually parked there amidst the mess of paper. Mainly pictures of Arlo and family, all blurry smiles and exaggerated gestures. But strangely today Nestor is unable to see them, presumably lost and submerged in the forever turmoil of Arlo's desk. Only scraps of the wood surface are noticeable around the edges, the entire surface flooded with shabby paper, spreading across to several low columns of cardboard boxes rising from the floor.

At the back of the desk, behind a narrow sign on the edge that reads 'Arlo Zamek - Manager', an original bulky site communication system juts upward through the swamp of paper. A curved, ungainly black plastic unit dominated by a long panel of switches, with an old headset hanging from a tall piece of metal. On the other side of the desk, a thick, curved metal arm with a monitor on the end manages to keep its head above the water. To the side of the monitor, arranged in a rough triangle on the floor, are three wastepaper baskets full of crumpled paper balls. Each individual basket having a number attached to the top: 5, 10, 25.

"And I'm proud that we can trust each other, Nestor. You and I, we understand each other, eh?" Arlo takes a puff from his cigar before moving to his desk and resting it in a round glass ashtray, perched atop a hefty pile of paper. "Coffee?"

Nestor shakes his head. Watching Arlo take one of the mugs on his desk, inspect it briefly, then pour himself some coffee from a dispenser perched on a utility unit nearby. Taking a sip, Arlo shuffles a few papers around to find a more convenient space at the front of the desk for the mug. Then he collapses into the slightly tattered, high-backed chair, exhaling deeply, staring back at Nestor.

"They're watching me. Been watching me for some time."

Nestor remains blank for a moment, then retrieves the notepad and pen from his overalls.

"'course I'm sure!" Lifting the cigar, drawing deeply. "Had my suspicions for the last couple of years but, just recently…"

Nestor scrawls on the paper quickly, holding it up to Arlo.

"Yeah, the company. Of course..." Arlo leans forward wearily, rearranging some papers to clear space for elbows. "You know what this means, don't you?"

Nestor glances away, frowning.

"Your operation? It's still not good news, eh?" Arlo waves a hand in the air, as though chasing an invisible fly. "I keep asking for you... But there's nothing I can do right now. I eh, I can't push it, you understand right?"

Nestor lowers his gaze to the floor as the disappointment lands. Another one, in a near monotonous long line of similar disappointments. With frustration building, Nestor notices his human hand beginning to tremble. A shaking met with the softest exhalation, almost a whisper, as a tiny amount of Psylinax is automatically injected into his system.

"I don't like it either, Nestor, but I don't have much choice right now. Too much heat. They're paying too much attention. To me. To the whole site. I even got Vinnia Fairchild coming out again. It's just a tour she says. Yeah right, just a tour..."

Arlo puffs on the cigar as Nestor scribbles further: *make the request again.*

"Are you listening, Nestor? Or are those eh..." Arlo spins a hand round in the air, "...hearing circuits fading as well?"

Nestor shakes his head, staring off through the window, watching orange light spin and bounce.

Arlo raises his voice, adopting his more typically ebullient tone. "'course I'm going to ask again but what I'm trying to say is, right now, it's not so easy, eh? I need to cool it for a while. I mean, I want my team to be 100% but I got to be careful here. You're not the only one, eh? I can't keep rocking the boat more than I already have, can't keep making demands, attracting more attention. I need to protect things, eh? The business?"

Nestor flicks over a piece of paper and scrawls again, showing it to Arlo.

"What did they say?" Arlo shrugs. "Does it matter? They say what they always say. You don't need to speak to hold a street vac. It's not a priority repair, you've been doing alright without it for so long now it doesn't matter. And then there's the new cuts this year. The usual stuff…"

Nestor droops one shoulder and begins to stand. Arlo immediately holds up a hand.

"Wait, Nestor. I know it's disappointing, always the same response. I get it, I get it!" Adopting a quieter tone. "But we got another option. Just wait a minute, hear me out."

Nestor lowers himself back to the seat.

Arlo glances warily at the office door then clears his throat, talking quietly. "Look, if we can increase the supply… To Laszlo? Maybe we can get the repairs done… elsewhere? Privately, y'know?"

Nestor stares ahead. Lined eyes weary with age, with fatigue and the never-ending reflection that with Arlo there must always be another condition. The way it has always been.

"It's the best I can do right now."

Nestor opens his mouth then closes slowly, as though forgetting that words will not come. He taps the pen several times on the notepad, as though unsure what to write, staring at Arlo. Both separated by at least fifty years, a body of life-saving embedded cyborg technology and now a draining, uncomfortable silence.

Nestor nods his head softly and places pen and paper in a side pocket. He rises from the seat and slowly moves to the door.

"Oh and, Nestor…"

Metal hand already on the door handle, turning slowly.

"You gotta watch your levels?"

Nestor looks over his shoulder.

"Your consumption charts? You're not going to make the new limits with these numbers."

Nestor watches Arlo lift his short chubby frame from the chair, sighing and wincing in slight pain as he steps closer.

"Look, eh… When I was younger, just starting in the collection business, I used to take time out. Every day. I'd go to the edge of the city and just sit for a while. Y'know, let the stress fade a little. That routine helped me, made me react to things differently. Why don't you try it, might help bring your usage down? 33 isn't far from the edge of the city, you got Paulson Glen nearby, on the other side of the Terrace. You can go up there after your shift every day? Try and… recharge."

Nestor reflects briefly on the idea, feasible of course and might even have some benefit, perhaps bringing his worrying Psylinax consumption down closer to currently required levels. But for how long? How long before those levels are reduced even further? What then for Nestor, the longest serving and most heavily transformed collector in the whole hub? He's long given up on the dream of ever being Psylinax-free. And then there's the exhaustion to think about. At the end of most shifts, all Nestor can think about is returning to base quickly and moving to early downtime.

Even so, the thought strangely intrigues Nestor. He retrieves the paper and pen, scribbling quickly.

"Your time?" Arlo grins and chuckles slyly. "Look, I'll sort out the paperwork. You keep Laszlo happy. I'll worry about Bade. Just eh, try and keep things low key, y'know? Not so obvious? I don't want other collectors getting suspicious. Don't want them blabbing to Vinnia that you're getting special privileges, know what I'm sayin'?"

Bade looks up from behind his many screens when Nestor and Arlo step back into reception. He nods as Nestor passes his desk, shuffling towards the main door.

Arlo calls out behind, "Safe shift collector!"

But Nestor doesn't respond, already slipping back along the pathway and stopping for a moment to let a short cylindrical utility droid pass by.

When he reaches his bay, he brushes a hand across the bullet cart and pulls open a large panel on the side, inspecting a row of tools all attached neatly.

Whatever the thinking, whatever the deep frustration and conflict inside, it sinks back to noise as thoughts return immediately to the start of the shift. It allows for nothing else, focusing Nestor entirely on last-minute equipment checks and the cleaning duties ahead.

***

Under steadily lightening grey sky, a lonely bullet cart travels silently, casting two bright steady beams in front. In the modest cab, Nestor holds the steering bars lightly, almost letting the vehicle drive itself.

As he drifts, he makes shapes with his mouth. Attempting in vain to hum along with the jazz music playing in the cab, concentrating on each note as much as the deserted road in front. Ignoring the few scattered delivery vehicles and transporters interrupting the solitary mood.

Nestor has always enjoyed cab time since the last round of limb replacements. His pain-free metal legs now considerably more suited for any journey, long or short, far superior to the endless aching and trembling discomfort of old flesh and blood. Even on the relatively short section 33 commute, the difference has been nothing short of remarkable. Every shift starting without pain. No stiffness. No aching. But, just as Nestor begins to feel overawed by the difference, a humbling voice rises inside to remind him. There's no pain because there's no feeling, either good or bad. No feeling left at all.

Foot steady on the acceleration plate, Nestor slips off the main route and travels under several sprawling concrete spiders that carry roads overhead in all directions. Navigating familiar lanes that edge section 33, he bypasses several commercial sites, every one of them drowning in a huge ring of makeshift, dilapidated worker camps. Each haphazard home jammed together, permitting only narrow and disordered spaces between.

Once upon a time, the random tents and coverings were few and transient. A distant memory, but one that Nestor can still remember, even though its age means it has the quality of a dream to it. Just enough for Nestor to doubt whether the images are accurate.

Slowing to avoid a few of the dishevelled inhabitants standing at the side of the main road, Nestor avoids meeting the stare of the several few weary souls that lift tired and dirty faces as the cart passes.

Awake. But still asleep...

Instinctively, Nestor lowers the volume of the music as he passes and looks straight ahead – something every collector is trained to do while moving past any of the worker camp areas. As he passes by, he hears the voice of Lynette 24 from earlier: *"You don't mess, they don't mess."*

Nestor moves from private to public territory, steering the bullet cart onto a narrow, unmarked road that runs parallel to a large canal. The dark water flows gently between two wide sloping concrete banks, each broad grey line fringed with a thick stripe of grass and wild undergrowth.

The canal runs straight, eventually disappearing into a curving concrete structure further along, an artificial hill that carries the single road up and over the water. Passing in front of several luxurious, sleekly designed apartment blocks rising skyward from the crest of the hill. The new exclusive development: Eden Terrace.

Nestor slows the bullet cart down, slipping into a low gear and trundling over an uneven grassy area, steering onto gently declining concrete. As he straightens out, he notices another larger vehicle ahead. A small capacity white transporter, parked at an awkward angle back from the large gates, through which water passes underneath Eden Terrace.

Nestor activates the locks in the cab and approaches cautiously, bringing the vehicle to a stop close, but not too close. As the bullet cart whines quietly, Nestor carefully surveys the scene through the windscreen. He waits patiently, nervously, for any sign of life around the seemingly abandoned vehicle.

It's right to be cautious. Nestor has experienced some of the canal area history first-hand across the years, all the smuggling, the robberies, the murders. Here in the cab, Nestor knows that while those terrible recollections may fade, trauma always finds a way to survive in flesh or even metal. Always lingering just beyond, in strange dreams and actions, eased only through Psylinax.

Yet, in recent times, with the all-seeing wall cameras of Eden Terrace now tirelessly scanning the luxury apartment complex, the crime level has dropped considerably. The monitoring, the increased security on the ground, the presence of huge work teams for months, forcing most of the crime out of section 33 entirely.

Content that the scene appears to be clear, Nestor disengages the engine and opens the door, heavy safety boots stepping carefully to concrete. He slides open a tall panel just behind the cab and unclips a short metal baton, gripping it tightly in a metal hand.

Then, just as he quietly lowers the panel in place, he hears it. A twisted, barely audible cry for help, followed by a terrible mix of gasping, groaning, then silence again.

Trembling at the sound, Nestor creeps towards the abandoned vehicle. Staring through the cab window and noticing the door on the other side is wide open. Holding the baton in front, Nestor moves round the front of the vehicle, following the sound of horribly laboured breathing.

As he turns, the full sight is revealed. A motionless body slumped against the side of the vehicle. Legs spreadeagled, arms hanging limply at the side, hands resting open on blood splattered concrete. Clothes ripped and punctured, with blood draining from terrible wounds underneath. Eyes narrowing then widening, peering from a horribly swollen, blood-stained face, pleading as Nestor approaches.

"Help…"

Nestor recoils immediately at the sight, old skin freezing in sudden terror. The shock succumbing to a terrible, violent, disabling trembling. The baton drops to the concrete and rolls away, Nestor, having no choice but to clamp his metal arm to his one remaining flesh and blood limb, in a vain attempt to stop the shaking.

Barely moving, with a dying breath. "Call… Please…"

But Nestor can't speak, can't react, can't move in any way. Metal limbs rooted to the spot in fear, supporting an upper body now quivering violently.

Several large doses of Psylinax are administered immediately. The drug taking hold quickly, pacifying and soothing. Several terrible seconds of softly diminishing frenzy pass, then Nestor attempts to speak.

"Help…" Eyes looking upward, distant. "Please…"

Nestor reaches a softly trembling hand forward but it's too late, the driver slips to complete silence. The patches of skin not drenched in blood already, turning a sickly grey.

Leaning closer, eyes drowsy, heavy, laced with Psylinax and sadness. Nestor covers his mouth with a human hand while he reaches out with metal fingers, touching bloody skin uncertainly. From somewhere inside, swimming on the heavy dose of Psylinax, he hears a blood-curdling scream followed by several gun shots. He flinches, studying the blood on his metal fingertips, seeing the pattern there.

Suddenly a burst of static leaps from the nearby cab, drawing Nestor away from the corpse. He stretches up, moving along the side of the transporter, looking inside. Incredibly, the entire dashboard and all the electronics underneath have been stripped away, leaving only empty spaces and bare chassis behind. Broken shards of curved plastic and a small assortment of ripped cabling lie scattered on the floor.

Another burst of static, this time accompanied with a faint voice. "2-40?"

Nestor climbs up and stretches inside, placing his metal arm under the seat. Touch sensors eventually locating a small, circular communications device.

"2-40, have you reached your destination?"

Climbing down to the concrete, Nestor examines the simple device. A cheap, generic model, not company branded. A sign that suggests the driver might be a low-level trader, working for a small organisation.

Static. "2-40? Can you confirm arrival?"

Instinctively, Nestor lifts the device to his mouth as though to answer. Then he pauses, realising his mistake, dropping his head before switching the device off completely. After a moment, he places it on the concrete, next to a bloody, motionless hand.

Walking to the rear of the vehicle, he tips the two metal locks at the bottom of the large roller shutter door. Strangely, neither lock was fully secured, which may explain why the rear of the vehicle shows no signs of forced entry.

Nestor rolls the door upwards, just enough to reveal what's inside. Columns of small brown cardboard boxes all stacked equally from wall to wall. A few at the front have been disturbed, as though quickly investigated then discarded messily. All scattered on top of each other, creating a chaotic flurry of packaging and…

…shoes.

The frown gives way to a flicker of a smile as Arlo's words echo from earlier. *"If we can increase the supply… Maybe we can get the repairs done…"*

Nestor reaches up to the bottom of the metal door and lowers it gently. He turns to look at the bullet cart parked further along the concrete. There's no space for all this stock, the cages inside the bullet carts designed for only a few bulky items at the most. The fluid tanks could hold many but, as the shift hasn't even started yet, they're all full of liquids.

And Nestor needs all of this if there's any chance he's going to speak again. So, it's time. Time to return to the cab and message Laszlo. He'll know exactly what to do.

***

Nestor sweeps the power mop over the side of the grey concrete column. The large head spinning briskly, scrubbing the smooth concrete, slowly fading one arm of a large dark X symbol sprayed on the surface.

"What a mess. Every fucking pillar…"

Nestor pauses, looking over his shoulder, startled by the voice and unaware that a security guard is standing behind him.

"Why do they keep doing it?"

Nestor powers the mop down but the guard shakes his head.

"No. Don't stop. I want to watch it disappear."

Nestor flicks a switch and returns to the cleaning, perhaps a little self-consciously, moving the power mop over the rest of the graffiti. The weight of the stare from behind creating a small burn.

"You're the collector in this section, what's your name?"

Nestor moves his mouth but there is no sound, just the low drone of the cleaning unit. He gestures to his mouth before powering down again, propping the mop against the column and searching for pen and paper.

Stepping closer to the side. "You can't speak?"

Nestor scribbles messily, showing the guard his name.

"Nes-tor?" The guard smiles, holding out a hand. "I'm Inspector Callum. Call me Maurice though. I'm new here. Pleased to meet you…"

Nestor places the paper and pen in his pocket and hastily removes one of the thicker work gauntlets, holding out a metal hand.

Maurice recoils at the sight, his brow furrowing painfully, mouth twisting with distaste. "You're a fucking robot…"

Unnerved, Nestor hastily removes the other gauntlet, dropping it to the floor and stretching out a human hand.

Maurice steps back, a mixture of repulsion and confusion. "A fucking robot. Why'd they put a robot…"

The sight of the outstretched human hand has no effect, Maurice is unable to rip his gaze from the metal, the colour draining from his face. Putting his hand on another pillar with a large cross scrawled across it, Maurice bends over and heaves, vomiting violently on the ground.

Nestor quickly pulls on his tough work gauntlets, stepping slowly across to the retching security guard.

Choking. Heaving. One uniformed arm raised out as a warning. "Don't you fucking come near me…"

Nestor pauses, then retreats softly, lightly. Uncertain.

Maurice turns to look at him, eyes glassy, chest heaving, wiping his mouth with the back of a hand. "Didn't anyone tell your company that Mr Matthews fucking hates robots?"

Nestor casts his eyes downward, unsure what to say even if he could speak. He stretches out his arms, holding gloved hands up, trying to calm.

"What are you looking at? You'll clean this mess…" Maurice stretches up, the expression on his pale face hardening as he moves closer, threatening. "You're the fucking cleaner? You… You fucking clean it up before anyone sees it!"

Nestor trembles. His gloved metal hand reaching over, reassuring his shaking human arm.

"Clean it up and all the other mess." Maurice leans further in with threat, words drenched in spit. "Don't think I didn't see you earlier. I saw everything you were doing down there."

Nestor looks away, unable to contain a sense of guilt. Stress rising inside, necessitating a small dose of Psylinax.

"I've been watching you. Robot…" Stepping back slowly, Maurice spits a small amount of saliva that lands on Nestor's overall. "You better get this place clean and fast."

As Maurice moves away, Nestor nervously retrieves the power mop, wheeling the cylindrical power unit over to where the puddle of sick drapes down the pillar and gathers on the ground. He switches it on quickly, cleaning the mess.

Through the sound of the cleaning, Nestor hears Maurice howling back at him. "And stay out of sight! We don't want to see you, especially when Mr Matthews visits."

As Nestor concentrates once more on gradually disappearing paint, he watches Maurice from the corner of his eyes. Climbing a flight of concrete steps in the adjacent section, up towards a gate in a tall perimeter fence. He waits there for a moment, adjusting his helmet and uniform, before the gate opens and he steps inside.

***

Under late afternoon light, the bullet cart whines quietly on the grass, waiting on the next move.

Nestor sits inside, staring through the windscreen. Hands gripping the steering bars, jazz music playing softly in the cab. His lined face seemingly an age older in the mirror after a long shift, drained from the work and the incident with Inspector Callum. Even so, a sliver of restless energy remains, just enough to fuel a fog of hazy, uncertain reflection. Enough of a spark to consider meandering thoughts and vague ways forward.

To return to the Citi-Clean hub for downtime, or?

Again, Nestor hears an echo of Arlo speaking from earlier. Rising and falling words creating a deeper, stranger resonance:

*"Every day. I'd go to the edge of the city and just sit for a while. Y'know, let the stress fade a little. That routine helped me, made me react to things differently. Why don't you try it, might help bring your usage down?"*

Nestor glances wearily at the time on the dashboard, watching the backlit figures dance and melt, the unavoidable symptoms of higher than usual levels of Psylinax. The blur. Then focus. Blur. Focus.

After a moment, Nestor slowly releases the brake, edging the bullet cart forward then stopping again as the front wheels hit the side of the narrow road. Pausing only for a second, he steers the cart to the left. Following the canal further along then up and over the Eden Terrace rise, exiting the invisible territory of section 33.

The unmarked road on the far side meanders away from the canal, snaking through light forest towards a busy main road with late afternoon traffic passing either way.

Nestor carefully steers onto the carriageway that heads out of the city, speeding up to maximum, following broken painted lines on the concrete ahead. The bullet cart zips along silently, following the terrain as it ebbs and flows, heading steadily into hilly landscape.

Not far along, Nestor turns off the main road to follow an unmarked trail, a curving route that hugs the sides of several large hills. Climbing higher, Nestor acknowledges a boldly painted and badly damaged sign for Paulson Glen as he passes.

The music in the cab slides to silence. Leaving only the sound of tyres on uneven, dirty terrain to interrupt the quiet, peaceful ambience. Sunbeams flicker through blankets of tall, thickly gathered tree and shrub, all passing through late summer glamour.

Breaks in the cover offer more distant views, Nestor shifting his gaze left and right, the tranquillity around now soothing and energising him. The sight of distant hills and undulating fields, all earthy shades. The main highway far below, the traffic moving like metal ants.

In scattered places the road cuts deeper into the sides, creating modest vehicle passing places in the undergrowth. A few of those places, situated in more scenic areas, are accompanied with broader cleared sections, enough space for a handful of vehicles to park off the road. As Nestor passes, every single one of these areas is empty and overgrown. The whole place seemingly deserted.

Navigating the winding road, Nestor creeps up and along the side of the main hill. As he drives, he wonders whether this is the place Arlo talked about? Could this be the actual place that Arlo used to visit every day, all those years ago?

Glancing through the trees, Nestor sees several small, brightly coloured buildings, all situated in a large clearing, higher up. Deciding instinctively to park there, Nestor carefully navigates the remaining turns before bringing the bullet cart to a stop in a wide parking area.

Activating the rear camera on the bullet cart, Nestor adjusts one of two joysticks either side of a small screen in the dashboard, focusing the area across the broad dirt road.

He leans closer, studying the image. Patiently scanning what appears to be a long-abandoned café and trinket shop, with overgrown eating and play areas either side. Once bright pastel colour panels, used liberally as a decoration across the whole site, lie broken and scattered. All covered in years, perhaps decades, of dirt.

The few of the panels remaining in place are covered in old X symbol graffiti. Some arranged in consistent rows, others irregular and daubed seemingly at random. But even those marks are drowning, losing the relentless war with Nature, encroaching mercilessly through time. Each painted symbol losing all impact and meaning in such a deserted place.

Deactivating the screen, Nestor turns the handle on the door and gently steps to the ground, the higher than usual levels of Psylinax washing through his system, requiring him to concentrate doubly on every action. He locks the cart behind and slowly turns to face the café across the road, flinching immediately when he hears a sound like a gunshot.

He stumbles back against the side of the cart, his arm immediately trembling, a reaction met swiftly by a small whisper of body machinery. The system intelligently administering yet another micro dose.

Trembling only slightly, Nestor watches the buildings across the road for any signs of life. But nothing follows. Only silence.

Quietly, Nestor retrieves the short baton once again from the side of the cart, gripping it tightly in an unwavering metal hand. He steps across the road cautiously, shuffling towards the derelict building then off to the side, drawn to a large open and overgrown space.

Several panels of small wooden fence stand limply against the years, gradually disappearing in a quicksand of wild grass and shrub. Dotted across the uneven green space, a scattering of worn metal shards, all pointing skyward at different angles. Most of them dull and bare, but a few still retaining flickers of once bright colour. Lying discarded around the edge, the wreckage of several painted wooden and metal panels, most daubed with fading dark crosses.

Barely anything remains of what once stood there. The roundabouts, swings, climbing frames, now all gone. Ripped away for salvage, the remains hidden through time, smothered by Nature.

Nestor moves back along the porch, running a hand across the side of the building. Brick. Naked concrete. Rough, damaged plaster.

"Leave... her... alone!"

He stops immediately. Hearing sounds of struggling. Terrible words, loud and shocking. A scream, fading.

Silence.

Frozen in the main doorway, his metal hand raised, gripping the sturdy baton. Remaining human skin cold and quivering. Afraid to continue, yet too afraid and confused to step away. Are the sounds real? Tired eyes screwed shut then wide open. Chest rising and falling quickly. Sharp, shallow breath.

Nothing more. Just, glimpses of.

Fighting the tension, Nestor indicates his presence, hitting the side of the doorframe with the baton. But only silence and a slight breeze blowing through broken windows answer.

Nestor steps forward, heavy safety boots crunching quietly over years of debris. A shadowy interior revealing itself in a decaying riot of naked brick, broken plaster and exposed wooden beam and panelling. A floor of dirt and fragments, scraps of vinyl the merest of indications that the concrete was ever covered. The only feature standing, a damaged counter running along one side of the room. Everything else, every piece of equipment, every scrap of useful metal, most of the shelving even, all seemingly ripped out a long time ago. Leaving only outlines in dust and ruin across filth-covered walls.

Nestor crosses quietly to one of the large, empty window frames, warm late afternoon air turning colder as it seeps inside. Once, this modest dining area must have been a noisy, vibrant place. But now, only a solitary broken oblong table-top and several damaged chairs, all caked with dirt and grime, remain to tell their story.

Content that no-one appears to be here, Nestor drops his metal arm and closes his weary eyes. Imagining the space around him, hearing the voices, the smiles, the colours. Instinctively, a soft smile creeps across his heavily lined face.

His eyes flicker open. A shuffling sound, from somewhere further inside. Turning slowly, Nestor focuses on a doorway that leads deeper into the building. Watching quietly, waiting. Expecting.

Nothing appears.

Frowning, stepping slowly across. Nestor raises the baton once again, holding it out in front. Standing in the doorway, he taps on the inner wall, waiting for any response or further movement.

Nothing.

He peers quietly around the edge of the broken doorway. A short, gloomy hallway there revealing nothing except debris and two other open doorways.

Nestor moves forward cautiously, stepping into the nearest room. A much brighter space, late afternoon light pouring in through ruined window frames. The ceiling and roof damaged completely in places, making the sky visible. Ruins of white paint, plaster and tile mingle everywhere, meeting ripped outlines of low sink and storage. Somehow, in the wall to the side, an external door remains in place. Windows either side fully open, fragments of glass mixing in shattered debris across the floor. Scattered over the surface of two walls, ragged edges of metal and plastic pipes poke mournfully from broken concrete.

Safety boots crunch dust, plaster, fragments of glass as Nestor hears voices. The people working there? Shouting. Advising. Even joking. Busy doors opening, swinging, never closing. The hum and clatter of kitchen machinery and the heat, the heat…

Nestor stares at his human hand, as though waiting on it to catch fire. His skin warms and crawls as he glances through burning fingers, seeing a short bundle of stained paper hidden under a hill of fine debris. He uses the baton to disturb the material on the floor, revealing what appears to be an old calendar. Drawing it closer, Nestor leans down and lifts the square bundle of paper, tipping the dirt on top away.

Turning the calendar over, weary eyes widen in shock. Nestor sees an image of a bird, almost identical to the image fixed on the ceiling in his sleeping alcove. Dark plumage, broken by sparks of bright colour. The posture and position, the branch and forest behind, almost identical. Almost.

Leaning the baton against a nearby wall, Nestor rifles through the other pages, each containing an image of a different animal. Then he slowly returns to August, clearing the dirt and dust from the image, as much as he can.

August…

Nestor reels uncomfortably from a strange shock. A confusion that forms somewhere between coincidence and significance. That inner electricity that upsets each beat, each thought, leaving almost no space to breathe, to think.

When he lifts the baton, Nestor hears a shuffling sound in the doorway behind. Sharp, stuttered breath passes as he looks warily towards a shadow in the doorway. The shadow of a large black dog sitting there, staring at him quizzically and peacefully, through one healthy dark green eye.

***

"Good morning 33…"

Lights flicker on but Nestor is already awake. Staring up at the faded, torn calendar image fixed on the alcove ceiling above, replacing the image he had before.

"Weather is… sunny. Chance of rain… 0%."

He swings his legs towards the floor. Heavy, dirty boots still wrap around metal feet. A grubby grey utility suit still wraps around curved metal legs. For the first time in however long, Nestor had slept in the clothes of yesterday.

He exhales deeply, taking several controlled healing breaths as he stares across the room, finding an invisible point to focus. Today there will be no inspection. Today there will be no ritual.

He gets to his feet and slowly removes his clothes. Letting the tough garment fall to the floor, revealing simple under-clothes and a near empty Psylinax tank and circuitry. Instinctively, Nestor places both hands on top of the hollow chamber.

***

Nestor taps a metal hand on the thick plastic ledge in front of him, waiting patiently for the service droid to return from deep inside the storeroom.

Over his shoulder, back across the bays, the controlled chaos of the shift change window rolls as usual. The clamour of loading cages and removing tanks, the spin of orange and red light, the whine of bullet carts firing up and down, mechs shouting and gesturing.

Nestor waits patiently at the hatch, leaning forward with his tired body trembling. After a few moments, a cylindrical utility droid slips back along the smooth floor, moving towards him.

"Nestor 33. Your weekly quota is exhausted."

Nestor shakes his head softly, casting weary eyes downward. He glances at his arm, trembling more noticeably now as it rests on the ledge. He looks up, staring at the ungainly droid, all flickering light and circuitry, then retrieves his paper and pen.

"Nestor 33. Your weekly quota is exhausted."

Nestor nods several times while he scrawls his response, eventually holding it out in front of the droid's visual circuitry. A red circular light scans and pulses as it interprets several scribbles across the paper. *There must be some mistake, some error with the allowance? A recount is required.*

"Nestor 33. Recount requires elevation."

A solitary collector standing in the queue taps Nestor on the back, politely gesturing at him to hurry. Nestor acknowledges nervously, his body shaking more noticeably. He scribbles another message with his metal arm, his human arm now unable to control the pen properly.

"Nestor 33. Cannot interpret."

Nestor crumples the paper into a ball and gasps, slumping to the wall at the side, away from the other waiting collector who reaches out towards him.

"Hey, are you okay?"

Deep in conversation with her mechanic, Lynette 24 glances across the bay area and sees Nestor struggling near the storeroom hatch. She holds up a hand, stopping her mechanic in full flow. "Wait… Hold on. I need to… Nestor?"

She moves across the smooth concrete floor quickly, pausing briefly to let one of the laden utility carts pass in front. Heading straight towards Nestor now leaning against the white wall, struggling at the side of the hatch.

"Nestor? What the hell…"

Nestor stares at her, a mixture of confusion and distress, skin pale, almost chalk white. A steady metal hand waving a pen above, a quaking human hand struggling with paper below.

Looking at characters forming. "A… R… Arlo? You need to see Arlo?"

Nestor sighs with relief, struggling and just managing to place paper and pen back inside one of his overall pockets.

"Nestor 33. Do you require medical assistance?"

Lynette holds out one metal hand, gesturing at the droid in the hatch. "No, it's alright. I've got this…"

Lynette pulls a metal arm up and behind her neck, gently lifting and supporting Nestor. After reassuring the other collector standing at the hatch, they walk slowly along the outer path. Moving carefully beside the wall, edging towards the main office.

Bade looks up immediately, initial shock giving way to concern, leaping from his desk to assist Lynette as she guides Nestor to a chair.

"Saw him at the hatch. He needs a shot. Wants to speak to Arlo. Where is he? Ah need to talk to him…"

"Arlo is in a meeting. You can't talk to him right now, he's with…"

Lynette pulls Bade closer. "Look at him. No way he'll get through a shift like that. Give him a shot. I'm sorting this with Arlo now."

Lynette throws the door to the office wide open and strides inside, focusing Arlo behind the large desk and ignoring the woman sitting opposite.

"Arlo…"

Shocked, Arlo leans back in a creaking chair, rubbing his hand over his shirt nervously and placing a short cigar cap into a nearby ashtray. "Lynette… Eh, a problem here?"

"Yeah. You could say that."

Arlo coughs awkwardly, looking towards Bade now standing anxiously in the doorway. "Bade? I'm, we're, busy here, eh?"

Bade shrugs, scanning the room warily before meekly slipping away.

"Great…" exasperated, Arlo rubs his forehead and neck, sighing.

Now leaning over the desk. "I've got Nestor 33 outside Arlo, and he's not in a good way. Found him near the hatch this morning, he's struggling. Won't make it through the shift…"

Rubbing the back of his neck, Arlo glances nervously at the woman sitting in the chair opposite. "Vinnia, this eh, this is Lynette 24. One of the collectors you were enquiring about, that move from section 45?"

Finally, registering the somewhat cold and tense atmosphere in the room, Lynette steps back from the desk. She turns to Vinnia, all cropped fair hair, dark suit and carefully applied make-up hiding narrow, suspicious eyes. An open folder on her lap, containing a bundle of large papers.

"Hi…"

Vinnia smiles with a slight twist of performance, just enough to disguise any shade of irritation. "Morning. I'm Vinnia Fairchild."

Lynette nods meekly, brushing gloved metal hands across the front of her overalls.

"Arlo?" Vinnia closes the folder in her lap. "Something you need to attend to, personally?"

Arlo and Vinnia meet each other's stare, the former eventually pulling his gaze away, frowning. After an uncomfortable pause, Vinnia unexpectedly rises from her seat, placing the folder on top of other papers on the corner of the desk. The sudden movement enough to cause Arlo to bolt forward from his chair, one arm stretched out apologetically.

"Eh, you stay here, Vinnia. I'll deal with this, eh? Won't be long." Arlo makes an ushering-out gesture to Lynette.

"This Nestor 33. Wasn't he one of the collectors I was due to meet on my previous visit?"

Arlo clears his throat again. "Eh, I'm not sure…"

Vinnia straightens her crisp sky-blue blouse and dark fitted jacket, then retrieves a round black cap with a blue flash from the back of the chair, placing it at an angle on her head.

"I would like to meet this collector again…"

Arlo frowns. "But our accounts, the report, eh? There isn't a lot of time?"

Lynette clears her throat, commenting calmly, carefully. "Nestor is our longest-serving collector. Scrubbed more crosses than anyone in the team… and 33 is the Eden Terrace section."

"Ah, Mr Matthews. I see." Vinnia raises her eyebrows, noting the information and giving Lynette a soft smile in response. "A valuable employee, Arlo, I'd like to hear what he has to say."

Lynette opens the door and steps into reception, moving sideways to let Vinnia pass to where Nestor is sitting, with Bade crouching beside. The latter gets to his feet quickly and moves away, having already administered an emergency shot of Psylinax. Arlo loiters behind near the office door, restless and apprehensive.

"Nestor 33?" Vinnia holds out a largely human hand, only one index finger covered in a tight-fitting material, suggesting a metal substitute beneath. "You won't remember me. I'm Vinnia Fairchild, Regional Director for the East."

A dishevelled but recovering Nestor looks up. Cloudy, tired eyes peering from heavily lined skin, narrowing at first then quickly widening. His expression transforming from seeming indifference through gentle shock, towards a soft, warm smile. Nestor shuffles and straightens in the seat, holding out a trembling human hand to meet the gesture.

"Lynette 24 tells me you are the longest serving collector in the hub?"

Nestor glances at Lynette, casting his eyes downward with a flicker of modesty.

"Is this true?"

Lynette steps closer, whispering to Vinnia. "Nestor can't speak."

Vinnia fixes Lynette with a quizzical expression, glancing back towards Arlo then leaning closer to Nestor. "Really? And why is that, Collector? I imagine that with your age you are largely modified?"

Nestor nods softly. Removing the paper and pen from his pocket.

"I see. So, your vocal circuitry hasn't been repaired. This is a recent malfunction?"

As Nestor writes the word 'no' on the paper and holds it out, Arlo coughs loudly. "Delays, Vinnia."

"Delays?" Vinnia spins round, fixing Arlo. "The eastern workshops? *My* workshops, Arlo?"

Uncomfortable. Floundering. "We've had other priorities in the hub, Vinnia. All the restrictions, eh?"

"The service budgets are still healthy. A more rural location, perhaps."

"Well, eh…" Arlo shakes his head in slight frustration. "Maybe it's something we can discuss later, eh?"

A hollow sadness, neither angry nor abject, releases and seeps through Nestor as he finally acknowledges what he locked away years ago. After all, Arlo has never been a man of his word. Why should all those persistent requests for vocal circuit repairs have been met with anything other than lies?

But still, through the trembling, the final acknowledgement is no comfort, the crush of disappointment is bitterly real. For through all the lies, Nestor could never remove a tiny sliver of hope. The tiniest belief across the years that, no matter how unlikely, for this one request – this one *vital* thing – Arlo would do right. *For him.* Nestor 33. The longest-serving employee in the hub who never missed a shift. The most trusted collector who never questioned. Who played – and still plays – all Arlo's games of moving scrap and contraband. But no. Nestor sees it now. Old, lined eyes suddenly clear. The request to repair his vocal circuits really was just the same as the hundred other Arlo conversations after all. Every single one packed with self-interest, with deceit.

Nestor fixes Arlo calmly, watching him squirm as he disappears back inside his office, unable to blind with his usual truculence and empty assurances.

"I see…" Vinnia stretches up. "Bade, is Nestor 33 prepared for his shift?"

Ruffled slightly, Bade looks over to the group. "Yes, Director. I've administered an emergency shot and authorised additional supplies. It should be ready. Talk to the store droid…"

"Good." Vinnia smiles. "Then have a safe shift, Collector…"

***

Nestor stands on a curved ledge that juts out from the concrete canal bank, fishing for debris with a long-hooked pole and net. He carefully dips the pole under the surface of the flowing water, drawing it along a partially submerged row of thick metal bars, revealing the rubbish that gathers at the barrier. Slowly, Nestor drags the debris closer to the edge, scooping it up and fashioning it into piles at the side of the canal. Eventually placing it in one of two cages in the nearby bullet cart, one for incinerating, the other for anything of even mild salvage potential.

Sometimes, Nestor retrieves other items from the water. New, important things. Goods carefully packaged for short nocturnal trips along the canal, weighted carefully and skilfully to float hidden under the dark surface of the water.

Packages designed to stop and await collection at the large crescent entrance gates – the 'gates of paradise' as Arlo calls them – where water flows underneath the Eden Terrace.

And there is no more conscientious collector than Nestor 33, who retrieves those bundles quietly and obediently from the canal and places them in his bullet cart, later transporting them to several private contacts along various work routes. Those extra grey duties that can only be trusted to a few of the collectors, or so Arlo says. The trustworthy ones, the collectors who keep their mouth shut. And, of course, there is no more silent collector than Nestor 33…

Today, the canal water flows steadily, the long pole and net moving in the water freely. Revealing only the more typical and mundane daily detritus, the usual combination of natural and worker junk. A broken folding chair, scraps of blanket and clothing, random pieces of rotten board and a miscellany of large metal parts and brackets. Some rusted irretrievably, some good enough still for the salvage cage.

As Nestor combs and cleans, he does what he always does and wonders. Reflecting in precise moments as he pulls certain pieces of debris closer. Wondering which one of the dark crosses scrawled across the city was once the owner of these abandoned things.

"You!"

Nestor steps back from the canal edge, startled by the ferocity of the bark from somewhere above. Glancing up, he sees Inspector Maurice Callum staring down at him. Nervously, Nestor carefully lowers each long pole to the ground nearby.

Gesturing over his shoulder. "Seen the mess up here?"

Trembling, Nestor nods, stepping forward and retrieving paper and pen.

"Stop. Don't come any closer." Maurice holds out a hand quickly. "Just stop what you're doing now and get all this shit cleaned up here. Mr Matthews is visiting today. Weren't you informed?"

Nestor shakes his head, returning pen and paper to pocket.

Maurice spits on the ground. "Just get the front cleaned up fast then make yourself scarce. I want you as far away from the terrace as possible today."

Nestor watches Maurice step back from the edge and disappear. He waits for a moment, listening to the sound of his boots scuff across concrete. Reassured that he has moved away, Nestor quickly gathers up the last of the debris, sorting and dropping most into the large cages which he will return to later.

With the debris secured, Nestor returns to the bullet cart. Removing a set of thick gauntlets and dropping them on the wide seat in the cab. The vehicle powers and whines as Nestor carefully reverses along the edge of the canal, the steeply rising concrete at the side eventually levelling. Switching gears, Nestor steers the vehicle to the right, slowly climbing towards the narrow road that rises ahead and skirts past Eden Terrace.

Moving silently, Nestor slows as he nears the large development, staring through the windscreen at graffiti hastily scattered across many concrete surfaces. Several dark crosses are scrawled across a low wall that runs beside the road, and at least one dark cross adorns each of the pillars in the large alcove behind. Several crosses even decorate the ground, all at different angles, each of a different dimension.

Standing just ahead, gesturing impatiently, a dark uniformed figure. Maurice Callum's sneering expression partially hidden by the shade of a visor. He marches to the side of the bullet cart as it powers down and bangs several times on the window.

"I want all of this gone by the next inspection. Move it!"

Nestor flinches in his seat, tiny pulses of Psylinax seeping into his system, keeping the growing tension in check. Opening the door softly, Nestor watches as Maurice recoils, stepping back immediately. His face already twisting with apprehension, repulsion. Unable to disguise his own instinctive disgust at the mere sight of Nestor and what he represents. That haunting fusion of old flesh, strong metal and heavy plastic.

Walking backwards, pointing in every direction at the crosses, Maurice continues to scold. "All gone!"

Nestor watches him walk away, following the same route as the day before. Moving further off towards a short flight of steps that cuts into an incline, leading up to an imposing security gate and fence. Keeping his head bowed, Nestor continues to observe, watching him waiting briefly near several security cameras at the gate.

When he disappears, Nestor moves to the side of the bullet cart and pushes a wide panel open and across, revealing various pieces of cleaning equipment clipped within. He removes several of the parts and fits them together, propping the mop against the cart.

Moving to the other side, Nestor lowers a short ramp to concrete and guides a dirty orange power clean unit to the ground. Wheeling it to a nearby pillar and connecting a thick power cable to the generator in the cart, the unit hums into life. Then Nestor connects mop and tank, pointing the power mop at the first of the crosses, fingers on the trigger.

Pausing to stare at the two lines, scrawled hastily in black, he pulls on the handle trigger with his human hand and starts to clean, watching the mop spin and the paint transform to dark rain.

***

Not for the first time that day, Nestor disappears in a seemingly endless moment. The circular cleaning movement, the power mop spinning, spiralling, mesmerising. The gentle whir and hum of Citi-Clean machinery. The sound of water flowing across concrete, wood, metal, plastic. The vaguely medicinal smell of cleaning fluid, even the vanishing graffiti. One cross. Then two. Then twenty. Everything appearing and disappearing, flowing, strangely timeless and…

Tired…

Nestor screws heavily wrinkled eyes together. Briefly shaking his head, trying to invigorate, struggling to find the energy to obliterate the last few crosses on the long yellow panel before him. The old black paint, having faced the elements with confidence for years, now unable to withstand the focused Citi-Clean assault, disappearing almost instantly.

Releasing the handle trigger, the power clean sinks to a barely audible whirring, disappearing into the low background hum of the generator. Nestor slumps, lowering the bulky pole to the grubby orange unit, propping it up on the side. A modest puddle of water forming underneath the mop, soaking into the ground.

He steps backwards on the dirt, metal limbs whirring. Casting his gaze sideways, he examines the group of other brightly damaged panels assembled there haphazardly. Each one lifted from its resting place of years by gloved metal and flesh hands, brought to the front of the building to be inspected and scrubbed free of every single piece of graffiti. Each slice of material might be damaged and broken, but at least it's clean now. Enough to reveal the colour from under years of ruin and neglect. Each one bright, fresh, warm in evening light.

Nestor looks over to the large black dog, relaxing on the remains of the wooden porch, where it has spent the last few hours observing the whole operation. A few times, Nestor had noticed the dog slowly walking away, wondering where he might go, whether he should stop cleaning and follow him, even whether he would return. But he always came back. Returning several minutes later to collapse on the exact same spot. Lowering his head to his paws again. Never sleeping. Always awake. One eye. Watching. Almost as if…

Nestor recalls the scene that had greeted him on his arrival. The dog seemingly asleep in the main doorway, bolting upright when the bullet cart pulled over at the front of the building. Skipping excitedly across the ground, jumping to greet him when he opened the door. As if the dog was waiting for him, expecting him to return.

No. Impossible.

Likely just the promise of food. After all, hadn't the generous remnants of the daily Citi-Clean rations been devoured the moment Nestor placed them on the ground? Or was it just the company of a kind stranger, perhaps the first ever known living here among the ruins?

Yet, as Nestor smooths a dark glove across his head, vainly flattening several tufts of silver hair there, he cannot stop a deeper, gentle smile breaking across his lined face. A look that doesn't go unnoticed by the nearby dog, who raises his head and quickly stands up on all paws, responding to

Nestor as he shuffles closer. Warmly gazing up towards him through one healthy eye, padding forward then turning away, moving round the corner of the building.

Instinctively, Nestor reaches into an overall pocket and removes the pen and notepad. He starts scribbling, mock frowning as the dog reappears and walks closer.

Scribbling and holding the page out: *what is your name?*

The dog sits and casts a quizzical gaze, watching the movements. One eye shifting from page, to Nestor, and back again.

Nestor opens his mouth wide in response, as though laughing. He points directly at two words on the page.

*Your... Name...?*

Suddenly, the large dog barks violently, taking Nestor immediately by surprise. Recoiling, he nervously hides pen and paper inside a pocket while his system responds with a tiny sliver of Psylinax.

The dog quietens but remains strangely agitated. Whining as it retreats along the porch, padding quietly to the corner of the building. Turning to Nestor and barking twice but different this time. As though impatient, encouraging him to follow.

Uncertain, Nestor pauses before curiosity soon spurs him forward, cautiously stepping along the remains of the wooden porch. Instinctively, he holds a hand in the air, gesturing at the disappearing dark shape to wait. The dog eventually stops, near thick undergrowth that edges the play area at the side. An area Nestor is already familiar with, having retrieved the damaged and abandoned boards from here earlier.

Stepping onto dirt and scuffed grass, limbs whirring as boot follows boot over gently uneven ground, Nestor walks along the remains of the fencing that must have once outlined the entire space. Few of the low white wooden fence panels are standing, most are reduced to scattered fragments, lost under the weight of Nature.

The dog barks somewhere ahead, announcing its presence even though invisible, lost amidst a collage of overgrown shrubs. The same blanket that slows Nestor considerably, limited to navigating a narrow pathway hidden in the mass.

The ground dips gently, causing Nestor to stoop lower and push on through an area that, from the outside, must look impenetrable. Perhaps, once upon a time with old and aching flesh and blood limbs, it might have proven so – but not now.

Increasingly curious, Nestor moves steadily through overlapping branches and an overhanging blanket of green and broken light. Eventually reaching an old wooden gate hanging partially open, submerged deep within tree and shrub branch. A battered red metal 'Private – No Entry' sign hanging beside the remains of two sturdy locks, only just attached to the splintered wooden edge of the gate. Signatures of forced entry, lost somewhere in time.

With a metal arm outstretched, Nestor pulls and rips at the branches draping around the damaged gate. Clearing enough space to push a metal shoulder against the old material, the gate cracking and groaning before eventually moving backwards, creating a narrow space to pass though.

Nestor takes several more steps before the shade of overhanging tree and shrub gives way to a panorama of wide evening sky. He finds himself on a natural ledge, covered only in grass and weed, with a considerable drop in either direction. A few larger rocks sit embedded in the ground, convenient enough to sit on and look out over Paulson Glen and the dusky carpet of hill and field beyond. Or, to the other side, the scattered dapple of the edge of the city, pinpoints of light in hazy shadow, the concrete peaks of Eden Terrace even.

Entranced by the view, Nestor begins to lower himself instinctively to one of the rocks, causing the dog to stop and look up from where it is digging furiously. Barking excitedly, Nestor rises in response and slowly walks to the side of the large rock, crouching carefully to investigate the deepening hole underneath. Further seconds pass in industry, the dog eventually sitting back when its paws reveal the edge of a dirty metal box buried there.

Nestor reaches out to the dog, patting him on the head, stroking dark and dust-covered fur, encouraging him to move away as he kneels in front. Then he reaches into the ground with a metal hand, breaking the remaining layers of earth, scooping the dirt out and scattering it behind him.

Eventually, the top edges of the box are completely revealed. An old design, some modest container once used for food, with barely discernible imagery and labelling on top. Perhaps an indication that the container was already old when it was placed in the ground.

Nestor wipes both hands on his overall and sits back, looking at the dog studying his face from nearby. Frowning, he removes a small rag from a side pocket, brushing soil from metal fingers. Dropping the rag to the ground, he reaches forward with his human hand, touching the surface of the box.

And at that precise moment he freezes, hearing a voice inside. A woman. Soothing words, spoken from somewhere.

*"It's so beautiful here, isn't it?"*

***

The remaining flesh and blood parts of Nestor move restlessly in the confines of the sleeping alcove, as the dream loops one more time.

In the cab now. Powering up the bullet cart. Hearing the growing whine of the engine. Louder. Louder. Music playing, the volume low, just enough to hear. Everything dark inside, except for the tiny spillage of dull blue and green screen.

Outside, only darkness. Except for the narrow portion of road illuminated by headlight. A thin slice, like a door ajar, just enough to glimpse the road and the building beyond. Each stream converging and dancing, broken as a huge, ominous shadow moves left and right. Always back and forth. Back and forth. Then it stops pacing and stands in the beam, looking directly towards Nestor through one burning red eye. Barking viciously. Baring huge, terrible fangs.

Cowering. Sinking, as thin, elongated shadows seep through the doorways of the ruined building behind. They file along the ruined porch of the café and gather in a short line at the front. All of them. *Is that people, it must be people?* Standing. Waiting.

Foot down now. Nothing. The engine doesn't respond. Still whining, louder and louder. Boot to metal again. Still nothing. Just the music, the barking, the whine of the engine, grey faces peering...

As if by some invisible signal, they all walk towards where the dog angrily paces and lashes back and forth. They gather at the front of the cart, moving slowly closer. Closer still, enough to see their faces. Except Nestor can't. He can't see them. Can't see their faces even as they peer into the cab.

Boot to metal. Nothing.

Then mouth opening. The shape of a scream. Silent and terrible.

A buzzer…

Cold light flickers across a white room.

"Good morning, 33."

Glistening, yellowing eyes reveal themselves in a trembling, fearful face as Psylinax streams into a system that hasn't slept.

A shaking hand reaches up quickly, tracing lines between a few remaining pictures on the low ceiling above, moving and skipping as a spider moves and skips across its own thread. Pointing to each picture, tracing an outline, moving to the next. Then back again, tracing different routes.

"Weather is… good. There is zero per cent chance of rain."

Nestor breathes deeply, grasping the Citi-Clean logo on his grubby utility suit, before dropping his arm to the bed where it settles among several discarded images. Exactly where Nestor had ripped them down and scattered them the night before.

Several moments pass before dirt-covered safety boots lower to polished white floor. Nestor studies them briefly, touching the dirt still crusted underneath. Then he raises his head, staring over to the metal box lying open on the table. The contents arranged in a line across the surface, exactly as he left them the night before.

An old dog chain with a return tag, a blue headscarf wrapped tightly around it. Five pictures, some folded over, all ripped from various times and sources. A beautiful bird on a branch. A hilly and sunlit landscape. A long table, dressed for a party, laden with various plates and bowls of food. Children on a climbing frame waving. A petite hand resting on a window with sky behind, taken from inside a moving vehicle…

Nestor recalls the shock when he reached out to unwrap the headscarf. How a flurry of strange, garbled voices had near paralysed him. Disturbing echoes lunging from some invisible place, forcing him to rip the cloth away with his metal arm and throw it to the table. Watching in confusion as it floated mysteriously in the air, dropping like a simple feather.

And then, reeling backwards. Across the room. Unable to stop a huge and terrible emptiness pouring forth. Seeping from every scrap of old, remaining skin while the Psylinax gauge ticked lower dutifully. Sudden tremors eventually easing, but nothing more than that. Nestor's feet still on the edge of some vast inner chasm, a landscape that hadn't even existed seconds before. The items and images from the metal container reaching out, reaching *through*. Calling out to the abandoned shadows still wandering around inside him. Stories never entirely removed, just hidden within the polite walls of the everyday. By time. By metal. By one shift after another.

And the images. How he couldn't rip tired and fearful eyes away. The similarity between the pictures there on the table and the jumble of images in the sleeping alcove uncanny. As though all these years he sensed the same things too, but only darkly. Never sharply defined, never illuminated clearly. Just the same persistent whispers from somewhere in the shadows.

"You have… one new message 33. Playing…"

The cloud of uneasy, reflective silence breaks to the sound of Arlo clearing his throat and making several other guttural sounds. Grumbles that Nestor had long come to know indicated displeasure, unhappiness, anger.

"Eh, Nestor... What the hell was that all about yesterday, in front of Vinnia? That whole stunt you pulled in the morning? As if that wasn't bad enough, you're crawling in just before curfew last night. Damn it, Nestor, she saw it. We're in the office, she saw it! Alright, I get it, I know, I said take some time... I didn't say take all the fucking time! What is wrong with you?"

Nestor shivers, lifting his metal hand close, studying the dirt and grime crusted across the many plates and gears. He scrubs some of the dirt with a shaking human hand, watching the powder disappear.

"You blew it... You embarrassed me, Nestor. You and eh Lynette. Whatever happened to *our* loyalty, *our* history, eh? I'm done, I'm done with you... For now, anyway. I don't want to see you until Vinnia leaves. Don't come to the office – hear me? You need anything you get one of the crew to talk to Bade. Like, Lynette, get Lynette to talk right? I mean, that's all she fucking does, is talk..."

Nestor stands up slowly, whispers of legs whirring and clicking.

"Just think about what you did, eh? What I've done for you over the years? Maybe you've been here too long? Think about it... I've protected you all this time, Nestor!"

A metal arm reaches over the table, lifting the chain, the headscarf, the pictures. Touching and examining, Nestor holds each item for precious moments, as though trying to feel, to absorb and reveal every last impression.

"And this is what I get, this is what you give me, eh? It's unacceptable. Completely unacceptable you hear? Listen, I'm telling you... you'd be dead if it wasn't for me, Nestor. Dead!"

***

The surface of the water breaks quietly as the long metal pole dips under the surface and drags. Probing and dislodging whatever lies underneath which, so far that morning, is proving to be the usual meagre assortment.

In a strange, troubled peace, Nestor slowly trails the pole through the water, glancing towards the empty cages in the rear of the cart. The material recovered so far still lying in a modest haphazard pile on concrete nearby. Twisted metal that might be part of a small bicycle, two damaged and filth-covered folding chairs, several connected shards from old wooden pallets, a section of old blanket and a collection of assorted branches and driftwood.

Not that the lack of any contraband or salvage matters now. Not since the excoriating message from Arlo earlier that morning, all bile and blackmail. Where he'd used the entire capacity for any individual message to pour out his anger and frustration at this seemingly bitter betrayal. And not a hint of that anger for Vinnia and the other faceless colleagues closing the net around him. Sifting through the records, studying every communication, piecing one inconsistency together with another. No. The anger was not for them.

It was all for Nestor.

The most trusted, most loyal and longest-serving collector in the entire hub. A collector who's scrubbed more graffiti from the banks of the canal and the surrounding 33 area than anyone else, in any other section in the city. A collector who's survived long enough to see the worker camps in the commercial district grow to become miserable towns of their own. Who witnessed the first mark in the ground where the luxurious Eden Terrace now stretches towards the sky. Who's done everything he was asked to do across years, all the special business, every day without complaint.

And the one thing he did ask for. The one surely reasonable request…

No. It doesn't matter now.

Not since Nestor had shuffled into his bay that morning to see Vinnia stooping over the mech, discussing the process of fitting part of the new filtration system in the side tank. She'd come to say farewell, to check Nestor had recovered from the events of the day before and to enquire whether he had adequate Psylinax for the shift ahead.

And she asked him, if there was anything else he wanted to say, anything else he wanted to mention while she was there on site. Instinctively, Nestor shook his head from side to side. But then he stopped, his expression dropping just enough for Vinnia to ask again, stepping closer so her words wouldn't be lost amidst the din of the shift change.

"Are you sure? There's nothing you'd like to mention before I leave?"

Unable to meet her gaze directly, Nestor had reached into one of his chest pockets, removing the pen and notepad. Trembling, he leaned against the rear of the cart, quickly writing several words. Tearing the small sheet and placing it in the palm of his human hand, which he held out in a farewell gesture.

Vinnia had shaken his hand with neither warmth nor gratitude. Calmly retrieving the paper at the same time and staring at Nestor. She had managed a strangely tense half-smile, her manner serious, perhaps resigned, even cold.

With head bowed slightly, Nestor had watched Vinnia leave. Studying her as she walked away and stopped, reading the words on the paper.

*Ask Arlo about the shoes…*

Nestor drops the net back to the concrete and steps closer to the metal gate, dragging the long fishing pole with him. He manages a tired, delicate smile as he watches the water bubble and pour beyond the bars. Dropping somewhere below and flowing underneath Eden Terrace.

No. It doesn't matter now. None of it.

Doesn't matter whether Nestor fills the salvage cage once, twice, three times or more. Doesn't matter whether the net lands a catch that's travelled all the way down from somewhere upstream. Another driver losing their cargo, circumstances either mysterious or meticulously planned. Skimming from countless organisations, jettisoning their contraband in the water. Moving downstream, point to point. None of it matters.

Nestor smiles quietly, reflecting on different items now. The few precious things stored in a dashboard compartment. A collection of worn images. A ragged old headscarf. A dog chain with a return tag. And the voices, sounds of someone else, somewhere else. The place on the return tag. A place across the region, where the dog must be from, the owner there. A place he is compelled to go to. Today. Now.

Securing the cages in the rear of the cart, Nestor returns to the cab and powers up the engine, switching off the main display on the dashboard and lowering the volume on the light jazz that fills every space. Releasing the brake, he reverses back along the concrete edge carefully. Eventually turning the vehicle and crawling up the gentle grassy incline to the narrow road. Building a small amount of speed as the road rises, towards Eden Terrace.

As the cart levels out and moves towards the edge of the apartment area, Nestor sees a uniformed figure running out from the network of concrete alcoves. Sprinting towards the cart, gloved hands waving a baton back and forth. Angry, frantic gesturing to stop immediately.

Nestor slows the vehicle, pulling in towards the side and watching with increasing anxiety as the dark figure approaches the cart.

Banging violently on the window. "Get out!"

Unnerved, Nestor powers the cart down with a trembling hand. Unlocking the door, he slowly swings whirring legs round, letting heavy safety boots reach the ground gently. He looks towards the irate inspector. Confused. Uncertain. Shivering.

"What have you done? You missed... Mr Matthews? You..." Callum shakes his head, part fury, part disbelief. "Fucking come with me..."

Nestor doesn't move, holding out a quivering arm in a gesture of calm, trying to see the eyes hidden behind dark rectangular shades.

Callum raises the baton to one side of Nestor's head. "Lower your hands right now, robot, don't fucking push me. You've no idea what you've done..."

Nestor lowers his arms slowly, staring at the ground, sinking backwards, appearing contrite. Whispers of Psylinax slip into his system, vainly trying to balance the unease.

"Don't you realise? You missed one. You fucking missed one... And Mr Matthews, he was here today. He saw it. He fucking saw it..."

Nestor reaches towards the pocket with pen and paper.

Shrieking. "Leave it! Hands where I can see, robot. I said stop!"

Callum lashes the heavy baton down and across, striking a metal arm that instantly recoils from the blow. Nestor slumps backwards against the side of the bullet cart.

His metal limb registering no feeling, no pain, but the remaining flesh elsewhere now cold with fear, new tremors demanding a sharp injection of Psylinax.

"You need to see. You fucking come with me…"

Maurice pushes the baton into Nestor's chest then moves to the side, forcing Nestor up and forward, angrily pushing him on.

"Move!"

The baton circles to his back and lashes across metal legs. Machinery whirring and pausing, no pain, just awkward moments of recalibration. Nestor glances at Callum, a painful and pleading expression. His mouth opening and closing in silent words.

"Don't turn round – walk! You'll see what you've done!"

Nestor shuffles forward, half his body trembling, fearful. Arms raised to the side, dark baton in his back, boring through the utility suit. Into the ragged border where skin meets metal, pushing him forward.

"Across here. Move!"

The inspector marches Nestor through the alcove, eventually stopping next to a pillar at the back of the area, the one closest to the open space that leads over to one of the security gates. The one pillar most easily seen from inside the luxury complex itself.

Without warning, Callum forces Nestor to the ground, metal legs impaired slightly and unable to counter-act in time. On hands and knees, Nestor flinches as a heavy boot meets his side, old flesh hurting immediately.

"Look!"

Nestor gasps horribly on the ground, crawling forward to where Callum is standing, pointing with the baton at the pillar.

"Here!"

In pain, Nestor slowly attempts to look up.

"Fucking look!" Maurice forces the baton under Nestor's jaw, pushing upwards.

Nestor opens his eyes, seeing a solitary large X displayed on the surface, his mouth moving instinctively in fear, forming soundless words.

Another blow, Nestor clatters back to the ground.

"You missed it! And he saw it. Mr Matthews fucking saw it! He was taking guests into the complex. He saw it from up there. All of them, they all saw it…"

Nestor lowers his head, trying to see from the corner of blurring vision without meeting the terrible gaze from behind dark shades.

Crouching down. "He was so fucking angry. Called us before he left. Said we were getting lazy. Said that seeing one of the crosses was as bad as seeing a thousand of them. That no-one would want to live here if it was covered in graffiti. Kept blaming us, everyone in security, everyone. And all the time it was your fault, a fucking cleaning robot…"

Nestor crawls back from the pillar, a gesture that doesn't go unnoticed as Callum gets to his feet and stabs a boot violently several times into his side. Nestor slumps forward, holding out a metal arm in vain.

"It's not me, not my fault. I didn't miss it, you did. A fucking robot!"

In pain, Nestor watches Callum return to the pillar and pace round it, the presence of the symbol scrawled across the concrete making him oddly nervous, unhinging him further. For a moment he forgets about Nestor crawling away, metal legs gradually stretching out, moving in the direction of the bullet cart.

*"How could you miss it? You clean here every day, every fucking day…"*

Ignoring Callum pacing round and round, lost in some disbelieving rage, Nestor slowly gets to his feet. Cold metal limbs whirring and clicking more audibly, perhaps indicating some light damage, he half-drags and half-stumbles towards the vehicle.

"Unless… Unless you didn't miss it…"

Callum glances over to where Nestor has made it across the alcove.

"Stop! You can't leave!"

An exhausted Nestor looks over his shoulder, seeing Callum jogging forward.

"You knew didn't you? You fucking knew!"

Footsteps quicken to a sprint, reaching Nestor just as he nears the side of the bullet cart.

"You knew."

Gathering his last dregs of strength, Nestor spins round, metal hand stretching out, grabbing and twisting dark uniform. Callum screams in panic, sickened by the mere contact, disabled by his own repulsion. He instinctively lashes at the arm with the heavy baton, one vicious blow then another. Strikes that have no immediate effect as Nestor slowly draws him closer and closer.

Hysterical, Callum drops the baton and brings flailing gloved hands to one of several small devices on the side of his belt. He feels for a small lid and flips it open, pressing a button underneath which instantly turns red. In the distance, warning sirens fire near the front of the security gate and elsewhere across the whole site.

The sound interrupts Nestor, as though waking from a dream, he reaches up with a shaking human arm and pulls the metal hand away. Collapsing back against the driver door, staring at it in disbelief, mouth gasping silent words.

Scrambling across concrete to a safer distance, Callum regains his former loathing and aggression. "Oh, you're fucked. You're fucked now, collector!"

As Callum gloats from the concrete, Nestor touches the front of his utility suit with a shivering human hand, feeling damp material, fluid leaking from damaged gauges and circuitry underneath.

"They'll be here soon, collector! Take you away. Offline is the only place for robots that pull this kind of shit."

Callum staggers to his feet and retrieves the baton from nearby. Moving quickly towards the cart, he is unable to catch Nestor who has already climbed inside and locked the doors behind him.

"Get out!"

Nestor ignores the frenzied face in the window as he powers the engine and switches into reverse. The cart moving and whining backwards, orange light spinning behind. Light jazz briefly drowning the sounds of violence from outside.

"Stop the vehicle! Out!"

Undeterred by the ferocious strikes across reinforced glass and clean white metal, Nestor engages the forward drive and steadily pulls away. The bullet cart eventually leaving Callum slicing the air in frustration as several of his uniformed colleagues reach him. Nestor glances in the mirror, watching them gather round, a couple looking straight at the escaping cart and speaking into various communication devices.

Nestor leans forward in the seat, head and arm shaking, gripping the steering bars tightly as he navigates the road that leads away from section 33. Feverishly checking the mirrors for any sign of pursuing vehicles.

When the bullet cart finally mingles with other traffic on the highway and the Eden Terrace complex grows more distant, Nestor breathes several painful sighs of relief and rubs weary, tortured eyes. As he drives, he makes several exaggerated shrieking gestures, intense movements, completely silent.

Nestor glances at the large compartment in the centre of the dashboard and reaches across, opening it to reveal the metal container inside. He lifts the worn box and places it on the seat, resting his hand on the grubby, marked surface. As though drawing strength from the mere touch.

*"It's so beautiful here, isn't it?"*

But any magical recuperation is dashed as he winces, leaning forward again, opening his mouth in silent discomfort. Finally sensing the impact of the struggle, of every single blow. Bruised, remaining flesh burns and shivers, as Nestor pulls open the top of the utility suit and places a quivering human hand inside. Exploring. Checking. Sensing each bruise, each impact. Feeling damaged and damp skin across his ragged torso. Fluid seeping from the cracked Psylinax gauge. Tiny, inconsistent movements of the machinery, struggling, breaking…

It doesn't matter. Not now. None of it matters. All that matters is to find the dog, return it home and, maybe, discover something else. Someone else.

Nestor slows the bullet cart and steers off the highway, following the dirt road into Paulson Glen as it curves round and rises gently. Navigating the winding route and passing the large sign covered in overhanging branches, Nestor notices a couple of unmarked transporters in one of the larger passing spaces. He slows down, checking for other activity as he passes but sees nothing, no-one. He increases his speed and continues, following the track carefully, meandering up the side of several small hills.

Afternoon sun filters and flickers through woodland; light and shadow dance inside the cab. Through cracked glass, glimpses of sky and distant field combine to ease the pain just enough. Enough to assist the damaged Psylinax machine inside. Enough to take the edge from each bruise, to soothe the worst of the tremors, but not enough to eliminate the pain and the shivering entirely.

Reaching the buildings, Nestor swings the cart round in front of the ruined café and reverses, powering down in the same space as the day before. He checks through the windscreen and the cracked side window, the area seemingly deserted as usual, before activating the forward camera to inspect more closely. Scanning the porch and side areas first, Nestor returns focus to the main doorway, perhaps disappointed not to discover the dog lying there, waiting for him.

Sitting back for a moment, Nestor opens the metal container and carefully lifts the items from inside. He studies each briefly before finding pockets for everything and returning the metal container to the large dashboard compartment. Deactivating the monitor, Nestor fastens the top of his utility suit around his neck and steps outside.

The place is quiet and peaceful. Only the sound of birdsong, distant machinery, his own heavy boots on dirt. Still quivering, Nestor stretches and straightens but regrets it immediately, as hot blurry aches instantly sharpen.

He reaches out to the side of the cart, feeling several new scratches and depressions around the slim door behind the cab. Opening the panel, he removes the short metal pole from inside and grips it tightly in a whirring metal hand. As he closes the door, Nestor drops the baton at his side, having neither the strength nor the will to hold it in front.

Moving slowly and awkwardly across the track towards the low porch, Nestor lifts the dog chain from a side pocket. Letting it drag across the ground, he listens for the merest hint of a sound in response. Perhaps, if the dog sees?

Stepping carefully across the broken porch, Nestor peers through the main doorway into the ruined café. Eyes cautiously scanning the dim available light within, checking for any sign, any movement. Pausing for a moment, he taps the pole on the external wall, but receives only silence in return.

Nestor steps to the centre of the completely shattered space. The floor a scattered litter of wood, plaster, glass and scraps of natural debris blown in to root or rot. He steps towards one of the large empty window frames, feeling the lightest touch of a breeze from the still day outside. He glances back towards the bullet cart parked at the front, checking to see if its appearance had brought the dog out from its hiding place but no. Nothing. Not a sound. Not a sign.

"Nestor?"

Surprised by the voice, Nestor turns quickly, the soft female voice vaguely familiar. He takes several nervous steps forward, looking directly towards the tall figure standing in the gloom further back. A woman in a small-peaked cap and thin black shades, wearing a tight-fitting dark suit with green edges and flashes. Draping from her shoulders, a long gown-like garment stretches almost to the floor. The style more utilitarian than luxurious, lightly padded material covered in repeating patterns, all various shades of grey.

"I'm sorry." Taking a long breath and exhaling deeply, then removing her dark shades. "Sorry it always comes to this. That we find ourselves here once again."

Frowning, head shaking more in confusion than pain, Nestor opens his mouth wide in surprise. Vinnia? Why is she here? Didn't she leave earlier that day? How does she know about this place? He steps quickly across the floor.

"I wouldn't come any closer if I were you. Protocol…"

Nestor stops instantly, looking at his metal hand and letting the pole drop to the floor. He watches it roll and nestle among dust and debris.

Vinnia tips her head, noticing the stained chest section of the utility suit. "I see you're damaged?"

Nestor feels the material then looks towards her, nodding softly.

"Your levels must be very low by now. But we've brought an emergency supply."

Hearing vehicles drawing closer, Nestor glances over his shoulder and watches as the two unmarked transporters he saw earlier park on the road outside. One stops at the front of the building, the other parks diagonally in front of the bullet cart. White-clothed medical and support technicians step out quickly, a few carrying bulky cases of various sizes.

"You have to stop this. Three times now, four?"

Holding in both hands, Nestor brings the chain closer as a young man in a white tunic walks through the hall doorway at the rear. He marches towards Vinnia, making a formal nodding gesture before handing over the old metal box retrieved from the bullet cart. Whispering a short message then retreating to the back of the room, Vinnia studies all sides of the container, rubbing the surface with gloved hands.

"I don't know how you keep finding this…" Vinnia sighs deeply. "I'm not sure how this happens. We have the best mechs, the most rigorous processing. But even our best engineers don't understand it. I find it strange, a challenge even…"

In the main doorway, a child-sized cyborg hulk partially decloaks and lowers itself to the floor from somewhere above. Having the appearance of an insect, dark heavy armour down one side, it flashes briefly in places, rows of distorted orange symbols and writing. The guardian raises an arm covered in weaponry and points at Nestor, while a small drone attached to the cyborg silently floats upwards and begins scanning the whole room.

"You've upset some important people, Nestor. These imaginings of yours…"

Nestor kneels on the floor, crushed suddenly by an invisible weight that floods outwards. A numbing pain worse than each bruise, worse than the broken gauges, the tremors. Something much deeper, something that cries out from his very core.

"It seems Arlo has made more than one mistake…"

Vinnia steps closer, crouching down and holding the metal container out in front of Nestor.

Whispering. "Thank you for your honesty earlier today. Arlo and I… we had a very long conversation."

Nestor shivers. His mouth moving in silent words instinctively, unable to pacify the growing mix of confusion, despair, sadness.

"But this situation. The situation we have here…" Vinnia exhales. "It's time to put these things away. Again…"

Nestor glances around the room, now full of technicians and support staff. Groups of faces and several modest stacks of heavy plastic boxes stretch along the nearby walls. Everyone watching, some of them recording and taking notes.

Vinnia places the container on the floor and stands up. "Nestor?"

Slowly, he pulls the small bundle of images from a pocket and begins tracing the outline of each subject with his human hand. One twisted, gnarled finger following the edges in each image, movements sinking behind weary, stinging eyes. Taking these final moments to remember, to force last, desperate impressions onto infinity itself before dropping each image into the metal box.

Now the scarf. Holding the thin, ragged material in both hands. Bringing it closer to his face, inhaling the dust of years, of decades, like a timeless hand reaching out and waiting. The touch, that deeper something that can never leave. Gripping the material tightly for a few seconds, pressing it deep into old skin, then folding and placing it in the open container.

Finally, the chain. The reason he came back. The reason nothing else matters. To find the dog that led him to the items in the first place. To find the dog and return it home. To find it and, perhaps, to find a person who knew. A person who knew that he wasn't Nestor at all.

Vinnia places a hand on his shoulder and reaches down, lifting the metal box from the floor and closing the lid.

"Is that everything?"

Nestor nods briefly, unable to look up as Vinnia passes the container to one of her staff.

"Good..."

Nestor reaches into his pocket, causing a few of the technicians to shout and leap forward. Instantly, Vinnia holds up her hand, watching calmly as Nestor withdraws his pen and notepad and starts to write.

Hand trembling, he scrawls words across the small sheet of paper: *I am not Nestor 33*.

Ripping it from the pad, holding it out for Vinnia to read then dropping it to the floor. Another page follows, the same words, tearing it off quickly and letting it fall. Then another and another, over and over, discarding each piece of paper on the ground.

"Nestor…" Vinnia bows her head before making a forward gesture with a gloved hand.

In a moment they circle around him in force. Disabling each of his metal limbs instantly, rendering them entirely useless. They attach various pieces of restraining and monitoring equipment to each limb, cutting through heavy canvas material at one shoulder and injecting twice.

A large group of white-clothed people carry him from the building. Ignoring his fading struggle and the pen that drifts in air. Still writing, still attempting to form the same words.

Through the haze he hears another voice, someone speaking from behind the wall of white, a rough voice he knows well.

"Don't worry, Nestor, eh? They'll make it better. You won't be out for long. Going to get your voice back after all, be good as new…"

The words fade away as they lift him up the steps of the transporter, enveloping him in a brightly lit operating space. As the doors close firmly behind, Nestor thinks only of the notepad lying somewhere in the café. Nestled among the ruins and fragments, lost among the debris.

Cold now…

A mask.

Piercing white light succumbing to shadow then complete darkness.

A darkness that breaks only with a faint artificial voice.

*"Good morning 24…"*

# About The Author

Born in Scotland, Barry A. Coates has written both fiction and non-fiction on a variety of subjects from an early age.

All stories in **The Book of Orphans** created and captured during 2022.

Contact the author:

**Web**: https://cabinetofshadows.com/
**Twitter**: @BarryACoates

If you enjoyed this book, please support the author by leaving a review. Thank you.

Printed in Great Britain
by Amazon

28428041R00205